THE NINE LIVES OF CHLOE KING

THE NINE LIVES OF CHLOE KING

THE FALLEN
THE STOLEN
THE CHOSEN

LIZ BRASWELL
writing as Celia Thomson

Simon Pulse
New York London Toronto Sydney

This book is a work of fiction. Any references to historical events, real people, or real locales are used fictitiously. Other names, characters, places, and incidents are the product of the author's imagination, and any resemblance to actual events or locales or persons, living or dead, is entirely coincidental.

SIMON PULSE
An imprint of Simon & Schuster Children's Publishing Division
1230 Avenue of the Americas, New York, NY 10020
This Simon Pulse paperback edition June 2011

For information about special discounts for bulk purchases, please contact
Simon & Schuster Special Sales at 1-866-506-1949 or business@simonandschuster.com.
The Simon & Schuster Speakers Bureau can bring authors to your live event.
For more information or to book an event contact the Simon & Schuster Speakers Bureau
at 1-866-248-3049 or visit our website at www.simonspeakers.com.
The text of this book was set in Fairfield.
Manufactured in the United States of America
12 14 16 18 20 19 17 15 13
Library of Congress Control Number 2011922984
ISBN 978-1-4424-3570-4
These titles were previously published individually by Simon Pulse.

Contents

THE FALLEN

For John Ordover and Dave Mack, good friends and the sine qua nons of my career and marriage

Prologue

He never tired or lost her trail.

Not since she'd first seen him an hour ago in the bar, when his sleeve had fallen back and revealed an ornate black brand. Scrolls and curlicues of ink and scar tissue spelled out the familiar words: *Sodalitas Gladii Decimi.*

And so she ran.

She took a deep breath and looked ahead, leaping over piles of garbage and puddles with the precision of an acrobat, propelled by her terror. Which street did this alley connect to? Was there a public place close by—even a twenty-four-hour gas station—where she would be safe?

Finally the smell of open, wet air told her an exit was ahead: a barbedwire-topped gate blocked the far end of the alley.

She prepared to leap, triumph and freedom singing in her ears.

Then something burned into her left leg, ripping through muscle.

She clung to the gate, her leg dangling uselessly below her. She reached to pull herself up, hand over hand, but a near-silent whir announced a second attack. In an instant, she fell.

"Trapped, I'm afraid," said an irritatingly calm voice.

She desperately tried to push herself along the ground, away from him—but there was nowhere to go.

"Please . . . no . . . ," she whimpered, pushing herself back up against a wall. "I'm not what you think. I'm not *bad*. . . ."

"I'm sure you don't believe you are."

She heard a blade, fine and small like a dagger, being whisked out of its sheath.

"I've never—I would never hurt *anyone*! Please!"

He cut her throat.

"Id tibi facio, Deus," he whispered, putting the side of his left hand to his heart, thumb in the middle of his chest, pointing up. A gentle sigh escaped the dying girl; a thin ribbon of blood trickled down her neck. Tiny marks of an expert assassin. He bowed his head. "In allegiance to the Order of the Tenth Blade. *Pater noster, rex gentius.*"

He adjusted her head so that she looked more comfortable and closed her eyes. Then he wiped the tiny silver blade on a handkerchief, sat back on his heels, and waited.

When she woke up, he would kill her again.

One

As soon as she opened her eyes that morning, Chloe decided that she would go to Coit Tower instead of Parker S. Shannon High, her usual destination on a Tuesday.

She was turning sixteen in less than twenty-four hours, with no real celebration in sight: Paul spent Wednesdays at his dad's house in Oakland, and—far worse—her mom had said something about "maybe going to a nice restaurant." What was a "nice" restaurant, anyway? A place where they served blowfish and foie gras? Where the wine list was thicker than her American civilization textbook? No, thank you.

If Mom found out about the Coit Tower expedition, Chloe would be grounded, completely eliminating any possibility of dinner out. Then Chloe would have a *right* to feel miserable on her sixteenth birthday, at home, alone, punished. The idea was strangely alluring.

She called Amy.

"Hey, want to go to the tower today instead of physics?"

"Absolutely." There was no hesitation, no pause—no grogginess, in fact. For all of Amy's rebel post-punk posturing, Chloe's best friend was a morning person. How did she deal with the 2 A.M. poetry readings? "I'll see you there at ten. I'll bring bagels if you bring the crack."

By "crack" Amy meant Café Eland's distinctive twenty-ounce coffee, which was brewed with caffeinated water.

"You're on."

"You want me to call Paul?"

That was strange. Amy never volunteered to do anything, much less help with group planning.

"Nah, let me guilt him into it."

"Your funeral. See ya."

She dragged herself out of bed, wrapping the comforter around her. Like almost everything in the room, it was from Ikea. Her mom's taste ran toward orange, turquoise, abstract kokopelli statuettes, and blocks of sandstone—none of which fit in a crappy middle-class San Francisco ranch. And since Pateena Vintage Clothing paid a whopping $5.50 an hour, Chloe's design budget was limited. Scandinavian blocks of color and furniture with unpronounceable names would have to do for now. *Anything* beat New Southwest.

She stood in front of the closet, wearing a short pair of boxers and a tank. Even if she still hadn't gotten her period, Chloe was finally developing a waist, as if her belly had been squeezed up to her breasts and down to her butt. Hot or not, it wasn't as though any of it really mattered: her mom grounded her if she so much as even *mentioned* a boy other than Paul.

She threw herself in front of the computer with a wide yawn and jiggled the mouse. Unless Paul was asleep or dead, he could pretty much be located at his computer 24/7. Bingo—his name popped up in bold on her buddy list.

Chloe: Ame and me are going to Coit Tower today. Wanna come?
Paul: [long pause]
Chloe: ?
Paul: You're not gonna guilt me into it 'cause I'm not gonna be around for your birthday, right?
Chloe: :)
Paul: *groan* ok I'll tell Wiggins I got a National Honor Society field trip or something.
Chloe: ILU, PAUL!!!
Paul: Yeahyeah. Cul8r.

Chloe grinned. Maybe her birthday wasn't going to suck after all.

She looked out the window—yup, fog. In a city of fog, Inner Sunset was the foggiest part of San Francisco. Amy loved it because it was all spooky and mysterious and reminded her of England (although she had never been there). But Chloe was depressed by the damp and cheerless mornings, evenings, and afternoons and liked to flee to higher, sunnier ground—like Coit Tower—at every opportunity.

She decided to play it safe and dressed as if for school, in jeans and a tee and a jean jacket from Pateena's that was authentic eighties. It even had a verse of a Styx song penned carefully in ballpoint on one of the sleeves. She emptied her messenger bag of her textbooks and hid them under her bed. Then she stumbled downstairs, trying to emulate her usual tired-grumpy-morning-Chloe routine.

"You're down early," her mother said suspiciously.

Uneager to pick a fight this morning, Chloe swallowed her sigh. *Everything* she did out of the ordinary since she'd turned twelve was greeted with suspicion. The first time she'd gotten a short haircut—paid for with her *own* money, thank you very much—her mother had demanded to know if she was a lesbian.

"I'm meeting Ame at the Beanery first," Chloe responded as politely as she could, grabbing an orange out of the fridge.

"I don't want to sound old-fashioned, but—"

"It's gonna stunt my growth?"

"It's a gateway drug." Mrs. King put her hands on her hips. In black Donna Karan capris with a silk-and-wool scoop neck and her pixie haircut, Chloe's mom didn't look like a mom. She looked like someone out of a Chardonnay ad.

"You have *got* to be kidding me," Chloe couldn't keep herself from saying.

"There's an article in the *Week*." Her mother's gray eyes narrowed, her expertly lined lips pursed. "Coffee leads to cigarettes leads to cocaine and crystal methamphetamines."

"Crystal *meth*, Mom. It's crystal *meth*." Chloe kissed her on the cheek as she walked past her to the door.

"I'm talking to you about not smoking, just like the ads say to!"

"Message received!" Chloe called back, waving without turning around.

She walked down to Irving Street, then continued walking north to the southern side of Golden Gate Park, stopping at Café Eland for the two promised coffees. Paul didn't partake; she got him a diet Coke instead. Amy was already at the bus stop, juggling a bag of bagels, her army pack, and a cell phone.

"You know, real punks don't—" Chloe put her hand to her ear and shook it, mimicking a phone.

"Bite me." Amy put down her bag and threw her phone in, pretending not to care about it. Today she wore a short plaid kiltlike skirt, a black turtleneck, fishnets, and cat-eye glasses; the overall effect was somewhere between rebellious librarian and geek-punk.

The two of them were comfortably silent on the bus, just drinking coffee and glad to have a seat. Amy might be a morning person, but Chloe needed at least another hour before she would be truly sociable. Her best friend had learned that years ago and politely accommodated her.

There wasn't much to look at out the bus window; just another black-and-white-and-gray early morning in San Francisco, full of grumpy-faced people going to work and bums finding their street corners. Chloe's reflection in the dusty window was almost monochromatic except for her light hazel eyes. They glowed almost orange in the light when the bus got to Kearny Street and the sun broke through.

Chloe felt her spirits rise: this was the San Francisco of postcards and dreams, a city of ocean and sky and sun. It really was glorious.

Paul was already there, sitting on the steps of the tower, reading a comic book.

"Happy pre-birthday, Chlo," he said, getting up and lightly kissing her on the cheek, a surprisingly mature, touchy-feely act. He held out a brown bag.

Chloe smiled curiously and then opened it—a plastic bottle of Popov vodka was nestled within.

"Hey, I figure if we're going to be truants, why not go all the way?" He grinned, his eyes squeezing into slits zipped shut by his lashes. There was a slight indentation in his short, black, and overgelled hair where his earphones had rested.

"Thanks, Paul." She pointed up. "Shall we?"

"What if you had to choose just one of these views to look at for the rest of your life," Chloe said. "Which one would it be?"

Amy and Paul looked up from each other, almost intrigued. The three of them had been sitting around for the past hour, not really doing much, with Chloe's two best friends occasionally exchanging giggly glances. That had grown old real fast.

Half of Coit Tower's windows showed spectacular, sun-drenched San Francisco scenery, the other nine looked out into a formless, gray-white abyss.

"I'd wait until the sun cleared before making my choice," Amy said, pragmatic as ever. She swirled her cup of coffee for emphasis, mixing its contents. Chloe sighed; she should have expected that answer.

Paul walked from window to window, game. "Well, the bridge is beautiful, with all the fog and clouds and sunset and dawn—"

"Bor-ing," Amy cut in.

"The Transamerica Pyramid is too sharp and weird—"

"And *phallic*."

"I guess I would choose the harbor," Paul decided. Looking over his shoulder, Chloe could see colorful little sailboats coming and going with the wind, dreamy, hazy islands in the distance. She smiled. It was a *very* Paul choice.

"Definitely *not* Russian Hill," Amy added, trying to regain control of the conversation. "Fugly sprawl with a capital *Fug*."

"Made your decision just in time, Paul . . ."

As they watched, low clouds came rolling down from

the hills, replacing each of the nine windows, enclosing the views in a white, total darkness. What should have been a beautiful blue day with puffy white clouds, now that they were out of Inner Sunset, had rapidly given way to the same old stupid weather.

This wasn't exactly what Chloe had expected for her sixteenth-birthday-school-blow-off day.

To be fair, she always expected more than life was likely to give: in this case, a golden sunny *Stand by Me/Ferris Bueller* these-are-the-best-days-of-our-lives sort of experience.

"So dude," Amy said, changing the subject. "What's up with you and Comrade Ilychovich?"

Chloe sighed and sank down against the wall, taking a last swallow from her own cup. Like Amy's, it was spiked with Paul's birthday present to her. Paul had already drunk his diet Coke and was now sipping directly from the amazingly cheesy plastic vodka flask. Chloe looked dreamily at the black-and-red onion domes on the label.

"He's . . . just . . . so . . . *hot*."

"And *so* out of your league," Amy pointed out.

"Alyec is steely-eyed, chisel-faced young Russian," Paul said with a thick cold war accent. "Possibly with modeling contract. Sources say Agent Keira Hendelson getting close to his . . . *cover*."

"Screw her." Chloe threw her empty cup at the wall, picturing it smashing into the student council's blond little president.

"You *could* be related, you know," Amy pointed out. "That could be a problem. He could be a cousin or nephew or something of your biological parents."

"The old Soviet Union's a big place. Genetically, I think we're okay. It's the getting to actually *date* him that's the problem."

"You could just, I don't know, go up to him and like, *talk* to him or something," Paul suggested.

"He's always surrounded by the Blond One and her Gang of Four," Chloe reminded him.

"Nothing gained, nothing lost."

Yeah, right. Like *he* had ever asked anyone out.

Amy swigged the last of her coffee and belched. "Oh, crap, I've got to pee."

Paul blushed. He always got nervous when either Amy or Chloe discussed anything like bodily functions in front of him—so usually Chloe didn't talk about that stuff when he was around.

But today she felt . . . well, odd. Jumpy, impatient. Not to mention a little annoyed with both him *and* Amy. This was supposed to be *her* birthday thing. So far it sucked.

"Too bad you can't do it standing up, like Paul," she said, watching him blush out of the corner of her eye. "You could go over the edge."

Now, what had made her say that?

She stood up. Leaning against the stone wall, Chloe peered down. All she could see was swirling whiteness and, off to her left, one water-stained red pylon of the Golden Gate Bridge.

What would happen if I dropped a penny from up here? Chloe wondered. *Would it make a tunnel through the fog? That would be cool.* A tunnel two hundred feet long and half an inch across.

She climbed up into a window and dug into her jeans pocket, hunting for spare change, not bothering to put her other hand on the wall for balance.

The tower suddenly seemed to tilt forward.

"What—," she began to say.

Chloe tried to resteady herself by leaning back into the window frame, grasping for the wall, but the fog had left it clammy and slick. She pitched forward, her left foot slipping out from beneath her.

"Chloe!"

She threw her arms back, desperately trying to rebalance herself. For a brief second she felt Paul's warm fingers against her own. She looked into his face—a smile of relief broke across it, pink flushed across the tops of his high cheekbones. But then the moment was over: Amy was shrieking and Chloe felt nothing catch her as she slipped out of Paul's grasp. She was falling—*falling*—out of the window and off the tower.

This is not happening, Chloe thought. *This is not the way I end.*

She heard the already-muffled screams of her friends

getting fainter, farther and farther away. Something would save her, right?

Her head hit last.

The pain was unbearable, bone crushing and nauseating—the sharp shards of a hundred needles being forced through her as her body compacted itself on the ground.

Everything went black, and Chloe waited to die.

Two

She was surrounded by darkness.

Strange noises, padding footsteps, and the occasional scream echoed and died in strange ways, like she was in a vast cavern riddled with tunnels and caves. Somewhere ahead and far below her, like she was standing at the edge of a cliff, was an indistinct halo of hazy light. It rippled unpleasantly. She started to back away from it. Then something growled behind her and shoved her hard.

Chloe pitched forward toward the light and into empty space.

This was it. This was *death*.

"Chloe? *Chloe?*"

That was odd. God sounded kind of annoying. Kind of whiny.

"Oh my God, she's—"

"Call 911!"

"There's no way she could have survived that fall—"

"GET OUT OF MY WAY!"

Chloe felt like she was spinning, her weight being forced back into her skin.

"You *stupid shithead*!"

That was Amy. That was *definitely* Amy.

"We should call her mom. . . ."

"What do we say? That Chloe is . . . that Chloe's *dead*?"

"Don't say that! It's not true!"

Chloe opened her eyes.

"Oh my God—Chloe . . . ?"

Paul and Amy were leaning over her. Tears and streaky lightning bolts of black makeup ran down Amy's cheeks, and her light blue eyes were wide and rimmed with red.

"You're a-alive?" Paul asked, face white with awe. "There's no way you could have—" He put a hand behind her head, feeling her neck and skull. When he pulled it back, there was only a little blood on his finger.

"You—you didn't—oh my God, it's . . . a . . . miracle . . . ," Amy said slowly.

"Can you move?" Paul asked quietly.

Chloe sat up. It was the hardest thing she could ever remember doing, like pushing herself through a million pounds of dirt. Her head swam, and for a moment there was two of everything, four flat gingerbread friends in front of her. She coughed, then began puking. She tried to lean to the side but couldn't control her body.

After she finished heaving, Chloe noticed that Paul

and Amy were touching her, holding her shoulders. She could just barely feel their hands; sensation slowly crept back over her skin.

"You *should* be dead," said Paul. "There is no. Way. You could have survived that fall."

She was struck by what he said; it seemed true. Yet here she was, alive. Just like that. Why was she so unsurprised?

"Help me up," Chloe said, trying not to notice the confused and frightened looks on her friends' faces. They helped Chloe lean forward, then slowly rise on shaky legs. She pointed her toes and bent her knees. They worked. Barely.

"Holy shit," said Paul, unable to think of anything else to say.

"We should get you to a hospital," Amy suggested.

"No," Chloe answered, faster than she meant.

"Are you in*sane*?" Paul demanded. "Just because you're not dead doesn't mean you don't have a concussion or something. . . . You can't just fall two hundred feet and walk away without *some*thing happening."

Chloe didn't like the way her friends were looking at her. Shouldn't they be overjoyed? Thrilled that she wasn't dead? Instead they were looking at her like she was a ghost. "Yeah. We're going. No arguments," Amy said, stubbornly setting her pointy chin.

She and Paul helped Chloe up, one at each shoulder. *My devil and my angel,* Chloe thought ironically. *Well, my nerd and my wanna-be outsider.* Her head pounded, and she wanted nothing more than some aspirin.

And time alone to *think*.

She managed to get time to think in the emergency room, though she wasn't exactly alone. After Amy made a big hysterical deal about her *friend* and the *accident* she'd had, the reception nurse took one look at the healthy-seeming girl and relegated the three of them to the waiting room, behind a line of homeless people with visible damage: broken arms, scraped-up faces, oozing sores.

Paul took over filling out the contact information and paperwork, but after an hour of playing Guess the Symptom in her head, Chloe finally lost it.

"Look, why don't we just get out of here," she hissed. "I'm *fine*."

"As if," Paul said, reaching for a three-month-old *Vogue*.

"Don't touch that," Amy said, smacking his hand down. "Germs." Then she turned to Chloe. "You fell like a million feet onto your *head*, Chlo."

Another half hour passed. They watched the muted news flitting by incomprehensibly overhead, stories about Iraq and Wall Street and some girl's body found in an alley.

Finally, at four o'clock, the staff was ready to let in the girl with no visible injuries. The reception nurse put up her hand when Amy and Paul tried to follow.

"Only family," she said.

Amy turned to Chloe, wrinkling her freckled nose and smiling. It was a "cute" look that Chloe knew she had practiced in front of the mirror for hours, but it just didn't work with her friend's regal nose. "You'll be okay, I promise."

I know. I am *okay.*

"Thanks. For everything." Chloe gave her a lopsided smile, then went through the big, double-swinging metal door.

"If you and your friends are lying about your 'accident,'" she heard the nurse saying to Amy and Paul, "her parents are going to owe their insurance company a *whopper*. . . ."

As soon as the door swung shut behind her, Chloe scanned the hall for the exit.

She wished she had money for a cab, but she had to take the bus instead. As soon as she was inside her house, Chloe ran into the bathroom, tore off her clothes, and turned on the water. After a long soak she finally began to feel normal again, as if a few minutes of downtime by herself were all she really needed. *To recover from a two-hundred-foot fall.* She wrapped the towel around herself when she got out and looked in the mirror. There was a slight bruise on her temple and some dried blood on her scalp that was kind of fun to pick at. That was all.

Chloe wandered out and sat in front of her computer,

where her day had begun just a few strange hours before. She called up Google and then paused, her normally super-speed fingers hesitating over the keyboard. *How do you research "chances of surviving a crazy long fall onto pavement"?* A few minutes of surfing unearthed the interesting but useless fact that *defenestration* meant "the act of pushing someone out a window" and that almost no one besides Jackie Chan had easily survived a fall of much more than fifty feet.

Chloe got into bed and contemplated the ceiling. There was no way around it: she should not have survived her plummet from Coit Tower. Maybe this was the afterlife, and she was being eased into it slowly with familiar people and places?

She dismissed that quickly, though, picking some more blood out of her hair. *Heaven would be cleaner,* she thought decisively. But something strange had definitely happened. She should not be alive.

It was really a miracle.

Thinking in the autumnal afternoon light, Chloe drifted off to sleep.

She dreamed:

She lay in a comfortable hollow that was soft but did not move the way a mattress should when she shifted position. It was hot but not unpleasant; the sun's rays were tangible on her skin, caressing her back into sleep. Something licked the side of her face, rough and quick: *Get up.*

Chloe rose from the sand, dusted herself off. She shielded her eyes and looked to the horizon. This was no beach: it was a desert, empty and vast—but familiar and not frightening. The dunes were golden and the sky a dark empty blue, foreshadowing a chilly night when the sun finally set, half a day from now. They were heading to the north, down the river.

Below her hand was the lion that had woken her; it nuzzled at her fingers. They were all lions around her, female and maneless, the real power of the pride. Four of them. She was upright and awkward; when they finally started moving, the great cats had to slow their normal pace so she could keep up. Their beautiful shoulders rose and fell in a languid, powerful rhythm.

A vulture circled in the sky, hoping to feast on whatever they left.

When Chloe woke up, she was ravenous.

In the first moment of wakefulness after opening her eyes, before remembering her fall or being brought home, Chloe thought about what might be in the fridge. The rest came back to her as she got up. She was stiff, but even the bruise on her forehead was already fading.

She was surprised to see that the clock on the microwave read six; she had napped for over four hours. *Doesn't feel like it.* She opened the fridge and surveyed its contents, most of which were ingredients for whatever complicated gourmet dinner her mother was planning next. She pulled out a couple of yogurts, a pint of macaroni salad, and an old carton of lo mein. If falling two hundred feet didn't kill her, this probably wouldn't, either.

Chloe sat at the table and ate, still not fully awake, still not fully thinking, just enjoying the feeling of the food hitting her stomach and filling it.

The door slammed open and Mrs. King threw herself in. She opened her mouth to say something, then noticed the demolished feast on their table.

"I fell off Coit Tower today," Chloe said without thinking.

She hadn't planned on telling her mother immediately. She'd wanted to think it over first, plan the right approach—but she hadn't come up with one. Apparently her subconscious had.

"I know," her mother said in a low, angry tone. "I just came from the *hospital*, where you were supposed to be waiting for me. But no, you decided not to stay there, just like you *apparently* decided not to go to school today."

Daughter and mother looked into each other's eyes, not saying anything for a moment.

"*What* has gotten into you?" Chloe's mother finally yelled. "Is this the week you decided to get all of your teenage rebelling out at once?"

"Mom!" Chloe shouted back. "I *fell off Coit Tower.* Doesn't that mean anything to you?"

"Besides the fact that you were acting like an irresponsible idiot?"

But Mrs. King's eyes flitted to the light marks on her daughter's face, the uncomfortable way she was sitting, the black blood on her scalp.

"Are you okay?" she finally asked.

Chloe shrugged.

"That's why I left," she mumbled. "There wasn't anything wrong. They wouldn't listen to me."

"I'm glad Amy and Paul had the good sense to ignore you and bring you in." Mrs. King sighed. "Though I could kill them for encouraging your 'day off.'"

"Paul wasn't going to be around for my birthday," Chloe said, feeling like an idiotic, self-pitying brat as she said it. "I wanted to celebrate it with my friends."

Her mother opened her mouth to say something about that, but closed it again.

"You could have been killed," she said. She was quiet for a moment. "It's a miracle you weren't."

"I know."

There was another moment of silence. Chloe stared at her empty plate, and her mother stared at her. Mrs. King readjusted her black-rimmed glasses. Chloe could almost see her mom's thoughts tumbling around in logical lawyer circles: *She should be dead. She's not. I should be grateful. I'm angry with her. She's not dead. Therefore she must be punished.*

"We're going to have to talk about this. About your behavior and your punishment."

"Obviously," Chloe said with heavy irony, suddenly irked. "Mom, I should be *dead.*"

"So? You're not. Be grateful. I have some steaks. . . . I'll make them in an hour, after I do some paperwork."

"Did you *hear* me? I could—I *should* have been killed!!!"

Her mother opened her mouth to say something but didn't. She ran her fingers through the wispy bangs that framed her face, pushing it out of her eyes. Her hair was thick and blond, as far from the color and texture of Chloe's own hair as it was possible to get.

Chloe turned and stomped up to her room.

Maybe *she* was the one on drugs.

It was the only explanation Chloe could think of to explain such a blasé reaction. Maybe it was shock? Maybe she really didn't care. Chloe bitterly considered how easily her mom could have been rid of her. She would be free to throw dinner parties, go to gallery openings, and maybe pick up a really cool boyfriend. The kind who stayed away from complicated situations like *daughters*. Especially adopted ones.

She thought about the father she could barely remember, gone when she was four. *He* would have cared. He would have rushed her *back* to the hospital, no matter how much she protested.

Chloe sat on her bed and carefully opened the middle drawer of her bureau. It was the only old piece of furniture in the room, ancient, solid, and oak. Perfect for hiding the only real secret from her mom.

A little gray mouse sat up on his hind legs and looked up at her expectantly.

Squeak!

Chloe smiled and put her hand down next to him, letting the mouse run up it. Her mother absolutely forbade all furred pets—supposedly because of her allergies. But back when her mom had gone on a rampant extermination phase, convinced that the house was overrun with vermin from their less cleanly neighbors next door, Chloe had come home from school one day and found the baby gray mouse in a live trap. With Amy and Paul's help she'd installed a light in her bureau. Now Mus-mus had a water dropper, a feeder, and an exercise wheel. This was a whole little world her mother knew nothing about.

She took a Cheerio out of the sandwich bag she kept under her bed and carefully held it out to him; the little mouse grabbed it with its front paws and sat back, nibbling as if it was a giant bagel.

"What should I do?" she whispered. The little mouse never stopped eating, ignoring her. "My mom is such a bitch."

Calling Amy was the only thing to do, really—Chloe could apologize for acting so weird after she and Paul had taken her to the hospital, thank her for it, then get into the nitty-gritty of how bizarre it was to be alive and discuss why she had survived. Amy would probably offer some explanation involving the supernatural or angels—useless but entertaining. Chloe smiled and picked up the phone, dropping Mus-mus carefully back into his cage.

Seven long rings . . . Amy's cell phone was on, but she wasn't picking up. Chloe tried three more times in case the phone was buried at the bottom of Amy's bag and she couldn't hear it. On the fourth try Chloe left a message.

"Hey, Ame, call me. I'm—uh—feeling better. Sorry about the total rudeness today. I guess I was in shock or something."

She tried her at home.

"Oh, hello, Chlo-ee!" Mrs. Scotkin answered. There was a pause; she must have looked at a clock. "Happy sixteenth birthday in six hours!"

Chloe smiled despite herself. Amy must not have told her anything. "Thanks, Mrs. Scotkin. Is Amy around?"

"No—I think she's working on the Am civ project with her group tonight. Try her cell."

I did, thanks. "Okay, I will. Thanks, Mrs. Scotkin."

Chloe frowned. She went to the computer and checked all of Amy's aliases, but none of them were on. Maybe she really was doing homework? Nah. Paul was on but afk—Chloe didn't really feel like talking to him anyway. She needed *Amy*. She had almost died. It would be her birthday in four hours. Her mom was crazy. And she was All Alone.

She wandered around her room, picking up little things—pieces of bric-a-brac, stuffed animals—and putting them back down again. Her gloom gave way to restlessness; the room suddenly seemed very small. Too small for good brooding. She moved up and down on her toes like a ballerina.

Chloe stood for a moment, indecisive, then grabbed her jacket and banged down the stairs.

"Where are you going?" her mother demanded, like someone on a TV show.

"Out," Chloe responded, just as predictably. She even slammed the door behind her, just for good measure.

Three

The night was chillier than Chloe expected. She stood for a moment in just her T-shirt, letting the moist air brush against her skin and lift the hair on her arms. It smelled surprisingly good; clean and wet as a cloud. Then the wind changed direction and she could hear and smell traffic at the same time: exhaust, acrid and dry even in the dampness, bit at her nose. Chloe sighed and put on her jacket.

Okay, Spontaneous One. Where to now?

She had set herself up for a *really* spectacular punishment later (though she hoped her near-death experience might help cut her some slack), so the night was not to be wasted. Then it came to her: *The Bank.*

Normally she would never, *ever* consider trying to get into the club without spending several hours dressing and redressing with Amy, going through everything in both their closets and sometimes even Paul's. Jeans and a tee were just embarrassing.

Chloe didn't care; she was going to do it. She was going to get into the club, by herself, dressed like the Creature from the Gap Lagoon. She just *needed* to dance right now.

It was a Tuesday, so there wasn't much of a line outside the club; its Christmas-from-hell orange and black fairy lights barely illuminated the otherwise empty street. One bored bouncer half sat on his stool, wearing tiny round black sunglasses that didn't reflect anything.

Chloe swaggered up to the velvet rope, unsure of what she was going to do. Everyone else in line was dressed in something sparkly, revealing, or all black—and was at least half a decade older.

Before she could think about it, Chloe sashayed past them and was asking the bouncer directly: "Hey, can I get in?" Just like that.

The giant man looked up at her and down, pausing at her scuffed black Converses. He cracked the barest hint of a smile. "I like your shoes. Those are *old* school, baby," he said, and unhooked the rope for Chloe.

"Thanks, man," she said in what she hoped was an equally cool voice. It was just like she'd passed a level in one of Paul's video games. Charon of Inner Sunset had just let her into the Dancing Afterworld.

The floor wasn't large, but it was surrounded by black mirrors that made it look twice as big and crowded. Clinging to the far wall and snaking around to the door was the enormous bar for which the place was famous: its surface was covered in thousands and thousands of shiny copper pennies, shellacked into permanently flowing streams that ran all the way from a vault in the wall down to the floor.

During the day, when people vacuumed and cleaned and tried to remove the eternally beery stench, normal lights probably illuminated unpleasant details on the copper river—inky blots where people declared their fleeting love with Sharpies, worn and chipped places where coins had been hacked out, a night's work for the prize of a single penny. But for now it gleamed like an ancient god of wealth had just overturned his big pot of money. Bright, harsh golden lights bounced over it without shining on the patrons surrounding the bar, keeping their faces romantic and half lit.

The music was typical house with just a touch of electronica. No Moby *or* Goa here. Paul would have threatened to walk out, ears covered, before sidling up to the DJ to check out his equipment. It *should* have been the three of them there, not just her alone. But the music throbbed loudly, and Chloe felt like she could go out and dance by herself—she had almost died today; she could do anything.

She went to the bar first, leaning against it and surveying the scene. A few people were dancing and dressed badly, but otherwise it was a pretty hot crowd. What looked like an entire fraternity was loudly but good-naturedly arguing about sports, waving their beers, making an out-of-place businessman and his model very uncomfortable. There was one particularly hot guy across the floor, hanging around in the back, drinking quietly and people watching, just like her. He had black hair, dark skin, and light, light eyes. Exotic. She ducked her head to follow his movements as he ordered a beer, talked to a friend, and wandered into the crowd, but soon she lost him.

She waited patiently, but he didn't return. No one took his place, either; there were a few runners-up, but the hottest guy in the club had disappeared.

"Buy you a drink?"

He appeared at her side, smiling at her surprise and embarrassment. Up close he was even better looking, with full lips and a light spattering of darker brown freckles across his nose.

Chloe was just about to say No, thank you, like she did every time some twenty-something tried to pick up her fifteen-year-old self. But, "Absolutely!" was what came out instead.

"What'll it be?"

"Red Bull and vodka."

He nodded his approval and clinked her drink with his beer glass when the bartender handed it over.

"It's my birthday in two hours!" she shouted into his ear.

"Really? Cheers!" He sounded British. They toasted each other again and drank. "Happy birthday!" He kissed her delicately on her cheek. Chloe felt her stomach roll over and her mind play dead. An enormous grin spread over her face, completely destroying her cool. She had gotten into the club with no hassle, a drop-dead gorgeous guy just bought her a drink—this was turning out to be a pretty great birthday after all.

After another drink they started dancing. He moved in small sways and tiny circles perfect for avoiding other dancers in the tightly packed space. For one song he just put his hands around her waist and let her move, the center of his attention. When they walked through the crowd for a drink or a break, he would very lightly touch his hand to her back or shoulder, leading her protectively but not possessively.

"I'm Chloe!" she shouted at one point.

"I'm Xavier!" he shouted back.

At twelve thirty Chloe decided she was turning into a pumpkin. Near-death experience or no, her mother was going to kill Chloe *herself* if she stayed out all night. Xavier walked her out.

"Let me be the first to wish you a happy birthday," he said, kissing her gently on the lips in the dark parking lot. His mouth was warm and moist but not wet, and he was a hell of a lot more delicate than the few guys her own age Chloe had kissed. He pulled a card out of his wallet. It was actually engraved: *Xavier Akouri, 453 Mason St., #5A, 011-30-210-567-3981.* It took her a moment to realize that it was an international cell phone number she was looking at.

"Aren't you going to ask for mine?" Chloe asked.

He smiled and lowered his head so their noses were almost touching, looking directly into her eyes. "And would you have given me your real number? *You* call *me* if you want."

Her stomach did another flip-flop. Before she knew what she was doing, Chloe grabbed him around the back of the neck and held his head still while she kissed him. He actually let out a little moan. It drove her wild. His hands came up around her hips. Chloe reached around up and under his shirt to feel the skin on his back, kneading his muscles and clawing him with her fingernails. He moaned again, from pleasure or pain, it was hard to tell. But he took one of her legs and wrapped it up around his waist. Chloe felt herself sliding in closer and closer—

What the hell am I doing?

She opened her eyes and saw a handsome Euro kissing her, which might have been fine, wonderful, even—but she was inches from having sex with him in the middle of the parking lot.

"I'm sorry." She disentangled herself from him and backed off, breathing heavily. She ached and throbbed with want.

Xavier looked confused. His eyes were heavy lidded, and little beads of sweat held on like silver around his brow. His hair was tousled.

"I—I can't do this right now," she said.

To his credit, Xavier nodded, albeit reluctantly. "Do you—do you want to come back to my place?"

Chloe opened her mouth to say something. She realized it was very close to, Yes, I do—but managed to choke out, "I'm sorry," again, quickly turning and walking away. She ran all the way home and then once around the block for good measure, hoping to work the desire out of her body. Would her mom notice a look in her eye, a flush on her cheek? She could say it was from running.

When Chloe came in, her mother was reading on the couch, shoes off, glass of red wine on the table near her. Untouched. She was trying to make it look like she was just staying up late, not staying up for Chloe. Their eyes met.

"I'll be up in a little while," Mrs. King finally said. "I just want to finish this chapter."

She's actually going to be cool about this. Chloe couldn't believe it. And from her tone, it was like the late night out hadn't even happened—like maybe it would never be brought up again.

"Okay. G'night," Chloe said as gratefully as she could.

She staggered upstairs tiredly, taking her clothes off as she went. She could smell parts of Xavier on her shirt, his hands dangerously close to her breasts when they rested on her waist, his lips on her collar when he was kissing her neck.

She put on boxers and her oversized Invader Zim

T-shirt and fell into bed, holding her stuffed pig, still wondering what had happened. Teenage hormones, as they always said, or had it been an up-with-life reaction to her near-death experience? She thought she had heard of such a thing. . . . She clutched Wilbur more tightly and fell asleep.

Four

It was several hours into the next day, during first-period American civilization, when it suddenly hit Chloe: what she had done—or almost done—the night before, never mind the part about not dying. She had forgotten it all for a short, happy while.

This wasn't surprising; her brain barely began working before nine. The hours between being woken by her crappy old clock radio and second bell usually passed in a painless, mindless blur. Her mother, once upon a time playing the happy single mom, used to make her pancakes with syrup smiley faces and ask her about what she was doing that day. Eventually she gave up trying to communicate with her just-awake, mumbling daughter, filling the coffeemaker and setting the timer the night before instead. Chloe always tried to remember to grumble "bye" on her way out as Mrs. King did her morning yoga in front of the TV.

Holy crap. I almost had sex with a stranger in a parking lot last night.

Chloe felt tingles when she thought of Xavier; she could remember wanting him that badly but not the feeling itself. She idly tried to sketch his lips in the margin of her notebook. Where had she put his card?

". . . the same boot, for either foot. I don't think any of you kids today with your Florsheims or your tennis shoes could possibly imagine the suffering those soldiers marched in. . . ."

Neither Paul nor Amy was in this class, so it was triply boring. *What the heck is a Florsheim?* Chloe tried to cover a yawn, but it was so huge that it felt like her jaw had opened up wider than it was supposed to, like in *Alien*. Her teeth snapped back together when it was done, way too loudly. She looked around to see if anyone had noticed—no one except for Alyec, who was watching with raised eyebrows. She blushed but grinned back, actually looking him in his beautiful ice blue eyes. He smiled and made a "sleepy" gesture with his hands on the side of his face. Chloe nodded, and they each went back to note taking or doodling before Ms. Barker took notice.

When the bell rang, Chloe gathered her stuff and prepared to go to the library—it was such a bitch: she had *second* period free. Last year Amy had had first period free and often slept till eight before bothering to come in. As Chloe passed by the popular lockers, she saw Alyec and waved. He was, of course, surrounded by the beautiful people.

Chloe thought about their little interaction in class and her success with the bouncer the night before and walked right up to him, ignoring the others.

"Didn't Am civ *suck* today?" Once again there she was, doing something she could not believe. First there was falling off a tower, then making out with a stranger, and now going directly up to the most-wanted guy in the junior class and talking to him. She could feel the vicious glares of his coterie impaling her backside, but somehow she wasn't the least bit nervous. Not even a heartbeat.

This is great. I should almost die every *day.*

"Oh, man," Alyec said in an accent that was fading but still had foreign overtones. "Watching you—how do you say—moan? Yes? That was the most exciting part of the hour."

"I wasn't moaning, I was *yawning,*" Chloe said with a shy smile. "But if you find a way to make me moan, I'll let you watch all day." *Did I just say that?* She could see a whole bunch of jaws drop in her peripheral vision.

"You're hilarious, King, you know that?" He said it with a genuine laugh.

The second bell rang. "I've got to get to the library—but we should hang sometime."

Keira looked like she was actually going to growl; her lips were pulled back over her teeth.

"Absolutely," Alyec agreed. "Catch you later, King."

"See ya." She strolled past the other girls, trying not to look too smug but unable to keep from smiling a little.

Chloe thought about Xavier for most of her time in the library, staring out the windows and dreaming a little. She did the same during math and lunch. She thought about him more than her fall. It was kind of like her mom said—she fell, she survived, here she was. She was staring into space, pizza halfway to her mouth, when a familiarly annoying clap on her shoulder jolted her back to reality. Gobbets of bright orange oil flew across the table.

"Oh my God, is it *true*?" Amy threw herself into a seat next to her. "I mean, *happy birthday*, but ohmygod, is it really *true*, did you really flirt with Alyec right in front of Halley and Keira and—and everyone?"

"Yeah, I guess I did," Chloe said with a smile.

"How are you feeling?"

Chloe shrugged. "Fine, I think. A little weird. Last night—"

"Look, we gotta talk," Amy interrupted, leaning in close and looking her right in the eyes. "Something *big* is going down with me. I want to discuss. Dinner?"

Bigger than a near-death and near-sex experience? But Chloe bit back a sarcastic response; Amy really did look worried. And more intense than usual.

"Okay—"

"Cool! See you in English!"

Chloe watched her friend leap up and run off, safety pins and chains jangling as she went, unkempt chestnut hair bouncing. She turned back to her pizza and wondered when life would get back to normal. The grease had congealed into little solid pools of something like orange plastic. Chloe sighed and pushed it away.

Normality seemed to reassert itself at Pateena. As much as she hated sorting the clothes when they came back from the cleaner, there was a soothing familiarity in the folding and the straightening, the random tirades of the manager, the trendy customers. Nothing sexy *or* supernatural. Just a lot of jeans and overpriced old basketball shoes.

Chloe couldn't help noticing one customer who came in, though—just when she thought she had finally beaten her hormones down. He wore black cords, a ribbed black tee, and a black leather jacket, straight cut, like a regular suit jacket. But there were no hints of the über-goth about him: no tattoos or jewelry or fangs or anything. The outfit, which would have made anyone else look like a wanna-be Johnny Cash, worked perfectly on him; he had very dark brown hair, very slightly tanned, healthy skin, and deep brown eyes with beautiful long lashes.

The kicker, though, was his handmade black knitted cap with kitty cat ears.

Here was a handsome guy with a sense of humor. He thumbed through the polo shirts, frowning.

"Looking for a Halloween costume?" Lania asked him nastily. Chloe groaned, still unable to believe that the little alterna-bitch was allowed to operate the cash register and *she* wasn't. Just because the other girl was two years older. If Chloe had a dollar for every customer Lania insulted, she would finally be able to afford a new mountain bike. A *nice* one.

But he just chuckled. "No, I'm afraid it's for an actual meeting with actual executive types." He looked pretty young to be in business, but this was San Francisco, after all. He was probably a programmer or graphics designer or something.

Chloe went back to her work, wondering what Xavier looked like in the daylight. How many drinks did she have? Just two or three. She *could* have been beer goggling. Maybe those sexy freckles were actually bad acne. . . .

"Excuse me." The guy in the kitty hat carefully stepped around her, his purchases clutched to his chest. Apparently Lania had decided to let him pay.

"I like your hat," Chloe said.

"Really? Thanks!" He took it off and looked at it, as if he was surprised she'd noticed.

"Did your girlfriend make it?"

He grinned. "No, I did."

Chloe couldn't help being impressed. Besides Amy, almost no one she knew—not counting her mother's trend-happy friends—knitted, and those who did never really finished anything. Except for some of the stitching, it looked pretty professional.

"I found the pattern on the Web," he continued. "If you knit, I'll give you the URL."

"No thanks, I can't. My friend Amy can, but I'm a complete spaz with my hands."

"Oh, you should totally take it up. It's kind of fun," he said, only a little embarrassed.

Chloe steeled herself for the usual touchy-feely sensitive guy discourse that was sure to follow, about how the movements were soothing, about how he felt in touch with people from long ago, about how some native culture or other did something spiritual with knitting needles, how he might want to open a shop someday, how it was good for teaching underprivileged kids self-esteem. . . .

But he had already turned to go.

"Well, see you," he said with a cute little half smile as he reached for the door. His eyes crinkled the upper part of his cheek, the skin pulled taut by a sexy scar that ran from the outside of his eye to just below his cheekbone.

Chloe waved and watched him go. Part of her was a little insulted; was she not a hot young girl who had attracted the notice of two hot guys in the last twenty-four hours? And Mr. Kitty Cat Man didn't even care. It was her *birthday*, for Christ's sake. Before her imminent grounding, didn't fate owe her something?

Then her butt vibrated.

She had to carefully dig her phone out of the back pocket of her own vintage jeans, which were men's and had a pre-worn white rectangle in the back where someone had once carried his wallet. Once in, her phone fit fine. Getting it out when she was any position but vertical was almost impossible.

Text message: *carluccis @ 7—a.*

Carlucci's was the place she and Amy had first met when the Scotkins had moved into the neighborhood. Maybe she'd get some decent pizza today after all. The best part of her job was that Pateena paid her in cash under the counter at the end of every day. She'd have a whole twenty to blow on a Make Me One with Everything pie.

The rest of the afternoon passed without incident, except when Chloe had to hide a pair of faded purple velvet pants she just knew Amy would love. Usually the owner didn't have a problem with employees "saving" items for themselves. Marisol was the coolest boss she'd ever had. She even let Chloe use the shop's machine to hem her own jeans and stuff. But if Lania saw the pants—or liked them herself—she was bound to make trouble. Chloe stashed them under a pile of polyester bowling shirts when she left.

As she approached the restaurant in the damp fog, the windows of Carlucci's glowed like they were lit with gas carriage lanterns, a restaurant out of time. Really, it was just a little Italian pasta place with candles set in old

Chianti bottles like every other little Italian pasta place in the world, but it was hers and Amy's, and it was cozy, and sometimes the insane old owner even remembered them.

When she opened the door, there seemed to be even more candles than usual.

"Happy birthday to you . . . ," Amy sang, wisely giving up after one cracked phrase. Her eager face was lit manically by the glow of seventeen candles around the crust of a Make Me One with Everything pie. "Blow quickly," she added. "Carlucci thinks I'm going to burn the place down."

Chloe laughed with delight, something she couldn't remember doing for days. She took a deep breath.

I wish . . .

I wish . . .

It used to come to her easily: world peace, an end to all of the environmental disasters in the world, the ability to fly, a dog. Wishes seemed to get more complicated as she grew older: for her father to come back. To know who her biological parents were. For a brother or sister. Come to think of it, maybe her recent jonesing was some sort of replacement-male-love sort of thing. *Ewww . . .*

"Chloe?"

She broke out of her reverie.

I wish for a new mountain bike.

No, wait, *world peace.*

She blew, trying not to get spit on their pizza. Chloe saw with amusement that Amy had also pre-ordered the requisite three cans of Nehi grape each.

"You're the best, Amy."

"Hey, no problem." They didn't hug; Amy hated things like that. Instead they sat down and began the serious business of shoveling sausage-onion-pepper-tomato-pepperoni-caper-black-olive slices into their mouths as fast as humanly possible. Chloe groaned with pleasure.

"This pizza is the best thing that's happened to me all week. Well, except for last night." She swallowed and looked at Amy, but her friend wasn't biting.

"Yeah? You mean the fall? That *was* some freaky stuff."

"No, afterward. Last night. *After* my mom pulled a major freakage." But Amy really wasn't listening. Chloe sighed, finally giving in to the desperate-to-share, distracted look on her friend's face. "Okay, what's more important than my life on my birthday?"

"Paul and I made out last night!" Amy blurted, suddenly covering her mouth as if she hadn't meant for the words to escape.

Chloe found herself choking. It took half a Nehi to restore normal breathing and swallowing. Of all the things Amy could have said, that was definitely the one she'd least expected. Sure, Amy and Paul had been gazing a bit at each other yesterday—but holy crap, they had all known each other since third grade. It would be like dating a brother. A *really geeky* brother.

"You did *what*?"

"After we took you home, we hung out at his place." Easily pictured: Amy and Paul in his tiny room, surrounded by bookshelves packed with records and his turntable equipment. Lounging on the floor. "I mean, it really freaked us out, you know?" Amy looked her in the eyes. "You really could have died. I mean, the fact that you lived is just—amazing. Like you were given a second chance or something." Chloe silently pleaded that Amy not get into her angel crap; suddenly it was *not* the time. "It sort of, it sounds dumb, a total cliché, but it was just sort of like we realized how death almost touched us. Say things while you can, you know? In case you never get a chance to." She took a deep breath. "So then we were talking about, you know, deep things and life, and uh, then . . . Well, and then . . ."

"You sucked face?"

"Basically, yeah." Was Amy blushing? "But that's not all. I mean, I really care about him, you know? We grew up together, he's like family, so there's like that kind of love, but I never found him sexy before. . . ."

"Oh my God," Chloe said. "Are you telling me you find him sexy *now*? Still? Twenty-four hours later?"

"I don't know. I mean, maybe."

They chewed in silence for a while. Suddenly Chloe's obsession with sexy club guy and flirting with Alyec faded. With Xavier it had been just a kiss, albeit a long and deep one, and if she never saw him again, that was all it would ever be. And Alyec was just a flirt. *This* was serious. This affected the Trio.

If they weren't serious, or if they were and it failed, or if it was just a weirdness from last night and one of them didn't feel as strongly as the other, the once-solid friendship of the three of them was doomed. Chloe didn't relish the thought of being the friend in between after the "divorce." Terribly awkward. Chloe was sure this was going to be a total disaster.

After dinner Amy grabbed for the check when Carlucci left it on the table.

"Will miracles never cease? First I survive the fall and now this . . . ," Chloe said, preemptively ducking. But Amy just frowned a little and walked her home, chattering about Paul the entire time. Only as they neared the Kings' residence did she seem to remember Chloe.

"Was there something you wanted to say before?" she asked.

"Oh, uh, no biggie. I mean, not like *this* biggie." Chloe unlocked the door and pushed it open. "You want to come up? We can—"

There was a crowd of people, well dressed, talking and hanging around the Kings' dining and living room. Hors d'oeuvres were being passed; champagne was being poured into glasses. Paul was there with his parents, and Mr. and Mrs. Scotkin, and other people who were neighbors or familiar faces.

"Oh, crap," her mom said, turning around and seeing her. "Surprise!"

Five

Two glasses of champagne later, Chloe began to enjoy herself. Even though she suspected that the party was some sort of psychological ploy on her mother's behalf to make her daughter feel loved, wanted, and appreciated, she had done an excellent job, and Chloe felt all three. She wondered when her punishment for skipping school and leaving the hospital was going to kick in or if that, too, had been canceled in some sort of amnesty.

Mrs. King could not, however, give up the traditional elements of a birthday party, i.e., an old-fashioned frosted cake and sharing embarrassing photos and pictures of a much younger, and often naked, Chloe.

And of course, a toast.

As soon as her mom began to tap on a glass, Chloe looked around for the quickest way out of being the center of attention. No one was budging; she was trapped.

"As many of you here already know," Mrs. King

began with a sniff, "we aren't exactly sure when Chloe's birthday really is."

Chloe closed her eyes. She was going to do it. She was going to tell the whole story.

The crowd waited expectantly.

"She was born somewhere in the countryside of the old USSR. By the time *we* found her, the only thing the Soviet officials could give us was a document with some scribbles and a sickle-and-star stamp."

Mrs. King pointed to the tattered paper, matted and framed above the dining room table.

"David and I wanted a baby so badly . . . and we were *so* lucky. Chloe was the most beautiful little girl we had ever seen. And she has grown in grace and beauty and intelligence in every way since." Chloe almost groaned aloud. Amy gave her a look, sympathizing with her horror. "And even though we have our little . . . fights, I couldn't be more proud. And if your dad"—*had stuck around*—"were here, he would feel the same way. Chloe, I love you. You're the best thing that has ever happened to me. Happy sixteenth birthday!"

Everyone clinked their glasses and hugged her. Chloe mumbled thanks, just glad that the worst part was over so quickly. As soon as the knot of people around her loosened, she dove for the table of hors d'oeuvres, filled up a plate, and stood in the corner behind a tall plant so she could enjoy the caterer's specialties in peace.

A pair of people walked by, dangerously close. Chloe froze—they didn't seem to have noticed her.

"Remember how badly they were fighting toward the end?" Mrs. Lowe whispered.

"Yes, Anne's toast was so diplomatic," Paul's dad responded. "Considering how he just took off like that."

"Did she ever wind up getting a divorce?"

"No . . . it was like he dropped off the face of the planet. He's never sent a penny for Chloe. Of course," he considered, reflecting, "I don't think Anne or Chloe is suffering."

They were both silent.

"More champagne?" Mrs. Lowe finally suggested.

Chloe chewed contemplatively on a celery stick. Back when her father was still around, when she was young, they also used to celebrate her adoption day, which was just a few weeks later. They hadn't done it since her father left, though.

She left the safety of her plant to try and mingle; the revelers were here for *her,* after all.

"So where's the hired magician?" Paul whispered, approaching her and looking around surreptitiously. "I thought there would be clowns and pony rides and stuff."

"She's not *that* bad," Chloe said, surprising herself with her defense of her mother. It was an amazingly nice little party; one of her mom's friends was playing a cello in the corner, which was kind of weird but lent a sophisticated air to the whole thing. Like they were rich and she was a debutante or something. There was even a little American sturgeon—not endangered, her mother said proudly—caviar. And most importantly, a beautiful white-and-chrome Merida mountain bike with electric pedal assist for the more tiresome hills in San Francisco.

What do you know. I got my wish. She felt a little guilty about the whole world peace thing, though. *Maybe next year.*

Paul was tapping the bottom of his champagne glass nervously.

"Um, Amy told me," Chloe said quietly.

He instantly looked relieved, letting out a deep sigh.

"So you're okay with that?"

"With what?"

"With us . . . having . . . you know . . ."

"Well, no," Chloe said, licking caviar off her fingers. "I mean, seeing as I've had this crush on you since we were nine and—"

"O-*kay*." Paul held up his hand. "That's enough. Message received."

Amy wandered over.

"Hey, guys," she said a little nervously. She and Paul exchanged shy—*shy!*—smiles. Chloe watched their two hands "accidentally" brush each other. Amy smiled, glowing a little. Chloe shuddered a little. *Oh God. Fine. I will be the cool best friend.*

• • •

I will be the cool best friend.

Chloe repeated her little mantra through English the next day as she watched Amy and Paul try very hard not to watch each other. Who cared? Why were they trying to keep it a secret? It wasn't as if anyone in the school actually gave a rat's ass about this particular trio of friends or what went on between them. Mr. Mingrone turned to sketch a giant scarlet *A* on the blackboard. When Amy used the opportunity to toss Paul a note, Chloe put her head down. The plastic desktop reeked of old glue, the sharp tang of pencil lead, and other, less identifiable but equally unpleasant odors, but anything was preferable than watching Paul and Amy.

I will be cool.

Paul was nominally on the school newspaper, which allowed him (and Amy and Chloe) access to the club's better computers and equipment, as well as the old ratty couch and semiprivate room. Almost no one used it until after school, which allowed the three of them to hang there during the day if Paul was around. Chloe decided to use sixth period to catch up on some much-missed sleep.

Chloe knocked tentatively on the ancient, solid-oak door, praying that she wouldn't catch her two best friends making out.

"Come," Paul called, using his Captain Picard voice. Amy was definitely not around.

In fact, when Chloe went in, Paul actually appeared

to be working on the paper, sitting on the edge of his desk and looking over an article.

"Crunchy cheese-baked scrod every Wednesday for the next *month*." He sighed, throwing down the lunch schedule. It was Paul, Amy, and Chloe's private opinion that the only reason anyone read *The Lantern* was for the cafeteria menu and Sabrina Anne's often-banned column.

"Why don't you get your mom to pack a lunch? PB and kimchi. Breakfast of champions." Chloe threw her book bag, and then herself, onto the couch.

"Yeah, right." Paul kicked his legs under the desk.

It was strange having him look down on her like that. Or maybe it was just an overall change in his demeanor since the whole hooking-up-with-Amy thing. He seemed calm and confident, like he was relaxing on a throne instead of perched on a desk. Actually, he looked pretty good today. He was wearing a simple black T-shirt and baggy jeans that complemented his square, compact body better than any of the bowling shirts or DJ wear he often sported.

Uh, what? Chloe suddenly realized she was *admiring* Paul's looks. Good ol' Paul, with the harelip scar that tugged his mouth when he smiled. *Kind of endearing, really . . .*

Chloe shook herself.

"So what's been going on?" she asked quickly.

"Between you almost dying and Amy? Not a whole lot." He looked at her with faint amusement in his dark brown eyes. Chloe felt her palms sweat. It was a small room, secluded from the rest of the high school; their aloneness was a very palpable third presence in the room with them.

It's just because Amy likes him, she told herself. *A competition thing.* In the still air of the room she could just smell the deodorant and soap he used and underneath, a saltiness that she realized was probably his skin. The way he was sitting there, it would be so easy just to walk over and push herself against him; they would be the same height. She could wrap her arms around his neck like she had with Xavier and pull him in—

"Robble robble, blah blah blah—hey, King, you listening?"

"Yes!" She leapt up, trying to shake off the desire. "No. I mean, I gotta go. I, uh, forgot to hand in my essay to Mingrone—shit, I hope he hasn't left yet."

She grabbed her bag and made for the door.

"I think he said we have until tomorrow," Paul called after her. The door slammed between them.

I will be cool.

Yeah, right.

At work Chloe forced herself to seriously look over every guy who came in. Including a few who were gay. Things were very bad indeed when she found herself almost kissing her best friend. Who seemed to be her other best friend's boyfriend.

Marisol didn't help anything by putting the Eurythmics'

"I Need a Man" on the shop speakers. Chloe jumped guiltily when she heard the chorus.

"Is it that obvious?"

"Honey, you're *dripping* hormones all over my nice clean floor." The older woman smiled at her. Chloe wished her mom was more like her manager. She always seemed to understand Chloe's moods immediately and unless there was a sale coming up, was often ready to talk and listen.

"Who put on this old shit?" Lania screamed from the shoe section, hands over her ears in horror.

Chloe and Marisol exchanged "what can you do" looks. "Go get yourself a boy, girl. You're not concentrating; it's obvious your attention is elsewhere," Marisol said in a lighthearted voice.

As Chloe patiently ripped through the hem seams of more jeans, she reflected on what her boss had said. Maybe she *could* get it "out of her system." Maybe she was due for a nice boyfriend.

Or a visit to Xavier.

Once Chloe had found the right street, she pulled the crumpled card out of her back pocket. *I'm going to have to get better at this.* She imagined herself in a business suit, somewhere in a steel-and-glass future, shaking someone's hand and pulling out her own card, all rumpled and greasy. She checked the address against the building. Xavier must have had a little money or have been crashing with a friend who did: it was a *nice* old house, three floors, dark wood and bay windows on a street with soft green trees and no traffic. Of course, both sides of the street were stuffed with parked cars—rich neighborhood or not, this was still San Francisco.

The front door was propped open and there was a hand-scrawled note to FedEx posted over the buzzer. The lobby smelled of lemon wood cleaner. There was only one apartment per floor; Xavier had the attic. With gables. Chloe had always dreamed of living in a real old house like this instead of her bug-ugly vinyl-sided ranch. She climbed the stairs, letting her hand trail along the smoothly polished rail.

But in the half-light of the stairwell Chloe began to question what she was doing: going to some foreign older guy's apartment by herself at twilight without anyone knowing where she was. He could turn out to be anything: a rapist or murderer. A vampire, even.

She paused briefly, but an image of herself kissing Paul pushed her forward. *I won't go in. I'll stand in the hallway and ask him if he wants to go out. Maybe grab a coffee.*

His door was dark wood with molding and a little brass-and-glass peephole at eye height. She raised her hand to knock . . .

And realized the door was pushed open just the slightest bit.

"Uh, hello?" she called out, stepping back.

"Help . . . ," a choked, wheezy voice called from inside. *"Help me!"*

Chloe hesitated on the doorstep. It could be a trap. He could kidnap girls and rape them and sell them into slavery and . . .

"Please . . . someone . . ."

Chloe pushed open the door and stepped inside.

The apartment smelled of sickness and decay, which was strange against the clean, antique furniture and expensive, modern lighting. In each gable was a carefully designed nook for reading and sitting—*just like I would have done.* Chloe made herself follow the sound of wheezing.

Lying under the lintel to the bathroom was a very different Xavier.

He was wearing the same clothes from the club two nights ago, but they were torn and pulled like he had tried to rip them off his body. His face had bubbled up like the rind of a diseased grapefruit. His cheeks and forehead were swollen and red, with white liquid, lymph or pus, oozing out of giant sores.

"Help—" He was trying to scream, but his throat was swollen so badly, he could barely breathe. He groaned and twisted, trying to crawl out of his skin. He flopped onto his stomach and Chloe got a look at his back. Long, oozing cankers and welts, like claw marks. Exactly where she had scratched and kneaded him outside the club.

Chloe backed up slowly.

Must call.

Without thought, like she was walking through syrup, Chloe found the handset of a cordless phone in the living room, resting on top of one of those expensive giant HEPA filters from Sharper Image, like the one her mom had. She dialed 911.

She recited the address when a brusque, disinterested voice came on. "There's someone here. Covered in sores. Can barely breathe. It looks like he's dying."

It looks like he's dying.

"We'll be right there, ma'am. What's your telephone number?"

"I don't—" She looked at the card and gave them his cell. After hanging up she went back to Xavier. He was hissing and coughing and his eyes were crusty and half shut. She wondered if he could see her, if he would recognize her.

Exactly where she had scratched him.

Chloe waited until she heard sirens approaching, and then she ran.

Six

Friday passed normally, and Xavier wasn't mentioned in any obits or police beats, so Chloe was determined to have a normal weekend, too. Hormone free. Guy free. Falls-from-towers and formerly-hot-now-sick-strangers free.

She got up on Saturday, poured herself a big box of Lucky Charms, and watched new (really crappy) cartoons for a couple of hours. It was sunny out, so she drew the shades, just like she used to when she was young so she wouldn't be tempted to leave the glowing light of the television for the great outdoors.

At two she met Amy at Relax Now. Chloe had casually suggested to Amy the night before that they treat themselves to manicures with some of her birthday money. Amy objected at first, calling it a middle-class, bourgeois ritual of the Burberry-knockoff set. Chloe told her to cut the crap and enjoy it; they had never done it before and might never do it again. Besides, she was paying.

And Amy actually seemed pretty cheerful, looking over her nails as they dried. She had talked the most artistic seeming of the women there into painting the lower half of all her nails black, then putting a single clawlike black stripe in the middle of each one. She flexed and re-flexed her fingers under the little lamps.

"Grrr," she said.

Chloe was still having hers worked on. She'd opted for the hot paraffin, vitamin-wrap, extra-super-cleany options and was drilling the woman doing it with a battery of questions: Could fingernails be dirty even if they didn't look it? Could you carry diseases under your nails? What about toxic fungi?

"Yes, yes, and yes," the woman replied, zealously buffing. "I knew a girl once, she went to a place—not here, a *dirty* place—she got a pedicure and had to have her whole toe removed afterward. Nasty infection. Anyway, this will take care of all that. You could eat with them now."

Chloe felt relieved. And guilty. She hoped Xavier was okay. She had to somehow check on him later.

It *was* kind of funny, though, that she'd managed to spread something diseaselike to her partner before she'd ever even had sex. Funny in a loose sense of the word, of course.

"This is *perfect*," Amy said, admiring her nails. "We're going to the Temple of Arts tonight—this will freak the shit out of all the vampire role players there."

"Cool. I haven't been there in so long." Chloe didn't have anything planned for that evening, except for cooking with her mother (mother-daughter time), something she was anxious to get out of. And it would be an excellent way to get over whatever weird rush she'd felt with Paul earlier that week. The three of them just hanging out would be a good thing. "I promised Mom I'd help her with some weird and complicated recipe tonight, but I should be done by nine or ten."

"Oh." Amy stared more intently at her nails, blushing. "I meant, like, just me and Paul. Like a date."

"Like a *date*?" It had been just a casual, high-tension kissing session before. . . . When had their status changed? "Oh." Chloe fidgeted, prompting a smack from the woman working on her. "Oh. That's cool. No problem."

I will be the cool friend.

"How about tomorrow? We could totally get together tomorrow," Amy suggested eagerly.

"Nah. I'm taking my new bike for a ride." Disappointment and embarrassment and anger raged through her brain, making it difficult to sound casual.

"All day?"

"Yeah," Chloe said firmly, staring at her nails. *"All day."*

At home Chloe began to feel bad about breaking her "I will be cool" mantra when Amy obviously was already embarrassed by the whole discussion. And she had kind of acted like a baby. Of course she and Paul wanted to spend time together. They were *dating*, dummy.

Chloe finally e-mailed:

You wanna hang Sunday night? Rent a movie or something . . . xo, C.

That didn't stop her from being grumpy about it, though. Chloe drowsed on her bed, visions of Xavier, Alyec, and—yuck—Paul spinning around in her head before her mom finally demanded her help with dinner. She was silent in the kitchen.

"Is something wrong, Chloe?" Her mother was in a rare, selfless good mood.

"No." She smashed a clove of garlic with the side of her knife for emphasis.

Her mom looked at her sideways but didn't say anything.

Dinner was fabulous if weird, as all of her mom's Saturday night attempts tended to be. While Mrs. King napped on the couch in the living room afterward, Chloe channel flipped, pausing at some sort of nighttime soap she never would have normally given a second thought to, but a handsome couple was making out on the beach at night. Chloe watched them wistfully, imagining sand under her own head and lips against hers.

"How was your bike ride, Chlo?" Amy asked in line for lunch on Monday.

"It was great." It really had been. And if she hadn't been so preoccupied with how pissed she was at Paul and Amy and how she really wanted her own boyfriend, it would have been perfect. She had never noticed how many goddamn happy couples there were all across San Francisco before. Making out in public. Everywhere.

She felt in her pocket for a quarter that wasn't there and tried to find something interesting in what the lunch hag was doing. "You never replied to my e-mail."

"Sorry about that," Amy continued bravely. "My phone ran out of juice. I didn't get the message until this morning."

"No problem." Chloe realized she couldn't watch the pot of reddish glop—"chili"—being stirred around by the woman with the mustache. The beans looked suspiciously like cockroaches. She turned her head, but there was nothing else to look at in the small line but Amy.

"You—you want to hang after school today?" Amy got her like a deer in headlights. Her big eyes were trembling: *I'm really sorry,* they said. "I suck, I know."

Chloe resisted.

"Please? I'll make it up to you. You and me and Paul, we'll go watch the sea lions, like we used to. I'll buy you an ice cream. *Please?*"

Chloe couldn't help smiling. This was Amy, after all. "Oh, all right. But I want two flavors, swirled."

"You're on!" Amy agreed, grinning.

Whap—their moment of reconciliation was interrupted by a pile of red mush hitting Chloe's tray with a sickening, definitely unfoodlike sound.

"Next!" the lunch lady screamed.

As she and Amy left the lunch line, they ran smack into Alyec.

"King!" he said, smiling. "When are we going to hang out?"

Chloe watched his curvy, exotic lips. Smiling at *her*.

"This afternoon? My friends and I are going to go down to the pier and watch the sea lions. Want to come?" Amy looked askance at her, surprised.

It was the lamest, lamest thing she could have ever imagined saying to Alyec. But when the words came out of her mouth, they were confident, and she looked him in the eye.

Alyec raised his eyebrows; it really did sound corny. "Sea lions, eh? Well, why not? It's free."

"It's a date," Chloe said casually as she headed off to a table. Amy trailed, her mouth hanging open.

Paul and Amy were trying to behave, Chloe could see that.

Amy was sitting on his lap in the glowy late-afternoon sunshine, contented smiles on her and Paul's faces. There was no actual making out going on. *So why do I feel like vomiting?*

"Arp!" a sea lion barked.

She licked her cone, using her tongue to carefully pick up the chocolate with an equal amount of vanilla.

The bay was dark blue and the bridge an ancient,

rusty red. Little islands in the distance faded in and out of view as strings of perfect sailboats floated in front of them. The crowds of tourists weren't even that bad.

It was almost perfect. Almost. Alyec wasn't here.

And why should he be? Why should anything I want ever work out? Come on, this was *Alyec*—as Paul said, "He is steely-eyed, chisel-faced young Russian." Why would he show up for a lame-ass double date with three of the out crowd?

"Hey, look at that one!" Paul wasn't pointing at a sea lion; he was pointing at one of the few tourists. But this one was a beaut: he wore a hat that said Frisco on it and a T-shirt that said Alcatraz and was trying to take a picture of the pier with a tiny, bright yellow disposable camera.

It was the most exciting thing that had happened since they came.

And now the sun was beginning to set. The night ocean breezes picked up, brushing a strand of dark hair into Chloe's face. She brushed it out of the way impatiently.

"You wanna go somewhere, get coffee?" Paul asked eventually.

Chloe sighed. *Ah, I am now officially a third wheel.*

"Where are the sea lions? Or are you talking about the fat tourists?"

Chloe spun around. Alyec was walking up the pier,

hands in his pockets, frowning as he tried to make out the animals in the dimming light.

"Over there." She pointed casually at the water. It took every ounce of her will not to jump up and shout his name joyfully. *I am cool,* she repeated, finally for a different reason. He was drop-dead-gorgeous casual tonight, button-down open over a T-shirt, no socks. The approaching dusk made his blond hair look like it was streaked with honey and brown.

"Oh! I see them now!" He actually looked interested; his face lit up. "Very cool. We didn't have any of those in St. Petersburg. Or maybe once we did, but they were all eaten."

Chloe introduced Amy and Paul. Alyec shook their hands formally. "Amy—I think I saw you at that café with the chicken. You were reading some of your poetry?"

Paul looked a little annoyed. Amy blushed. "I do some readings now and then."

There was a long, awkward pause. A single sea lion noiselessly slipped into the water. Others soon began to follow.

"Well, this was fun," Alyec said, looking around. "But maybe we should do something else now? It's getting too dark to see the lions."

Chloe tried not to giggle. It sounded so cute coming out that way.

"We were going to get coffee," Paul said.

"Okay. Then what?"

"A club?" Amy suggested.

"Excellent!" Alyec pointed at her like she had just picked the correct amount for a washer on *The Price Is Right*. Then he looked serious. "The one thing I really miss about my old town is the dancing. Every night, if you wanted. No cover, either."

"I don't know about going dancing tonight—" Whatever Paul's reasons were, they were cut off by a sharp jab in the side from Amy's elbow.

"Sounds great," she said. "Chloe?"

"Absolutely." She imagined dancing with Alyec like she had with Xavier. Then she thought of Xavier in the parking lot and Xavier on the floor of his apartment, covered in sores. She beat the guilt down as fast as she could. "Um . . . anywhere but the Bank!"

Alyec, Paul, and Amy all looked at her.

"It sucks on a Monday night," Chloe continued lamely. *And Tuesday and Wednesday and Thursday and Friday.* In fact, she would be happy if she never went back there again.

To Chloe's relief they settled on the Raven, a place that played a lot of good dance music but didn't have a dance floor. What they *did* have was a lot of comfy old couches and a tendency to serve to those who were underage. Also a dartboard, which Alyec and Paul instantly commandeered.

"Look at them," Amy said, giggling. Paul was closing one eye and aiming. Alyec had his arms crossed and a serious expression on his brow. "They're like cavemen."

"I don't think Cro-Magnon men used darts to bring down woolly mammoths." Chloe sipped delicately from her Hoegaarden. Alyec was impressed by her choice but hadn't offered to buy it for her. Which was a shame, since it was five bucks.

"I think he fits in well," Amy said, meaning Alyec and the trio of friends.

"I don't want him to fit in well," Chloe said with a little more passion than she meant. "I want him to come over here, drag me outside, and kiss me like he really means it." She took a couple of big gulps.

"Oh my God, Chloe gets shallow. You really *do* want a handsome caveman."

"I like talking," Chloe protested. "Talking is good. Later. *After* the making out."

"Well." Alyec sat down next to her, coming over the back of the couch. "I have taught your friend a little lesson in the finer points of losing."

Paul just growled and sat next to Amy, who turned so she could lean on his lap. Alyec put his arm behind Chloe on the back of the couch, touching her occasionally to emphasize points. She wondered if he realized that he was driving her crazy. *Probably. That's how he wound up with a crowd of worshipers in the first place, isn't it?* Chloe made a mental note that no matter what happened, she would not end up in that category. Chloe was different from them, the Keiras and the Halley Dietrichs of the world.

Paul challenged Alyec to darts twice more, never winning. Amy panhandled for jukebox quarters. Chloe watched Alyec, sipped her beer, and occasionally moderated Amy's music decisions. At ten Amy's mom called and insisted she come home from whatever scandalous thing she was doing. All four parted ways at the street corner outside, but Alyec didn't offer to see Chloe home.

"See you in Am civ tomorrow," Alyec said. "Thanks for inviting me out today." He kissed her lightly on the cheek, then turned and disappeared into the night.

It was nice. A *nice* kiss. Very *nice*. Too *nice*.

Chloe felt like screaming.

"You could just wear a T-shirt that says I'm Easy," Amy suggested.

In the end, Chloe was glad to walk home by herself. The air was dry and a little chill, just the way fall weather should be. Quick little winds pushed leaves around and around on the pavement, making dry scratchy noises. Clouds skittered across the moon. *Very Halloweeny.* For the first time in days her thoughts drifted away from Xavier, her fall, and even Alyec: she wondered what Amy would do for a costume this year. They were always spectacular, complicated, and often puns: last year she'd been a Big Mac Daddy, with a red wig, clown shoes, and gold chains. Paul had worn jeans and a jean jacket with a pin of a DNA helix that said Selfish Gene. Chloe had just worn a vintage evening gown and a half mask, one that Amy had helped her take apart and put on a stick so she would look like a Venetian attending a ball.

"Hey—*smile*, sister!"

Chloe broke out of her reverie to see one of San Francisco's many friendly street people approaching her. He was tall and probably in his twenties, with blond hair in stupid white-man dreads. His clothes were grubby. Chloe forced a smile at him and kept walking.

"Hey, sister, can you spare a dollar or two?" He ran alongside her and put out his hand. "I really need a beer." He flashed a toothy grin at her. His honesty was refreshing—and amusing—but Chloe suddenly realized there was no one else on the street with them, and all of the shops were closed for the night.

Her Spidey sense, as Paul would have called it, tingled. She picked up the pace.

"Sorry," she said.

"Come *on*." He grabbed at her hand. "You gotta have a dollar or two. Everyone does."

Chloe pulled her hand away. "I'm sorry, I don't."

"I'll bet you do." He grabbed her harder and spun her around.

"Let go of me!" She yelled it, looking him right in the eye, just like they had taught her in the self-defense class she and her mom had taken. He put his other hand over her mouth. It stank of old body, dog, and pee.

"Come on, don't be like that. We can have a little fun." He leered at her.

Suddenly she was *angry*, all fear gone. Rage burned in her: who did he think he was? What gave him the right to do this to *her*—to anyone?

Chloe bit down on his hand, catching a thick piece of palm meat. She ground her teeth down and pulled back her head, ripping something loose.

"Holy *shit*—mother*fucker*!" He pulled that hand away, stared at it dumbly, thick ropes of blood gushing out of it. Then he whacked her in the face.

It hurt *bad*. Chloe didn't care. She spun around. Using his hand to balance herself, Chloe leapt up and kicked him on the chest.

Which was odd, because she didn't know a single martial art, and she'd actually been aiming for his crotch.

He stumbled backward, winded.

Chloe waited.

"You little—" He dove at her.

She leapt easily out of the way and grabbed his hair as he passed. She yanked back hard on it so he lost balance, then spun and kicked him in the side as he fell. She channeled all her rage at the world, at her friends, at Alyec, at her dad who'd left her, at her bad chemistry grade into that kick. There was a very satisfying sound of ribs breaking. He rolled onto his stomach and she kicked him on his other side.

"Fucking—bitch—," he wheezed. "I'll kill you—"

Chloe backhanded him on the side of the head. He went out immediately. Blood trickled out of his ear and down his jaw.

She stood there, panting. *What now? Call 911 anonymously for the second time in a week?*

Nah. He didn't deserve it. She turned and started walking home.

The night was the same as it was when she began her walk: beautiful, cold, and quiet. Chloe whistled a little tune, still full of adrenaline, realizing something strange.

She had enjoyed *every second* of the fight.

Seven

Her mother didn't come home until late that night, after she was home and asleep, so Chloe was spared the almost inevitable confrontation about the bruises and scrapes on her cheeks. She slept dreamlessly until her alarm rang and managed to hide her face from her mom until she got out of the house.

"What the hell happened to *you*?" It was blunt, but at least Amy didn't start off with any is-your-mom-hitting-you bullshit. She was smoking a clove cigarette this morning, trying to look cool by casually dropping it and stepping on it as they approached the school.

"I walked into a door. *Again,*" Chloe answered tragically.

Amy hit her.

"I was attacked by a bum last night, walking home." She wasn't sure if it was a good idea to tell the truth, but after not bothering to mention her night at the club *or* Xavier, Chloe was beginning to feel uncomfortable with the number of omissions and half lies she was telling her friend.

"Oh my God. Are you *okay*? Wait, what am I saying. This is the Chloe King who survived a fall from Coit Tower." Amy raised one eyebrow and shook her head.

"I beat the living shit out of him," Chloe couldn't help bragging.

"Yeah? Which episode of *Buffy* was that? Or more importantly, what was he on?"

"Hey! I attribute it to my awesome strength, lightning-fast reflexes, and that self-defense course I aced."

"Uh-huh," Amy said, nodding and pretending to agree. "So. What was he on?"

Why didn't Ame believe her? Was it so unbelievable that she'd managed to defend herself successfully from an attacker? Chloe thought back on the fight. The man had been large, six-foot two or so, but skinny. He had obviously been living on the streets for a while. She tried to play the scene through Amy's eyes. It seemed believable, almost like a scenario from the self-defense class—up until, with no training, she's done that high kick onto his chest. And instead of running away, she had finished the fight.

Chloe sighed. "Probably smack or something."

The predictable appearance of crunchy cheese-baked scrod on Wednesday was a surprisingly reassuring thing. Though it made Chloe want to retch, lunch seemed to indicate that everything was normal. Sure, Amy and

Paul tended to disappear from the scene every available moment—Chloe was convinced that someday one of the face-sucking couples she passed in the hall before class would turn out to be them. She'd taken to walking between classes faster, head down.

Amy *did* manage to find five minutes on the walk between school and work on Wednesday to talk, bringing a latte for her friend, the first of many what Chloe called "gilfts": guilt gifts. They chatted about this and that, but it was always the same problem.

Chloe wanted to *talk* about things—like the fall. Like her fight with the bum. Like Xavier, for Christ's sake. But she and Amy had been so apart recently that it took a few minutes of rapid reacquainting before Chloe felt comfortable enough to *really* talk, and by then one of them—usually Amy—always had to leave.

At Pateena's, Marisol had turned on the old black-and-white television—one of four throughout the store that played trippy visuals to trance on the speakers. Some dumb sitcom was playing while she set up the tapes. Chloe absently watched it while taking her break, scanning the obituaries again, looking for Xavier. The TV show was something about a normal guy and his hippie wife and the comic mayhem that ensued as a result of their differences.

Chloe suddenly envisioned a different version of her mother: a slightly ditzier, San Francisco hippie version who dragged her daughter to horrible things like drumming circles and Goddess nights. Maybe she owned a bookstore. She would be kooky but easy to talk to and would have relevant things to say about boys when Chloe opened up to her over a mug of homemade chai. Nothing negative. Nothing like "don't date them," for instance.

From what little she remembered and had been told, her dad was more that type of person. A modern do-gooder, a legal defense aide who worked with immigrants by day and took his wife to benefits and galas for nonprofits by night. Chloe tried to picture him at Carlucci's with her, the gray and hazy areas of his face pieced in with old scrapbook photos. He would tell her that boys were terrible things and that he should know, because he had been one. He would blush but try to remain supportive when she talked about Xavier. He would be interested that Alyec was Russian. He should be, considering it had been *his* idea to adopt the orphan of an ex-Soviet state. Right now Chloe felt like she had *no one* to talk to.

"Hey."

A pair of black knit kitty cat ears appeared above the rack where she was working. The guy wearing them stood on his toes and waved at her.

"Hey," she said, smiling.

"I think I'm going to buy a whole *suit* this time," he said. "Or maybe just a jacket," he added.

"Lania is our queer-eye-for-every-person girl. She

can help you pick out something professional *and* stellar if you don't mind the constant bitching."

"Oh." In the flash of sunlight his eyes were almost green and very deep, like an expensive glass paperweight.

Chloe desperately tried to think of some way of continuing the conversation.

"Hey, um, I think I want the pattern for your hat after all," she said. "My friend Amy knits, and she owes me a birthday present."

"Oh! Absolutely!" He gave up his tippy-toe routine, seeming to suddenly realize he could simply walk around the rack. He wore a dark green shirt with jeans and black square-tipped European-looking shoes. Very much the clove cigarette type: dark and mysterious. His shoulders were larger than they had seemed the other day, and he held a copy of James Joyce's *Ulysses* under his arm. "I'll bring it by."

"Sure, that would be great."

There was a silence between them for a moment.

"Or," he added, "I could take you out for a coffee after work sometime and give it to you."

Chloe smiled. "*That* would be great."

"How 'bout tomorrow?"

"Absolutely!"

"I'm Brian, uh, by the way."

"I'm Chloe. Pleased to meet you." She made a serious look and held out her hand. He shook it.

"Chloe—like 'Daphnis and Chloe,' the Greek myth?"

"One and the same," Chloe said, surprised he knew of it.

"You know," he said, glancing at the newspaper section she held, "not everyone who dies winds up in the obituaries."

"What? Oh." She blushed, thinking furiously. "I—I guess I'm just morbid. I, uh, like to see how old people are when they die and stuff."

"Try the crossword instead," he suggested, smiling. "It looks impressive and high-falutin' when you do it with a pen."

Chloe grinned. "Maybe I'll just do that."

She stayed late to help Marisol lock up, checking her watch nervously. Now that the new season of television had once again begun, Wednesdays were *Smallville* and takeout night, her mother's attempt to connect to her daughter via cable's younger generation. One of her more successful attempts, actually, since Chloe loved dumplings and Michael Rosenbaum. Plus since the unexpected birthday party she and her mom seemed to be getting along better, something Chloe didn't want to screw up.

By the time she helped Marisol pull the chain gate down, it was seven forty-five. There was *no way* the bus was going to get her home in time. Three miles on the bus took forever.

"Here." Marisol handed her a ten-dollar bill.

"I only stayed an extra hour," Chloe protested.

"Shush!" The older woman pushed it into her hand and closed her fist around it. "Take a cab home. I got a ten-year-old, and someday she's going to be your age. It freaks me out watching you and Lania. Be safe."

"You have a daughter?" Chloe felt twice as embarrassed taking the money now, having just found out about an important part of her boss's life that she knew nothing of before.

"Yeah. She's at her dad's this week. Lazy son of a bitch loves his little girl, at least. See you tomorrow." Marisol tossed her long brown-black hair over her shoulder like a younger woman, like a girl, like someone who didn't have a ten-year-old and an ex-husband and a business. When she crossed the street, she kind of bounced.

Chloe looked at the ten in her hand and thought about the differences between her mom and her boss, and the little ten-year-old she hadn't known about until today, who split her life between her parents. Like Paul now. Chloe didn't even have that option.

She looked around: the streets were devoid of regular cars, let alone cabs. The faintest curl of cold air hit her nose, sharp and electric. When it faded, Chloe noticed the city-made warmth, the biological smell of trees and dirt and humans, men and women running about and excited, glad the workday was over.

Chloe began to trot, methodically jogging like she

did in gym to do as little work as possible and not get noticed. Her breasts bounced uncomfortably in her not-designed-for-jogging bra.

Then, without thinking, she opened up her stride and *ran*.

She ran like her body had been waiting its whole life to actually run, as if she had been held in check up until this moment. She didn't even have to think about the movement of her arms or the placement of her feet and legs the way Mr. Parmalee was always shouting. She ran with wide steps, eating up the vanilla slabs of concrete below with hungry feet. And when her steps weren't wide enough—she leapt.

Houses passed in a blur, parked cars looked like they were moving. She jumped over fire hydrants and small bushes, not like a normal long or high jumper, but springing with her arms held curled at her sides to break her fall if she mislanded.

She never did.

When she crossed the street, she did it in the middle of the block and leapt onto the hood of a car that blocked the pedestrian walkway. She was gratified to hear the alarm go off in whoops. From there she found herself using a *parking meter* as a step closer down to the sidewalk, her left foot delicately resting on it for a moment while her right foot reached for the ground.

The energy, strength, and speed she felt were just like in the fight with the homeless guy—but they lasted longer. Not just an adrenaline burst. And there was no rage, no flight or fight—just the pure joy of movement, of almost flying through the deserted night.

She cut through an empty lot, pretty sure it was a faster route home. Even though there was no moon that night and no streetlights in the area, she managed to leap over dead tires, puddles of broken glass, and unpleasant-looking plants without nicking herself on a single obstacle.

When she finally leapt up the steps to her house and let herself in, she wasn't even winded.

"Just in time," her mother said, smiling. She was laying out cartons of Chinese.

The clock on the TV said 7:57.

Eight

"Hey, Alyec," Chloe called, waving to him across the hallway the next morning.

"Hey, King." He waved back, but he turned around to continue his conversation with Keira. Chloe could almost *feel* Keira's smugness as he dismissed her. It was infuriating. Chloe slunk away as if she had never stopped. Yeah, she should probably be happy about Brian. But Alyec was *hot*. Sexy. Drop-dead gorgeous. Covetousness inspiring. She snuck one look back to watch his wheat blond hair (or was it rye? What did they grow in Russia?) fall over his brow in waves like the fringe on an expensive pillow. *Maybe I should tell him that I'm a Ruskie, too.*

Or maybe, she thought, maybe she should choose one guy and stick with him. Either pursue Alyec or continue with Brian.

Nah . . . this is way more fun.

"Hey." Paul waved at her from the river of teenage

traffic that was going the opposite way, down the left side of the hall. He jumped into a free space next to her. "Take any long falls from tall buildings lately?"

"I base-dived the Transamerica—does that count?"

"We were thinking about going to the arcade at Sony later," he continued. *And since when did he and Amy become a "we"?* Amy and *she* were a "we." Amy, *Paul*, and she were a "we." Should she just assume from now on that whenever either one of her best friends used that pronoun, they were only referring to themselves? "Wanna come?"

Oh, now I'm being invited *places by them. Pity the third wheel.*

"No thanks, I've got plans." She didn't know if hazel eyes could look cold, but she tried her best, making her face go flat with lack of emotion. She had practiced it in front of a mirror. The expression looked good with her high cheekbones.

"Plans?" Paul asked. His eyebrows raised almost to his spiked bangs.

"Yeah, *plans*. Maybe another time."

And she walked away.

Of course, she knew it wouldn't drop like that; she was *hoping* it wouldn't. It came during math in the form of a single-character text message on her phone from Amy: *?*

She responded: *thanks 4 the invite, tho.*

Amy: *whats ur prob biyatch? @ least cometo my reading fri 7 @ b.rooster Puhlleeeeeeeezzze :) ! ucan bring alyec.*

Yeah, right, if she wanted to make sure that Alyec never wanted to hang out with her or her friends again. Amy's poetry could have that effect on people.

Chloe put away her phone, not wanting to deal.

Brian showed up at Pateena's precisely at six.

Chloe was leaning in the doorway, carefully searching through the obituaries. No mention of Xavier. "Where to?" Chloe asked, shoving the paper into her bag.

He seemed to have dressed up a little. His pants were something soft, black, and matte that almost looked like velvet. Wool? Velour? Chloe found herself resisting the urge to reach out and feel it. *I wonder if he likes dancing. . . .*

"I was thinking . . . the zoo." He looked at her expectantly, his brown eyes wide.

"The *zoo*?" Mugs of coffee and an intimate dinner melted away. "Isn't it closed?"

"Nope. Not until eight. And I'm a member, so we get in free."

The zoo . . . Come to think of it, she hadn't been there in years, even though it was reasonably close by. And no one had ever offered to take her there before.

"All right, but you're buying me a souvenir drink cup."

"Hey, *you're* the one with a job."

"*You're* the one who asked me out."

"Touché," he admitted. He was so easy to talk to! This was, like, their third conversation and they were already bantering like old friends. "Okay, one souvenir drink cup for you. But if you felt like the evening went well, I wouldn't object to you purchasing a stuffed monkey for *me*."

Chloe grinned. "It's a deal."

There were no crowds outside the zoo gates, only families leaving, and all Brian had to do was wave his card at the guard and point to Chloe and they waltzed in. So much better than the heat, lines, and crowds she remembered from experiences there as a kid. It was also kind of cool going there at dusk: the overhanging trees gathered shadows under them, making the place seem more wild.

"Are you in college?" she finally asked casually, looking at a map. He didn't look *that* much older than her. . . .

"Not yet. I'm taking a couple of years off."

"So, what did you need that suit for?"

"Twenty questions!" he said, laughing. "I'm looking to major in zoology. Hence, uh, the zoo. But that's kind of a difficult program for an undergrad degree, and competition is fierce. I wasn't exactly a . . . *scholar* in high school, so I thought I would get some experience by working at a zoo or animal rescue league or something like that. I'm in the interviewing process right now. You'd be surprised how many people want crappy, low-paying jobs that involve shoveling a lot of animal—well, *crap*."

Chloe smiled. "Sounds cool to me . . . I've never had

a pet more interesting than a goldfish or a beta. My mom's allergic."

"I have four cats," he said smugly, watching her envy. "Tabitha, Sebastian, Sabrina, and Agatha."

"Four?"

"Oh, that's nothing. When I was little, we had . . ." But his brow furrowed, and he looked away distractedly.

"When you were little . . . ?" Chloe prompted him.

"We had a lot. Of pets," he finished lamely. "Lots of cats. Rare breeds, too, like Cornish rex and Maine coon."

They wandered the paths randomly. Chloe *loved* seeing the zoo like this, for free, with no pressure to see all of the top animals, to see every square inch before it was time to go. They could pause as long as they wanted to watch a pair of simple mallard ducks that wandered into the aviary and skip the exhibits they didn't care about without feeling guilty.

But Brian was much quieter than before, except when he was pointing out interesting factoids and habits of the various animals they saw. He chewed the inside of his lip when he thought she wasn't looking, as if trying to decide whether or not to say more.

"So you had lots of pets when you were young?" Chloe prompted when they stopped to get her a diet Coke in a plastic monkey-shaped cup. He ordered one of those cappuccinos from a machine, something Chloe wouldn't have done if she were *starving*.

"Yeah, uh . . ." Brian's face fell, completely losing the animation it had when he was talking about the meerkats and the cassowaries. "My mom's dead," he finally said. "And my dad and me—we don't really get along. He's got this apartment he keeps here in the city—where I live, for now—but he does a lot of work out of his other house in Sausalito. We don't talk much."

He shook his head. "But that's *way* too much information for a first date. You probably just want to make sure I'm not some kind of freak."

Chloe laughed. "I have a secret mouse," she volunteered, lightening the mood.

"What?"

"A secret mouse. His name is Mus-mus. From the Latin name for mouse, you know? *Mus musculus.* My mom doesn't know I keep him in a drawer of my bureau."

"You keep a *mouse*? In your *bureau*?"

"Yeah," she said a little defensively. "Mom wouldn't let me otherwise."

"That's so . . . cute." He looked at her in wonder, as if that was the most charming thing anyone had ever said. They wandered out of the concession area, Chloe sucking noisily on the straw that impaled the monkey's head. A sign pointed to penguins, otters, and lions.

"Hey . . . ," Chloe said, remembering bits of the dream she'd had after she fell off the tower. "Let's go see the lions. I . . . dreamt about some recently. . . ."

"Yeah?"

"Yeah." She looked down as they walked, trying to match her stride to his, but Brian's legs were much longer. "My dad's gone, too," she said. "And my mom's kind of a bitch."

"*Every*one's mom is a bitch when you're sixteen." He laughed. "I just would have liked to have known mine."

"How did you know I was sixteen?" Chloe asked, suddenly suspicious.

"I didn't." He shrugged. "It was more of a general comment. Not you in particular, but when 'you're' sixteen, meaning everyone."

He took the tiniest sip from his cappuccino but still managed to get a foamy mustache.

"The day after I turned sixteen, I almost punched my dad out," Brian continued. He straightened up and looked her in the eye, daring her to disbelieve him.

"That would be *so* much more effective if you didn't have milk all over your lip," she said, laughing. She reached over with a napkin and carefully wiped it off, trying not to drag it across his mouth too hard. She was doubly glad she had a manicure: it made the gesture twice as sexy. Denim dust under the nails would *not* have been attractive.

He blushed, and his hand went through his hair, dislodging a lock that made a Superman-style curl in the middle of his forehead. *With glasses and a dye job, he'd make a very passable Clark Kent.*

He's so . . . cute*!* Chloe thought again, and it wasn't for the last time that night. She wondered what the chances were that someone so much like her, so cute and so charming and so funny, could have randomly met her at work. If she had been in the back that day, or if Lania hadn't been so mean to him, or . . . it never would have happened. And while mentioning Xavier and his subsequent sickness with him was not the sort of thing one did on a first date (*or ever, really*), Chloe could definitely see talking to Brian about other things. Her mom, her dad, Paul and Ame, her near-death experience . . .

"Well, there they are," Brian said, indicating the big yellow cats.

Chloe put her hand out to the rail. She had always sort of dismissed lions before as the popular and inevitable members of any zoo tour. Common, even. But she looked at them more closely now. One female rose and walked languidly over to a water trough. Every step was casual; her shoulders moved up and down slowly. There was no mistaking the power in her muscles. Somehow Chloe wasn't surprised when, after taking a gentle lap and letting the droplets hang from the fur around her mouth, the lion turned and looked directly at her, golden eyes into her own hazel ones.

"I never realized how beautiful they were before," Chloe whispered, unable to turn away.

Brian was saying something, spilling off factoids

about the big cats, but she wasn't listening. She could feel her dream again, like it was real.

". . . know all about these guys. In the wild they eat like ten *pounds* of meat a day, sleep up to twenty *hours* a day, and can run up to fifty miles an hour. . . ."

You need a desert, Chloe thought at them. The lioness showed no sign of hearing or caring about her. She wandered back over to the other females and let herself down onto the ground, lazily and heavily. She bit at her paw.

"Uh, Chloe? Chloe?" Brian asked, waving his hand in front of her.

"What? Sorry?"

"I was trying to impress you with my *National Geographic*–like knowledge of the big cats."

"Oh, sorry. Very clever." Chloe turned for one last look at the lionesses. "These don't just kill people, like Siegfried and Roy's tiger?"

Brian snorted. "Lions aren't usually as dangerous as tigers. But they're not house cats, either. They can get annoyed or pissed off—and even the friendly ones, like these, don't know their own strength compared to humans. They can accidentally kill a zookeeper while trying to play with him."

"Oh." Chloe thought about that last fact, and Xavier.

"We should probably go; it closes in like ten minutes."

"Oh yeah. Of course." Chloe shook her head. "I have to get you your monkey!"

Brian smiled shyly. "You don't really have to. . . ."

"Of course I do, silly. This was a *great* idea for a date." She grinned.

"Date . . . ?" he asked, surprised. Chloe hit him playfully on the shoulder. As the twilight deepened and they headed back to the main entrance, Chloe felt a surge of energy jolt through her, making her skip, babble incessantly, and touch Brian as she talked, without embarrassment or reserve. She even bought him an extra-big monkey, one with long arms and Velcro so he could wear it around his neck.

They made it out just as the gates closed.

"This was great—thanks for suggesting it," Chloe said honestly. Her bus was coming; he was going in the opposite direction.

"Oh, cool. I'm glad you enjoyed it."

She waited. He seemed to be looking anxiously for the bus. "Can I see you again?" Chloe finally asked, a little annoyed that *she* had to be the one to bring it up. Hadn't she bought him a monkey, after all?

"Oh—yeah—of course. If you want." He looked down at her, unsure.

"Of course I do! Didn't I just say this was, like, the best date ever?" The bus stopped and opened its doors. "Aren't you going to kiss me?" Chloe asked, the first real flirty thing she had said all evening.

He leaned over and kissed her delicately on the cheek.

"Good night, Chloe," he said softly, and turned around and walked away.

Chloe climbed into the bus, feeling her cheek with her fingers, wondering if this was as close to a normal guy her age as she was ever going to date.

As soon as she was sure he wasn't looking, at the last moment she dove off. There were *other* ways to get home. She took off her jacket, tied it around her waist—and ran.

This time she concentrated on more and more outrageous leaps, sometimes running along a line of parked cars, bouncing from roof to roof. When she turned off the street and started running through tiny parks, fences proved no issue: she vaulted over short ones and leapt as high as she could onto chain-link ones, throwing herself over the top and jumping all the way to the ground, sometimes as far as twelve feet.

A pit bull strained on its leash in the courtyard of one run-down condo complex; a beautifully groomed old yellow Lab barked at her, nipping at her legs as she streaked by. Even Mrs. Languedoc's nasty little shih tzu howled like a wolf at her when Chloe finally ran up her own driveway.

"Kimmy, what's wrong with you?" Chloe heard her neighbor scold the dog.

Chloe wandered over to the cheap picket fence. This time she was breathing heavily, and her lower stomach was cramping—Chloe wondered how badly she would pay for this exercise session tomorrow. She stuck her hand between the plastic slats to let the dog nose her.

They had never been particularly good friends in the past, but Chloe had occasionally thrown it raw hot dogs, trying to get it to shut up when Mrs. Languedoc was away.

Kimmy growled, backed away to a safe distance, and began barking again.

"Whatever." Chloe shrugged and went inside.

"How was your study session?" her mother called from the table, where she was paying bills on her laptop.

It took Chloe a moment to remember exactly what lie she had told.

"Lousy. We got *nothing* done." She threw her jacket into the closet with disgust. "I just don't see why Lisa keeps inviting Keira along. All she wants to do is gossip and bitch."

"Well, if you need help"—Chloe's mom looked over at her and smiled—"I was great at trig."

Of course. You were freaking great at everything.

"Thanks." Chloe gave her a weak smile and went upstairs to the bathroom.

Blood.

On her boy panties, in the front part of the cotton crotch. Bright red. Her ten-dollar *nice* boy panties.

Her first thought was that she had ripped her hymen during one of the gigantic leaps off fences she had taken, legs spread wide.

Then as she felt more wetness on the inside of her leg, she realized what it was.

Holy shit. She finally got her period.

"About time," she muttered, and started rooting through the bathroom cabinet. That must have been what set the dogs off. They must have smelled the blood on her. She finally found a box of tampons—another thing that, if she didn't like her mother's brand, she would have to start paying for herself.

I have to call Amy, she thought. Chloe smiled.

And then she got a cramp.

Nine

"Hey—where were you last night?" Amy demanded. Once again, the bus had arrived early or someone at the school had arrived late, and they had to wait *outside* for the first bell. It was a brisk fall morning, and, like many other students, Chloe had not dressed for extended outside lounging; she stamped her feet and balled her fists into her pockets, considering bumming a cigarette.

"I had a date," Chloe responded coolly. It was easy in this temperature.

"With Alyec?"

"No. Someone else."

Amy regarded her for a long moment. She was going sort of mod today, sort of Austin Powers, in a big purple fake-fur coat and goggles.

"What the fuck, King?" she finally said. "First you don't even answer when I invite you to my poetry reading and now you announce this little secret life—"

Chloe knew how she *wished* she could respond. Like

the people on TV who always had a good answer, the proper words, just enough righteous indignation:

"*I* have a secret life? Since you and Paul started dating, it's like neither of you exist anymore. We haven't really seen each other except for my birthday, and suddenly you're pissed that I won't come to your poetry reading you so *graciously deigned* to invite me to?"

Or at least the heartfelt, emotionally genuine pre-mutual-crying speech:

"Amy, I've really felt abandoned recently. I know that you and Paul have suddenly become very important in each other's lives, and I respect that—but *we're* friends, too. A lot has been going on in my life I haven't had a chance to tell you about—and you're my best friend. I really need you sometimes, and lately I feel that you just haven't been there for me."

But, "I'll be at your poetry reading," was what she actually said, grudgingly, looking at the ground.

"Oh." Amy looked confused, then relieved. "Thanks. Maybe you'll tell me about your secret lover *then*?"

"Yeah. Whatever." There was a long pause. Chloe sensed that this was a crux of a moment, what could be the beginning of a serious rift. For a second it was breathtaking, like she was poised at the edge of a canyon, at the top of a tower, ready to jump: no more annoying, pretentious Amy *or* weirdness with Paul, just a slow parting of ways behind her. In front were Alyec or Brian, the new things she could suddenly seem to do, the freedom and excitement of the night.

But she wasn't ready for that yet. An image came to her mind of the lionesses in her dream and at the zoo. If they were human, they wouldn't even let something as small or foolish as this waste their time.

"Could you ask Paul to come a little later?" Chloe finally asked. "Give us some girl time to catch up?"

Amy's face softened.

"Yeah, of course! Totally. Come by at seven."

"Will do."

They were silent for a moment, awkward in their emotions.

"So . . . like my coat?" Amy finally asked.

"How many Muppets died to make that thing?" Chloe shot back, grinning.

Chloe was in a state of mental panic when Alyec called out to her in the hallway. She didn't hear him, overwhelmed by what she had just promised. Ame's poetry readings were something not to be believed.

Chloe thought madly about tiny FM radios that she could hide in her ear and pull her hair over to hide, about getting very badly drunk or stoned, about getting one of the loopier Wiccans at school to put her into a trance before the reading. *Anything* that could get her through it with her sanity intact and a straight face.

She and Paul used to sometimes have to hold hands during them, squeezing for strength and distraction during the bad parts, keeping the other restrained if she or Paul couldn't fight the urge to giggle or get up and run screaming from the café. Somehow she didn't think that would be happening with Paul *this* time, however.

Maybe I can puncture my eardrums. . . .

"Hey! Chloe!"

She finally looked up and realized that Alyec had been waving to her and calling her name for a few minutes. He ran down the hall to catch up with her.

"Sorry." She shook her head. "Lost in thought."

"No problem." He looked her up and down. Suddenly Chloe was self-conscious about her second-day jeans and her Strokes T-shirt with the bleach hole. Even her undies were the last ones before the wash: nasty, unsexy thongs. "I tried IM-ing you last night, but you weren't on."

Me? You were IM-ing me, *you hunka hunka icebergy love?* He smiled at her, a little puzzled, a little expectantly. Chloe immediately began to come up with some non-ego-shattering lie she could tell him about why she wasn't around that would keep him calm and interested, that would cut the conversation short and move them on to pleasanter topics.

Then she noticed how close he was standing, very much in her space, looming over and looking down at her. Kind of obnoxious. Like she was the kind of girl who *enjoyed* being loomed over by the sexiest guy in her class in the middle of the hall.

"I had a date," she answered, shrugging.

"Like, a study date?"

She almost laughed at his quick assumption. "No, a *date* date." She turned and began walking to her next class.

"Wait, what?" He ran to catch up with her again. "Who?"

"Brian. You don't know him."

"Does he go to Mary Prep?"

A wicked gleam came into her eye. "No," she answered casually. "He's not in high school."

"King, you are one hell of a tease." He sighed.

"Tease?" She turned and faced him finally. "Uh, I don't see anyone else making demands on my time."

"*That* is definitely teasing," Alyec called after her when she walked away again. "If I understand English properly."

She waved *buh-bye* at him over her shoulder.

Reflecting on the encounter later, Chloe had to admit she was thrilled with the way Alyec had no inclination to keep their little tête-à-tête silent. He was obviously after her, loudly, in the middle of the hall and didn't seem to care if anyone—even Keira and her gang—heard him. The whole school now knew that Alyec Ilychovich wanted Chloe King.

It was a nice feeling and made her feel even cozier with the cold day outside and her inside the thick-wood-and-velvet café, hands wrapped around a hot cider. She snuggled back into her seat, pretending to not see the microphone and spotlight being set up in a corner.

"He-e-e-y!" Amy came in, looked around, waved to the people setting up, kiss-kissed them on their cheeks, and told them she would be with them in just a few minutes. Even though it was a little thing, Chloe was pleased that her friend cared enough to put off what was a fairly adoring crowd to spend time with her. Which did not stop Chloe from putting her hand up just in time to prevent Amy from air kissing her, too. There *were* limits. *The pretension ends here.*

"So . . . what? *What?* What are all these things happening in the life of Chloe King?" Amy turned and screamed, "I'll get a tea, over here, Earl Grey, with lemon!"

"Well, first things first." Chloe shifted back and forth uncomfortably. "What kind of tampons do you use?"

Amy's jaw dropped. "Oh my *God*. You finally got your *period?*"

Chloe winced, trying to draw her hair down over her face. She felt the tips of her cheeks, right under her eyes, go hot and pink.

"Tell the entire world," she mumbled.

"Oh. Uh, sorry. I'm just . . . amazed. And glad you're, like, normal and stuff. No weird tumors or something." Amy's eyes went glassy. "You're a woman! You've finally joined us in the cycle of life and—"

"Save the goddess shit for later. I'm uncomfortable and cramping."

"Try 'slenders.' You have to change them more often, but that's what I used until I started having sex. . . ." Her friend's face suddenly furrowed. "Jeez, you're going to have to start taking all that stuff seriously now. Maybe go on the pill. Condoms break, you know, and you could get pregnant—"

"Thanks for the sex-ed speech. I only needed the relevant part. 'Slenders.' I get it. Thanks." She looked at her cider and admitted, "Besides, it's not like I've even had actual intercourse yet . . . and it doesn't look like it's a possibility anytime in the near future."

"Yeah, Paul and I haven't had sex yet. Even if we were at that point, he's, you know, old-fashioned and stuff."

Chloe shuddered. Thinking of Paul having sex made her think of Paul having a penis, and Paul's penis was definitely something she never wanted to think about. Much less Amy *and* Paul having sex. Together.

"I know you two are serious, and I'm happy for you," Chloe said slowly, "but it would be nice if you kept some parts of it . . . to yourself, you know?"

Amy blinked. Her blue eyes made her look extra innocent. "Who else am I going to talk to about it?"

"You can *talk* to me about it," Chloe said, "but just censor the dirty parts, you know? This is *Paul*. And besides"—she came up with a brilliant excuse—"do you really think he would want *me* knowing these things about him? He gets all blushy about a trip to the *doctor*."

"I hadn't thought about that," Amy said after a long

moment. She fiddled with the hand charm on her necklace that had lost its silver tarnish long ago from other nervous musings. Chloe smiled; she remembered when her friend first got it, years ago, from her grandmother. . . . "Well, what about *you*? What happened to Alyec?"

"Nothing. He's still on my 'watch' list." Chloe grinned like a very self-satisfied cat over the rim of her cup. "It's just that I met this other guy, Brian. He comes to Pateena now and then. Totally cute. He's working a couple of years before applying to college. I think you'd like him; he knits his own hats. He took me out for coffee last night." She didn't feel like telling her the part about the zoo; there was something strangely private about it. In a nice sort of way. Not meant for sharing, not even with Amy.

Hey, he never gave me the hat pattern, she realized.

A size-zero girl in all black brought over a mug of tea with slices of lemon on a saucer. Amy busied herself preparing the tea exactly as she liked it, and Chloe watched more people come in, filling the dark corners of the café like large, quiet rats.

"I think that fall affected you more than we thought," Amy finally said.

"What are you talking about?" Chloe said, a little offended by the cavalier way her friend spoke.

"Come on—*two* guys? One is the most popular in our class, the other not even in high school? You? *Chloe King?*" Amy shook her head. "That's not like you at all."

Good thing I didn't tell her about Xavier, Chloe decided.

But it gave her pause: Amy was right. It used to be that Chloe never would have gone after *any*one in the popular crowd, no matter how cute or nice. And a guy not at their high school? *Any* high school? Two years older than her? Old enough to vote and look at porn? *Fuggedaboutit!* And what exactly about going to a club by herself and picking up a stranger and making out with him in back?

Chloe looked at Amy's necklace again, suddenly brought back to the girl she was at Amy's party when they were both thirteen. A very different girl.

"I'm blooming," she answered with a hint of irony in her voice.

"Exploding, more like." She winced at Chloe's look. "In a *good* way," she quickly added. "What's Brian look like?"

"Tall, dark and brooding, handsome, brown eyes, mysterious smile . . . He didn't kiss me good night, though."

"Gay," Amy decided.

"I wasn't exactly getting a 'gay' vibe," Chloe said defensively.

"All right, maybe he's just shy."

"Hey." Chloe suddenly really *saw* her friend's necklace. It looked suspiciously like a cat, lying down, a smug little smile on her face. She furrowed her brow and reached for it.

"Don't you remember? Nana gave it to me when she came back from Egypt. For my bat mitzvah."

"Yeah, yeah. But what is it supposed to *be*, exactly?"

"Um . . . a cat goddess of some sort, I think." Amy pulled it out and tried to look at it. "Bastet or something? It was back when I was totally obsessed with cats, when I got Pharaoh." That was the original name of the all-black kitten she'd rescued from an alley. Now he was huge and fat and just called Kitty.

"Ma chérie!" a draggle-haired *Moulin Rouge* extra in a long white silk scarf called to Amy. "We await your presence."

"Yeah—give this to Paul when he comes, will you?" Amy fished a brown, letter-sized bag out of her giant denim one. "He left it at my place Wednesday night."

After her friend joined the other poetry weirdos, Chloe pulled the package closer to her so no one would take it or sit on it. *Left it at her place Wednesday night.* The three of them used to watch cheap DVD rentals at Amy's midweek when everything was getting too stressful, usually Bollywood musicals. She was the only one with a TV in her room. They would pop popcorn and watch gold and pink dancers twirl and sing and elephants march by and feel like they were at the edge of another world, somewhere far more interesting, beyond Inner Sunset. Chloe wondered what they watched last night, or if they just made out.

She opened Paul's package: comics. Wednesday was comic day, something he had drilled into her since they were nine.

She flipped through them—some starred recognizable characters like Batman and Green Lantern, others were just as brightly colored but with superheroes she had never heard of. Some were called things like *Hellblazer* and filled with amazingly disgusting scenes of people and demons doing extreme violence to each other. Chloe had learned a long time ago to avoid looking at those.

She pulled a couple out; there was at least another fifteen minutes before the readings began. *Batman* was familiar but way too short, and the ads were more intriguing than the plotline. She opened another one about a woman called Selina Kyle and followed the four-color panes through her adventures leaping and running across the Gotham City skyline. Chloe grinned, thinking of herself.

Then she frowned.

Is that it? Is that what I have? Superpowers?

She had never thought of it that way before. It sort of added up, though, if you looked at it from a comic book point of view: She'd survived a fall that should have killed her, she'd fought a guy—with no previous training—who was twice as big as her and used to living on the street, she could run for miles without getting winded and jump hurdles like a track star—when she used to have all the physicality of a slug. And here she'd been assuming that part of it was just some sort of growing spurt. . . .

"Hey, since when did *you* become a comic mooch?" Paul asked, sliding into the booth across from her.

"Since I was bored out of my mind." She showed him the comic book she was reading. "Do any of these guys have, like, more subtle powers? Besides flying?"

"Selina Kyle doesn't *have* powers," he said with a little bit of smugness. "Neither do Batman or Robin. John Constantine is . . . questionable. Aquaman can breathe underwater, which I guess is subtle, but he can also talk to fish. Why?"

"Just wondering." She watched as he carefully put the comics back in their Mylar bags and slid them gently into the brown bag. "So, how long is this horror scheduled to last?"

"An hour and a half."

Chloe groaned. The lights dimmed and people clapped politely. The man with the scarf gave a little introduction. Chloe almost wished she still had a comic to look at. The poets were theoretically in order of who signed up first, but they tended to let the least worst go last.

Which meant that Amy was usually second or third.

If I'm a superhero, Chloe idly thought, *I should definitely get some better clothes. Clingier. Spandex. Tank tops and bike shorts.* Where did superwomen keep their extra tampons, anyway? Her foot tapped; she tried to keep it quiet through the first few readings. She would have given almost anything to be able to run outside. She hoped one of the poets' clove cigarettes would fall and catch the place on fire.

"And now, Amy Scotkin, reading three of her works."

"Whoo-hoo!" Chloe shouted, cupping her hands to her mouth like she was at a sporting event.

"Go, Amy!" Paul shouted.

Amy blushed. "My first one, 'Night Swan.'"

"Holy crap," Chloe whispered in horror. "She's doing the 'Swan' again? All thirteen verses?"

"Hey, a little support and positive thought might be welcome here," Paul suggested.

> *Lo, my lover lies asleep*
> *In a twin bed with black satin sheets*
> *In the gable nook of our hallowed nest. . . .*

Chloe clenched and unclenched her hands the entire time, her fingernails tingling. She looked over at Paul; he sat still—*trying* to look serious, she thought.

> Call, call! *My night black swan!*
> *Weep for the love that is lost*
> *The scarlet threads of shame and shadow*
> *That flow betwixt my breasts . . .*

Thirteen verses and approximately fifteen minutes later it was over. There were still two more Amy "specials," but the last one was new, so at least it was an unexpected horror. And there was a break just two poets later.

"Holy shit," Chloe said as she and Paul went up to the bar afterward to reorder. "I think it gets harder every time."

"Yeah, some of those poets were atrocious," he agreed.

"And what about her new masterpiece? What gothic shit was she listening to when she wrote 'Daylight Incubus'?"

"You didn't like it?"

Chloe turned to stare at her friend. "Um—hello? It *sucked*, Paul."

"I don't think it was that bad," Paul demurred.

"If you mean that it wasn't any better or worse than any of the other stuff she's done, I agree."

"Why did you bother coming if you're just going to trash her?"

He didn't say it nastily—it wasn't a challenge. It almost sounded like a genuine question.

"Because that's what we always do, Paul!" Chloe said, exasperated. "We keep on trying to get her to drop this shit and do the stuff she's good at, she ignores us, we keep coming here to support her, she reads her poetry, and we—well, commiserate."

"She's my *girl*friend, now, Chlo," Paul said softly. Like it was supposed to shock her.

And it did.

"That doesn't change everything. Or at least it's not supposed to." Chloe spun on her heels and walked away, ignoring the tea that was set in front of her. *Has everyone gone insane?* It seemed like she was just getting back into sync with Amy, and Paul suddenly went off the deep end, taking this whole girlfriend-boyfriend thing way too seriously. He had always been a harder person to get to know than Amy, sometimes difficult to read, but these dreadful readings used to be their bonding time. He used to relax.

"Hey, good job," she said, kissing Amy on the cheek. "I gotta take off."

"Oh! Thanks!" Amy grinned. "See you tomorrow!"

Chloe stormed out into the cold, hands balled up into fists in her pockets again. She didn't feel like running; she felt an almost uncontrollable rage. Paul had always been kind of secretive and weird about his girlfriends before—but this was beyond beyond. His and Amy's relationship was the worst thing that had happened to the three of them.

And it's kind of your fault: they got together 'cause of the fall.

Chloe sighed, some of the steam going out of her. She unclenched her hands and realized she had been clutching a crumpled-up piece of paper in her pocket. She pulled it out and read it under a streetlight, assuming it was a permission slip or note or something. Her eyes widened when she realized what it actually said.

Chloe:

Your life is in danger. Be wary of the company you keep. Be prepared—and ready to run. The Order of the Tenth Blade knows who you are. . . .

A friend

Ten

Normal people called the police. That was what normal people did in situations like this with weird notes and death threats and things like that.

Too bad I'm not normal.

It was probably just a joke. Right? Chloe had been terrified in fourth grade when she found a note in her cubby telling her that she'd better "watch out." And that had turned out to be Laura Midlen's idea of funny. But somehow this seemed less amusing than that incident.

My life is in danger? Did that mean someone found out about Xavier? Maybe he was after her? That didn't make sense, though: she hadn't meant to hurt him, and it wasn't worth killing her over. What was the company she kept? Paul? Amy? Nothing strange about them or dangerous . . . Whoever wrote the note probably meant her new friends: either Alyec or Brian. More likely Brian since Alyec was a known factor, a normal high school kid with roots in the community. She didn't really know anything about Brian besides what he had told her. . . .

Then again, he could also be the "friend" who was warning her. But he hadn't been in the café—in fact, Chloe didn't really know anyone at the Black Rooster except by sight. When was the note slipped into her pocket? Maybe it wasn't even meant for her.

She checked the locks on the doors several times before going to sleep—or *trying* to go to sleep. She felt pretty sure she could handle a daytime attack by a street thug, but a nighttime ambush would be another story.

The next Monday at school Chloe was even grumpier and sleepier than usual. She kept looking up suddenly, jumping at noises, and seeing things out of the corners of her eyes. All for what was probably just a prank. As soon as she got a free period, she went to the newspaper office.

"Hey, Paul," she said, making straight for the couch.

"Chloe," he answered uneasily. He was sitting at the computer, playing some bright-colored and contraband video game.

"I'm wiped. Do you mind?" She threw herself into the couch.

"No. Go ahead." He stood up and played with a pencil for a minute. "I . . . might have overreacted Friday night. . . . Are we cool?" he finally asked.

Even through her sleep-thick haze, Chloe smiled. Paul actually cared if she was angry at him! Then again, she had a complete right to be.

She raised her arm to give him a thumbs-up.

"Cool." He threw his bag over his shoulder. "Just close the door on your way out, okay? It's already locked."

But Chloe was already asleep.

She woke up perfectly, precisely forty-five minutes later, *almost* in time for phys ed. Which was really odd because usually once Chloe was out, she was *flat* out until someone woke her up. The second, warning bell rang and dozens of classroom doors slammed shut, students trapped inside, being forced to learn.

She stretched and yawned and scratched herself, rolling her head and shaking the stiffness out of her shoulders—she hadn't moved from the position she'd fallen down in, and it wasn't really the most comfortable of couches.

She slumped out of the room, pausing to pick up the obituary sections of the local newspapers lying around and remembering to make sure the door was closed like Paul had said. She started down the hall toward gym, possibly her most-hated class. *Although,* she considered, *maybe I could surprise them with a thing or two.* But probably not. The one thing every TV show, book, and comic book had ever suggested about people with special powers was to never reveal them to the outside world. At the worst she could be kidnapped and dissected by the government. At best Mr. Parmalee would insist she go for a drug test.

"Chloe King!"

Alyec was coming down the empty hall. She smiled.

"What are *you* doing at this end of the school?"

"I am going for my flute lesson," he said, somewhat embarrassed. He held up a small black case. "I have always wanted to learn it, but there was no money or opportunity in Russia."

"Funny, I would have picked you for a boner," she said.

His eyes widened.

"*Trom*boner? You know? That and trumpet are what all of the popular guys play."

"Well, I am not a normal popular guy. And anyway, if I am so popular, how come you haven't asked to see me since the sea lions?" There was a sexy little smile that he was just hiding. Chloe felt a shiver run through her body. "How's *Brian*?"

"He's great." *Except for that whole lack-of-kissing-and-phone-calls thing.*

"Oh yeah? You really like him, huh? *I* think you're just playing hard to get."

"Awww, what's the matter? Keira not enough for you?"

"Nope," he answered, grinning. Then he leaned over and kissed her. "She is just a stupid little girl," he whispered into her ear, brushing it with his lips.

Although such things had been placed far, far from her mind since—well, since her period began, Chloe felt the desire she had felt with Xavier rise up through her again. She turned her head so they were cheek to cheek, her lips against his jaw.

"We should go somewhere," he whispered, kissing the tops of her cheeks over and over again.

"Janitor's closet," Chloe breathed, pointing.

They both broke for it. Unlike on TV, this one was filled with actual janitorial stuff—mops and buckets and bottles of cleanser—and there was no real room to stand. They looked at it, then at each other.

Chloe giggled. Unlike the time with Xavier, this was playful and fun. Alyec threw himself against the back of the closet so he would bear the brunt of their weight and pulled her in after him as she closed the door.

Everything was very close and warm. She could smell all the disparate aspects of Alyec: his cologne, the fabric softener on his clothes, his toothpaste, the shampoo or gel in his hair, his skin and his breath.

Also Lysol and Mr. Clean, but she tried not to think about that.

He put his hands around her face and kissed her full on the lips, the way she had been aching for Brian to do the other night. He didn't stop, not even to breathe, feeling every corner and surface of her mouth with his own.

The way a girl should *be kissed,* was Chloe's last coherent thought.

When they stumbled out into the bright light of the hallway later, it was, fortunately, still empty. Alyec had to clap his hand over her mouth once or twice when they were in the closet because she was giggling and making him giggle, too. But no one had come by. She pulled and adjusted her shirt.

"You are one sexy girl, Chloe King," Alyec said, kissing her one last time on the cheek. "That was powerful stuff in there."

She *felt* pretty sexy. But . . .

"Well, and now you can tell all your friends that. How you finally cornered Chloe King and you had the time of your life." She smiled weakly.

Alyec frowned. "Do you really think I'm like that? Chloe, I was serious about Keira. She means *nothing* to me. And I'm *not* a complete dick."

Chloe nodded. She hoped, of course. In nice-guy competitions Brian had him definitely beat. She reshouldered her bag and then realized Alyec was empty-handed.

"Where's your flute?" she asked.

They looked back into the closet and saw the black case sticking out of a bucket.

Getting out of gym was easy—as soon as she and Alyec parted, she ran for the nurse's office and made a big deal about how she was *bleeding* and this was her *first period ever* and she was cramping and had spent the whole time in the bathroom. The nurse was brusquely sympathetic and promised to speak to Mr. Parmalee before it was officially filed as a cut. She also recommended that Chloe get her gyn exam ASAP. Chloe agreed and left, limping a little as if she was still in pain.

She had texted Amy earlier about meeting for lunch—in the corner of the cafeteria near the pay phones. It wasn't a desirable area, but at least they would be left alone. She planned on showing her the note. Maybe even telling her the truth about . . . *Well, about what?* Running really fast? Kissing Alyec in the closet? Whatever. Anyway, Amy loved mysteries—she had gone through a whole *Harriet the Spy*/*Nancy Drew*/Agatha Christie stage that had lasted a lot longer than those of most little boys and girls who were interested in being detectives. Even if she had no idea what to make of the note, at least it would be entertaining. After all, maybe the note wasn't even meant for her. Maybe it was a mistake.

Chloe looked up and around the cafeteria, then at her watch. They only had twenty minutes for lunch today, and five of them were already gone. Amy hadn't texted her back, but that didn't mean anything. One of them always said "meet me here" and the other one just showed up. It had always been like that. Unless there was a problem—that was the only reason for a response, if one of them couldn't make it.

She checked her phone. No messages.

At 12:35 she finally gave up, realizing Amy wasn't going to show.

• • •

She had the whole evening to herself, sort of a nice change from recent events. And sort of not. Chloe did some desultory straightening of her room and read a little of *The Scarlet Letter* for class. She went to the computer and surfed for a while, downloading MP3s and seeing what her favorite celebrities were up to. Then on a whim she searched on AIM for Alyec Ilychovich . . . and there he was. Under Alyec Ilychovich. *He sure does have a lot to learn about hiding your real identity and other American things.* Chloe smiled and added him to her buddy list. His account was private—*such a popular guy!*—so she sent him an invite from oldclothesKing, one of her more common aliases. Then she went on surfing.

There was an e-mail from Brian on her Hotmail account:

> Chloe,
>
> I really enjoyed our playdate the other night. But I never gave you the pattern!
>
> Do you like ska? Downtime hosts Kabaret Saturdays, no cover. No penguins, but it should be a cool night otherwise. If not, maybe you have an idea . . . ?
>
> —Brian 415-555-0554

She smiled. He was just so . . . perfect. It was almost like he could sense she was lonely and sent this. She called him but got his answering machine.

"Hi, this is Whit Rezza—if you're looking for Peter

Rezza, you can reach him on his cell, 415-555-1412. Leave a message, thanks!"

"Hey, Brian, it's Chloe. I'd *love* to go out on Saturday—not a huge fan of ska, but I like it enough. Just going to have to figure out what to tell my mom first; she's not big on me and guys. So this is a possible 'yes,' and . . ."

The electronic sound of a door opening came from her computer. She looked over; Alyec was online. A second later there was a *beep* as he accepted her invite.

"And I'll call you or e-mail you later, okay? Bye!"

She would have to remember to call before her mom came home; on the home phone bill it would only appear as a local call, but on her cell phone the bill listed every number. And her mom went through the bill *very* carefully each month, demanding to know what unrecognizable phone numbers were. She said it was for budget reasons . . . *ha!*

Chloe spun back in her chair so she was facing the computer. There was already a message from Alyec.

Alyec: Miss me yet?

She giggled.

Chloe: Only your lips. The rest of you—well, whatever.
Alyec: Shallow girl! I have a brain, too, you know.
Chloe: Yeah?
Alyec: And more . . .

Chloe flushed. She had felt a lot of his body—fully clothed—in the closet. She wished it was summer so they could go to the beach and she could rub oil all over his broad shoulders. Or that they could date like normal people. *Too bad I'm not normal,* she thought for the second time in a week.

The phone rang.

Chloe: Hang on, brb.

"King residence," she answered.

"Hey—uh—Chloe—was that you who called?" Brian's voice came from the other end. "My dad has caller ID and callback on this thing."

"Yeah, it was me." She was still flushed, thinking about Alyec and his body and the closet, and suddenly found herself thinking about Brian. More specifically, her on top of Brian, holding him down while she kissed him. *I'll bet I could do that with my new strength, too. . . .*

He must have heard something funny in her voice.

"Are you okay?"

"Yeah, I'm fine. Why?"

"Oh. You just sounded—never mind. So, you still want that pattern?"

No, I want you, *you dillhole.*

There was a beep from the computer:

Alyec: I'm waiting. . . .

Or Alyec. I want Alyec, too. It was funny right this moment, the two guys on two different means of communication. But soon, if her life was anything like TV—or even real life—it would all get very complicated without a decision. *But not yet. Not just yet!*

"Yeah. Should we try for Saturday?"

"Uh, sure. That's fine. I mean, it's great!" There was a long pause. "Chloe? I, uh . . ."

"Yeah?" She waited to hear him say that she was too young for him, that they had to break up, that he didn't find her attractive. She sucked in her breath. *So much for* me *making a decision.*

"Uh, nothing. I just think you're cool, that's all."

"Oh." She grinned. "Thanks."

"Yeah, so call me about Saturday, okay?"

"Absolutely."

There was another beep from the computer.

Alyec: Chloe King is so full of herself that she lets Alyec Ilychovich, one of the most popular guys in class, hang on the telephone. Or computer. Or whatever.

"All right, then, bye."

He hung up sounding excited, pleased, and embarrassed. Chloe ran back to the keyboard.

Alyec: Doopy doo, doopy doopy doo . . .
Chloe: *All right, all right!* Jeez, can't a girl pee?

Alyec: I'll bet you were talking with your other boyfriend.

Chloe froze. Now would be a good time to say something.

Chloe: If by talking you mean urinating and boyfriend you mean toilet, then yes.
Alyec: Your sexy talk is leaving me all hot.
Chloe: Ewww! I didn't know you were into stuff like that.
Alyec: Hey, we foreign boys are weird.
Chloe: At least you have nice lips.
Alyec: Oh, and you don't even know the half of what they can do.
Chloe: Yeah? Want to give me a hint?
Alyec: I can blow up balloons really fast.
Chloe: Now who's being the tease?
Alyec: Why? What do you want me to do with my lips?

They typed back and forth furiously for several hours, taking breaks to go get drinks, or more bathroom breaks, or to IM other people. Alyec told her that Jean Mehala was just asking him if he had any desire to join the Junior UN. *I am the junior UN!* And Lotetia wanted him on the dance committee, which he might just do; most of the music at the dances sucked.

Chloe: It must be neat being so wanted.
Alyec: Yeah? And exactly how do you want to be wanted?

There was a noise behind Chloe, the slightest scratch of a throat. She jumped and spun around, expecting a murderer or something awful.

It was worse. It was her mom.

"Who is that you're talking to?" Mrs. King demanded. She was wearing her driving glasses and looked stern and real mommish for once. Her gray eyes narrowed, and she gripped her attaché like an ax.

"How long were you standing there?" Chloe demanded.

"What was it you two *did* at school today that was so exciting?" From the set of her lips it was obvious that she had a pretty good idea already. She must have been standing there for quite a while. How had Chloe not heard her?

"Nothing," Chloe said dully.

"Making out in a *janitor's closet*? During *class*?"

"It was only gym. And besides—it's not like you let me go out on actual *dates*."

"This is precisely why!" Her mother hit the computer screen violently enough to make it ring. "You are *grounded*, young lady! For the next week at least!"

"That's so unfair!" Normally Chloe would have been thinking about how badly she'd screwed up right then and doing whatever she could to make up for it—lie, apologize, finish out the normal teenage fight, and act good for the next week—but real anger was growing inside her, and she found she couldn't think. "Everyone else *dates*—and I have to lie and sneak around, even with *nice* guys like Brian. . . ."

"Who's *Brian*?" her mother demanded. Her hands shook with rage.

"What does it matter? He's totally great, but you won't let me date *him*, either!"

"It seems like you're doing well enough, whoring around like—" She fell silent.

Chloe just looked at her, eyes like coals. She couldn't hear; rushes of blood and fury rose in her. For the first time since she was a child, she had the almost overwhelming urge to hit her mother.

"Take. That. Back."

Mrs. King bit her lip.

"I'm—sorry. I didn't mean—that was way too harsh. I apologize. I shouldn't speak to you like that." She played with the hammered silver earring on her left ear, tugging at it.

"You're going to give me the whole 'how hard it is to be a single mom' speech now, aren't you?" Chloe spat.

"No, I—"

"Are you going to 'keep me' from dating when I'm in college? Jesus Christ, Mom, I'm *sixteen*. I have a job. I get good grades. What psycho-pop book did you get this 'no dating' bullshit out of?"

"It wasn't a book!" Mrs. King said, her voice rising again. Then she fell back on her heels, suddenly tired, all energy and anger drained from her face. "It was the last thing your father said before he disappeared. He made me promise to never let you date."

Chloe's jaw dropped, but she had nothing to say. The man she had been glorifying and missing for twelve years was the one responsible for this?

"This is *bullshit,*" Chloe growled. She spun on her heels and pushed past her mother.

"Chloe, wait—"

She ran into the bathroom and slammed the door.

"FUCK!" she screamed. She clenched her fists, fingers aching painfully. She pulled back to punch the door.

And then she stopped.

There were claws where her nails had been. White and sharp and curved and beautiful, just like a cat's.

Eleven

She sat on the top of a chain-link fence, staring at the moon.

It was easy now, sitting like that on the balls of her feet with her hands just touching the rail. Now that she *knew* she was different.

"He made me promise to never let you date. . . ."

Why? Did he know something? Did it have to do with the claws?

Chloe lifted one hand and looked at it, trying to will them back. She bent her knuckles. She tried to remember the rage she'd felt. *What was it that she said that set me off?*

"Whoring around like—"

Sslt.

With the slightest of noises, the claws came out. They seemed to spring right from the bone, strong and sturdy as an extension of her hand. They didn't bend when she touched them, and the tips were razor sharp.

Xavier.

Maybe she'd scratched him with the tips. Maybe they were poisoned. Maybe they came out when she was all hot as well as enraged. *Is that why Dad didn't want me to date? Because I can accidentally kill people?*

She thought about what Brian had said at the zoo.

"Even the friendly ones . . . don't know their own strength compared to humans. They can accidentally kill a zookeeper while trying to play with him. . . ."

What if she had been face-to-face with her mom when she got that angry? Would she have lost control and tried to hit her? Would the claws have come out, scarring or killing her mother?

Suddenly her new powers didn't feel like fun anymore. They felt lethal.

So I can't make out with guys? But Alyec was fine. . . . It didn't make any sense.

A thousand mysteries, none of which were easily solved. Chloe felt an incredible surge of loneliness envelop her. Who could she talk to? Who could help her? Who would tell her that everything would be okay?

How can I even have a boyfriend?

Either he'd have to be *awfully* accepting and tight-lipped, or she would have to constantly hide things from him.

She stood up on the fence with ease: the trick was not to think about what she was doing and let her body just do it, she discovered. The roof of a nearby apartment complex hung just within reach. She leapt.

The sheer power in her body was phenomenal—as her legs flexed, she felt the way racehorses looked, all muscle and speed, no wasted movement or flesh. Her powerful thighs arced her easily over the gutter.

Landing was a little harder.

Chloe pitched forward, forgetting to compensate for momentum. She threw her arm out and managed to grab the base of an old antenna to keep herself from rolling off the roof. She lay against the tar tiles a moment, panting, scared to move, her feet dangling down. When she finally calmed down enough to think straight, she swung her left leg up and, bending her knee so she looked like a frog, pushed herself up onto the apex of the roof and swung her right leg over the other side so that she straddled it.

Not quite perfect.

Above her the stars glittered coldly in the dark blue sky. She looked out over the other roofs, the strange landscape with shingles and tiles for grass and chimneys and antennae for bushes and trees. Like the canopy layer in a rain forest, it was a whole area of the world she had never really noticed before. *Not before Coit Tower, at least.* And now it lay open to her. Some of the chimneys really were organic looking, like that kind of lumpy one—

Which was waving to her.

She stared harder. Chloe'd had better-than-perfect vision from birth, but, as on the night with the mugger, she realized she could see things far more clearly under the dim moonlight and night sky than she really should.

She waited and everything lightened, like in the viewfinder of a digital camera. She could see individual bricks and the mortar separating them.

The "chimney" elongated and straightened as the person stood up—balancing perfectly on the short wall that divided the roof space of one apartment building from the next. Then it crouched down, like a frog—*or a cat*—and leapt over the gap to the next building, landing so his—by the silhouette it looked more like a "his"—right hand came down onto the roof at the same time as his feet, ending in the same sort of crouch.

Oh, that's what I should have done, Chloe thought idly. *Spread my weight out across my legs* and *my hands so that . . .*

Then she realized.

This was him. The person from the note. *A friend.*

He was crouched very much like a cat on its haunches, arms and hands between his legs, watching her. He must be wearing all black, and his face was always in the shadows. He held up a hand—*paw.* What she was waiting for?

Chloe looked around. There was another house next to the one she was on, about ten feet away. An ugly, modern ranch like her own, with a tar roof. She started for it and then paused, scared. She looked up: he was still watching her. She took a deep breath and ran.

At the last moment she leapt, and instead of straight up like a high jumper, she stretched her body out almost like in a dive. She saw grass, sidewalk, and shadows pass far too quickly beneath her. Then her right hand touched the roof and her feet followed, landing in a perfect crouch.

Chloe had been holding her breath. She let it out and realized she was . . . *thrilled.* It was like the best free-fall ride at the park, no machinery necessary. Just her. She turned to look at the shadow figure across the street.

He gave her a thumbs-up, cocking his head. Then he leapt down off the roof on the other side, disappearing from sight.

"No!" Chloe cried, and looked around desperately for some quick way to get there, but there were no buildings that overhung the street or trees she could use to cross. She leapt down to the ground—without thinking this time; it was like she just decided to *fall*—and slipped down alongside the wall, landing with no sound. Her hands came flat against the pebbly concrete.

She ran across the street to the other side of the building. A single streetlight dimly illuminated an empty parking lot, gated shut. Someone had sprayed a colorful, huge tag on the brick wall that enclosed the far end. A plastic bottle rolled across the asphalt, pushed by an invisible breeze. Other than that and a billboard advertising Hankook Tires, nothing else was there.

What am I supposed to do now? For a few minutes it had looked like she had some strange sort of friend who could do the same things she could—and more. Who might be able to tell her who she was, why they were like this. What it all meant . . .

Ssst.

There was the faintest scratching noise above her. Chloe looked up and saw him crouching on top of a pole that supported a wire for the Muni electric buses. *I could have gotten across the street that way without coming down—but isn't it dangerous?*

As if to answer her question, he stood up and very carefully leapt onto one of the wires so that he never straddled the pole *and* it at the same time. Then he crouched down and sort of scuttled across it, using hands *and* feet to cling. He leapt up to the top of the billboard.

"How am I supposed to *get* up there?"

He jumped off the billboard, letting himself fall down its face. Ten neat rips in the paper lengthened as he fell, revealing the older ads underneath.

He had used his claws, she realized.

She walked over to the closest wood pole and tried swatting it. Nothing happened. She looked back at the shadow man and he crossed his arms impatiently. *Remember the jump,* she told herself. *No thought. Just* do. She leapt up and found herself clinging. Just with her hands and claws. *I'm gonna have the biggest delts,* she thought smugly. When she lifted her right hand for a grip farther up, her left hand and arm continued to supporting her; her claws were anchored deeply in the wood.

She quickly scuttled up the pole, using her legs at the last moment to vault herself up over the wires and onto the top. Chloe found herself grinning uncontrollably. The freedom of movement she now had—she could go anywhere—*anywhere*! Roofs, cliffs, tunnels, trees—all of those places outside normal human occupation. She could hide forever if she wanted or run across the skyline under stars, outside convention. *Free.*

She ran across the wire the way the shadow figure had but much faster and leapt to the billboard to meet him. But as soon as she landed, he took off for the gate, making an amazing leap to balance on its top bar.

"Hey!" she cried, laughing. A strange smell lingered behind him. He smelled like gasoline—like he'd fallen in a puddle of it. *An easy scent to follow.*

She tried to do the same as he did but wound up not quite making his last leap, falling into the parking lot, trapped—if, that is, she had been a normal human. She clambered up the gate and vaulted over it.

I could be a cat *burglar now.*

He was waiting for her, perched on a mailbox. But as soon as she recovered her breath, he was off again, running and leaping onto a fire escape, then climbing up to the roof.

Oh, you want to play, do you?

Chloe took off after him.

She chased him from rooftop to rooftop, from tree to telephone pole, neither of them ever touching the ground until they reached the park. Normally Chloe would never have even considered entering Golden Gate after dark—but obviously she was no longer a normal person. *Besides, he'll protect me if something happens.* Chloe felt sure of it.

It was mostly empty. Starlight wasn't enough to illuminate the paths, trees, and shadows, but her new night vision made everything, even the blackest dirt in the deepest shadow, glow like it was bathed in moonlight. The sidewalk gleamed like a fairy-tale road. She took to the grass instead, which was a little crunchy from the cold.

He paused near a bench under a ginkgo tree. He put his hands down as if to leap over it but instead straightened out so he was doing a handstand and then slowly let himself down the other way. *My arms aren't that strong,* was her first thought, before she realized what she had done that night already. He hooked his feet around a low branch and then pulled himself up into the tree.

Chloe ran forward, grabbed the top of the bench, and pushed, fully expecting to flip over and smash her face, arms, and body on the bench. But she straightened her hips when they were over her head and found herself doing a handstand as easily as if she had been a circus performer.

Suddenly there was a thud as all the weight in the world landed on her feet, bending and crushing her knees almost to her chin. And just as suddenly it was gone. Chloe lost her balance and tipped over onto the ground.

When she got up, she heard soft laughter, the first

noise he had made. He stood with his arms crossed several yards away: he had leapt down from the tree and used her feet and legs as a springboard.

"Funny," she said aloud.

He turned and ran again.

Chloe followed, straight into the trees and bushes, which had probably hidden a thousand muggers and rapists over the years. He darted from shadow to shadow, sometimes up a tree, sometimes over a shrub, always just keeping out of her reach. His scent was fading; if she lost sight of him, it would be over.

Suddenly she was at the other side of the park, in front of the exit. He was nowhere to be seen, and the scent trail was gone.

Chloe looked around, up trees and down the sidewalks, to see if he was hiding somewhere, waiting for her, ready to push her on again. But after five minutes there was still no sign.

"Come on," she called out plaintively. *"Please."*

With the excitement and the thrill of the hunt over, she suddenly felt lost. Just plain old Chloe King again, alone.

She started back the way she came, the shortest path through the park toward home, disappointed and sad.

Then she saw the oak tree.

About five feet up, its bark had been ripped to shreds by something with large claws, violently and deeply.

And under it, carefully dug in by single claw, was a smiley face.

Twelve

When Mrs. Abercrombie handed their quizzes back, Chloe had to remind herself: *Super-cat powers don't include the ability to do trig.* There was a big, ugly red D at the top of the page. Part of her fiercely didn't care; her life involved other things right now, more important things, like nighttime games of hide-and-seek and the fact that she wasn't like anyone else in class. Things like finding out about her past and what really happened to her dad.

But claws or no, Chloe was still Chloe, and she mentally calculated how much better she would have to do for the rest of the marking period to bring her grade back up to a respectable B. She snuck a glance over at Paul's paper and felt an evil satisfaction. He'd actually *studied* and only got a C.

When the bell rang, she got up and left quickly, giving Paul a quick "hey" in passing—but he was already making a beeline for Amy, who was out in the hall, waiting. Fortunately Alyec was also there, waiting for Chloe.

"Hey, Mamacita," he said. "How *you* doing?" The Spanish meets Joey from *Friends* spoken with a faint Russian accent was ridiculous, but his sexy face made it hard to take anything he said seriously, anyway.

"Hey." Unlike most other high school couples—note Amy and Paul—Chloe and Alyec did not kiss each other hello after class. They weren't even really a "couple"—which somehow made things sexier. They stood close without touching, faces inches apart.

"Do you want to go off campus for lunch, maybe?" he suggested. Chloe considered; this was strictly a no-no, grounds for detention, but it *was* a beautiful day out.

Just the sort for a picnic with a handsome Russian student. She pictured them on a hillside under a tree with a Red Delicious or two, somewhere between the Garden of Eden and something more wholesome, like apple picking. *Too bad there's no place like that around here.*

"Absolutely," she said, deciding that McDonald's would have to do.

This was the closest thing to a date she and Alyec had ever really had, Chloe realized. Their relationship was sort of reversed. And this was no relaxing, bucolic hillside: just a bench outside the McDonald's, and the air was redolent of *fry*. At least it was a nice day.

"So . . . what was it like growing up in Russia?"

Alyec shrugged. He was very carefully arranging his cheeseburger, opening its wrapper and folding it around the sandwich so that his fingers never touched it. Once it was properly (and somewhat daintily, Chloe thought) assembled, however, he opened his mouth wide and shoved in as much as he possibly could, like a normal teenager.

"The McDonalds there suck," he said, through a mouthful of meat. "They don't know how to do fries." Then he paused, reflecting. "Shakes were better, though."

"I'm *serious*, Alyec!"

"I *am* serious. They really are better. Not just McDonald's milk shakes, though. All ice cream and dairy."

"Yeah . . . ? And . . . ?" Chloe prompted him.

"And? It sucked. Nobody has any money, except New Russians. That's the mob. Everybody else—well, a movie costs a month's salary for most people. And a month's salary for many is like fifty dollars. A lot of people don't eat meat every day. So people drink a lot, you know?" His eyes narrowed, and for just a second Chloe thought she saw something deeper in them, something sad. But the moment was over and he shook his head. "At young ages, people start. I'll bet I could drink those football idiots under the table. But I don't," he added importantly.

Alyec poised over his remaining burgers and fries, deciding what to attack next.

Chloe dipped a single french fry into ketchup and chewed it slowly.

"How ever do you keep your girlish figure?" she asked.

"Sex," he answered promptly, setting about preparing another burger. In between he picked up a few fries *with a napkin*—and bit off their heads. Then he popped the remainder into his mouth. All without touching them. Chloe was tempted to ask if this was a Russian thing or if he just had obsessive-compulsive disorder. "No, I am just kidding. I do eat a lot, though."

"What was St. Petersburg like?"

"Ha—Leningrad? Well, it is a beautiful city, for Russian cities at least, not like San Francisco, of course." He threw up his arm as if indicating the most obvious beauty in the world, but she didn't know if he meant the sky, the fog, the bridge, the weather, or what. "Lots of domes and steeples. Gold now because of restoration work. In the summer it is light until two o'clock in the morning, and the sun is low the entire time, very pretty. But really, it sucks."

She couldn't tell if he was embarrassed about his past, secretive, or just honest: that was his old life, but now it was over.

"I thought it was hard to emigrate," she said, trying to draw him out.

"*I* got a rich uncle."

"Is he a . . . New Russian?"

"Yeah, kind of like that." He looked sadly at the empty wrappers and plates.

"Teach me some Russian," she said, lying down and looking up at him.

"Pazhoust," he said, leaning forward, his nose almost touching hers.

"What does that mean?" she whispered.

"'Please,'" he said, kissing her.

I should do that every *day,* thought Chloe as she waited for her bus home. While Alyec had not revealed himself to be a great thinker or philosopher or—er—someone with a sexy, mysterious, tortured past—he *was* an excellent kisser. The rest of the school day had passed in a dream—colors really did seem brighter and the future more optimistic.

And then Amy appeared.

"Want to hang tonight?"

Chloe took a moment to surface after she was torn rudely from her daydreams.

"Uh, what? No thanks. I really have to work on my trig. I'm in the danger zone," Chloe said coldly.

Amy stared at her a long moment, like a museum specimen she was trying to analyze. "What's your problem lately?"

"*My* problem?" Chloe felt an itchiness at her fingertips as her temper rose; she shrugged and twiddled her hands until it went away. *Clawing my friend's face off.* That's *a good way to end a fight. Especially with the whole school watching.* "What about *yesterday*? When I texted you about lunch and you totally blew me off?"

"I never got your message," Amy promptly denied. But there was a tiny hint of doubt in her voice.

"Check your mail," Chloe goaded. "Come on. Check it."

Making every movement flamboyant and impatient like she didn't have time for this sort of nonsense, Amy dramatically pulled out her phone and hit the buttons. "You see? There's no—*oh*." Her face fell. "That."

" 'That'? So you *did* get it!"

"I was going to get back to you," Amy said carelessly. "Paul and I were busy. We were—"

" 'Paul and I were busy'? What were you doing? Working on the newspaper or—hm, let me think—sucking face?"

"You—"

" 'You and Paul' are *always* doing something. It's like the two of you are one unit and you've totally forgotten everything else."

"*Oh*, so that's it," Amy said, nodding. "You're jealous and lonely—is that why you're whoring around with dumbasses like Alyec?"

There was that word again. *Sheesh, one of my "boyfriends" won't even kiss me.* Chloe opened her mouth to *really* let Amy have it.

But as she thought about the other aspects of her life—her claws, her mysterious nighttime friend, Brian—she realized how ridiculous this argument was. There were a lot more important things going on, and Amy had as good as abandoned her the day of her fall. This was *not* worth it.

"Whatever. There's my bus." She turned and walked away, leaving Amy openmouthed and speechless.

• • •

She had to talk to someone about it.

Chloe had repeatedly backed down from arguments for the sake of their friendship—and Amy still treated her like the bad guy. She couldn't even see how she was acting! *I'd love to tell you what's going on in my life,* Chloe thought bitterly, *but you really don't seem that interested.*

Alyec would probably tell her to shrug it off, that it wasn't important. She wanted to bitch and to brood, though; she didn't *want* to cheer up and stop thinking about it. She wanted to figure it out.

Chloe took out her phone and dialed Brian. If she only did it once, she figured, she could always tell her mom it was someone she needed to get homework from or a study group partner or something.

"It's Brian." His answer was so short and direct, Chloe almost didn't recognize his voice at first. It was very professional sounding—curt, but not self-important.

"Wow, did I just reach Enron or something?"

"Oh, Chloe! No . . ." He laughed, sounding more like himself. "I'm just waiting for callbacks from *everyone*—the zoo, the parks department, animal rescue—even the pound."

"Bad economy," Chloe said, the way she had heard her mother and her mother's friends talk about it.

"Ain't that the truth." He sighed. "So you, uh, want that pattern, right?"

Chloe had completely forgotten about it. "No," she said darkly, "I don't think I'll be needing that anymore."

"Oh." He sounded confused—but was that also *relief* in his voice?

"But I'd still like to see you again."

"Yeah?" he asked cautiously.

"Yeah." She laughed. "You want to go somewhere tonight?"

"Tonight?" There was a pause, like he was looking at his watch or a calendar or something. "Uh, tonight's not *great*. . . . I have to send out a bunch more letters and resumes and applications and stuff. I wanted to get them in the mail tomorrow."

Chloe's ears prickled. There was something odd about the way he was talking, strange pauses—whether it was her new, keen senses or just intuition, she had a feeling he was lying to her. *What's going on with him? He sounds like he's interested, but he keeps sort of putting me off.*

And then it occurred to her.

"You have a girlfriend, don't you?"

"What?"

"Tell me the truth. You have a girlfriend."

"No! *I have no girlfriend,*" he said with exasperation. "I haven't had one in *months*. Why?"

"You just sound like . . . I don't know . . . grudging about the whole thing."

He laughed softly. "Chloe . . . I don't mean to be. I'm just kind of anal and obsessive when it comes to setting a goal and a schedule for myself. I'm like a rat, you know? Can't get food until send out one more letter."

"Oh." Chloe looked around in embarrassment, but no one on the bus was listening. "I'm sorry. I've had a weird day. My best friend Amy and I just had this huge fight—" Something finally broke inside her. Chloe swallowed, trying to hold back the tears that were beginning. She turned her face into the window and rubbed her eyes with her knuckle, trying to bruise them away.

"What happened?"

"It's no big deal," she whispered, trying not to sound like she was crying. "It's just like . . ." *I have these new claws, there's this note that says my life is in danger. . . .* "Amy's dating my other best friend and doesn't have time for me anymore, and she doesn't even realize what a bitch she's being." It felt strange to finally say it aloud. She had been thinking it for a while, accompanied with all of the self-doubt that went along with too much introspection. But now it sounded *real.* And even weirder—he had asked her what had happened. He'd asked about what had happened between a girl he'd only gone on one date with and her best friend, whom he had never met. And sounded like he was actually interested. Like he kind of cared.

"I'm sorry. I mean, of course I'll see you tonight."

Chloe smiled through her sniffles. "Can you—are you free now?" She didn't want to tell him how hard her mom had been on her lately—that sounded so high school. Like she was a little girl not in control of her destiny or daily life. *Which is true, but it's fun to dream.*

"Yeah—want to meet at that coffee place by the playground, across from the Peet's?"

"That would be great. I'll see you in a few."

"Okay, be right there."

She got off at the next stop, calling her mom to say that she had to stay after school for extra help with trig.

Twenty minutes later she was hunkered down in a comfy, shabby old chair, sipping a mug of tomato soup while Brian sat across from her, looking concerned. *I could get used to this,* Chloe decided. Even though her own friends were—*had been*—really nice, Brian focused his attention on her in a way she had never really experienced before. The kitty cat hat lay on the table between them, and his hair, rather than being flat, greasy hat hair, was sticking up in tousled dark brown clumps that she longed to run her fingers through and straighten. He had another book this time, a collection of short stories by Eudora Welty.

"It sounds stupid, I know," she said, trying not to sniff. "But Amy's always been the constant in my life. My dad disappears, there's Amy. My mom becomes a complete bitch, there's Amy. Paul acts like a dick to me, there's Amy. Only she's not *there* now, you know? I can't rely on her. She doesn't even answer my messages anymore. And there are . . . other things in my life, too, stuff I want to tell her about. . . . Stuff we definitely would have talked about if things were, you know, normal."

"What kind of stuff?"

Chloe hesitated. She was aching to tell *some*one, and Brian seemed like the sort of person who would sympathize once he believed her. But it was a *big* secret and too soon. Maybe she could tell a *little*. . . .

"Well, like, I fell from Coit Tower," she said, just as abruptly as she had with her mom.

Brian stared at her.

"I mean, she was *there* and everything and took me to the hospital with Paul. . . ."

"What do you mean, you 'fell from Coit Tower'?" Brian demanded.

"I mean, I fell." Chloe indicated with her fingers and the large pepper grinder, making it look like a little person was walking off it and falling.

"From the top? Were you rock climbing?"

"Yes, from the top. No to the rock climbing. Just out the window."

Brian stared at her silently for another moment. Chloe began to feel a little uncomfortable.

"And you're . . . just . . . fine?"

"Pretty much." She shrugged and tried to look nonchalant. "But listen, we were talking about me and *Amy*."

"And not the fact that you didn't *die*?"

"I think I almost might have," Chloe allowed, thinking back and wondering how much more to reveal. "I was in this place, and it was all dark, and I was sort of . . . *pushed* back into life. Like another fall, off someplace very high."

"Have you told anybody about this?"

"That's what I'm here bitching about!" Chloe snapped. "See, Amy was *there* when I fell, and we never got a chance to talk about it. About what . . . happened, or seemed to happen. It's kind of weird and personal, you know? I really didn't want to talk about it with anyone else. Besides, she believes in the supernatural and stuff, so you know, she would definitely have some ideas about the whole thing."

"I can see why you'd be reluctant to mention it to anyone else. . . . You probably shouldn't, in fact," he said, taking a sip of coffee. It was plain American. Black. No milk, no sugar, no nothing. Chloe found that kind of sexy; it was rough and masculine. She didn't know anyone else who drank it like that except for doctors on prime time. "Your friend doesn't sound very thoughtful." He took a breath and seemed like he was forcing himself back on topic.

"She's never been really . . . *thought*ful." Chloe reflected on it. "She's an introvert and kind of self-centered, but then she'll suddenly come out of the blue and do something great for you when you least expect it." *Like skipping school to go to Coit Tower the day before your birthday.*

"You don't seem to be blaming Paul much for this or saying much about him," Brian observed.

"He's . . . a different kind of 'best friend,' I guess,"

Chloe said. "He's always around, someone you can watch TV for hours with without saying a word, and it's fine. Or sit on the bleachers with and make fun of the jocks. And sometimes he'll open up a little, like he has no problem admitting when he finds things beautiful, like art or nature or stuff. But he doesn't even talk as much as he used to; he's a lot more introverted and difficult. Almost cold. Since the divorce," she realized lamely.

Brian didn't say anything, just raised his eyebrows, like: *Duh.*

"But *I* need Amy, too," she said in a tiny voice.

Brian laughed.

"Of course you do. *She's* the one who can't seem to adjust or make time for you. Have you tried telling her that?"

"Uh, sort of. The squishy emotional thing is hard when there's already distance and you're pissed at someone." She changed the subject, suddenly uncomfortable. "So, anyway, uh, how's the job search going?"

"Oh." He crouched down over his coffee. His brown eyes narrowed and darkened, like he was trying to reheat it with heat vision. For just a moment he didn't look like happy, sensitive Brian. He looked like someone else entirely, someone a lot angrier. "Terrible. And my dad . . . my dad isn't exactly making it easier."

"How?"

"Lectures. Letters. Warnings about my future." He sighed. "He's very Victorian, does the autocrat-at-the-breakfast-table thing. He wants me to do something productive with my life. Like going into the family business."

"What's that?"

"Really. Boring. Stuff. A security company—corporate empire, really—everything from bodyguard supplies to alarm systems—mainly corporate stuff."

"Bodyguards? That sounds interesting!" Chloe leaned forward. She pictured Brian in something *Matrix*-y, black and neoprene-ish, with leather boots. For some reason she couldn't quite *un*imagine the kitty cat hat, but the rest of the image was extremely sexy.

"Most of what he does is contracts. Paperwork, negotiating with big clients, meetings, company analyses, layoffs . . . the usual corporate crap." He smiled wanly. "*Along* with the Kevlar, the Tasers, and the guns. Hence my interest in the whole fish and game department has dropped—did you hear about the cat they have to hunt down in LA? Not my thing at all. Back to guns and other weapons again. No thanks."

"A cat? Guns?" *Wouldn't a water gun work?* She pictured a little tabby up against a firing squad.

"A mountain lion," Brian explained, laughing. It was like he could see exactly what was in her mind. Chloe found herself falling a little bit more in love. "Horrible, really. It attacked a guy jogging by himself at night up in the mountains. He's in really serious condition."

"What was he doing jogging by himself at night in mountain lion territory?" Chloe asked archly.

"It wasn't in a protected park or anything. He was living in a new condo complex they built near the park, and he was just jogging around the neighborhood."

"So lions are supposed to know exactly where their park ends and where public streets begin and avoid crunching on all the big, juicy human hamburgers that stroll through their territory? So they're going to kill it!?" Her voice rose as she spoke.

"Chloe," Brian said, looking around nervously, "it almost killed a person."

"Whose bright idea was it to encroach on mountain lion territory with condos, anyway?" Chloe demanded. "Jesus Christ, what did they *think* was going to happen?"

"All right," he agreed, "it wasn't nice to destroy more of their environment. But the houses and condos are there *now*. They're not moving. How are you going to keep the lions from attacking people?"

"Big fences? Signs that say, Don't Jog at Night by Yourself, Dumbass?"

"You really don't feel anything for the guy who was almost killed?" Brian asked quietly.

"Of course I do." Chloe sighed. "The poor schmuck wasn't really doing anything wrong—aside from buying a new condo recently built up against parkland, which merits *some* kind of punishment. But is hunting down and killing the cat the right answer?"

"The problem is that it's no longer afraid of humans, and now it has a taste of their blood."

"So we have to exterminate anything that's not afraid of us. Yay us, evolved monkeys." Chloe snorted.

"I *said* I didn't want to work for them anymore," Brian mumbled defensively.

He shook his head, clearing the air and changing the topic. "What about *you*? What do you want to be when you grow up?"

Chloe sighed again. "I don't know. I've sort of already ruled out rock goddess and movie star. I really like working at Pateena's, fooling with the clothes and stuff. Seeing what people buy and why."

"So, fashion designer?"

She laughed and shook her head, sending her bob in a neat little flair around her head—which she knew was cute. "No, that's Amy. She's the stylish, crafty one. We always talked about teaming up after school someday—uh, when she finally gives up her dream of being a poet. She would design the fashions and I would manage the store or company: hiring, fixtures, accounts. . . ." Her eyes grew dreamy, then narrowed. "That's why it pisses me off that Lania gets to work the cash register. She sucks, and I totally want to learn that side of it."

Brian's face was blank for a moment. "Oh, is she that girl who keeps making fun of the way I dress?"

"Yeah." Chloe snorted. "Good customer relations, no?"

"No," Brian firmly agreed. "So are you going to get a job in retail out of school?"

"What are you, mad?" Chloe laughed. "I'm going to

college, dillhole. My mom's a lawyer. She'd kill me otherwise. And besides—retail isn't exactly the best way to realize your life's ambition. I don't think Mr. or Mrs. Gap started out dreaming behind a counter at five-fifty an hour. I'll go to college, and if I still want to do this, I'll get my MBA—isn't that what you do?"

Brian shrugged. "My old man always said that MBAs were charm schools for the slow. But he's old-fashioned and kind of an idiot."

Chloe looked at him, realizing something. "Are you the first one in your family to go to college?"

Brian blushed. "I'm not there yet. That's part of the problem. My dad is dead set against it. He thinks it's a waste of money and you don't learn anything *real*. You're a pretty intuitive girl, you know that?"

She smiled, but when she held his eye for a moment, he looked away. *That explains the books—they weren't just to impress me!*

"Feeling any better?" he asked.

"Yeah," Chloe admitted grudgingly. "I still don't know what to do about Amy, but at least I'm not all crazy about it anymore. I think . . . I'm going to have to give her some space to finally figure out for herself how she's acting, even though it's pretty lonely out there right now."

"You're not *completely* alone," he said with a faint smile.

She *had* told him about the tower, hadn't she? Just

like that. And he hadn't freaked out or disbelieved her—he'd just listened. Chloe hadn't told anyone else, not even Alyec. *Someone to talk to . . .* "Any more near-death experiences, emotional crises with my best friend, and fights with my mom, I know who to call."

"I'm your man," Brian said, giving her a thumbs-up and a wink.

For some reason, it gave Chloe pause. The gesture was familiar somehow.

"Uh," she said, a little unsure of what to do. "I guess I should get going before Mom realizes that I've overstayed after school."

"Yeah." He coughed. "Of course. I'm glad we could meet, though."

Are you? Chloe couldn't be sure.

He stood up and pulled the table out for her to make it easier to get up with her book bag and jacket, another completely Brian thing. He didn't do it with flare or a dramatic gesture, he didn't do it with a hello-I'm-being-chivalrous attitude, he didn't apologize for what might have been construed as a patriarchal gesture by some. He just did it. Courteousness without an agenda. *I could* really *get to like this.* Except for the whole not-seizing-the-moment thing. Was he shy?

Outside, Chloe threw her scarf on dramatically twice—what could she say, she was in full flirt mode and hoping Brian would notice. It was the only knitting project she had ever finished, with odds and ends from her mom's craft bin. In-your-face patchwork and ugly.

"You want to get together again soon?" he asked, shuffling his feet in the cold. "We don't have to do ska. I thought if you wanted, we could go ice skating or something—"

"Kiss me, you idiot," Chloe said, aware of the fall air, the crackling of dead leaves, the *life* in the environment. She reached up for his head.

Brian pushed her back, gently but firmly on the shoulders.

"What?" Chloe demanded, blushing and angry. "Is it because I'm in high school or something? You're only two years older than I am!"

"No—yes." He changed his answer, thinking it was an easy way out. Then he sighed and reverted to the truth. "No, that's not it. I—I just can't, Chloe. Not now."

"Why not?" She stamped her foot, not caring how little girlish it looked.

"I like you a lot—" he started.

"You're gay," she interrupted. "No, wait—*married*. That's why you said you didn't have a *girlfriend*."

"I'm not gay and I'm not married. Chloe, I really do like you. I—" He was about to try and get off with a platitude, but Chloe gave him a warning look. "I *want* you," he whispered. "I just—can't—right now."

"Does this have something to do with your father?" she asked. "'Cause he ain't watching right now, I can tell you that."

Brian's shoulders sagged and a shadow came over his brow. For the first time since she had seen him, he looked like an entirely different person: haunted, conflicted, and most of all *defeated*.

"So what now?" she asked, a little more gently.

Brian sighed. "I don't know."

Chloe wandered home glumly, too down to run. But as she walked past a familiar parking meter and car, it suddenly hit Chloe. The night with the other cat person. He had given her a thumbs-up, too, and turned his head like he was winking.

Thirteen

Chloe didn't have a lot of time to think about her realization immediately; it was pizza night. She and her mom did takeout fairly often, several times a week. But *pizza* was special and they ordered it rarely, keeping the nature of the occasion festive.

Once upon a time a year or so ago, Chloe had gotten all grown up and responsible for a month, trying to make dinner for them at least once a week, but that had been phased out as she and her mom started fighting over things more and more. *I should probably start doing that again.* . . . It was hard for Chloe to remember that her mom was a *person,* often exhausted and with her own troubles, but when she did, she was genuinely sorry.

And sorry she was such a burden.

They got a large pepperoni and split it with no mention of waists, calories, fat, or anything else. Rarely did a slice make it to a plate—one of them would scoop it up and shovel it directly into her face. The television wasn't on.

The whole thing was a little forced, but they were giggling—especially when her mom got a red Ronald McDonald smile on her face ear to ear from tomato sauce.

"Are you . . . okay?" Mrs. King finally asked when the laughter died down.

Chloe shuffled in her seat and played with one of the crusts on her plate, which she always saved for last, like a little pile of bread or pickup sticks.

"Mom, I want to go out," Chloe said quietly. "With . . . guys."

Or at least stop lying about it.

Her mother looked up at her, seemingly impressed with her daughter's new, mature-sounding tone.

"Look, I know you said it was like the last thing Dad asked before he left, but . . . he's *gone*," Chloe said, indicating the two empty seats at the table. "He hasn't been here for the last twelve years. I don't think he has a right to dictate my life from the past."

"I *never* agreed with your father's views about raising you," her mom said, ripping off another slice with more force than she had to. "We didn't agree on *anything* toward the end." She bit and chewed pensively. "Well, we probably didn't agree on anything in the beginning, either, but it was all hidden by the rosy mists of young love. And we both loved *you*."

Chloe didn't say anything, even holding her breath so she wouldn't interrupt her mom's train of thought.

"By the end, you were all that we had in common."

Her mother sighed and smiled sadly at her. "And we began to fight over you."

"So by keeping to the one last thing you disagreed with—you were still keeping Dad here somehow?"

"You watch *way* too much daytime TV," her mother said wryly, but didn't disagree.

"If he loved me so much, it would have been nice if he stuck around a little," Chloe muttered.

They were both quiet for a few minutes, chewing.

Then her mom sat up straighter and looked Chloe dead in the eye, coming to a decision. "You can't be skipping school and falling from towers and leaving hospitals and spending time with boys alone during school hours. Have you *seen* the news recently? About that dead girl, stabbed in the alley? They think her attacker knew her. It's bad enough out there, but you've also been lying to me—how am I supposed to be able to trust you?"

Chloe's first reaction was to argue that that wasn't fair, but unfortunately, her mom had a good point.

"All right," Mrs. King said with resolution. She spoke in her lawyer voice. "From now on, clean slate between us, okay? You can go out and do all the 'normal' things—and don't think I won't be talking with other parents to see what exactly is considered normal. But you can't skip school anymore. You have to tell me where you're going and when. And sometimes, now and then, I will be checking up on you. You don't have a very good track record, young lady." She frowned at Chloe.

"I want to be part of your life, Chloe, and help and protect you—" Chloe tried not to giggle at that part, thinking about what she had done to the bum. *"Capisce?"*

Chloe nodded. "Agreed."

"Good." Her mother took another huge bite of pizza.

"I got my period," Chloe said brightly.

Her mother choked.

At school the next day Chloe found herself reviewing everything she knew about Brian. The kitty cat hat, how he knew so much about the lions, how concerned he was that she might have talked about her survival of the fall with anyone else, like he was afraid of other people finding out her secret. And the thumbs-up just clinched it. *He really* must be *the other cat person!* She couldn't believe she hadn't realized it before. It all made sense, starting with their first meeting and her instant attraction.

But why didn't he just come out and tell her? And why wouldn't he kiss her? Did it have something to do with being cat people? Chloe felt sure he would tell her eventually, that all would be revealed in due time. She couldn't wait. Brian was everything she had hoped for: someone to talk to and someone who could tell her about her cat nature, who could teach her about it.

Making out would be nice, too, though, Chloe couldn't help thinking.

Gradually she thought about the less exciting parts of their conversation. . . . Like really, what *did* she want to be when she grew up? All the answers she'd given him were true, but were they correct? Was going into the fashion industry the right thing to do? Should she look for a higher cause, a nonprofit, something for the good of the world? And what about all those little kid dreams: fireman, astronaut, president. Could she really rule *all* of them out? Was she too young to narrow things down?

I might actually go talk to the guidance counselor, she decided. It was last period of the day; many teachers would already be warming up their cars or having their last cigarette break. And except for National Honor Society members—like Paul—the counselor was definitely an unutilized school resource. He would most definitely be free. Even if she chickened out of actually talking to him, she could go through all of the brochures outside his office. They had seemed kind of lame before, but some of them were put out by companies, she remembered, and spoke about careers within them. Paul had talked vaguely about publishing at one point, when he had given up on the music industry, and had taken a bunch of pamphlets.

She was walking by the newspaper office and found herself instinctively heading toward it—also probably because she was thinking about Paul—before remembering and continuing to walk ahead. She had *no* desire to see either one of the couple of the year.

Too late.

The door opened and Paul was walking out, a dollar in his hand, probably going to the snack machines in the cafeteria.

"Hey, Chloe," he said, a little surprised, but not upset.

"Hey," she said, and stopped walking. But she didn't say anything further, just stood there, looking at him, slightly bored and impatient.

"I heard you and Amy were fighting." He said it with faint surprise, like it was some other people he was talking about, like it was juicy school gossip. He was *almost* preppy today in khakis but with a slim, expensive-looking off-white shirt with red stripes along the seams and a tiny Puma insignia on the back.

"Um, yeah." She tried to sound cool. "Amy was pissed because I didn't want to go over to her place. She blew *me* off when I texted her about lunch and she didn't even read it."

"Oh," Paul said, shifting his weight from one foot to the other. "She didn't tell me about that."

"Quel surprise," Chloe muttered.

"Does it bother you that we're together?"

That was so Paul. Guarded, guarded, silent, then . . . pow! The direct, emotional kicker.

"It's a little weird," Chloe finally admitted. "But that doesn't bother me as much as her—and your—complete disappearance from my life. I mean, she always gets a little caught up in her boyfriends, and you always had the 'secret girlfriend' thing going on. . . . But this is different. We haven't hung out since that weird double-date thing with Alyec. I don't *want* to double date; I want to just hang with you guys like we used to."

Paul nodded, not saying anything.

"A lot has been going on with me recently and she hasn't. . . . Neither one of you has been around to hear it. It's like she doesn't even care anymore."

"I think," Paul said delicately, "she might be a little . . . concerned about your current choice of boyfriends."

Which one? Chloe almost asked.

"*Alyec?* What the fuck, man? I wasn't pissed or rude to her face about Ottavio or that loser Steve who brought fucking *ecstasy* into my mom's house and tried to sell it at my *Halloween* party."

Paul nodded again, getting quieter as she got louder. He did not disagree.

"Alyec is completely hot, doesn't take himself seriously, and doesn't deal drugs. Look, whatever," Chloe said, calming down. She could feel her fingertips beginning to itch again. "*I* think she's acting like a real bitch about everything, and frankly, I don't have time to deal with her shit right now. If she's not going to be around to lend an ear, at least she can keep her distance and shut the fuck up."

Paul raised his eyebrows. The movement didn't touch the rest of his face; he looked a Vulcan or something, with immobile, high cheekbones and eyes so dark you couldn't tell the pupil from the iris.

"I'm sorry about the ranting." Chloe sighed. "I gotta go."

"Chloe—" Paul stopped. "I'm sorry. Don't confuse me with her."

She softened a little. He sounded anxious, genuinely worried.

"I won't." She kissed him on the cheek, amusedly remembering how she'd had the urge to suck face with him a couple of weeks ago. No such desire made itself known now; just warmth and friendliness. *The way it should be.*

Paul smiled.

"Okay, well, see you later?" It was a question, a promise.

He continued on his way to the cafeteria—which was a relief; if he had gone back inside the newspaper office, Chloe would have suspected that he was going to call or text or e-mail Amy. Or worse, that she'd been in there the entire time. As Paul turned the corner, Chloe leaned forward and sniffed. She wasn't sure exactly what she was smelling *for*; if asked, she would never have been able to describe Amy's scent beyond the Anna Sui perfume she sometimes wore. She just assumed there would be some warm, vaguely familiar smell.

But there wasn't. Just Paul, his masculine, slightly acrid smell—not bad, just that he probably hadn't washed the gel out of his hair from yesterday. And his skin—images flashed through her head, but none of them matched or described the smell exactly. Ivory soap, sandalwood; something comforting and deep and good.

Oh, and underneath it all, a package of Cheetos he must have consumed a few minutes ago.

I could be a bloodhound, Chloe thought smugly. Then

she thought about Paul: he only ate crappy snacks when he was nervous. Either it was trig or her and Amy.

She continued on to the guidance counselor's office and began to look at the pamphlets, raising her lip at the army, ROTC, and other military ones. These she took and surreptitiously tipped into the recycling bin. Paul's cousin had been killed in Baghdad—he had joined the army because his father wouldn't send him to an American college and he didn't want to go back to Korea. Just like Brian, except he didn't mind guns.

"Ms. King. You are the *last* person I expected to see here."

Chloe tried not to look up with sneering surprise at Mr. McCaffety. He was *such* a guidance counselor, with visible dandruff and really ugly loafers.

"As opposed to, say, the kids who smoke up in the parking lot at lunch?"

"Good point," he allowed. He took a sip of coffee out of a mug that said World's Best Dad. A blurry shot of his twin daughters was framed beneath the words, an indistinct clue to his humanity, a life beyond these walls. "I meant to say I didn't really expect you to come here of your own volition."

Chloe shrugged, pointing at the rack of booklets. "I don't know what to do." *With my life, my boyfriends, my best friend, the threat on my life . . .*

Mr. McCaffety's eyes lit up.

"Well, I want to get out of here," he said frankly, "but why don't we make an appointment?"

"Okay," Chloe said, a little guardedly. She hoped no

one else heard about this. "I've got second period free Mondays, Wednesdays, and Fridays. . . ."

"Great. How's Friday?"

"Uh, okay, I guess."

"Anything I should research, know about before you come in?"

Research? He's actually going to look up stuff for me? Chloe blushed. "I'm kind of interested in the fashion industry. . . ."

"Ah. Design or corporate?"

"Corporate." This was really weird. He was taking her seriously. What she wanted to do with her life, seriously. Like she wasn't a dreaming little sixteen-year-old with delusions of grandeur.

"Excellent! Well, we'll see what we can find. I'll see you on Friday, then."

"Yeah, right," Chloe agreed in a daze.

"Hey." Alyec caught up to her as she was just about to board the bus back toward Inner Sunset. "Want to come with me across the street? I have to go to the comic store. We can hang out."

Wednesday is comic day. Alyec read comic books? Chloe couldn't help noticing that every new detail about the boy's personality and life revealed him to be—well, more boyish. *If it wasn't for the accent and the looks, he could just as well be an Alex having grown up in the Valley or Idaho or something.*

"I have to work today," she answered, looking at her

watch and trying not to smile. "If it's on the way and we're less than a half hour, I can walk with you."

"Oh, they have them bagged and up at the counter for me," Alyec said easily. He didn't *look* like a comic book reader, like the pale-fleshed males and females who were already hurrying together in a protective band out of the school. Paul was one of them, distinguishable by his slightly healthier skin tone. He waved to her as the group walked by. They were all laughing and arguing and loudly quoting movies and books and television shows. Chloe felt a quick pang of sadness as she watched them go. They were a little clan where everyone was accepted; if one was acting all bitchy—like, say, Amy—there were at least five others with whom one could take solace. *Plus they would probably think my claws were really cool.*

"I would be their goddess," she mused aloud.

"You would be *any*one's goddess," Alyec said without really listening. "Come on. I want to beat the rush." He took her by the hand and led her away. He was wearing a brown turtleneck sweater, precisely fitting jeans, and European-looking leather shoes and looked exactly like a model or a pouty-lipped god listening to the coolest new music on a Virgin ad.

"Do any of the other popular kids know you do this?"

"They accept it." He shrugged. "You and your friends talk about 'popular' a lot," he added, but didn't make a comment or conclusion.

Chloe waited outside the store, less from embarrassment

than claustrophobia; the tiny shop was packed with people. She also felt a little strange: here she was, an actual person with actual weird abilities. She worried that the comic readers could sniff her out or tell that she was different.

"Ach," Alyec said, emerging. "*Superman* looks like it totally sucks this week. Thank goodness for *The Punisher*."

"Well, that's what you get for reading kid stuff," Paul said, coming out the door behind him. To Chloe's surprise, Alyec didn't get upset.

"Yeah, I know." He sighed. "But you know, Superman is a symbol of America, so when I was in Russia, he used to mean everything to me. Rock music. Television. Money."

"Don't you mean truth, justice, and the American way?" Paul asked, a very faint smile on his lips.

"Yeah, whatever. Same thing." Chloe looked back and forth between them, her best friend and her boyfriend, who were really as different as the sun and Pluto, talking easily.

"I guess geekdom is the great leveler," she observed.

"You haven't seen anything yet," Paul answered, grinning. "Just wait until a convention. Well, I gotta go . . ." He faltered. *Pick up Amy,* Chloe realized. "Pick up Amy," he finally said, determined to keep things normal between everyone. Chloe was glad; at least the two of them could still communicate.

"C'mon." Chloe dragged Alyec, who had begun to flip through his brown paper bag of goodies. "I'll buy you some fries." He brightened up and went with her. Like a lot of the popular kids, he never seemed to have a book bag or backpack or anything, not even one of those messenger bags. Chloe wondered where they put all their stuff.

They stopped at the McDonald's a block from Pateena's and she kept her word, although she wouldn't let him eat any that she didn't hold in her lips.

"That's no fair," Alyec said, biting one and kissing her. "You get half."

She stuck a finger in the ketchup and licked it suggestively. "Hey, are you complaining?"

"No." He kissed her again, without a fry to entice him.

Chloe stopped, feeling someone watching her. There was a stopped footstep, a familiar smell. . . .

Brian, she realized.

He stood across the street, staring at the two of them. Hurt was plainly painted across his face.

"Hang on a sec," she told Alyec, who comfortably grabbed the fries and began tossing them down his gullet as fast as he could. She ran across the street.

"What's going on?" Brian asked heatedly, indicating Alyec. Once again, he was all in black, and his eyes were molten and focused.

"What do you mean?"

"With him? What are you doing? *With him?*" He tried keep quiet, but his voice grew louder and louder.

"Brian, you said you couldn't"—she winced at the clinical, grown-up-sounding words—"engage in a physical relationship with me."

He looked at her, uncomprehending.

"You won't kiss me!" she finally said, exasperated. "What are you? A friend? Then you shouldn't mind me dating someone. A *boy*friend?" She let the last word drop, not needing to add anything after it.

"I didn't realize it was so important to you—," he began haughtily.

"Don't give me that crap," Chloe retorted angrily. "It's the twenty-first century, I'm a sixteen-year-old girl, and wanting to kiss my boyfriend good night is not weird or horny!"

Brian let his head hang.

"I like you," she said, sighing. "I really do. But I asked you before—what now? What do you want us to be?"

Brian shook his head and walked away, eyes glassy.

Chloe watched him sadly but didn't chase after him. Alyec wandered over to her, seeming to not mind the incident. He was using the last fry to scoop up the last bit of ketchup. "Who's that, another boyfriend?" he asked, unconcerned.

"Uh, sort of," Chloe said, taken aback by his honesty.

"You haven't done anything with him." It was a statement, not a question.

"Yeah? How would *you* know?"

"He's still alive." Alyec grinned at her. "You would tear a boy like that up and spit him back out when you were done."

Chloe smiled weakly back.

Fourteen

Chloe spent the entire afternoon at Pateena's going over and over her and Brian's conversation. She thought she had been extremely mature and handled it surprisingly well, saying all the right things for once. But it had still been ugly and awful, and it had ended poorly.

Marisol noticed her gloom.

"Hey, what's the matter? You usually get this stuff sorted in the first hour," she said, indicating a pile of blouses.

"Remember when I had no one, and you told me to get someone?" Chloe asked, smiling wryly.

"Yeah?"

"Now I have two. One barely touches me and the other—well, he's not exactly Mr. Sensitive Man/Rocket Scientist."

Marisol whistled. "Ah, the tragedies and troubles of high school. *Two* boyfriends. My, my. Well, I tell you what: if you get this stuff done in the next twenty minutes, I'll buy you *un café* to ease your troubled mind."

Chloe couldn't help smiling; her boss was right. From an outside perspective, Chloe was bitching about an excess of good things, too many choices. *Too bad I couldn't combine them. I'd either have a neutered idiot or one hell of a sexy Mr. Right.* That didn't make the way Brian felt any less awful, though. But if he didn't want to see her with another guy, why didn't he say or do something? Was she coming on too strong? Was this new, confident, sexy Chloe too much for him? Did Brian feel he had to make the next move? And more importantly, did Chloe care about him enough to adjust for him? On the one hand, they'd only gone on two dates. On the other hand, she *really* liked him. Maybe it had something to do with him being another cat person. . . .

The coffee Marisol got her sped up her thoughts but didn't make the afternoon go any faster. Neither did "Torn Between Two Lovers," which somehow got played on the speakers at least three times over the course of the afternoon. It was weird how many customers could actually whistle or sing along to it.

Finally the sun began to go down and it was time to close up shop. Chloe called her mom to let her know she would be coming straight home after helping Marisol with the gate. Mrs. King thanked her for letting her know and said that she would be home a little later—they were taking out one of the other lawyers who'd just found out she was pregnant. Chloe didn't feel it was necessary to specifically mention getting fries with Alyec; that had been officially on the way to work from school, more of a detour than a destination.

Chloe steadfastedly refused Marisol's proffered taxi money this time, claiming she was just going down the street to the deli to wait for her mom to pick her up. As soon as Marisol was safely out of her line of sight, however, Chloe leapt up a bench, then a tree, and then onto a roof, determined to make it as close to home as she could without coming down.

One! she counted, making a running leap onto the roof of a nice, long attached condo. It was good for about a hundred feet. *Two!* She leapt off the side onto another house, which was much shorter and farther down than she expected, causing her to roll to break her momentum and keep her legs from breaking. She sprang up at the end, though, making an Olympic-style landing—except for the crouching, catlike, all-fours aspect.

Three! With barely a pause she straight jumped onto the garage of the next house . . .

. . . when she felt a sting on her left leg and felt something rip. She pitched forward, but instinct took over and she cradled her leg as she fell, missing the roof completely and landing on the sidewalk. She looked down and saw ropes of blood stream along her skin to the ground and a cold, sharp metal object with a tip buried in her flesh. She pulled it out, biting her lip at the pain, and held it up to the moonlight.

A throwing star, she realized with disbelief. *Like in ninja movies.* This one had ten points, five large ones, one of which was covered in blood and bits of skin, and five smaller ones in between these, either for decoration or to help it spin. There was something written on it, but before she could get a good look, Chloe heard a faint whir. She dropped her head to the ground against her arms—if she'd had ears like a cat, Chloe would have flattened them. Another shuriken flew by and embedded itself in a tire. *Sssssssht* went the air as it slowly deflated.

Chloe leapt up, flipped, and landed on top of the car.

"Excellent moves," said a voice from the shadows. "I can see someone has finally been training you."

"Who are you? Come out!" Streetlight glittered on glass and metal pebbles in the road. All the houses were dark or the shades pulled so tightly they might as well have been empty. Holes that might have once had trees and bushes in them were filled with beer cans and old toys. This was, as her mother would say, a bad area. A figure hid behind a car so rusted and old, it probably could just have been torn out of the boot that was locked to its right front tire.

A breeze stirred and Chloe sniffed it; this was *not* the cat person from the other night. For some reason she shivered. What was going on?

There was another, near-silent whoosh. Chloe crouched just in time to avoid another throwing star, this one aimed at her neck. She wondered wildly how many he had and turned to run.

Then she realized something: *He's using weapons that he has to* throw—*I'm only in danger as long as I'm* far *from him. . . .* Chloe turned back and ran along the tops of the cars *toward* him. She leapt down to where she thought he was hiding, yowling and screaming to scare him out into the open.

It worked: he threw himself out of her way and into the road.

"Well done."

Streetlight revealed him to be tall and skinny, with tautly outlined muscles on his legs and arms. He wore a dark, almost military-style outfit with a large belt—*for weapons*—and a loose black leather jacket—*for armor.* His hair was so blond it was almost white, pulled back in a ponytail. His eyes were a muddled blue. It was difficult to judge his age, but one thing was for certain: he didn't look entirely sane. His pupils were black pinheads, especially strange considering how dark it was.

He pulled out a dagger and crouched a little, a street fighter. *Like from the game Street Fighter.*

This is crazy, Chloe thought. *No one acts like this.* But it was obvious that the man was serious—and would have to be dealt with seriously.

He was waiting for her to attack. Someone threw a can out a window; it smashed onto the street before rolling into the gutter.

"Can I—help you?" she asked, unsure whether to run away or continue the dialogue.

"What's the matter? No urge to fight? The ancient instinct hasn't awakened in you yet?" the man sneered.

"I had kind of planned on a cocoa and an early bedtime, actually." She circled carefully, keeping a tree between them.

"You almost sound human." With a misdirection of his left hand, he threw the dagger at her with his right. Chloe jumped, but it tore her shoulder as it passed.

He had two daggers now, one in each hand.

"Where do you keep all those things?" Chloe demanded, touching her shoulder. Running now would definitely mean her death: by two quick blades, one in the neck and one in the back.

"I see no one has properly warned you about me," he said, almost disappointed.

"No, no one told me about a crazy blade-wielding psycho—" Then she remembered. *Your life is in danger. Be wary of the company you keep. Be prepared—and ready to run. The Order of the Tenth Blade knows who you are. . . .*

Order of the Tenth Blade? She thought about the shuriken. *Maybe it means that he only has ten blades?* Chloe somehow didn't think that was it. She wouldn't have been surprised if he had a tank hidden somewhere on his body.

"A pity. You should know your executioner."

Chloe shivered again; she felt the hairs on her arms and shoulders rise. Even if he was crazy, he was still serious.

"*My* executioner is probably all the trans-fatties in Oreos and stuff," Chloe countered. *He's going to attack—*

he's going to attack! Any second now . . .

"Id tibi facio," he whispered, and lunged.

Chloe jumped aside, a tenth of a second too late—once again he cut her, but shallowly this time. He didn't move like the homeless guy from the other night; he was fast and well trained—a professional fighter. *Killer,* she corrected herself. He wanted to *kill her*. She leapt again as he brought a dagger down on her and realized she had no time to think, only react.

Her left leg throbbed. It was still bleeding.

He went at her belly with a swipe; she leapt up and grabbed a tree branch, hauling her torso out of the way. He spun, keeping the momentum to hit her as she dropped back down, but she curled in a ball to avoid it. His heel ground against the sidewalk. Whenever she stepped backward, he stepped into her; whenever she leapt to the side, he was there with a dagger.

I have to attack him.

She ducked as he swiped a blade through the air above her head. When she came up, she brought her claws ripping up to his groin. They clanged on something metal.

He laughed.

She had to roll quickly out of the way as he threw a dagger down at her. Chloe saw little blue sparks jump away as it bounced off the pavement with incredible force. She shot out a foot, kicking him neatly in the calf. It made enough impact to give her a little hope.

Fight in, closer, her instincts told her. She was terrified but obeyed. Chloe waited until the last moment and then sprang forward, closing the distance between them, and tried to swipe him across the face with her claws. *Even if you get the slightest bit of flesh or eye,* she remembered her self-defense trainer saying, *the pain will be great enough to distract.*

Only if you hit, though—his arm came up immediately and his wrist blocked her. Chloe brought her knee up to his groin again, planning to shove *up* really hard, figuring that even if he wore some kind of ancient metallic jockstrap or chastity belt or whatever, it would at least hurt a little as it dug into his flesh. At the last minute, though, she leapt up and brought her foot *down* onto his cup and the other foot, too, pushing with all her strength. The way a cat disembowels.

She was rewarded by the first real response from her attacker: he groaned and caught his breath. Then he shot out his fists, one after the other, trying to slash her before she pushed herself away from him. He ripped right down her shirt and through her bra strap, drawing blood underneath in the soft part of her shoulder.

I'm going to lose this fight, Chloe realized, her stomach going cold. He seemed to be able to predict all of her moves—though if it weren't for the exercises the cat person put her through the other night, she wouldn't have survived as long as she had. She would have been lying on the sidewalk, blood running from her throat.

"Give up, blasphemy of nature," he growled. *"Demon!"*

As his slashing blades came closer, she slashed him back, batting at him with her claws and hissing.

He was waiting for that, apparently, and kneed her in the stomach.

Chloe fell over, unable to breathe. *He's trying to goad my instinctive reactions; as soon as I stop thinking and just react, he knows how to get me.* When she fought, he could beat her. He was a good *fighter*. . . .

This gave her the slightest shred of hope. She slowly drew herself up and faced him.

"So I don't scare you?" she asked. *Get a dialogue going.*

"Your kind doesn't scare me," he said with a sneer. "You only disgust me."

Chloe flicked a glance over his shoulder into the street. "Do *cops* scare you?"

His eyes widened and he turned.

Chloe hadn't thought he would actually do it. Before he realized there weren't any actual police coming, she kicked him as hard as she could in the stomach with the flat of her heel. She spun and did a backward handspring, putting her at least seven feet away from him.

Then she ran, not looking back and putting all of her effort into flight, satisfied with the heavy, thudding sound of his body hitting ground.

Fifteen

She took random paths home, sometimes doubling back and retracing her route for several blocks, sometimes running in circles. She considered finding a body of water to run through to hide her scent—before remembering that *she* was the animal; her attacker had obviously taken great pride in being a normal human. *Unless he's a dog,* Chloe mused. Who was to say that in a world where a girl could have claws, a guy couldn't have a muzzle and penchant for bones?

The thrill of the fight drove her; part of her wanted to turn back and finish it. To face death.

But she continued running.

When she finally felt it was safe—after pausing for a *long* time in public places like convenience stores and crowded Muni stops, waiting to see if he would reappear—she went home, carefully locking the doors behind her. She waited in the kitchen, listening.

After a while the adrenaline in her blood finally died down.

Chloe began to be afraid.

Just because she'd taken a labyrinthine path home didn't mean that he couldn't find her. Obviously he knew who and what she was—how hard would it be to find out where she lived? *How* did he know what she was, for that matter?

He could be coming for me now.

Suddenly she was terrified. It was one thing to be running free on the streets, between houses, out in the open—up to a police station or public place if she had to. But now she was trapped. The windows looked out on a black night spotted with pools of light from other houses and streetlights, which somehow just made the night seem darker, more likely to hide monsters, villains, psychos. Chloe had never really believed in them before, the people who came at you for no reason, from the outside, into your home—that was the stuff of horror movies and urban legends. Now she knew better. It was real.

Chloe turned on all the lights, but the corners still seemed dim and treacherous. She wanted to put on music or the TV, but she was afraid of not hearing him sneak up. She sat on the couch, paralyzed, certain that the next moment was going to bring him smashing into her house with a huge crash.

Just until Mom gets home, she told herself. *She should be here any minute. Just stay calm until she gets home.*

The thought reassured her.

And then she remembered the fight, the crazy, cold look in his eyes, the names he'd called her. What ancient, childlike habit made her believe that her *mommy* could protect her? She didn't even have the speed or claws of her daughter.

A second thought, more gruesome than this one, came:

If he comes here, it's my fault.

Not only could her mother probably not protect her, but Chloe would have led him directly home, if not now then later—and if her mom got hurt, it would be because of Chloe. . . .

What else can I do?

She reached for the phone. Maybe this guy knew her secret, but he was still a violent weirdo and she had the scrapes and bruises to prove it—she could describe him perfectly to the police and let *them* take care of it. If her attacker raved about Chloe being some sort of "blasphemy" and mentioned her claws—*especially* if he mentioned her claws—they would decide he was a crazy from whom she and the rest of society should be protected.

She dialed 9-1—

What about Xavier?

She paused. Whatever happened to Xavier, anyway? What if he had died? *Not all deaths appear in the obituaries.*

Her DNA was all over his lips and back and shirt. Her fingerprints on his doorknob and phone. If there was an investigation, she would at least be questioned, probably as a prime suspect. What if they examined her? Looked at her claws, checked her fingernails, x-rayed her fingers?

She cursed herself for not following up on him, seeing what had happened. If he hadn't died, the people at the hospital would have questioned him—"Yeah, there was this girl I met at the club; she was the last person I touched before I got sick. . . ." Typhoid Mary. Scratches and boils across his back where she had scraped him. Where her claws would have been, if she had known. She would make an interesting research subject. . . .

She put the phone back down.

I have a secret.

It didn't sound pretty, like a junior high secret crush or journal or juicy piece of gossip. The claws, the expanded senses, the speed, the freedom, the night—she hadn't realized they came with a price. Like the time she'd taken a pull from a bong, when the giggles were over and she'd realized she had *done something illegal*—that if they chose to, any of her friends could have told, and she would have had a police record or gone to juvie hall. She had a secret and it was *punishable.*

Silence overwhelmed the house. Once in a great while a car drove by and Kimmy the shih tzu would bark—Chloe thought about going outside to see if he still acted weird around her, but she couldn't bear the thought of opening the door.

There was a bang and a metallic-sounding scrape as someone threw a glass bottle into a recycling can.

More slowly than she had ever done anything, Chloe moved to the stairway and went upstairs. Every step was forced, every moment balanced. She listened for footsteps outside in the grass or on the pavement beneath the windows. The twelve steps took twenty minutes: she could barely hear over her own heartbeats and breathing.

When she finally got upstairs, she opened her drawer with what seemed like *way* too much noise.

Squeak!

Mus-mus ran from her. She put her hand down and he ran into the corner, cowering. Chloe frowned. She pulled a Cheerio from the sandwich bag and held it out to him. He stayed in his corner. It took almost five minutes for him to work up his courage—and then he only ran forward, grabbed it in his mouth, and ran back into the corner again.

"What's gotten into you?" Chloe demanded. He was her only friend in the house right now; she didn't have the emotional energy for *him* to wig out, too. "Come on!" she said, a little more annoyed, going to pick him up. Then she noticed her claws were still out.

He thinks I'm a cat now. A predator.

She made herself relax, calmed her thoughts, waiting until the claws disappeared.

But when she put her hand in, he still ran away.

Chloe was sitting on the bed, in the same position, staring at the closed drawer, when her mother came in hours later. Chloe didn't move when the car pulled up or the door opened or when she came upstairs.

"Hey." Her mom stuck her head in, face slightly flushed from drink and good times. "You're not in bed yet?"

"I'm going. *Now,*" Chloe said with a wan smile. Her tears had dried up a while ago, but they'd left scratchy, salty tracks on her cheeks.

She *knew* it wasn't safer now that her mom was home . . . but somehow still she felt like it was.

Sixteen

Chloe had no desire to go to school or work the next day—lying in bed under the covers definitely seemed like a superior option. *But not the safest.* Public places like school and work were absolutely the safest places to be, and in between she would make sure she was with crowds or other people.

And at home, tonight?

She never wanted to live through an evening of fear like that again. Thinking about it made her want to throw up. She hadn't slept much, jumping up at every noise and lying awake for hours, following each sound to its conclusion: cars driving into the distance, someone—possibly with a *different* malevolent purpose—striding down the midnight street, pausing, taking a piss, and then going on his way. A rat or something small and noisy pushed its food along the ground outside her window, into a hole, for what seemed like half the night.

She surfed the Web for a few minutes before getting ready, looking for alarm systems and door jammers and electronic sentries—most of which seemed to start in the five-hundred-dollar category. Chloe tried to come up with a way of suggesting it to her mom: "Uh, there've been a lot of break-ins recently, and I was wondering . . ." The easiest thing would probably be to get a bunch of those kids' toys that were supposed to guard your locker or room from a sibling and set them up all over the house.

But what about *her*? What if he attacked her again, more sneakily?

Thinking over the fight, she remembered how he had aimed for her throat and important joints—shoulders, knees—and finally the belly. She needed some sort of protection for those places: armor. Chloe took out the music box her dad had given her the last Christmas they were all together; where she kept all of her favorite pieces of jewelry, and the sparkly things she never wore. At the bottom, tangled up in a bracelet she got out of a cereal box, was a chain mail necklace she'd bought at a Renaissance fair Amy had dragged her to years ago. She put it on and looked at herself in the mirror. The steel links made a chain that was only a couple of inches wide, but if she wore it a little loose, then at least it protected the lower half of her neck, the veins and arteries there.

Chloe had no idea what to do about her knees and legs. She played with the idea of wrapping them with Ace bandages, the metal pins all stuck along more vulnerable areas. For her stomach and shoulders the closest thing to protection she had was a leather vest from Pateena's—very seventies and cracked in places. But it was a biker's, thick and strong. She dug it out of her closet and put it on.

Some call me a space cowboy....

Really, all she needed was a ten-gallon hat or a huge belt with a silver dollar buckle. *Actually* . . . She tilted her head. With her bob, a pair of feather earrings wouldn't look too bad, either. Maybe some thick black eye liner, clumpy mascara . . .

"Morning," she called, running downstairs and going right for the door. Her mother was doing a crossword—she never seemed to get headaches or hangovers from nights out.

Chloe realized she was breaking a major, major rule of their new "honesty" pact and felt guilty about it—but what was telling her mom going to accomplish?

"You doing anything after work tonight?" Mrs. King asked, trying to sound casual, not looking up.

Patrolling the perimeter? Setting little traps? Trembling in my shoes?

"Uh, no, not really . . ."

"I thought I would make lamb tonight." She tapped the pen to her lips. "A really nice cut. Will you be home by eight?"

An image flashed before Chloe of her coming in late and finding her mother dead on the floor, broken glass and blood everywhere, the smell of burnt lamb fat from the oven.

"Yeah, absolutely," Chloe answered quickly.

At school, she found she could doze for five minutes at a time—catnap—in class, without anyone noticing. While she felt the urge to snuggle down and sleep for much longer—especially in chemistry, when the sunlight warmed her chair and desk—Chloe found that even the brief five was refreshing. In gym she lucked out: they were watching a film about drunk driving. Chloe managed to sleep for the whole forty-five minutes.

She was woken in Am civ by her phone vibrating. She tried not to sit up quickly, annoyed and surprised out of a deep, dreamless sleep. The number was Brian's.

She wondered if he somehow found out about what happened to her the night before. Or more importantly, if he was going to tell her how much he really liked her and apologize for being so hands-offish and weird. Or maybe he was finally going to admit that he was the other cat person. All these things would be good. *Any* of them. She waited until she was out in the hall after class before calling him.

"You rang?" she asked, phone pressed tight to her ear so she could hear over the crowd.

"Yeah—Chloe, we have to talk." He sounded desperate, serious.

"Sure! Can you meet me before work, at the café near there, on the other side of the street?"

"You can't get out earlier?"

Chloe raised an eyebrow. "I'm in high school, remember? Not the 'real world.' Getting out early means calls to Mom and *consequences*."

"Oh. Right. Okay, then, two-fifteen?"

"I'll be there as soon as I can," Chloe promised. She put the phone back into her pocket.

"Hey, Chloe!" Alyec was waving at her. She smiled and sauntered over, swinging her hips in a half-cowboy-with-spurs, half-sexy walk. "Nice vest. So Keira says you're a complete slut. Is that true?"

Chloe's mouth opened—and then just hung there. She was too stunned to speak. Keira's closest friends were in earshot, listening raptly. Alyec was excellently maintaining a straight face, the still-foreign aspect of his expressions never too revealing.

Then Chloe laughed.

It was such a perfect, stupid high school moment, as far away from murdering psychos, supernatural powers, and mysterious fears as one could get. A complete breath of fresh air.

Alyec smiled, pleased to see her reaction.

"I hear you actually have to have sex to be one," she answered loudly. "You should talk to Scott LeFevre and Jason Buttrick and—well, the whole soccer team. Ask them about Keira."

The girl's two friends sped away like little bluebirds of unhappiness, eager to tell.

"You look so down," Alyec said, running a hand sexily through her hair. She pushed her head up into it, enjoying the feeling. *I hope I don't start purring or anything like that.*

"I . . . didn't sleep well last night."

"You should have called me. I would have come over, and *after* that," he said, grinning devilishly, "you would have slept like a baby."

"You're a complete ass," she said, genuinely meaning it.

"You love it, baby." He leaned forward as if to kiss her but stopped just before, so there was a barely a millimeter between them, and just stood there.

Chloe could smell his skin, clean and warm. It felt like she had just swallowed a double shot of cheap whiskey: burning coursed through her stomach and the rest of her body. She turned her face slightly to move her lips along his cheek—still not touching—almost overwhelmed by heat and desire. But she held back.

Alyec finally pulled himself away. "Whew, strong medicine," he said hoarsely.

"Catch you later, lover boy," Chloe said over her shoulder as she walked away.

This is way *too much fun.*

She saw Amy in the hall a couple of times. They didn't look at each other. Amy made a big deal of looking away. Chloe rolled her eyes. *With friends like this, who needs blade-wielding murderers?*

When the final bell rang, she jogged to the café, making sure she was on the side of the street with the most pedestrians, slowing down to tag along in groups, speeding up to pass on to others.

She breathlessly threw herself into the chair opposite Brian, where he was sitting, brooding, over a cup of something and a biscotti. He was looking even less goth than usual, with creased khakis and shined boots and a black hoodie with the number 10 in red across the front. His kitty cat hat was nowhere to be found.

"Hey," she said.

"Hi."

That was it for a few minutes while she ordered and they waited for her coffee to be brought over. It was tense; Chloe almost tapped her feet in impatience. When they were finally alone, Brian looked at her for a long minute, his brown eyes troubled. He absently fingered the scar on his cheek.

"I think you should stop seeing Alyec."

Chloe blinked.

She thought back to their brief telephone conversation, how serious he'd sounded and troubled . . . and realized that the last time he had seen her was with Alyec. It had nothing to do with him being another cat person. . . .

"Brian, I thought we already talked about this—" Then she stopped, thinking about what he'd just said. These days nothing strange or out of the ordinary—no matter how small—could be dismissed anymore as harmless. "How do you know his name?" she asked quietly.

"What?" Brian asked, flustered, not having expected that response.

"How did you know Alyec's name?" Chloe repeated, standing up. "Have you been following me? *Stalking* me?" she demanded.

He looked around, nervous at her loud accusations.

"Chloe, listen to me," he begged. "You really shouldn't see him. He's not . . . *safe.*"

"I cannot believe you, you . . . *freak*!" she said, slamming her fist down on the table. "You won't commit to anything like a real relationship, and after only a few dates you start accusing other guys of being dangerous? That's *pathetic*," she spat. "Not *safe*? What would you know about safe? Someone tried to *kill* me last night and you're worried about a goofy foreign sixteen-year-old?"

Brian's face went white. "Someone . . . attacked you?"

"Yeah! I could have been killed. I spent the whole night terrified—he knew stuff about me *too*, Brian. I only have room in my life for *one* crazy stalker."

"Are you okay?" he finally asked.

"Barely!" She took the vest and pulled it and her T-shirt aside. The deep gouge was clean but ugly. "Mofo had daggers and throwing stars and all sorts of weird stuff." She was furious but still owed him thanks. "If it weren't for the moves you taught me the other night, I'd be dead," she said grudgingly.

"That *I* taught you?" he asked, confused.

Oh no . . .

"You didn't . . . the other night . . . ? Come on, this is serious. *Please—*"

But he shook his head, shrugging.

When she realized he really meant it, Chloe was almost overcome with despair. Here she'd thought she finally had an answer to the insanity around her: not only was Brian a great guy, but he would have been someone who could teach her, who could protect her, who could tell her what she was.

And he'd turned out to be none of the above. Just some possessive, crazy freak.

"I have to go now," she said, pushing her chair in.

"No, Chloe . . . don't! Wait—"

But she was already out the door.

Seventeen

She stamped outside and stood there for a moment, unsure of what to do. The longer she stayed there, the more time Brian would have to pay the bill and work up the courage to go after her. Which was the last thing she wanted. For a moment, just a moment, she sobbed, feeling utterly lost.

Then she concentrated on what was she had left: the fact that Brian was a complete jerk. She was so angry, she could spit. She started walking—she had to do *something* with all of the rage inside her. Since it was almost time to go to work, she headed in that direction.

She balled her hands into fists and clenched and unclenched her hands, feeling the claws come in and out. It wasn't exactly soothing, but it made her feel better. Her shoulders felt tight, and Chloe wished she could run like the tiger on those gasoline (or was it oil?) commercials, stretching out with her front legs, leaping, springing off on her back ones. Then she thought about the mountain lions in LA—which made her think about Brian, which made her get all angry again.

"Hey, Chloe," a voice called from in front of her, waking her out of her thoughts. It was Keira, in something that looked like an actual tennis dress, complete with pom-pom socks. But she wore it over a pair of Mavi jeans. Even the other girl's smell made Chloe ill: it stank of seething hormones and irritation and, well, Keira.

She stood in front of Chloe casually, as if just to talk.

"Who exactly were you calling a whore today? In the hall?"

"Go *away*," Chloe said, trying to step around her. *Like I need this on top of everything else.* She felt like the fuse in her was half a centimeter from the pipe bomb.

"No, I'm really interested." Keira tossed her hair to the side, exhibiting all of its shades, roots, and layers. "Were you implying that *I* slept with Jason and Scott—and the whole soccer team?"

The bomb ignited.

Chloe turned, eyes flashing. She opened her mouth. A sound came out of it, deep and guttural and raw, from the bottom of her throat. Not exactly human. A warning.

Keira's face went white and she took a step backward.

Chloe walked around her, continuing to Pateena's. She was close to clawing the next person who tried to talk to her.

I'm going to pay for that later, though. As soon as she recovered, Keira would get on the phone to everyone and tell them what a freak Chloe King was, besides being a gossiping, lying rumormonger. But Chloe was pretty sure she wouldn't use the actual word *rumormonger.* It was several syllables too long for the field hockey star's vocabulary.

Chloe managed to calm down enough by the time she got to the store to punch in civilly and grab one of the doughnuts Marisol had thoughtfully brought in for them, even remembering to thank her. They were Halloween-themed ones from Dunkin' Donuts, covered in little black and orange candy bats and pumpkins. Chloe had forgotten about the holiday coming up; it was Amy's favorite.

She felt the urge to growl again.

Trapped within the store, the smell of recently dry-cleaned and bleached cotton and polyester enclosing her, Chloe found her thoughts similarly trapped. She *still* knew nothing about her attacker or the other cat person. She had no new way of protecting herself and her mom. She had no intention of telling her mother about the attack, either, which meant she was already violating the agreement between them. She had no one to talk to. Not anymore.

Chloe found herself attaching labels with the punch gun harder than she had to, putting holes in more than a few pairs of pants.

And this is where I met Brian.

"Awww. Is the little high-school girl all PMS about something?" Lania asked, pouting out her lip and looking down at her. "Whatsa matter, didn't get elected prom queen?"

Chloe considered how Lania's looks would improve with the addition of a plastic tag permanently fixed to her lower lip.

"Leave me alone," she muttered. It was almost a plea; why was it that when everything was at its suckiest, people like Lania and Keira suddenly decided it was their day for free torture? She didn't want to lose her temper again. Several people were in the store, and a leonine roar would certainly be noticed.

Lania shrugged, kicking Chloe's pile of jeans out of the way as she left.

Chloe took a deep breath, picked up another pair, and aimed the gun at it—but she was gripping too tightly and it misfired, jamming. Without thinking, Chloe raised it above her head to dash it against the floor—but stopped herself just in time.

She had to get out of here. Her mood was not improving.

Chloe carefully restacked the jeans, reset the gun, and found Marisol in the back.

"Uh." She coughed. Would she stick to her new honesty policy? "Marisol, I don't think I can keep working here today."

The older woman looked up at her, eyes narrowed, maybe searching for physical signs of illness, the only fathomable reason an employee would say such a thing.

"Are you okay?" she finally asked.

"Not . . . really," Chloe didn't give any further explanation. *Ask me no questions. . . .*

"Okay," Marisol said grudgingly. Her eyes flicked to a couple of black-and-white monitors that were linked to security cameras in the store. Chloe realized she was trying to tell her that she had seen the way she had been behaving. "I like you, Chloe. But I don't have time for crazy teenagers. This is a business I have to run, not day care."

"I understand," Chloe mumbled. *If only she knew what was going on. . . .*

"I think we'll be okay; it hasn't been that busy. Take the rest of the week. But I expect to see you back on Wednesday—if not, don't bother ever coming back."

"Thank you," Chloe said with all her heart.

"All right. See you next Wednesday." The woman turned her back; their discussion was over. Chloe grabbed her jacket and ran outside, rejoicing in the clean, fresh feeling of the sun on her.

But she still wanted to pound something. Where could she go? What could she do to shake this foul mood, this incredible rage?

Alyec.

He might not be the best conversationalist, but he would definitely take her mind off things. But where would he be? She had never seen him with a cell phone, wouldn't know his number if he did have one. She checked her watch—it was only three-twenty; there was a good chance he was still hanging out with his usual crowd of friends somewhere in or near the school.

Chloe ran all the way back and paused outside the main exit. Sniffing. Before she knew what she was doing, she had her nose in the air, trying to catch his scent. . . . *There!* Was that it? She waited as the breeze shifted direction, closing her eyes. A thousand different . . . not images exactly, but feelings and suppositions filtered through: Was that a cat? Was someone angry? Someone hadn't bathed in a while. . . . Something alien, animal, small . . . Squirrel? Rat? She couldn't name the scents; there was no vocabulary for them. But they were recognizable and learnable, like faces and sounds. She could have stayed there for much longer, letting these things fill her—like a dog, she realized, sticking its head out the window, or even that dumb little shih tzu, who always smelled up and down her arm before letting her pet him, as if to see where she had been and who she had seen that day.

There again! That *was* him! Like the smell of his skin this morning, masculine and unmistakably *Alyec.* She followed it, finding it hard not to also follow her instinct and move her head around against the building and even along the ground to follow the trail. But, there were still students around, and her reputation for weirdness had already been established enough that day.

Chloe paused at an intersection, checked the scent, and was rewarded for her guess: it led to the smaller basketball gym. She slowed down at the last minute, hearing other voices, smelling mixed signals, male and female.

She strolled in, like she had just been walking by, knocking on the door as she went.

Alyec sat like a benevolent king among his admirers and friends. Everyone was gathered around and below him, on lower risers, talking and laughing and tossing a basketball. Alyec was trying to learn how to spin it on one finger like the other Americans, causing a lot of giggles. Keira wasn't there. *Thank God.*

He saw her come in. There was no hesitation: he rose with the ease of a reasonably graceful human, tossed the ball to some cute little girl thing, and jumped down, slapping hands and giving high fives as he went.

"Gotta go, catch you all later."

Someone began singing, "Alyec and Chloe, sitting in a tree. . . ." It wasn't even mean, but it annoyed Chloe nonetheless. Who were these *little people* who just commented and talked about her life like that?

"Hey, beautiful." He didn't kiss her perfunctorily like other boyfriends might have—like Brian should have. Like all of their interactions, it was as if such a gesture was too banal for the two of them. He just raised his eyebrows, waiting.

"I want to do something *bad,*" she said, half joking.

He looked at her, trying to evaluate her mood. Then he took her hand. For a moment Chloe was afraid he'd taken what she'd said the wrong way; the last thing in the world she wanted was friendly physical contact. Right now the idea left her nauseated.

Alyec began striding down the hallway, pulling her behind him. "We'll blow your steam off," he said as she hurried to keep up with him. "I promise."

He took her to the tiny parking lot in the back of the school, to the even tinier seniors' parking section. The nearing-sunset light was extraordinary, both softening and carefully outlining every shape and color; its heat caused the smell of decaying leaves, tar, and dusty metal to slowly seep into the air. He led her to a tiny hatchback the color of dull copper, old and rusting.

"This is *yours*?" Chloe asked, surprised. "You're not a senior—"

"Is a *great* car," he said, lapsing into broken English in his excitement. "Rebuilt with eight-cylinder engine. Standard shift. Very pure."

"It's yours?" she asked again, noticing he hadn't answered.

"I have always loved the old hatchbacks," he said, taking out a key and opening the driver's side door. "There are a few problems, of course. Like, a few keys will open almost all models." He stuck his leg out of the car for balance and leaned in, fiddling with something underneath the steering wheel. "But you can get in and tinker and really know what you're doing, you know? No computers or that kind of crap."

There were a few short and unpromising-sounding clicks and growls, then something caught and the engine started. He leaned over and unlocked the passenger door.

Chloe opened it, having to pull harder than she thought; it might be a tiny car, but it felt like it was made completely out of lead, and the door didn't swing too easily. She fell down into the low seat, which still retained most of its original—leather? Vinyl? —cover, patched here and there with duct tape.

She looked at Alyec.

"This isn't your car, is it?"

He smiled at her and backed them out of the parking lot.

Chloe didn't know the first thing about cars and very little about actual driving—her mom had let her practice in the Passat once in a while, and she was signing up for driver's ed that spring. But even so, two things were apparent even to her: the little car was accelerating much harder and faster than it should have been able to, and Alyec had obviously not learned to drive in America.

They bounced forcibly up and down in the car; other than springs in the actual seats themselves, there didn't seem to be any form of suspension. She opened the window and grabbed the sill for support and found herself laughing. *Bonnie and Clyde!* Stolen car, infinite anger, open road. This was *exactly* what she needed.

She didn't bother asking where they were going; he seemed to have an agenda. They swung around corners so hard Chloe could have sworn that the two outside wheels lifted up, and while they didn't actually *run* any red lights, she saw them turn as they passed underneath.

Whenever that happened, Alyec kissed his fingers and touched the roof.

"Sometimes," he hollered—his window was down, too, and the engine was incredibly loud—"San Francisco really sucks. You have to get out! It's too . . . claustrophobic."

With a buzz they turned down the 101 and were zooming over the Golden Gate. It was a beautiful end-of-day panorama: the sky was darkening to a clear, pollution-free blue, and elongated puffy clouds rolled by, lit orange from underneath. The colors of the fading green hills in the distance deepened, and the water below looked violent and dark. The bridge itself glowed an almost rusty, bloody red.

"Ha!" Chloe laughed aloud, loving it. Alyec grinned at her and stepped on the accelerator.

They flew down the other side of the bridge and took the first exit, heading toward Sausalito. She and Amy used to go there all the time to shop and hang out along the water—but both had found it dull recently (as Paul always complained it was). Old people and weird tourists and boring shops. But Alyec wound down a road she hadn't been on and up a street that could only be described as *extremely* well paved, like out of a poster: tar hidden by a gravel-topped surface, the lanes curving gently down from the center of the road, where two lemony perfect stripes shone.

"Where are we?" Chloe shouted.

"Where all the rich assholes live," Alyec yelled back.

"I thought that was San Jose."

Alyec thought about this. "*Old money* rich assholes!"

He made a left and pointed. Chloe's jaw dropped at the sight of the house in front of them.

It was like an estate out of some English film, a giant stone-and-wood manor, rising several stories in the middle. Lower wings flanked either side. The roof was slate. The great lawn that sloped down the road had to be several acres at least and was protected by a tall and spiky old-fashioned fence, gate, and guardhouse. A gravel driveway gently rolled up from there to the front door, ending in a circular roundabout whose center was a fountain. Every piece of greenery was immaculately trimmed, and dotting the lawn were topiary and even the occasional fountain.

"Oh my God . . . It's *beautiful*," Chloe breathed. "I had no idea there was anything like this around here."

"It is not mentioned ever in *House and Country*, if that's what you mean," Alyec said wryly.

Christ. "Who owns this place? Bill Gates?"

Alyec shook his head. "Sergei Shaddar. He's the guy who bought the old market downtown and turned it into a multiplex. A true capitalist pig-dog. And a distant relative on the American side of my family." His face went dark for a moment. "He is the one who wouldn't put up the money to bring me and my family over."

"What a douche bag! I can't believe he spent it all on this instead."

"Yes, well, who knows," Alyec said airily. "Someday, maybe it will all be mine. He isn't 'married with children,' as they say."

He turned the car around and drove slowly back down the road, letting Chloe get one last good look at the beautiful house. She sighed. It was a complete world away from her and her troubles, a little fantasy kingdom of rich people and beautiful things and rich-people problems.

Noticing her silence, Alyec reached over and handed her a solid pewter flask with Russian words on it. She had no idea how he could have kept it on his person with the jeans he was currently wearing, extra tight around the ass. But she pulled from it generously. It wasn't vodka, as she'd expected, but something dry, deep, and stinging.

"Do you know how hard it is to get bourbon in Russia?" he asked when she coughed. Chloe gave him a smile, but it was weak. "Oh, you're getting all depressed."

"I wish—" She stopped, thinking about her birthday cake. "I don't know what I wish. I wish life was simpler," she finally said. "I wish we could hang out longer."

Alyec chewed his lip for a moment. "We need one last thing to cheer you up before you go home." Then he brightened.

"Chloe King, have you ever 'caught air'?"

Eighteen

In a dark room with no name, a circle of robed figures gathered.

Nine sat around an ancient wooden table lit by flickering lanterns that marked its circumference. Behind and above them, torchlight cast monstrous shadows onto the ornately tiled stone floor below.

A black-and-white monitor sat on the table, adding its sickly light to that of the flames; the main character in its silent movies was a girl engaged in all sorts of normal girl behaviors—as well as some that were not so normal.

One of the robed figures at the table spoke. "You see: already she has become dangerous—and it has been only days since she perceived her true nature."

"I hardly believe that defending herself from the onslaught of a street ruffian constitutes a dangerous personality," said another voice, old and female.

"But see who she keeps for her company," a third,

ancient male voice cackled. A skeletal hand reached forward. His fingers might as well have been just bone for all the good his dry, shrunken skin did; it clung to every detail, bump, and crevice. As if to magnify the deterioration, a bold ring with a giant black stone sat above the knuckle of the index finger. All looked to where he tapped on the glass of the monitor.

A young man was kissing the girl, on a bench outside a fast-food restaurant.

"Is the Russian still next in line?"

"We have no reason to believe otherwise."

"This is all moving too fast," the first speaker said, shifting in his seat. "Novitiate, you had said merely that the two knew each other. And that should anything arise, you would immediately . . . intercede."

"I did my best, Primary," a young voice from the benches said dully.

"Yet you failed. You also failed to positively determine whether she is the One the Rogue believes her to be."

"First you want me to befriend her, then you want me to see if she dies when I stick a knife in her belly. I didn't think that was part of my mission."

"Did she *tell* you anything? Anything strange at all—about her past, about some experience as a child, some miraculous survival or near-death experience?"

There was a long pause.

"No, sir," the novitiate said finally.

"I'm afraid you're far too close to the situation to be

able to react rationally. You are off the case; we will let the Rogue handle things his own way."

"But sir—let me try one more time. She's a good person—raised by *humans*. The Rogue will just *kill* her! He's mad—"

"Alexander Smith is a valiant member of the Order. He does his duties well and with zeal—let us not forget this. Above and beyond our own orders, he feels his way is directly ordained by God. Let him be, and God will determine the outcome."

"This is just murder, not the way of God," the young man spat.

"Novitiate, the Order of the Tenth Blade has *not* carried out its mission of protecting people from the feline scourge for a thousand years just to throw it away for the misguided urges of one infatuated adolescent! Am I clear?"

Another long pause.

"Yes, sir."

There was a moment of silence as everyone reflected on this.

"So our action is decided," said one.

"So it is recorded," said another.

"As we have done from ages past, as we shall ever do," chanted all of the figures.

Slowly they rose and filed silently out of the dark room. All except one—the young one who'd spoken, whose knees shook and who scratched at a scar on his cheek.

"It's all for the best, son," the oldest man said, hanging back and patting his shoulder with a skeletal hand. "I know it's hard . . . but there's no future there. Look at that poor Greek boy—you don't want to end up like Mr. Xavier Akouri, do you?"

Nineteen

In fact, Chloe had never "caught air" before, even though she had lived almost her whole life in San Francisco. Amy had tried once or twice, using the car Paul's brother let him borrow occasionally, a really tacky job with purple lights all over the place and a few too many spoilers. But as much as Amy pretended to be a badass, she'd never really gotten up the courage—or the speed.

Alyec had no such issues: he jammed the accelerator at the top of a good hill. But when they raced over it, the car just sort of bounced up and down. Alyec swore and tried again, swerving around corners and running a red light to build up speed. Winds tore through the windows. The city had just entered darkness and the lights were all on, but the afterglow of the orange sunset remained. It was a wild-feeling night.

I can't believe we're doing this. Chloe was so excited, she actually clapped as they approached the intersection.

"And . . . now!"

Suddenly she felt weightless. It only lasted a moment; her body strained against the seat belt and they crashed down *hard* onto the street again, causing her neck to whip forward and back.

She wasn't sure if all four wheels made it into the air, but it certainly felt like it.

It all happens a lot faster than on TV. She sighed, wishing they had gone slow mo through the movement, like they were on camera.

Alyec zoomed back to Inner Sunset. As they drove past the school parking lot, someone—with the build of a senior jock—was screaming, "Where's my *car*? Where's my goddamn *car*?" Alyec and Chloe sank down in their seats, giggling, but the owner's back was turned as they passed him.

"Where do you live? I'll drop you off before returning this."

"You don't know where I live," she said slowly, savoring the way it sounded, how it felt. He didn't know her other boyfriend's name, he didn't know what she really was, and he didn't know where she lived. Just a slightly more psychotic than usual average teenage boy. Simple. It was a nice thing.

"No, how could I?"

"Forget it," Chloe said, smiling, pointing where he should turn.

He slowed down as she tapped the windshield, indicating which house was hers.

"Hey," Chloe said, turning to look at him. *"Thanks."*

"No problem. You see? I'm not just a sexy boy. I also like doing dangerous and stupid things."

"Yeah?" She smiled.

"Yeah," he answered, leaning over. He very gently bit the bottom of her right earlobe, tugging it, deftly avoiding her piercings. Then he kissed her neck. Chloe shuddered. *"Next* time," he whispered.

Chloe's eyes widened, but she didn't say no.

Inside, her mom was wrestling with butcher's twine tied awkwardly around an incredibly primitive-looking hunk of lamb. She was tying a knot, holding one end in her teeth. Chloe went over to put her finger on the knot to make it easier for her, but Mrs. King shook her head emphatically.

"'Ot ohtil oo 'ash 'or 'ands."

Chloe sighed and ran them under the faucet before returning to help. At one time—during her brief stint as a vegetarian—the sight of meat like that, especially weird meat, especially weird meat from a baby animal, would have completely grossed her out. She couldn't help noticing her stomach growl, however, and had to actively resist the urge to pick off bits of the tastiest-looking raw fat and pop them in her mouth.

"There." Her mom put her hands on her hips and admired her work. She indicated the oven with her chin and Chloe opened it, feeling *very* nice heat waft out.

"Should just be forty-five minutes or so. I bought some couscous to go with it. Hey, are you feeling all right?"

Chloe looked up, surprised by the sudden change in conversation topic. Come to think of it, now that the wild car ride was over, she felt a little let down.

"Did something happen at work?"

Chloe took a deep breath. "I didn't go to work. I . . . hung out with my friend, Alyec. He gave me a ride home."

Mrs. King raised her eyebrows.

"Marisol gave me the rest of the week off," Chloe explained quickly. "I didn't feel like—I couldn't do it."

"Don't flake out on this," Mrs. King warned. "This is only your first job. If you get bored with this, and the next, and . . ."

Chloe just looked at her, patiently waiting for her to finish. It was probably the complete lack of *any* response from her daughter—much less an angry one—combined with Chloe's exhausted look that made Mrs. King trail off, giving up the lecture.

"Are you getting sick?"

No . . . But she realized she wanted to leave her options open. So she shook her head without saying anything, a weak protest at best.

They had a quiet night of lamb and couscous and a salad with feta cheese, working the Greek theme. Her mom let her have a glass of wine, something fruity, white, and Middle Eastern. It put Chloe right to sleep when she curled up on the couch next to her mom, who was flipping back and forth between CNN and Animal Planet.

Chloe knew she should have been more alert, but she was exhausted, her belly was full, and she felt cozy and warm.

"Well, what do you know," were the last few words she heard before dozing off. "Baby elephants suck their trunks just like human babies suck their thumbs. . . ."

When she woke up the next morning, Chloe was still on the couch but stretched out, with her own pillow under her head and her own comforter covering her. Her mom was already up and getting ready for work.

"How do you feel today?" she asked, leaning over Chloe and putting the back of her hand to her daughter's forehead. "When I tucked you in last night, you were burning up."

Chloe felt fine.

Holy shit, did I help Alyec steal a car and catch air with it yesterday?

How many more times, she wondered, would she be struck the next day by the weird things she had done the night before? And frankly, thinking about the car theft, she felt sheepish. What had gotten into her yesterday? Was she really that mad at Brian? He was just an idiot, after all. . . . Why did she do these weird things when she was around Alyec?

"Uh . . ." Chloe started to sit up, then fell back on one elbow, as if she were woozy.

Mrs. King sighed. "I'll call the school. I shouldn't have let you drink anything last night. Or I should have at least made it red. That's supposed to be good for headaches and colds." She fluffed Chloe's hair. "I'll call you later. Call me if you need anything—do you think you'll be okay at home by yourself?"

Ah, here it comes. Chloe saw the worry and the single-mom guilt shadow her mother's stony eyes. Should she stay home with her sick daughter? That was what *her* mother would have done. *Well, her mother didn't have a job, but whatever.* At least Chloe's mom was always very careful to keep her adult doubts and worries and psychoses to herself and never burden her daughter with them.

Of course, she couldn't help projecting sometimes.

And she would worry a hell of a lot more if she knew about the attempt on her daughter's life.

"Don't worry," Chloe reassured her, wondering vaguely how the whole mother-daughter thing had flipped around so quickly in the last few weeks and wondering when they would flip around away from each other again. "I'll call Amy." *Yeah, right.* "She can come over right after school with stuff if I need it. I'm probably just gonna sleep here for the next few hours anyway."

"Okay," her mom said, sounding unsure. She leaned over and kissed Chloe on the forehead. "Feel better."

And with the clank of a Coach purse, Italian attaché, and Kenneth Cole heels, she was gone.

Chloe waited on the couch for a while before deciding

what to do. There had been enough time since the attack for a little distance; she wasn't as terrified to be alone at home as she had been the first night. This day would be a good test: if her assassin meant to track her down and attack her at home, there would be no better time. She was by herself and the neighborhood was quiet.

But even if she *did* stay at home all day, it certainly wasn't going to be in a prone, vulnerable position lying on the couch. She could follow up on Xavier more, maybe call him. And what exactly *about* Xavier and Alyec? Were these urges—all the way from sexual to self-destructive to simply destructive—*normal*, or did they come with the claws, the speed, and the sudden desire to eat raw meat?

She flexed her hand and watched her claws *sslt* out. She held them up in a ray of sun that beat its way around the curtains and plants. On the one hand, the claws looked "normal": shiny, off-white, with little bits of calluses and dead skin around them at the base. On the other hand—paw—they looked as freakish and alien as the first time she'd seen them.

"What else do you bring?" she asked them aloud. Still no tail, thank God. That would have been harder to hide, and she couldn't imagine it suddenly disappearing somewhere up inside her body. She looked at her feet—her mom had removed her socks sometime during the night. Chloe hadn't even felt it—was that because she'd been dead asleep or because her mother's scent and touch and little sounds were familiar, nondangerous? Had she somehow known instinctually, even in her sleep, that she was safe? Amy's cat would often spend the entire day sprawled at the bottom of the bed. You could pet him as hard as you wanted and he would stretch, never quite open his eye, and continue sleeping.

Or did I just completely pass out? A much scarier thought.

She spread her toes pinkly in the sunlight. Then she flexed them. No claws emerged. Was this it, then? No more physical changes?

She got up and stretched, enjoying the feeling of morning warmth.

Then she went upstairs to brush her teeth and stuff. But before she did, she remembered one task she had to take care of: *Mus-mus.*

She went into her room and opened the drawer. Mus-mus came running forward, eager for a treat. Chloe dropped in a Cheerio. It bounced. The delivery and noise startled Mus-mus for a second, who was used to much gentler treatment. Chloe put her hand out slowly, extending a finger toward the little mouth. He leaned forward, sniffing. Then he squeaked, dropping the Cheerio, and ran away.

"You don't like cats, even nice ones . . . ," Chloe whispered. Just one more thing that came with her changes, along with the violence. She bit her lip, feeling a tear well up in the corner of each eye.

"Okay, Mus-mus." She reached forward to pick him

up; he was so desperate to escape her grasp that she had to extend her claws and very delicately close them around him like a cage. She held the mouse up to eye level, regarding the terrified little thing that had been her closest confidant as of just a few days ago. "Goodbye," she whispered. "And good luck."

Then she leaned down and opened her hand near the base of the bed. Mus-mus didn't hesitate at all, shooting forward and under the bed as soon as he could. Chloe sighed again, knuckling the tears out of her eyes. She carefully placed a little pyramid of Cheerios on the floor in case he needed a good start.

I'm gonna miss you.

She took a shower, trying to wash away everything she felt and start the day again. She put on her tank top and a pair of jeans, not bothering with undies. *Cats don't wear underwear,* she told herself but didn't even manage a smile. She adjusted her bra. *This cat has to wear something supportive on top, however.* She couldn't imagine having six or eight teats the size of her own.

Chloe wandered around, straightening some things, cleaning out the fridge for her mom, channel surfing. Overwhelmed by depression, she lay down on the couch.

Would I give up the claws if it meant no more crazy attacks on me, and life would return to normal, and Mus-mus would come back? Even if she had the choice, she wasn't sure what the answer would be.

• • •

A hesitant knock at the door jolted Chloe out of a long, dreamless sleep. She looked out the window, fingering the chain mail necklace at her neck.

It was Amy and Paul.

Chloe frowned, not sure she was ready for this. But she went downstairs anyway and opened the door.

"Chloe," Amy said. Her and Paul's eyes immediately took in the sexy tank she was wearing—and then focused on something particular near her left shoulder, causing them to gasp.

"Uh, your mom called us. Amy, I mean," Paul explained as Amy stared, still fixated on the wound from the other night. Chloe had cleaned it out in the shower and put antibiotic on it, but it was still huge, deep, and red. Healing fine, just ugly. "She said you were sick."

"Yeah, uh, come on in." Chloe opened the door all the way, turning to go into the room first. Her two friends followed meekly. "Want anything? Coke? Diet Coke?"

"Coke," Paul said absently.

The stillness in the room was museumlike; it was twilight and everything was dusky, dusty, dim. Like a grandmother's house. Noises dropped and disappeared into the room like drops into a flat black lake, absorbed instantly.

"What happened to your arm?" Amy finally asked.

Chloe turned from the fridge and tossed Paul his Coke.

"I was attacked on the sidewalk the other night," she answered flatly.

"By the bum," Amy supplied hopefully.

"No, someone else. Someone with a knife. Someone who seems to be *stalking* me."

All three were silent for a moment. Amy seemed to disappear into the gigantic puffy silver coat she wore—somewhere between pimp and London DJ chic. Her hair was up in knots and she had a thin lime green scarf thrown about her neck. Paul looked far more casual—though just as ill at ease—in jeans and a leather jacket, surprisingly normal for him.

"Is it someone you know?" Amy finally asked.

"No."

"Have you called the police?"

"Not yet."

Amy must have sensed something in Chloe's tone; she didn't follow up with the obvious, "Why not?"

"I guess we have a lot of catching up to do," Amy said slowly.

"Yeah?" Chloe asked, sounding like she didn't care.

"I didn't realize—you didn't tell me. . . ." There was a long pause. "I really haven't been there for you, have I?" Amy said softly.

"Not really," Chloe agreed, but there wasn't any malice in the way she said it.

"Paul told me how you felt." Amy suddenly laughed, forced. Paul looked down, embarrassed. "*Paul* told *me*. How *you* felt. That's a first." She was right: usually one of the two girls was demanding that the other talk to the impenetrable Paul. "I flaked, I know—and then I got pissed because you were dating Alyec. *And* this other guy. It was like you suddenly had this whole life apart from me."

"Hel*lo*?" Chloe indicated Paul.

"I know, I know." Amy sighed.

"I can leave . . . if you guys want," the boyfriend in question suggested, a little annoyed that he was being referred to as a distraction.

"I thought you would be overjoyed we were together, like celebrate it or something," Amy continued. "It's like—you know, perfect. Your two best friends, dating."

"I'm going to . . . uh . . . go to the bathroom," Paul said, getting up and leaving.

"That's pretty egomaniacal of you," Chloe said, sort of regretting that she hadn't minced words, sort of glad she'd said it the way she had. "I've never really dated *anyone* and you've had a string of boyfriends—and now you and my only other close friend have decided to see each other exclusively? How do you *think* I felt?"

"Is that why you suddenly started dating all these guys?" Amy said, heat rising in her voice.

"There aren't 'all these guys.' There's Alyec, who's fun and a great kisser, and Brian, who I met at the shop. Oh, and Xavier, this guy I met at the club the night after I fell when I was totally alone and felt weird and I tried calling you everywhere and you were busy with Paul."

Amy's mouth opened as if to say something, but nothing came out.

"I don't really count him," Chloe admitted. "I've only

seen him once since that night." *And he was at death's door.*

"Why didn't you tell me at dinner when—" Amy suddenly broke off, remembering the birthday pizza and how eager she'd been to talk about *her* experience with Paul the night before.

"You looked like you needed someone to listen to you," Chloe said quietly. "I didn't think what I did with Xavier was as important as what was going on with you two."

Amy's eyes grew wet and glassy.

"I'm *sorry*," she finally said, trying not to cry. "I know I haven't been there for you *at all*, and I felt guilty about it, but I was angry and busy with Paul, and the longer we went, the guiltier and angrier I got. . . ."

"It's okay," Chloe said, trying not to smile. Typical Amy. Overemotional but genuine to a fault—if you pressed her long enough. Amy grabbed her in a big bear hug that made Chloe grunt in surprise, the breath knocked out of her.

"Wait, isn't two attacks on you in one month kind of weird?" Amy suddenly asked, wiping her tears off.

"You don't know the half of it," Chloe said with a wry smile.

"Hey." Paul appeared in the doorway. "Why don't we walk across the bridge, like we used to?"

Amy and Chloe looked at each other. *Why not?* Chloe thought, trying not to focus on how "used to" was less than a month ago.

• • •

On the bus ride to Golden Gate, Chloe filled them in on the details of Alyec—minus the car theft—and Brian, focusing more on the latter and how she was really disappointed he'd turned out to be such a loser. Both her friends were disturbed when she told them about how he knew Alyec's name and told her to stay away from him.

"Isn't that a little weird, two stalkers so close together?" Paul asked, unknowingly echoing Amy's previous question. "You don't suppose . . ."

"That Brian hired a knife-wielding maniac to frighten me?"

"Or Alyec," added Amy quickly. She had granted that the popular boy might not be the root of all evil in the universe, but she hadn't given up hoping that he might be.

Chloe and Paul ignored her.

"Maybe you *should* call the police," Paul suggested in his "serious" tone.

"It's a little more complicated than that." Chloe sighed. She wasn't sure how much she was going to tell them, but she wasn't ready to say anything quite yet. *Maybe on the bridge. That would be the right place.*

When they got off, they slipped past the crowds of large, slow-moving people who were taking pictures and standing around in aimless groups like the Golden Gate buffalo. Paul stopped at a machine to get a bottle of Coke. Once upon a time he would have finished it when they made it to the middle, and the three friends would have written a note and sealed it inside, tossing it into the water below. When they were even younger, they'd pretended that they were on an isolated little island and the bridge led to another world and it was the beginning of a long journey and quest for the three of them, together.

But now they tried to look as normal and unthreatening as possible to the action-figure National Guard. The days of throwing harmless things off the bridge were long, long over.

"It's like we live under martial law," Amy muttered.

"Uh, I think they're here to protect *us*," Paul protested.

"I like your skirt," Chloe said, noticing the segmented and flaring jean mini Amy sported, almost like a loose tutu.

"Thanks," Amy said shyly. "I made it last week. I'm thinking about doing a whole matching set, like 'Jeans Princess.'" She pointed her foot and revealed, under the silver puffy coat, matching jean leg warmers, kind of like bell-bottoms without the rest of the pants attached. Chloe wasn't sure *she* would wear them, but it was definitely a cool idea.

"Your mom should totally let you work at Pateena's."

"*Tell* me about it," Amy said, kicking a rock. She kicked it again with her other foot and then really got into it, kicking it back and forth like a soccer ball before accidentally shooting it twenty feet or so ahead. She ran after it, puffy coat flying. Chloe laughed.

"Tuesday was our anniversary," Paul said.

"Yeah?"

"She made me a card. And wrote me a poem," he

added cryptically, no expression on his face. Chloe studied him for a moment before smiling.

"At least she didn't perform it in front of a crowd," she pointed out.

"Yeah," was all he said, with a heavily relieved sigh.

They caught up to Amy at the midpoint. She was already leaning over, spitting.

"I've told you that's a *myth,*" Paul said, putting his hands on his hips in exasperation.

"No, it's not," Chloe argued, leaning over and spitting herself. "If you get it just right with the wind—it really *does* fly back up."

"You two are disgusting," he said, turning around with his back to the rail. He pulled a cigarette out of his pocket and cupped his hand against the wind to light it. Red sunlight lit his face from below as if he was in front of a fire.

Unfortunately, when the wind blew the other way, the smoke completely overpowered her newly heightened sense of smell. She turned her head into the wind, trying not to gag.

"You gonna jump off *this* rail?" Amy asked, jerking her thumb at it.

Chloe smiled. "No, I don't think so. The boys in green over there wouldn't like it too much."

"Hey, I got it!" Paul suddenly said, holding his arms out like he was literally hit by an idea. "You're *supposed* to be dead! From the fall. And now, like in those Final Destination movies, death is doing everything it can to reclaim you! That *totally* explains the homeless guy and that guy who tried to kill you."

"Um, *thanks* for that heartening interpretation," Chloe said, "but if that were true, it wouldn't just be people after me—random things, like cars and—well, this *bridge* would collapse and try to do me in."

"Oh. Yeah." Paul took a step or two backward, looking at the ground.

"Anyway, like I said, it's a little more complicated than that."

"What were you *doing* walking by yourself at night, anyway? *Twice?*" Amy demanded, kicking the little rock between her feet and moving on across to the other side.

The three continued moseying along the bridge, long black shadows behind them. There were a few other people enjoying the sunset, and occasionally a cyclist would go whizzing by. Ahead of them the bridge was empty; they had it all to themselves, like the end of a movie. This was it. This was the moment. Here was where she decided how much to tell them.

Chloe took a deep breath.

A figure stepped out in front of them from the car side, blocking their path.

"Um, guys, you the know the weirdo with the blades—*not* the bum?"

"Yeah?" Paul and Amy asked; they were holding hands.

"That's him." She pointed.

The Rogue stood his ground and smiled.

Twenty

"Chloe King."

He held a dagger in each hand and wore no jacket tonight, just a black turtleneck that looked it was made of neoprene—or was hiding armor underneath. *Just the sort of thing Brian would wear,* Chloe noted distractedly. The pants and boots were the same as the other night; she could see his thick blond hair held back in a ponytail that just ended at the bottom of his neck.

"Hey," Paul yelled, thinking fast. "HEY!" he yelled, cupping his hands in the direction of the National Guard. But his words died in the wind.

"You think your human friends are going to help save you?" the man asked with feigned surprise. "Just because you keep company with them doesn't mean you're one of them."

"Ho-ly shit," Amy said, openmouthed.

"Um, *yeah* . . ." Chloe estimated the distance between

them—about twenty-five feet. Good enough for a head start? *What about Paul and Amy?*

"I have no idea what you're talking about," Chloe shouted back.

"They don't know your *true nature*?" the man asked, eyes widening.

"Do we all run in different directions?" Amy whispered, beginning to get really scared. "Or what?"

"They *should*." He walked forward slowly, looking Amy and Paul each in the eye, back and forth, like a cobra deciding where to strike first. "She's not really your friend. She isn't even your kind. *Our* kind," the man said, desperate to make them understand. "Her people want nothing less than the complete destruction of humanity. To rule the world. To defy God Himself."

"Chloe . . . ?" Paul asked. He wasn't referring to the killer's speech; like Amy, he was wondering what they should do. Without thinking or talking about it, the three of them began to back away slowly, at the same pace at which the man advanced.

"Run," Chloe hissed. "Run *now*!"

Paul and Amy ran.

The Rogue laughed, turning to watch her friends go. "How sweet—are you protecting them? Or protecting the truth about yourself!"

Chloe sensed this was it. And she was right: by the time he looked back and threw his daggers, she had already dropped to all fours and leapt at him. She heard the blades whoosh with deadly accuracy over her head; they would have been firmly buried in her stomach had she remained standing.

Two handsprings later she launched herself with a roar at his chest, not really thinking out her attack, just using momentum, movement, and surprise to gain the upper hand, if only for a second.

Just before her claws managed to sink into his flesh, he reached below her, grabbing and pushing, using her own weight to throw her over his head past him. She landed on the ground safely, not with a tuck and roll, but on all fours.

Flying daggers don't kill people, Chloe thought, leaping sidewise at the last minute to avoid one, grabbing the pedestrian rail. *People kill people.*

"It doesn't matter," he shouted. "Even if you are the One, I have blades enough for all of you."

What the hell does that *mean? And more to the point, why doesn't he carry a gun like a normal psychopath?* Chloe swung around so she was standing on the rail and lightly ran along it until she came to a slender blue lamppost. She leapt and clung to the sides, shimmying up it. A loud clank indicated a blade that must have just missed one of her feet, hitting the pole instead.

Chloe leapt to the next support without thinking, crossing ten feet of air right over his head. Shuriken whistled up into the sky behind her. She turned as if to leap back again, as if she were confused and frightened and not thinking.

At the last minute she dove right for him.

Finally her claws made contact with his flesh, skimming over some of the Kevlar or whatever he wore, sinking in where it ended. They struggled closely for a moment, landing together on the ground with a bone-jarring thud. Chloe concentrated on just digging in wherever her claws could reach and keeping her legs moving, hopefully doing some damage near his crotch. He tried to lock his own legs around her; they were very strong, almost stony with muscle. Just before her strength gave out, Chloe leapt away again. As soon as she was up, she turned around to face him, ready for his next attack.

There was a deadly whir that just skimmed her ears, followed by a clang of metal on metal. A throwing star shot by her head and bounced off the stanchion just above the Rogue, who was already getting up. Chloe spun around.

Standing on the other side of the Rogue, about twenty feet away, was Brian. He had a pained look on his face and another throwing star in his hand.

Brian . . . ? Chloe had a hard time processing what she was seeing, but there was no mistaking the weapon he held.

Pain and despair and rage beat down on her. She knew she should concentrate on the fact that she had *two* attackers now, but Chloe was suddenly exhausted by this unexpected betrayal. So much made sense now. . . . The note came back to her: *Be wary of the company you keep.*

He started walking toward her.

"Get *away* from me, you—*freak*!" Chloe screamed. "You *were* stalking me. I can't believe how real it seemed. . . . Nothing we did meant . . . anything!"

"Chloe, no! I . . ."

There was a scraping noise behind her. Chloe panicked and spun around. Her assassin was already up and advancing on her. He saw Brian and smiled.

She was trapped in between them.

Chloe looked around wildly; her only escape was off the bridge. She started toward the rail.

"No!" Brian shouted. "Chloe!"

But someone leapt at Brian, arms wide and claws extended. Chloe got a glimpse of furious ice blue eyes and a shock of honey hair before the two tumbled into an angry, kicking struggle on the ground.

Alyec. Alyec was the other cat person. She had misread *all* of the clues about both of them. Somehow she should have known. . . .

"I've got him," Alyec yelled. "Get that motherfucker . . . !"

Chloe felt new strength within her. *This* was her partner; he had her back. Now it was up to her. She turned to face the Rogue.

His turtleneck was torn to shreds on the right half of his body; black tatters and blood flowed down his skin. There was a strange tattoo on his arm, but she couldn't quite make it out. Blood dripped from the corner of his mouth, probably from his head hitting the ground. He wiped at it and spat out more.

She waited for him to say something profound, like in the movies, but instead he suddenly began throwing what seemed like dozens of throwing stars at her that appeared at his fingertips like roses from a magician's.

She danced and leapt and did handsprings and managed to avoid most of the shuriken.

"Another of my Order has come to watch and help with the cause!" He threw them harder and harder.

Chloe twisted and fell as a throwing star buried itself in her side.

"You thought he was your what—boyfriend? He was hunting you, just like I was." He laughed.

As Chloe struggled to get up, he reached down to the side of his pants and pulled out something that was smaller than a machete but larger than his previous blades. The pain in her side was like fire; every time she moved, it felt like her body was ripping apart.

He began advancing on her.

The wind whistled in Chloe's hair. She watched him come at her slowly, pain masking sound and thought. She could vaguely hear Brian and Alyec shouting obscenities at each other and the occasional muffled thump as one of them landed a blow.

There really *was* a very good chance that if no one helped her, she was going to die.

And then something inside her snapped.

How dare you?

"How *dare* you!" she screamed. Chloe ripped the shuriken out of her side and threw it to the ground, wincing at the pain. "What the *hell* did I ever do to *you*? Or *anyone*? I didn't ask for *any* of this!"

And she ran at him, blind rage eclipsing the pain.

He swung his blade down, but she lunged to the side and swiped her hand against his arm, raking her claws down it. He cried out, forced to switch the knife to his left hand. Chloe hadn't finished moving, though. She spun and kicked him on the back of his neck with her toes, smashing the Kevlar collar into his flesh.

"Fuck you," she screamed. "Get out of my *life*!"

The hot, blind rage was cooling, replaced with something much more cold and logical. She saw clearly ahead of time every punch, kick, and swipe—and followed up with an immediate counterattack. She never gave him time to draw another blade.

He backed up slowly until he was up against the rail. "How—many—others—have—you—killed?" With each word, she sent another kick into his stomach.

At the last minute he managed to launch himself so he was over the rail, keeping it between them.

"You fucking psycho," Chloe spat into his face.

Battered and bloody, he still managed a smile. "I do service for the Lord. His will be done."

"Yeah, well, tell that to the—"

And then he slipped.

Chloe was thrown off for a moment; this was something she hadn't expected.

"Chloe! Don't kill him!" Brian yelled. He tried to run over to stop her, but Alyec pulled him down to the ground again.

She leaned over, watching her assassin sway in the winds, struggling to hang on.

Finish him! Every part of her wanted to step on his fingers, to claw his face, to watch and smile as he slowly lost strength, slipped, and fell.

He tried to kill you! He hunted *you down, like you were prey!*

Even the human side of her agreed: this was a psycho who was better off *not* in the collective gene pool.

Then she offered him her hand.

I can't. Fighting is one thing—I can't kill someone in cold blood.

"You. On the bridge. Step away from the rail."

The electronically loud bullhorn noise made everyone spin. A helicopter rose up from below, aiming its spotlight along the bridge.

Chloe looked up as well—

And the Rogue fell.

Twenty-one

"No!" she cried, trying to grab after him. But there was only air.

"They're coming," Brian said, to no one in particular.

Chloe was still leaning over the rail, looking at the water in shock and disbelief. She doubted that he would come back the way she had from her own fall. It was like a book had suddenly closed and she would never be able to open it and read it again—find out why he was filled with hate. Instead of relief she felt a lack of closure, even a little loss.

"We've got to get out of here," Alyec said, grabbing Chloe's arm and pulling her away.

The two of them ran.

Although she was exhausted from the fight and felt some of her strength bleeding out of the wound in her side, Chloe still found a joy in running. When she leapt onto the handrail at the end to jump down off the bridge, tightrope running along its slick metal surface, Alyec was right behind her.

She chose to go up to the Marin Headlands; she leapt in between passing cars, up and over fences like she was flying. Alyec was beside her. He kept up with her, scrambling up the hill, jumping over rocks with an extremely familiar feline grace.

When she looked over at him, he grinned.

The other cat person.

A friend.

They crested the hill and started down the other side. The sky in the west was still its cartoon pink and orange; couples and families dotted the headlands watching it, cuddled in blankets and sipping from thermoses.

They had long outpaced the National Guard on foot, but the helicopter swept down the bridge and over the water, looking for trouble. The whole thing had Amy and Paul written all over it—still trying to save her after she'd made them go.

Chloe leapt. It didn't matter. The helicopter wouldn't be able to track her and Alyec. They were too fast. She felt like screaming with joy.

Alyec screamed instead—in pain—and went down on one knee, tumbling into the dirt.

Chloe stopped immediately and ran over to see him. He held his leg; a throwing star stuck out of it.

"Shit," he grunted, pulling it out and wincing.

"What the—?" Chloe turned around, looking for the attacker.

Brian stood twenty feet behind them, another star in his hand.

He began running toward them.

"That *bastard*!" Alyec growled, standing up with some difficulty.

Chloe put herself in front of him, between him and Brian. "Who is he? Why does he want to kill me?"

"He's a member of the Order of the Tenth Blade," Alyec spat. "I should have guessed before, the first time I saw him."

"Wait—Chloe—" Brian caught up to them. Chloe tensed, ready to spring.

"Coming to finish me off?" she demanded.

"I wasn't trying to *kill* you!" Brian protested. "I was trying to get *Alexander*!"

"Uh-huh," Chloe sneered. But . . . she really wanted to believe him. She wanted to believe that someone so close to her so quickly couldn't be capable of hunting her down and killing her. "And what about Alyec? Is he one of my 'race' that your . . . *friend* and you want to destroy?"

"I didn't mean to hurt you, but I had to stop you."

"Didn't mean to . . . ?" Alyec demanded, pointing at the blood running down his leg.

"I had to stop you," Brian reiterated. His brown eyes were wide, begging her to believe him. "If you keep heading down to the water . . . there are others, at least a dozen or more of . . . us, waiting for you, in case you do escape. Some with more . . . conventional weapons."

"Who the hell is the Tenth Blade?" Chloe demanded. "And what do you have to do with them?"

"Their only purpose is to kill people like us," Alyec said.

"Not all of you; that's not true. . . ."

"Tell that to the Rogue."

"Only the *dangerous* ones!"

"And what is Chloe? Dangerous?" Alyec growled and leapt at Brian, pushing past Chloe. His claws were fully extended; they were shorter and thicker than Chloe's. He was aiming for Brian's neck.

"STOP," Chloe said, pushing him out of the way and planting a firm hand on Alyec's shoulder to stop him. But he was angry, raging, out of control.

Without thinking, she took her hand and cuffed him on the side of the head to snap him out of it.

Like a cat cuffs her kittens, she realized after she did it.

Alyec shook his head, dazed, but stumbled back.

"Is that why you hung out with me?" Chloe demanded. "To keep tabs on me so they could kill me?" She looked Brian in the eye. So much made sense now—and it was a thousand times worse than she'd ever thought.

"No! I mean, I was supposed to keep track of you, learn about you, talk to you. Become . . . friends." They held each other's eyes for a moment; it was obvious he meant something else entirely. He hung his head. "Then I found out the Rogue was after you, and I wanted to stay by you and protect you—when I couldn't convince them to call him off."

"Don't believe him! Stupid monkey," Alyec said.

"I'm here talking to you, aren't I?" Brian shouted at him. "Why would I lie *now*?"

"I can't believe it." Chloe backed away from him. "I can't believe you're part of a group that wants me *dead*."

"It's more complicated than that, Chloe," Brian said tiredly. "Even Alyec can tell you that."

"Why did you warn me to stay away from him?" Chloe demanded. "Because you didn't want me learning the truth?"

"No. Alyec is a known . . . troublemaker. I didn't want you drawing attention to yourself, falling in with the wrong crowd."

"Looks like I fell in with the *right* crowd," Chloe said disgustedly. "Finally." She ducked down and put Alyec's arm around her shoulders to help him walk. "A couple of years of working out in the 'real world' so you could be a *zoology major*?"

Brian flushed with shame. "Chloe, I really liked—I really like you."

"Whatever," Chloe said, leading Alyec away.

Epilogue

Alyec lay on her couch, his injured leg raised. It wasn't that large a cut, but the shuriken had sliced through tendon, making it impossible for him to walk. Chloe's own wound on her side had stopped bleeding but continued to ache.

Dazed, exhausted from the fight, and unsure what else to do, Chloe took some taquitos from the freezer and put them in the microwave. She had maybe an hour before her mom came home and serious explanations began if Alyec wasn't gone.

"This sucks." Alyec swore, looking at the cut.

Leaning against the stove, Chloe put her hands to her face and finally began to cry.

"Hey, don't do that," Alyec said, pushing himself up and hobbling over to her. He put an arm around Chloe. "It's very confusing, I know. . . . But don't worry! Everything will be explained. There's so much you need to know—about who you are and where you came from. And you will be safe, I promise. There are these people you should meet now; I think you'll like them. . . ."

Chloe gave Alyec a small smile. Somehow she knew he didn't mean any of his friends from school. And that was fine by her.

THE STOLEN

For K. A. Kindya. Ra, Ra, Ra!

Prologue

She was back at the Golden Gate Bridge.

Paul and Amy were already gone. The highway spanning the bridge was empty of cars. The water below had stopped. Everything was silent, waiting.

Chloe wasn't surprised when Alexander Smith—the Rogue who'd tried to kill her before—seemed to drop out of the sky, a dagger in each hand. He was saying something but making no sound. She could tell he was going to attack and ducked, but her movements were so very, very slow. . . .

There was a scream as one of his daggers grazed her head. *But that didn't really happen,* she realized, confused. *That's not what happened last time. I was supposed to leap at him. . . .* He was coming at her, two more daggers in his hands, murder in his eyes.

Chloe couldn't make herself move.

But I won this fight, she told herself, panicking. *I've already been through all this and I won—*

The Rogue's arm shot out, dragging a blade across her face. Chloe leapt back just in time. *Did he scratch me? Am I bleeding?*

"Brian!" she called out, knowing her friend was supposed to appear. But wait, wasn't there some confusion? Had he been helping her or the Rogue?

Brian appeared, standing at an impossible angle on the rail. He looked serious and his arms were crossed. "Who is it?" he asked gravely. "Me or Alyec?"

"Help me!" Chloe screamed, trying to run away from the Rogue.

"You cause a lot of trouble," the Rogue said with a faint smile.

Then he drove a blade deep into her belly.

As she fell, she saw Alyec run and leap at Brian.

"No!" she screamed as the two boys went tumbling off the bridge.

The Rogue smiled, his face so close that his sour breath enveloped her. He raised the blade again, this time aiming for her neck.

One

"No!"

Chloe woke up covered in sweat and trembling.

"It was a dream," she said, letting her tense muscles sink back into the bed. She had fought the Rogue a day ago—and she had won, if you could call it that. He had fallen off the bridge when Chloe failed to grab his arm, and now he was the one who was dead. Chloe was okay. Alyec and Brian were both alive. Everything else was just a nightmare.

The room was bathed in a soothing half-light that could have been dawn but somehow *felt* like dusk. She wasn't home; the crisp richness of the bedding and the velvet fringe of the throw someone had tucked around her were definitely alien to the King household. Where *was* she? Slowly it came back to her.

Alyec had taken her to this place after the fight. His leg was injured by one of Brian's throwing stars. Brian had claimed that he was trying to stop them from running deeper into Tenth Blade territory, but Chloe still wasn't sure if that was true. . . . They had taken a taxi; she remembered looking out the window and seeing that they were on the bridge, the beautiful lights of San Francisco receding behind them. When they finally stopped, she was led through pitch darkness up to a house, where a short blond woman greeted and welcomed them, even though it was the middle of the night. She led them through narrow halls and—

Chloe sat up, remembering more from last night.

Something had passed them in one of the halls that still scared Chloe, even now that she was safely tucked in a luxurious bed.

The hall was dark and empty, and then, seemingly out of nowhere, a girl her own age drifted past them, silent as a black ghost. Her eyes gleamed in the low light, green and slit like a cat's. From underneath her straight black hair poked two giant ear tips, pointed, black, and covered with fur. She was gone as quickly and silently as she came.

Chloe had gasped and pointed and Alyec rolled his eyes and explained that the cat girl was just Kim. The other woman nodded nonchalantly. But even that simple explanation didn't make Chloe feel any better. She had no idea where she was or who these people were that Alyec had taken her to.

"I'll come by soon," he had promised after they stopped at a door.

"Go *away*, Alyec," the woman said sweetly, pushing

Chloe into the room. For some reason it was that maternal tone, the nice-but-ordering voice, that had set Chloe at ease again. Wherever they were, there were normal rules and people.

She couldn't see much in the tiny space except for a bed with about a thousand down pillows. She collapsed on it without asking.

"You have a nice little nap," the woman had said, clucking her tongue and pulling a velvet chenille throw up over Chloe's shoulders.

As exhausted as she was, Chloe hadn't been able to fall asleep instantly, and when she had, her dreams had all been nightmares: she was back on the Golden Gate Bridge, fighting for her life against the Rogue, the Order of the Tenth Blade's most lethal—and psycho—assassin. Sometimes in her half dreams Alyec was there, sitting on the side and watching like he had or fighting beside her. Sometimes Brian was there, helping her like *he* had—or chasing her the way she thought he had. Even though it had all really happened, it *still* didn't feel real. But it was.

Now that she was awake, Chloe was *still* tired and without answers to the questions that had been plaguing her nightmares: *Why me? What did I ever do to anyone?*

Chloe noticed a little side table that had been set up next to her while she slept. It was covered with a large doily and on it was a plate with various cold cuts and cheeses, slices of bread, and little cups of mustard and other condiments. A glass—*crystal?*—of water was placed next to a can of Diet Coke.

Chloe made herself the largest sandwich she could manage between two slices of thick brown pumpernickel, slathering it with mustard. It took only about a minute for her to gobble it down, maybe another to toss back the water and the Diet Coke. She let out a mighty burp (then looked around nervously, but no one was there). Somehow she wasn't as frightened as she should have been. Her belly was full, she was in a beautiful room, and she was safe. Strangely, she sort of felt happy.

Chloe looked around: the beams and floor planks were ancient wood, dark and polished just enough to keep the dust away, not so much as to be shiny. The room itself was small but cozy: there was an intricate Oriental rug in dark colors in one corner, on top of which sat a lightly worn velvet armchair. Over its back was another chenille throw. An old-fashioned floor lamp with a slightly cracked marble base and brass upright lit the room with a soft orange glow from three fake candle lightbulbs. If Chloe had the money—and the right house—this was exactly how she would decorate it.

She rose and stretched, feeling her joints and muscles snap into place. *Back to my old self, finally.* She pulled her cell phone out of her back pocket and turned it on. Three-quarters battery left. No one had left her a voice mail, not even her mom. *She must have bought that whole "I'm going over to Keira's" thing,* thought Chloe.

She called Amy and was a little surprised when she didn't pick up—both Amy and Paul had seen the whole Rogue-Alyec-Brian-Chloe mess last night—shouldn't they be worried?

Amy's voice mail beeped.

"Hey, it's Chloe. I'm fine. I'm staying with some . . ." She paused for a moment, trying to think of the right word. "Uh, distant cousins and friends. Don't call—I'm going to keep my phone off for a while. Save the battery. I'm safe, and I'll call you later."

Chloe then left a message for her mom, who wasn't home. "Hey, I'm going to be with Keira for a little longer. . . ."

She heard the sound of old-fashioned high heels clicking down the hallway outside her room, growing louder as they came closer.

"Um, love you. And, uh, I'll call you later—I'm turning off my phone. Okay, bye."

Chloe quickly shut off her phone and put it away. Soon a woman appeared at her door, finishing up a conversation half in Russian and half in English on a tiny cell phone dangling with charms. It took Chloe a second to realize that she was the same woman from the night before who had taken her to this room, just in more professional clothes.

"Yes," she said. "Two dozen. And tell Ernest thanks for the purple pens. The kids love them. Spaceba." She hung up and gave Chloe a weary smile. "Sometimes I feel more like an office manager than president of this little place. How are you feeling?"

"Uh, fine, thank you . . ."

It was hard to tell how old the other woman was; her body was Tinkerbell perfect, small and curvy with a tiny waist and amazing calves that were highlighted by what looked like six-inch stiletto heels. She had short, elfin blond hair and black eyes. The skirt and jacket suit she wore were a little flashy for Chloe's taste but obviously expensive. There was something more about her, though . . . the way she held her head, the way she stared without blinking, a certain smell that Chloe couldn't put her finger on.

Chloe knew this woman was just like her. A cat person.

"I'm Olga Chetobar," she said, extending a hand with long, perfect nails. One of them had a little golden charm dangling from the end. "I'm president of Firebird's, well, we call it 'human resources' department. We find and rescue, shall we say, *strays* and bring them home."

"Home?"

"Sergei will explain—he's very anxious to meet you." Olga checked something on her phone again.

"Thanks for the—uh, lunch," Chloe said, wondering if it would be rude to ask about a shower, new clothes, or getting in contact with her mom.

"Don't get used to it," the older woman said with a warm smile. "We all pitch in together around here. You will soon, too."

"I don't mean to be rude—it's great here—but when

will I get to go home? I think my mom is going to start to worry."

Olga held up her hand. "Sergei takes care of this. Your mother will be informed that you were witness to a potentially lethal crime—which you *were*—and are in police custody. Or federal witness protection. Or something. Maybe he already told her? I don't know the details—his people always do a good job, though. Come with me now." She looked at her watch, something expensive with gold and diamonds. "He is expecting you."

Chloe pulled on her Sauconys as fast as she could without tying them and followed Olga out of the room. They walked down a dimly lit narrow hallway, possibly the one from the night before. In the daylight she saw that the walls were decorated with reproduction vintage paper with little roses and stripes and things, and the floor was made up of little tiny planks of different-colored wood.

"Sorry we practically put you in the attic," Olga said over her shoulder as her tiny feet rapidly tapped their way toward a narrow stair. "We were a little unprepared and figured you shouldn't be disturbed for a while. This place can get busy and loud during the workweek."

Chloe had to double-time it to catch up, practically tripping down and around two flights of narrow stairs tightly clustered around a center well.

"What *is* this place?"

"Firebird Properties, LLC," Olga said crisply, proudly,

looking at her watch again. "A real estate and marketing company. Mainly we deal with investment and commercial properties, not so much with housing." Olga flowed off the stairs and was halfway down a new hall as she spoke; Chloe had to run to keep up. It was a much more modern area, with gray wall-to-wall carpeting and art prints framed on painted walls.

"Housing? Market? What . . . ?" Suddenly Chloe ground to a halt as she passed a big picture window on her left. She stared out.

They were one floor above ground; the first thing that was obvious was a huge lawn sweeping down, spreading out to the road. When she pressed her face up to the glass and looked directly down, she could see a fountain in the middle of a circular gravel driveway that led gently along one side of the lawn and downhill to the road. There was, as Chloe had guessed there might be, a gate at the end of it.

"This is that house," she said slowly.

"What house?" Olga asked, coming back to look.

"The one that Alyec showed me. When I was depressed. He drove me out somewhere near Sausalito and showed me this incredible house. . . ." It had been a wild day. The fight with Amy, the car that Alyec stole from the senior running back, the way Alyec liked catching air on the San Francisco hills, the escape from the city to see this huge old mansion. From the outside it was all stone and marble and as impressive as a museum.

And now she was inside.

"Alyec took you here?" Olga asked, faintly amused.

"I thought this was someone's house." *Like somebody really rich,* thought Chloe, though she didn't add that part.

"It is. A few of us live here full time besides Sergei. Me, Kim, and Ivan and Simone. But it is also the headquarters for Firebird and for our people. . . . Sometimes it is important to stay out of everyone's way, and this is certainly as nice a place as any. Nicer, even," the older woman reflected without a smile on her mouth, but her eyes danced. Chloe couldn't tell if the lack-of-facial-expressions thing was Russian or a cat-person attribute.

"You mean this is a place where—?"

"*Sergei* will explain," Olga said, shaking her finger. Then she spun and tapped away again. "Come!" she ordered.

Chloe followed.

There were offices in this part of the building, and actual people. It kind of reminded Chloe of her mom's accountant or their dentist, both of whom worked out of retrofitted nineteenth-century Italianate houses. When she was little, Chloe thought they were mansions—they were bigger than her, Amy's, and Paul's houses combined—and mentioned that freely, embarrassing the hell out of her mother.

"Who was that?" Chloe asked after she stepped aside for another person. He was a young, serious-looking man with brown eyes, who gave her a cursory smile as he made his way past her.

"That's Igor, director of sales."

Olga walked Chloe through a lobby with fresh, expensive flower arrangements and real paintings. She spoke rapid-fire Russian with a girl in a gaudy T-shirt with rhinestones and then brought Chloe up to a half-closed mahogany door. It bore a neat brass plaque with the name *Sergei* inscribed on it. It sort of reminded Chloe of a coffin.

Olga knocked at the door and then went in, beckoning Chloe to follow.

Inside was a large, beautifully appointed office whose main feature was a *huge* dark desk in front of bay windows hung with dark green velvet curtains. Behind the desk was a man who at first glance appeared to be far larger than he actually was. His body was extremely square, wide, and short, and so was his head. There were a few lines under his eyes, not quite bags, but he seemed like the sort of man who had gotten handsomer as he got older. His light blue eyes were overshadowed by huge orange-and-silver caterpillar brows.

He looked up from a stack of papers.

"*You* must be *Chloe*!" he boomed happily, throwing the papers down and leaping up. He came around to the other side of the desk in short but powerful strides, approaching her like a steam engine, his arms outstretched.

As ungainly as his build was, the suit he wore fit him

perfectly, immaculately, and, like everything else here, expensively.

"Welcome *home*, kitten!" he cried, giving Chloe a big hug. "Another one home! Another little bird back to the nest!" He kissed her on both cheeks and then held her out at arm's length. His strength was so great and his presence so powerful, Chloe found herself just sort of being manhandled, too stunned to resist.

"Let me see you!"

He looked deep into her eyes and face, examining her. After a moment he looked a little disappointed but tried to cover it with a smile.

"Well, you don't look like anyone I know—but that's even better. A new face is a good thing around here." He flicked her hair back in a paternal fashion. "And so pretty, too!" He chuckled. "We certainly are lucky to have you. I am Sergei Shaddar, leader of the Pride. And pleased as anything you have joined us."

Leader of the Pride? Sergei Shaddar? Suddenly it all clicked: *Sergei,* Alyec's distant relative, who hadn't helped his family emigrate. Owner of the mansion Alyec had brought her to. This mansion. It was all coming together.

"I have sent her records on to the department," Olga said softly.

"Blood work?"

The woman shook her head. "There is no need unless we find some sort of likely jumping-off point."

"A shame. I like the scientific stuff," he confided to Chloe with a grin. "It is so modern. A drop of blood and we know who your parents are! If we knew who your parents were, that is," he added. "So many orphans," he said sadly. "So few whole families left."

"I'm sorry?" Chloe said, trying to understand what exactly he was talking about.

"I'll go," Olga said, nodding—almost deferentially—to Sergei and backing out so that she faced him the entire time. She closed the door behind her.

"Chloe." Sergei put a meaty hand on her own. His short fingers suddenly developed claws, much thicker and shorter than hers. He pressed them against the back of her hand, indenting the skin but not breaking it, and looked at her seriously. "You are a daughter of the Kings of the Hunt. Goddesses were your ancestors. You are Mai. That is what we are called."

"Mai?" Chloe couldn't tear her eyes from his claws and touched them, picking up his hand and turning it over, staring at it in wonder. Sergei let her without questioning.

"People of the Lions. The Desert Hunters. Children of Bastet and Sekhmet."

Chloe vaguely recognized the last two names or at least Bastet—that was the cat pendant Amy always wore. "We're . . . Egyptian? I thought everyone here was from, like, Eastern Europe or something."

"No, originally we're from Egypt and other parts of

Africa. But then again, isn't everyone?" He chuckled. "Our race is thousands of years old, Chloe. We are gifted and different—and there are very few of us left."

"How did you find me?" Chloe felt a little embarrassed asking; he was giving her the lowdown on their history and she was all like, *Okay, but back to me.*

"There was no way of knowing for certain you were one of us." Sergei shrugged. He pulled his hands from her and waved them around as he spoke; the claws made little whistling noises in the air. They slowly retracted back into his fingers. "Usually we . . . show our true nature at adolescence, fourteen or fifteen or so. Alyec mentioned that you seemed . . . *different*, and when we looked up your records, we found out that you were adopted from the Soviet Union—Abkhazia, to be exact. Then we watched you to make sure. Alyec was told to intervene and instruct you in secrecy when things started getting complicated with the Rogue and the Tenth Blade."

A thousand questions were whirling in Chloe's mind.

"Why didn't Alyec just *ask* or something?" she demanded.

Sergei gave her a patient, pitying look. "Chloe King, if you were already upset by things that were going on with you and someone just said, 'Hey, you're secretly a lion woman, there's a whole bunch of us here in San Francisco, join us,' what would you have done?"

Freaked out. She nodded slowly.

"We would have speeded up things a lot more if we had known that Alexander Smith was after you and that you were *dating* a member of the Tenth Blade."

"We weren't dating," Chloe mumbled without thinking.

"What?"

"We weren't really dating," Chloe said more loudly. "He wouldn't even kiss me."

"Of course not." Sergei nodded as if this were the most obvious thing in the world. Chloe raised her eyebrow.

"Humans and the Mai can't—ah, how shall I say this. Uh, *mate*," the older man said, coughing in embarrassment. "It kills them. Like we are toxic."

Xavier! The guy she'd picked up at that club the night before her sixteenth birthday. They had made out in the parking lot, and when Chloe felt herself almost overcome with desire, she had left and gone home. Days later she went back to his apartment to see him: he was almost dead, covered in sores where her fingers had raked down his back. Chloe had even called an ambulance for him anonymously.

"Oh my God—" Chloe covered her mouth with her hand. "I made out with a guy at a club, and he totally had to go to the hospital. . . ."

Sergei raised his eyebrows.

"Is he going to die?" she whispered.

"Probably not, if you just kissed him," he said slowly. "But keep this in mind for the future."

Thank God I didn't kiss Brian, Chloe thought, and

then quickly remembered that she had no intention of kissing Brian ever again. *Or seeing him. Or thinking about him,* she thought. It had been a great relationship until the whole revealing-he-was-a-member-of-the-Tenth-Blade-thing. Chloe went over the facts in her head again; she couldn't help it. He'd claimed he was trying to save her from the Rogue at the fight on the bridge—but some of his shuriken had come perilously close to her own head. And then there was the one that he'd neatly buried in Alyec's leg when they were running away. . . . He'd said he was trying to stop them. To protect them from Tenth Bladers hidden in the Marin Headlands. But he never had liked Alyec. . . .

And now Chloe began to understand why.

"Anyway, think of it, Chloe! You have a real family now—people who are related to you by blood and who share your heritage! And you know what?" He pounded his fist on the palm of his other hand, causing Chloe to jump back. "*I'll* sponsor you. You can't live *here* all the time—"

"What about my mother? When can I go back?" Chloe didn't want to offend Sergei, but all of this family talk did bring Chloe's mind back to her mom.

Sergei sighed and shook his head. "Not anytime soon, I'm afraid. The Tenth Blade is trying to track you down. They believe you killed Alexander Smith; the streets are crawling with their agents. If you leave, you will be dead before you get halfway across town."

"Can I call her at least?" Chloe thought it might be best to ask this before admitting that she already had. . . .

"I'm sorry, Chloe, but no. Even if the Tenth Blade hasn't tapped her lines, they are almost certainly monitoring her every move. And if your mom called the police, then her line is *definitely* tapped."

"But . . . won't she be suspicious? Where does she think I am? Oh my God—what are my *teachers* going to think when I don't show up on Monday?"

Sergei ticked off his fingers. "Your mother is being informed that you are part of a federal witness protection program and that she will be allowed to speak with you as soon as it's safe. Your school has been informed that you have come down with mono and will be out for a while." Sergei smiled. "We have even given them an address to send your homework," he added, satisfied with himself.

Chloe flinched. *Did it have to be mono? The kissing disease? Couldn't it have been Ebola or mad cow or something you don't get from sucking face?*

Sergei fixed her with unamused eyes, noticing her reaction. "It is the most logical debilitating sickness for a teenager to come down with."

"It's just that everyone's going to think, well, whatever . . ." Chloe said, resigned.

Everything sucked. She couldn't talk to her mom; she couldn't even tell her mom the truth; the whole school would be laughing at her; and she was stuck here for a while. It wasn't that she wanted to *leave*, precisely, but she wanted the option. And then there was the idea of an entire city blanketed with men who wanted to kill her. Whose purpose was to kill her. Her, Chloe King. Sixteen and harmless.

"I didn't kill him!" she said, the anger in her voice surprising even her. "When he slipped, I tried to *help him back up!*"

"Why would you do that?" Sergei asked, genuinely surprised.

"I don't know, I just . . . I don't know. It seemed like the right thing to do." Chloe shrugged helplessly; she couldn't explain it. *It's just what you do.* "Who *are* these people anyway?"

"The Tenth Blade exists solely to wipe us out," Sergei said, putting his hands back on her shoulders, a black and serious look in his eyes. "They believe the Mai are evil, sent by the devil or some such nonsense. They only tolerate us here because it is harder to kill people out of hand in America than elsewhere. . . ." His eyes glazed as he thought about another time and place. Then he refocused. "And as long as we don't draw too much attention to ourselves, we are more or less safe." He spat viciously. "We have to hide like *rats* here." He waved his hand around the room, a room that Chloe personally didn't think would be out of place in the White House, much less a place for rats. "They fear our power. We are stronger, faster, and quieter than they—we should be revered, not annihilated."

He was silent for a moment, seething.

"Well, I'm sure Olga is having someone make up a real room for you," Sergei said, lighthearted again in a flash. "I have to go to a meeting now, but you should go to the library and learn the history of our people. Simone and Ivan will be notified about our newest resident. You have complete run of the place. Goodbye, Chloe, and welcome!" He gave her one last bear hug and then ushered her out, pushing her lightly on the back.

"Wait! One more question!" Chloe begged.

"Yes?" He paused just as she was over the threshold.

"Why are so many people here on a *Saturday*?"

"This is *real estate*!" he said as he began shutting the door behind her. "We never really close!"

She just stood there, dazed for a moment, thinking about everything Sergei had said. *Blood tests? Goddesses? Thousands of years old?* A fax beeped somewhere, breaking her reverie. This was a strange place for ancient hunters to gather.

The girl in the ugly, sparkly T-shirt told Chloe how to get to the library and then ignored her.

Chloe wandered off. She felt disoriented and ghostly in this half-modern, half-old place; not properly belonging but somehow connected with it. There was no one around she knew, nothing familiar, yet she was probably safer than she had been anywhere for the past month. A refugee in the home of the people who really were her family. *Her . . . pride . . .* It was all too much, yet so far they all seemed painfully normal. Olga with her cell phone and Sergei with his businessman's attitude. Chloe realized she was expecting them to act secretive and weird, like vampires.

And to *not* be involved with stuff like real estate.

The library, like everything in the mansion, was spectacular and perfect and right out of an English costume drama: built-in wall-to-wall bookshelves, infinitely high windows between parenthetical pairs of infinitely long velvet drapes that were just a touch faded. She walked along one immaculate bookcase, looking at the titles. Most of them were classics or encyclopedias—though there was a case devoted to modern books like *Bridget Jones's Diary*. One shelf had a pair of bookends in the form of Egyptian cats—Bastet, Chloe realized, and it *was* the same one on Amy's necklace, a house cat with a slight smile and an earring. The other was a lion with her teeth bared. In between the two were books with titles like *The History of the Mai, Essays on Mai Origins, Res Anthro-Felinis*. Chloe picked one up and flipped through the pages, already bored and intimidated by the old-fashioned font and paragraph-long sentences.

She sighed and threw herself into a chair.

Two

"What do we do *now?*"

Behind them another helicopter was circling the bridge. They had been hovering like pissed-off dragonflies off and on since Friday night. Paul and Amy hoped that the National Guard had caught up to Chloe and whoever was attacking her and split them up—but almost a day had passed, and it didn't look like there had been any resolution.

Paul thought he'd seen a body fall from the bridge, but he didn't say anything about it to Amy.

"Well?" his girlfriend demanded again.

Paul sighed.

"I don't know—what do *you* think we should do?"

"Call her mom . . . ?" But even as she suggested it, Amy trailed off, knowing that it probably wasn't the right thing to do—or, more importantly, that it wasn't what Chloe would want. She ran her hands through her chestnut hair in exasperation, pulling on the roots. It was a leftover habit from when she was younger and tried to flatten her big, often frizzy hair every chance she got. "What do you think it was all about—*really*?"

They'd had this conversation several times in the last twenty-four hours, but somehow Amy was never satisfied with Paul's answers.

"I don't know. Drugs? Gangs? Some weird psycho game of tag?"

"Maybe it's got to do with her real parents or something. Maybe she's actually some sort of Russian Mafia princess."

Paul gave her a lopsided smile. Silently they started to walk home, not holding hands or anything. Like they had in the old days, when the three of them were just good friends. Before Chloe almost died from falling off Coit Tower. Before she and Amy got into that weird little snit they were in for days—and had just patched up. Before Chloe started seeing Alyec and Brian . . .

"You know," Paul said slowly, "a *lot* of weird shit has happened with Chloe in the last couple of months, don't you think?"

Amy shrugged. "Seems to me she got her period and turned into a total bitch. For a while, at least," she added hastily. Chloe might have been a bitch, but she was still Amy's best friend, and she was still missing.

"No, it's more than that." Paul frowned, crinkling his long white forehead. "I mean like her fall and the bruises on her face and her random absences from school—not to mention being totally incommunicado about general Chloe life issues."

"She was going to tell us everything," Amy remembered. "On the bridge . . . She was just about to explain *something. . . .*"

". . .when that freak with knives showed up." They looked at each other for a long moment.

"We were talking about her crush on *Alyec* when she jumped off Coit Tower," Amy suddenly pointed out.

"She didn't jump, she fell," Paul said, surprised at the way Amy said that. She was the only person on the planet who probably knew Chloe better than he did, and it was a really weird thing to say about their friend. At no point in her life, even at her gothiest moments, had Chloe *ever* seemed the suicidal sort. *A jackass, sometimes, but never suicidal.* Jumping up onto the ledge to get more attention had been a *little* rash, but they had been drinking, and it wasn't completely out of the range of typical Chloe behavior.

"Whatever," Amy said quickly, dismissing it. "Her life started going crazy after that. I'll bet it has something to do with him."

"That's insane. How could *thinking* about him have anything to do with getting mugged or whatever?" Paul asked. He tried not to laugh or smile but couldn't stop his dark eyes from twinkling. Fortunately Amy wasn't looking directly at him.

"No! Think about it." She began counting off facts on the tips of her black glitter fingernails. "She was mugged right after we all split up at The Raven, then became a total hag when she started actually dating Alyec—and he's Russian, just like her. Maybe he's got her into something *bad.*"

"What about *Brian,* then?" Paul demanded. "As long as we're accusing random people of having somehow screwed up Chloe's life and sent assassins after her. Brian, the mysterious sort-of boyfriend who never kissed her, who isn't in school, and, most importantly—*who we've never seen?*"

Amy stared at him with blank blue eyes, at a loss for an answer. He was about to add a few more salient facts that proved she was a complete wacko with insubstantial—*crazy*—arguments, but then he noticed Amy's lips trembling and tears forming on her lower lids.

"She'll be okay. The National Guard is out there. We can call the police if you want or her mom later—let's say if we haven't heard from her in a few hours. Okay?"

Amy nodded miserably, and they continued walking home.

Three

Amy looked into the bottom of her locker hopefully. Nope, nothing. She was always making cute little notes for Paul and slipping them into *his* locker. Sometimes they were quick scrawls—*See you in English!*—and sometimes they were really intricate things she made the night before with cloth and her glue gun and stuff.

Not. Once. Had he ever done the same for her. She didn't want to outright *ask*—but how strongly did a girl have to hint? Now that she was finally dating a nice, nonpsycho boy, she figured she should cash in on some of the perks that were supposed to go along with it. She was being stupid, she knew, and selfish: Paul did all other kinds of nice boyfriendy things, like buying tickets ahead of time for movies they wanted to see and getting her a coffee at the café if she asked. And he would talk to her for *hours* on the phone about all sorts of things. . . .

But once, just once, Amy wished someone would treat her exactly the way she wanted them to. All that stuff about the Golden Rule and karma and stuff—her do-gooding didn't exactly seem like it was making its way back to her yet.

She closed the door dejectedly. Then she kicked it, hard enough to leave a dent with her steel-toed combat boots. Things were so up in the air and uncertain these days. Chloe was still gone. Amy cursed herself for not hearing the phone when she'd called; it had been jammed at the bottom of her backpack and she had been outside, looking for Chloe, of all people. Amy started checking her voice mail about a thousand times an hour, hoping to hear something from her friend, but nothing.

She was definitely worried about Chloe. No doubt about it.

But she also felt a little . . . left behind. It was like she had made the decision to go out with Paul and now all these strange and mysterious things were going on in Chloe's life that Amy *still* wasn't in on. . . .

Alyec's famous barking laugh echoed down the hall. Amy looked: he was slamming his locker closed and waving goodbye to his friends Keira and Halley—very non-Chloe friends—and balancing his flute case on top of his notebook. *Off for a music lesson.*

Amy realized this was her perfect opportunity to thoroughly interrogate the untrustworthy jerk. She snuck along twenty feet behind him, keeping her back to the lockers, Harriet the Spy style. She needn't have bothered, though: Alyec was too busy waving to people in the main corridor to notice her.

As soon as he turned down toward the music wing, Amy double-timed her tiptoeing until she was almost four feet behind him. She didn't have to do it *too* quickly, though: he was dragging one of his legs a little. *What is that, some kind of new cool-guy walk?*

She smoothed her big dark red hair back and put on her best frowny face. She wished she could do the cold-blue-eyed thing—she had the eyes for it, after all—but somewhere between her freckles and "aristocratic" nose, she tended to come across more goofy and pleasant than aloof.

"You could just, I don't know, talk to me like a normal person," Alyec said causally, without looking behind him.

After she got over her surprise, Amy was so angry at being caught out she almost stamped her foot.

"Where's Chloe?!" she demanded. "I swear to *God*, Alyec Ilychovich, if you fucking *hurt* her . . . !"

A couple of students toting big, cumbersome instrument cases turned the corner, giggling and holding sheet music.

Alyec easily scooped an arm around Amy and pulled her into an empty practice room. He put his hand over her mouth and held a finger to his own. They stood there, his ice blue eyes locked on her own blue ones, insisting that she stay quiet until the two other students had passed.

He watched out the door to see if anyone else was coming and then took his hand away from her mouth.

"If you're not going to talk to me normally," Alyec said with a faint smile, "at least don't go throwing a psycho fit about it in public."

The room was mostly dark, on an inside wing with no windows. It was small and cluttered with the sort of desks and chairs small groups of students would sit in while practicing. In just a few minutes some teacher would come in and flip on the lights and the next period would begin. But for now it was just the two of them, and they were very alone. Alyec's chiseled-perfect face was inches from Amy's.

"You . . . *jerk*!" Amy lifted up her foot to stamp on his toes. He very neatly spun her away so she was at arm's length.

"She is home sick today, that is all," he said patiently.

That was what all the teachers had said when Amy had asked them, too.

"I *know* she said she was safe, but I *saw* what happened on the bridge," Amy said, sticking out her chin.

Alyec's blue eyes widened, and for once he didn't have a comeback.

"What's all this about?" she demanded. "Why was someone trying to kill Chloe? Twice? You know. I *know* you know."

He opened his mouth, looking for something to say. "She really is just sick at home. With her mother," he repeated lamely.

There was a long, tense moment between them, Amy glaring at him, *daring* him to lie again. He finally looked away.

Amy slammed her fist up into his stomach.

"*Jerk!*" she said again, stamping out into the hallway as he leaned over, hand to his belly. She knew she couldn't have done any real damage with her small wrists and the "artist's hands" that Chloe always made fun of, but at least he looked surprised. Amy spun around.

"Chloe is my best. Friend. *Ever,*" she hissed. "If anything happens to her because of you, I'm getting my cousin Steve to beat the living *shit* out of you—and anyone else you know!"

She turned and left, adrenaline—if not exactly triumph—ringing in her ears.

Four

Chloe was snoozing, *The History of the Mai* resting on her lap, its old leather cover making her sneeze occasionally in her sleep. This was her second time trying to get through the dense text since she'd arrived, and the second time it had put her promptly to sleep.

She was dreaming again. This time a cat as large as a person walked toward her quietly. Chloe waited for it to tell her something useful or do something. . . .

"Am I disturbing you?" it said.

Chloe jumped, finally awake. She was *not* dreaming. The weird and ghostly visage that had terrified her the night before was standing patiently before her. *That's just Kim; she's a freak,* Alyec had said.

And boy, was he right.

She was a skinny and oddly built girl, willowy and sleek. Her hair was shorter than Chloe's, shiny, full, and black—almost blue-black, almost Asian. She had high cheekbones.

And velvety black cat ears.

Big ones. The size they would be if a cat's head were blown up to human proportions.

Her eyes were an unreal green, slit like a cat's, completely alien and lacking the appearance of normal human emotion. She wore a normal black tunic-length sweater and black jeans. She was barefoot; her bony toes had claws at the end and little tufts of black fur. Chloe couldn't help thinking about hobbits, except the girl was drop-dead gorgeous. She seemed about Chloe's age, but it was hard to tell.

"Uh, no, I was supposed to be reading anyway," Chloe said, running a hand over her face, trying not to stare.

"I'm afraid I gave you a bit of a scare when you arrived. I'm sorry—I do not usually expect, new, ah, people to be wandering around late at night."

"Hey, uh, no problem. My bad." Chloe kept on trying to look elsewhere, not sure what to say, still trying not to stare.

"I am—"

"Kim, yeah, Alyec told me."

The other girl looked annoyed. "My name is *Kemet* or Kem, *not* Kim. No one calls me that, though, thanks to people like Alyec." She sighed, sinking gracefully into the chair next to Chloe. "*Kemet* means 'Egypt.' Where we are from originally, thousands of years ago."

Chloe made a note to ask her about that later, but something else intrigued her more.

"Is that your given name?"

"No." Kim stared at the floor. "My given name is Greska."

"Oh." Chloe tried not to smile.

"You can see why I wanted to change it."

"Absolutely."

There was a moment of silence. Kim was looking into Chloe's face as curiously as Chloe was trying to avoid staring at the other girl.

"So we're from Egypt originally?" Chloe asked, trying to break Kim's icy, blinkless gaze. She closed the book. "I . . . uh . . . hadn't even gotten that far."

"We're first recorded, or history first mentions us there: 'Beloved of Bastet and guarded by Sekhmet.' " Kim took the book up and flipped to a page with a map on it and an inscription in hieroglyphs. "We were created by her, according to legend."

Chloe didn't know where to begin with her questions—*Created by? Ancient legends? Kim is my age and she can read ancient Egyptian writing?*

"Most of us in this pride are from Eastern Europe—"

"Wait, 'pride'?"

"Yes." The girl looked up at her coolly. If she'd had a tail, it would have been thumping impatiently. "That is the congregation our people travel in. Like lions."

"And Sergei is the leader of the . . . Pride?"

"No, just this one in California. There are four in the New World. Well, were. The one in the East is also primarily made up of Eastern European Mai." Kim flipped a few pages and showed another map with statistics and inscriptions, lines and arrows originating from Africa and pointing toward different places: migration routes to lower Africa, Europe, and farther east. "The pride in New Orleans tends to be made up of Mai who stayed in sub-Saharan Africa the longest. They like the heat," she added with a disapproving twitch of her nose.

"And the fourth one?"

"It was . . . lost," Kim said diffidently. "Anyway, we have been driven all over the world, away from our homes. Our pride managed to live in Abkhazia for several hundred years after we left the Middle East for good." She pointed to a little area shaded pink to the northwest of Russia, on the Black Sea. "The people there remained polytheistic long after the Roman Empire declined, Christianity swept the world, and Baghdad was destroyed by the Mongols."

"I get the feeling that there's a 'but' in here somewhere. . . ."

"Many Abkhazians were driven out in the middle of the nineteenth century to Turkey by domestic warfare with the Georgians. We got caught up in it and families separated, some staying, some fleeing, some going to the Ukraine or St. Petersburg. And then again, not so long ago, just when some started to move back and reunite with lost branches, there was new violence."

She put the book down and twitched her nose

again—more like a rabbit than a cat, Chloe decided. It seemed to signal a change in emotion.

"I'm an orphan, just like you," the girl continued bluntly. "My parents were killed or separated during the Georgian-inspired violence in 1988, before the Wall fell. They say I had . . . a sister . . . ," she said slowly, looking at Chloe with hope. "A year older than me. When I saw you come in, I thought we looked alike—and . . . maybe . . ."

Maybe a little, except for the ears, was Chloe's first, defensive reaction. If you took away the ears, they actually *did* look a little similar: dark hair, fair skin, light eyes, high cheekbones.

What if it were true? Chloe had *always* wanted a sibling, especially a sister; Amy was the closest she had, but it still wasn't quite the same, like someone you could whisper to in the middle of the night or talk about your crazy parents with. Someone who you could scream at when she borrowed your favorite piece of clothing without telling you and then brought it back reeking of cigarette smoke or just plain ruined.

Someone who could tell you it was okay when you suddenly grew claws.

So maybe she's a little freaky, but a sister is a sister. . . .

"There wasn't any mention of siblings when my parents adopted me," Chloe said gently. "My parents told me they asked—they kind of wanted siblings to raise together."

"Ah, Slavic bureaucracy. Who knows what they recorded and what they didn't?"

"They never said anything about a place called Abkhazia either. . . ."

"The issues surrounding it and the country itself are not commonly known to Western . . . ah . . . normal people."

"Well, I've always wanted a sister," Chloe said softly, hoping to cheer up the other girl.

"I have been looking for years." Kim sighed. "Sergei has a whole department dedicated to trying to track down all of our relatives: parents, family trees, missing cousins. . . . We even send things out for genetic testing to establish relationships."

"Wow. That's impressive." Actually it sounded a little nuts, like a more proactive version of Amy's grandmother and her family tree obsession.

"It's *survival,* Chloe," Kim said, fixing Chloe's eyes with her own. "There are very few of us left."

Both of them were silent for a moment.

"Ah, Chloe!" Sergei came bounding in, arms outstretched as if he was going to hug her again. She shrank reflexively back, not from distaste but fear of being squeezed to death. "My meetings are over, and it is time for lunch." He stopped short of actually hugging her, giving a casual, uninterested nod toward Kim. "I thought you could join me. We'll get some nice salads or whatever you young kids eat today. And I can show you what we do here."

"Sure, if you don't mind. . . ." She turned, but Kim was already silently padding out of the room, again, like Olga, backing away, facing Sergei until the last minute before turning.

"Also, I told Valerie and Olga to scare you up some clothes. What are you, size eight?"

Chloe jumped. A brief worry that he might not be taking care of her in a strictly fatherly fashion must have flashed over her face.

Sergei chuckled. "My family were leatherworkers, Chloe. In Sokhumi. I grew up among vests and coats and saddles and knowing how to fit a customer." Sergei put his arm around her shoulders and began to lead her out.

"Uh, can I ask one question? If it's not rude?" she ventured.

"Anything, Chloe."

"Why does Kim—I mean, do we all . . . I mean . . . the ears?" She made a motion with her finger.

Sergei rolled his eyes. "Kim is a very religious person. She is following a particular path to bring her closer to the Goddesses. In her beliefs, it is what we all looked like a long time ago."

"She . . . *wants* to look that way?"

"Something like that. She's a very intelligent and pious girl, but kind of . . . zealous." The older man said it in the exact same tone Alyec had said "a freak."

"Do you worship—?" She wanted to say "the Goddesses," "ancient Egyptian gods," or some such, but it was hard while they passed copy machines and short-sleeved cubicle slaves at messy, piled desks.

"It is hard for anyone who grew up in the shadow of the Communist Soviet Union to really worship anything," he said gently. "I follow Sekhmet as best as I can. Olga was raised sort of Russian Orthodox, with some worship of Bastet, too."

They stopped in an office of slightly calmer people with bigger desks. Chloe recognized Igor, shouting in Russian on a phone. Standing next to him was an assistant, a boy about Brian's age, with trendy thick glasses and a look of resigned hopelessness.

"Is everyone here . . . Mai?" Chloe whispered.

"To the last one. I built up this little real estate empire so everyone could have a place to work with their own people if they chose."

"Does everyone . . . in the pride . . . work here?"

Sergei shook his head. "Valerie, Igor's fiancée, is a model. Simone is a dancer. And Kim does her own thing, as they say. But it's difficult for us to hold down corporate jobs—people can sniff out the wolves among the sheep, or the cats among the . . . well, you know. We don't fit in."

Chloe looked at Igor. He seemed like a normal overworked human male. His tie was thrown over his shoulder and his shoes were trendy. He took notes with a pencil and played with a desk toy as he spoke. But the way he arched his back, and the way the light hit his brown eyes and made them glow for a moment, and the way he swung his head to look at Sergei and Chloe and didn't blink—taken all together, there was indeed something very different about him.

Igor put one hand over the receiver and held out the other when he saw Chloe and Sergei standing there.

"Hello," he said in an accent that was noticeably Russian. *Or noticeably something.*

"I'm Chloe." She felt something strange poke her on her skin as she shook his hand— and realized that his claws had come out and were gently pricking her. *A secret greeting,* she realized, trying to do it back. She pressed too hard, though, underestimating her strength. Igor pulled back his hand, grinning ruefully, and sucked on the pad of his palm where she had drawn blood.

"I've never done that before," Chloe said, blushing. "The handshake thing."

Sergei thought it was hysterical.

"That's my girl. A man-eater!" He slapped her so hard on the back, she almost pitched into Igor's lap. But he was already shouting back into the phone.

"Igor is my right-hand man. I'd be helpless without him," Sergei confided. Somehow, Chloe didn't believe that. "Right now he's working on an old, uh, massage parlor near Union Square. We plan to put franchises in it, like Starbucks. Maybe a Quiznos."

"That's terrible," Chloe said before she could stop herself. "I mean, that must be very profitable." She paused. "But I mean, it might have a bad history, but at least the place has, you know, an interesting one. Not a strip-mall-y one."

"Ah, you're one of those." Sergei sighed. "If it's any consolation, we just worked with the city to turn the space next to a vacant lot into a city-subsidized child-care center for low-income women and the lot into a community garden for them."

"Hell of a tax break," Igor whispered, holding his hand over the receiver again.

Sergei frowned at him, and the boy went meekly back to work.

"At least consider a bookstore," Chloe pleaded. "Even a Barnes & Noble."

"Look at this, I have my own little spiritual adviser." Sergei fluffed the hair on her head. "Maybe we'll put you to work while you're not in school—like an intern. Then you can make your voice heard. Heh. Come, let's order lunch." He whirled his arm around Chloe's shoulders, and dragged her with him.

Five

"The emergency meeting of the Order will now come to session."

It was a lot less formal than most of the meetings Brian was forced to attend: in daylight, no less, and in normal street clothes. *Well, street clothes for me. Suits for all of these old—*

"Purpose?" his father asked ritually, for the stenographer to take down. Brian watched in disgust as his dad, Whitney Rezza, flexed his fingers, admiring the ancient gold ring and his own manicured fingernails. Metrosexuals had nothing on *his* dad. He'd practically invented the style.

"To determine once and for all what to do about Chloe King," said The Nonce. The Nonce was Edna Hilshire in real life and a dead ringer for Dame Judith Anderson. Her age, short hair, dry wit, and sharp, piggy little brown eyes all made her seem as powerful as she was—so were most of the inner circle of the Order.

Rich, white, and mostly middle-aged. Brian's grandfather, the venerable Elder of this Conclave, was *ancient*. He at least seemed to understand Brian's hesitation to go along with the group about Chloe, if not forgive it. *Or permit it, more importantly,* thought Brian.

"Directly or indirectly, she is responsible for the Rogue's death." This was said by weaselly Richard, the little yes-man Brian's dad loved to keep around. Richard—Dick—might be Whit Rezza's favorite, but almost everyone else referred to him as Dick*less*. He was doing all he could to become leader someday. It was a position that Brian had once hoped for and had almost been guaranteed, due to his lineage, but then things had changed. *Everything* had changed when he met Chloe.

Brian had never chosen to be part of this world of Tenth Bladers, unlike Richard, who chose to join of his own free will. There was something about secrecy, rituals, devotion, and danger that seemed to draw people in at every age, Brian reflected bitterly.

Brian never would have chosen this life for himself. If he'd ever had any choice, that is. That was how he'd somehow wound up at a committee meeting determining the fate of the only girl he'd ever felt strongly about. Maybe even loved.

"She is *not* directly—or even *in*directly responsible for his death," Brian repeated tiredly for the thousandth time since that night, when he had returned home from the fight on the bridge. He ran his hand through his dark brown hair, normally full, now lank with exhaustion and sweat. "Alexander Smith came to *kill* her, and she defended herself. What's more, when he slipped off the bridge *by his own actions*, she put out a hand to *save* him."

"I find that highly unlikely," Richard said primly.

"Shut up," Brian snapped at him. "You weren't even there."

"Easy, Novitiate," Edna said. "You are almost out of line." But she said it with a faint smile. "While I, too, find it hard to believe that *any*one, Mai *or* human, would try to help someone who just tried to kill her, the only witness we have at present is Brian."

"Whose views are obviously prejudiced," his father stated in the rich, stirring tones of a leader. "Let it be noted that I will not allow love for my own son to interfere with the facts of the proceedings."

Like it's ever interfered before, thought Brian.

"There is no proof of the Rogue's death," Ramone, the minute-taker, offered. He was a tall, gaunt young man, every inch the Librarian he was supposed to be—except for his healthy skin tone and fairly radiant brown eyes. He wasn't much older than Brian but already sounded ancient. "I have gone through police and hospital records. No bodies have washed ashore, or been trawled, or—"

"That means nothing," Brian's father said again. "He fell. Defending himself."

"From a girl who was defending *her*self!" Brian protested.

"Strike that last statement," Mr. Rezza ordered Ramone. "It is of no consequence and out of order."

"You know, it was *you* people who first put me onto her case," Brian said angrily.

"Yes, and we expected you to follow, befriend, and observe the Mai in question. We did not ask you to become her advocate!"

"Let us turn to the mother," Edna interrupted politely, clasping her hands on the table. She too wore a ring of the Order, but it was smaller, in an orange gold that was different than that of Brian's dad's. "Is she safe?"

"For now." Brian didn't miss the look his dad gave Edna: *We'll discuss it later,* it said.

"Well, that is one thing we can be grateful for." The old woman leaned forward, spreading her hands. "Let us continue tracking Chloe, much more closely this time, using someone, ah . . ." She glanced in apology to Brian. "Not *directly* involved with her heretofore. As long as we know where she is, we can make our decision at any time, and meanwhile, we can watch to see if she does anything else violent."

"That seems reasonable," Ramone said.

"All right," Brian's dad said. "Agreed. Brian, you are off the case. *Really.* If you are caught anywhere near Chloe King again—there will be consequences."

Like what? You'll dock my allowance? You'll ground me? You'll somehow let Mom get killed again? Brian's dark brown eyes burned with a rusty fire deep within. His father had punished him enough already for an entire lifetime. He couldn't possibly do any more.

"Where was she last seen?"

"Running away from the bridge. The National Guard was alerted to the Rogue's presence by her friends," Brian mumbled.

"Her *human* friends," Edna said. Brian nodded.

"She wound up on the Marin Headlands, but I lost her there."

"Was anyone else with her?"

His father looked him straight in the eye. His were a rheumy old blue like a dark sky with clouds; Brian had gotten most of his looks from his mom.

Brian thought about Alyec, the drop-dead gorgeous "other" boyfriend of Chloe's, the high-school student, another Mai. One who could touch and kiss Chloe and not die from doing it, unlike Brian.

His nemesis.

"No," he said slowly. "She was completely alone."

Six

"Take these over to Misha," the feral receptionist flatly ordered Chloe, dropping a stack of contracts into her arms.

Chloe sighed and began the task of trying to find yet another hidden office in the archaic complex that was Firebird. It was strange to go from a halogen-lit bright copy room with faxes, computers, copiers, and phones, for instance, to a tiny bathroom with a pull-chain toilet and a steam radiator that took up half the room.

Sergei had followed up his own suggestion that she intern a bit around the office to alleviate boredom and was paying her a fairly decent ten bucks an hour. Fine, she couldn't actually go out and spend anywhere, but the thought was nice. And she was learning a lot about the business of real estate, most importantly that this was one thing she definitely did *not* want to do when she grew up.

She knocked on a door she thought was Misha's, one

of the in-house paralegals, but instead walked in on Igor and his gorgeous blond fiancée, Valerie, staring at each other starry-eyed on a couch.

"Uh, sorry," Chloe muttered, hastily closing the door. She was looking up and down the hallway again, trying to figure out where she was, when her cell phone rang. She had accidentally left it on after checking her voice mail, listening to *more* messages from Amy. *Well, at least she's properly worried. Teaches her for ditching me for so long,* Chloe couldn't help thinking.

She looked at the caller ID and sucked in her breath.

"Hello?" she asked quietly. No one had said anything explicitly against her using the cell phone, but somehow she suspected they wouldn't be particularly thrilled about the idea, either.

"Chloe? It's Brian."

From his voice it was obvious he didn't know what to expect; he sounded hesitant but urgent. The scene at the Marin Headlands flashed through her mind again: running with Alyec, Alyec falling, a throwing star sticking out of his leg. Above the two of them Brian, with another throwing star in his hand.

"What do you want?"

There was a long pause; she heard him swallowing, could picture his brooding, handsome face as he tried to come up with the right thing to say. She could practically see him frowning a little, his brow knitting over his dark, bottomless eyes.

"Are you okay?" he finally asked.

"I'm fine. I'm with some people who are protecting me."

"You . . . found the Pride, then."

She shouldn't have been surprised by his deduction; who else would it be? The police? The federal witness protection program, as Sergei had told her mom?

"Yes," she answered evenly. "And they're going to try to find out who my parents are, too. What happened to my biological family." *Why am I telling him this stuff? Why do I still want him to know about my life? About me?*

"Oh." There was another pause. Chloe was a little disappointed, but after all, he couldn't really say, "That's nice," or "Good for you," when the people involved were outright enemies of his organization. Whatever his personal beliefs were, the group he belonged to had only one intention: to wipe out the Mai or keep them under control. It was still hard for Chloe to understand.

"Chloe, I really was trying to help you on the bridge."

"Really? By almost cutting Alyec's hamstring in half?"

"I told you," he said impatiently. "If you two had kept running that way, you would have wound up right in the middle of an outpost. And believe me, there may not be many members as psychotic as the Rogue, but there are more than enough members of the Tenth Blade who wouldn't think *twice* about taking down a pair of Mai. Especially one that was somehow involved in the death of the Rogue."

"I didn't . . ." But she trailed off when she realized

what he'd actually said. He hadn't said that she had killed him. He hadn't even said that she was responsible for his death. "Well, you had no trouble targeting Alyec. Why weren't you able to get the Rogue in the throat?"

"Chloe," he said a little pleadingly, a little sadly. "Do you think it's easy to just *kill* another person? Even if they're doing something awful? Especially if he's a . . . friend of the family?"

Chloe didn't want to listen to this. He should have just wanted to save her and not given a thought to anything else. *That was* what she wanted—or at least that was what she wanted to hear.

"Even *you* weren't ready to let him die," he said quietly. "I saw you give him your hand."

He had a good point. Why had she tried to help save her own assassin? *Because it seemed like the right thing to do.* So why did she blame Brian for not automatically coming to her aid and killing for her?

"I have never killed anyone," he added. "Not human, not Mai, not anyone. And I don't want to start."

"You could have done something," Chloe muttered, feeling childish and not knowing why.

"It looked like you were doing a pretty good job yourself."

She could hear the smile in his voice, beyond the sadness. For just an instant, she wished she could see him. She could just imagine him reaching over and stroking her cheek at that point or touching her hand. . . .

And suddenly she realized something.

"I know why you didn't want to kiss me," she said slowly, not caring that it had nothing to do with what they were just talking about. She remembered her conversation with Sergei that morning and with Alyec, days ago, when he'd first seen her with Brian.

"You haven't done anything with him." It was a statement, not a question.

"Yeah? How would you *know?"*

"He's still alive." Alyec grinned at her. "You would tear a boy like that up and spit him back out when you were done."

He had been deadly serious, not speaking metaphorically at all. She thought about what had happened to Xavier and the time Brian had almost thrown her away from him when she was trying to steal a kiss.

No wonder Alyec wasn't jealous of Brian! He knew there was no future in it.

"I'm sorry. I really did want to. I mean . . ." He paused. "I do."

"Was it all an act?" she whispered. "Just so you could keep an eye on me?"

"No, Chloe, I swear it wasn't," he said desperately. "I didn't mean to fall in love with you."

And there it was, hanging in the air. He sort of choked out the last bit quickly, at the end, as if he hadn't meant to say it, as if it had just come out of nowhere.

Chloe opened her mouth to say something, but no

sound came. Her ears twitched; familiar footsteps came stomping down the hall.

"I have to go," she said.

"I—" He seemed to know that now was not the time to push. "I'll talk to you later. Be careful, okay? You're a . . . wanted woman these days."

Chloe smiled at the double entendre.

"I will."

She flipped the phone closed just as Alyec barged into the room.

"Chloe! Love of my life!" he cried, flinging his arms open dramatically. Chloe flinched; this was a poor time for him to be throwing words like that around.

"Hey, who were you talking to? Paul? Amy?"

Hearing their names come out of his mouth was strange. Their weird double date a couple of weeks ago aside, the four of them had never really hung out. They weren't two couples, or four friends, or anything like that. Paul had the comics thing with Alyec, but Amy absolutely hated him. Chloe wondered if he even knew how she felt about him.

As Alyec put his notebook and books down on a chair, Chloe couldn't help staring at his perfect body. Not too muscled, but broad shouldered and well defined. It was like he might fall into a fashion magazine without even realizing it. Alyec was probably the hottest guy in her school. But Alyec's bodily perfection so soon after a talk with Brian was only distracting and even a little upsetting.

He noticed her mood immediately.

"Talking to a secret *lover*, maybe?" he asked, grinning. He cocked his head knowingly at her, coming close as if to take her in for a kiss. Then he grabbed the phone from her.

"Hey!" she shouted. "Give it!"

He laughed and danced around her, holding it high above his head, at least two feet out of her reach. She jumped and leapt in a completely human fashion, pulling at his arms and forgetting all of the cat training he had led her through on that mysterious night when Chloe first learned what she could do as a Mai.

"Let's find out who you were calling . . . if you have another boyfriend. . . ." Just as he flipped it open and started hitting the menu keys, Chloe made one last desperate leap to stop him. The phone was almost in her grasp. . . .

"Hey! Catch!" he shouted suddenly to Igor and Valerie, who were walking by. As Alyec tossed the phone, Igor reached out and caught it gracefully. *Catlike reflexes,* Chloe thought. He and Valerie smiled at the other couple. Chloe ran at them. Igor spun and tossed the phone back to Alyec seconds before Chloe reached him. Valerie laughed and they walked on.

"Give it," Chloe growled, beginning to lose her temper.

Alyec responded by flipping open her phone and looking through the incoming calls list. He danced away as she frantically tried to throw herself against him. But when he saw Brian's name, he hesitated. Then he closed the phone and handed it back to Chloe, trying to maintain a cheerful, playful look on his face. But Chloe hadn't missed the moment of hurt.

"I wasn't telling him where I was or where your secret base camp is," she said defensively.

"I didn't think you did," he said, a little sadly. Silence hung between them for a moment. "I'm hungry. Let's go see what's around," he said, trying to muster up a little bravado. He picked up his books again. "You really *should* call Paul and Amy," he added quietly. "They're worried about you."

There it was again, those two names out of his mouth. Like he really was a close member of her life now, someone who had met her mom, taken her out on dates, and fed her chocolate during her period, and not someone she had done everything to keep her mom from meeting, who had taught her how to extend her claws, to climb trees, and run on rooftops at night.

Chloe put the phone in her back pocket and followed him out of the room.

Seven

Paul was happy just staring at Amy.

They were at Café Eland, and his girlfriend was animatedly talking about her day. He never really got over how she *sparkled*. Chloe was pretty, too, but different. Sort of reserved, held closely inward. Though she would be the last to admit it, Chloe King was an introspective person, prone to occasional insight and moody sulks, which was why her semi-disappearance from his and Amy's life—before her *real* disappearance three days ago—didn't surprise or upset him as much as it did Amy.

But with Amy, what you saw was what you got. If she was feeling something, no matter what it was, you knew it immediately. There was no guessing her moods or mind games. And even if some of her ideas and leanings were passing beyond the border of eccentric and well into the country of the insane, at least she had amazing amounts of energy to put into it.

Her dark red hair—almost back to its natural color,

Paul noted—was framing her face and bouncing gently as she waved her hands around and spoke excitedly. He looked deep into her beautiful marble blue eyes, smiling, his harelip scar barely tugging his skin.

"And *then* he put his hand over my mouth and dragged me into the room!"

She said this so loudly that not only did Paul come to, but half of the café stopped for a moment to listen.

"Wait, what?" He shook his head. He knew he should have been listening, but Amy talked a *lot*. All the time, in fact. He couldn't help tuning out once in a while.

"Alyec!" she repeated with exasperation. "When I told him that he had better not have hurt Chloe. He *grabbed* me and dragged me into the music theory room."

"Why did you do that? Why *would* you do that?"

"Blame the victim, why don't you?" Amy huffed. "Typical male."

Even though he was confused and impatient to find out exactly what had happened, Paul thought over his next words carefully. "Did he hurt you?"

"No," Amy admitted grudgingly. "But he grabbed my arm and put his hand over my mouth!"

"Did he threaten you?"

"Yes!"

Paul waited, staring steadily at her with his dark brown eyes, raising one of his perfectly rectangular eyebrows.

"No," Amy finally said under his scrutiny, looking down at her coffee and kicking the table leg like a little girl. "But he *might* have. If there hadn't been other people nearby."

"So wait—you accused him of doing something to Chloe in the hall in front of other people?"

"No, I'm not an *idiot*. There were just some band geeks walking by."

Paul sat back and stirred his tea slowly, not wanting to look her in the face while he digested everything. Paul could be enigmatic, but sometimes he was just so stunned by what Amy said or did that it took a moment for him to adjust.

"But he knows *something* about what's going on," Amy said desperately, unable to bear his silence. "When I told him what we saw on the bridge, he got all surprised and weird and stuff."

Paul reached for the zipper under his neck and loosened it a little, playing with the tag as if it were a tie. It was his new Puma running jacket, sleek, with red stripes going down the sides. When he wore it, he fit in perfectly with the older, "real" DJs at the clubs he liked. It was like his personal superhero costume.

"Amy," he finally said, "you shouldn't have done that. If he's innocent—and let me remind you that you still don't have any real proof of anything—then it was crazy and mean. And if he *is* involved somehow, how is confronting him like that going to help?"

Amy frowned. "I told him if he hurt Chloe, I would kill him."

Paul tried not to smile. "Very John Constantine of you."

"You're a *jerk,*" Amy said, so distracted she sucked hot coffee up through the stirrer. She tried not to react, maintaining her dignity. Paul sighed inwardly, knowing he would just have to wait it out. *We have time for what, one, maybe two more mood swings tonight?* While it occurred to him that this was a little tiresome sometimes, he wasn't sure he'd have it any other way. For now he would stay. They would talk. And later they would make up.

Eight

Chloe and Alyec had Firebird's lounge to themselves that night. Sergei had made it very clear that there were to be no boys anywhere near Chloe's bedroom, and she knew that meant Alyec especially. So the lounge was as private as they could get.

The lights were dimmed, candles were lit, and she and Alyec were lying on the floor, eating some post-make-out Chinese.

"It's better than going to a restaurant," Alyec said, delicately stuffing his face with lo mein. His skill with chopsticks was extraordinary. "No one else is here, and we can do whatever we want."

Chloe was clumsier with her own set of chopsticks and had to resort to tipping the mostly empty carton of fried rice into her mouth while digging at the bottom with a single stick, making it fall in great clumps into her mouth.

He sucked up a last noodle as lasciviously as he

could without getting soy sauce all over everything. Then he leaned forward and kissed her, briefly licking her teeth with the tip of his salty tongue.

She rolled over to him and kissed him more, holding the back of his head so he couldn't pull away. He didn't try. He mouthed his way off her lips and down to her neck; as he traced the delicate veins on her skin there, she felt her claws extend. She threw her head back, enjoying it.

"Chloe," he whispered, pulling back and smiling gently at her. "I have to go."

"Tease!" she said, only half pretending to be upset. She felt her claws retract again.

"Mom's giving me a ride home," he said apologetically. "I should go find her unless you want to keep making out and have her walk in on us. . . ."

"No, I understand." Chloe sat up, sighing. "It's just that I don't really get to see you anymore. Now that I don't go to school—I mean, I used to see you at least off and on all day."

"I know," he said, kissing her on the forehead. "It was one of the few reasons I looked forward to going."

"How long were you interested in me? I mean, before we really talked?" Chloe asked, her face brightening.

"A *long* time before I knew you were Mai."

"If I was human, what would you have done?"

"The same thing I did with Keira Hendelson. *And* Halley Dietrich. Nothing. Not that I wanted to!" he added quickly when she raised her hand to hit him.

Chloe backed down and began to pick at the fried rice again, trying to make the two chopsticks work. "Do you hate humans? The way Sergei seems to?"

Alyec shrugged. "It's hard to hate six billion people all at once. Sometimes it is difficult being in both worlds. Like . . ." He shifted position as he really thought about it. Chloe tried to remain as casual and silent as she could; this was the most he had ever really talked about his feelings. "Like I'll be listening to music or whatever at my locker, slapping hands with someone, and that will all be fine—but at night, you know, when the sun sets, I get that urge to *run*, explore the night, chase after something. For a while I can be tricked into thinking I am completely human, but there is no denying that other, completely different world we inhabit."

"Why aren't you in danger going to school like this? By yourself? Won't the Tenth Blade try to kill you?"

Alyec shook his head and stuffed another dumpling into his mouth, the moment of reflection over.

"We're at kind of a stalemate. If they out-and-out killed *me*, it would mean instant retribution from the Mai. War. Newbies, prideless Mai, don't count—like you before we got you. Because technically you are not under any protection. In this 'modern' world, the Tenth Blade doesn't tend to attack members of a pride unless they hurt or kill a human."

"It all seems a little . . ." Chloe looked for a word, thinking of *The Godfather*. "*Archaic*."

Alyec shrugged. "How is this fantastic bedroom of yours I'm not allowed to see?"

He wasn't changing the subject because it made him uncomfortable; he was really just done with it and moving on to other things.

"Oh, it's pretty cool. Usually after everyone's gone to sleep, all the girls come over in their skimpy jammies and we have pillow fights until we're all basically naked."

Alyec's eyes lit up for a moment, and then his face fell. "You're lying," he realized.

"You think?" She popped another dumpling into her mouth. It was scallion and vegetable, and she was secretly relieved she still liked that kind. Chloe had been experiencing a quiet but growing fear that she would become a complete carnivore the more time she spent with the Mai. "Sergei wanted to give me a real room, like with a four-poster bed and all this wonderful stuff, but I asked to stay in the first room. You know, the little gable they let me nap in. I love it. Everything is sort of dusty pink and green. It's the bedroom I've always dreamed of," she said shyly. "Kind of like living in my own version of a Gothic novel."

"Like *The Scarlet Letter*?"

It was what they had been reading in English when Chloe was forced to disappear. She felt a brief pang of sadness as she thought of Mr. Mingrone sketching little *A*'s on the blackboard.

"No, more like, I don't know, *Wuthering Heights* or something."

"Oh. I think we have to read that next year." He gathered up his garbage neatly and stuffed it into one of the plastic bags the delivery came in, making sure to put lids back on the little dishes of soy sauce so they wouldn't spill. Chloe watched him, amused. When he was through, Alyec leaned over and kissed her gently on the lips. "Goodbye, Chloe King. I'll see you the evening after tomorrow?"

"What's tomorrow? A prom committee meeting?"

"As a matter of fact, yes." He winked and kissed her again. He squeezed her hand and left.

Chloe sighed, watching him go, then began to blow out all the candles. Her evening of romance—her couple of hours of normalcy—were over. She gathered up the bags of garbage and went in search of the kitchenette to throw them out. For a moment she happily imagined that this was what college life would be like: a hard day of classes, a cheap date in the dorm's common room, and then borrowing incense from a next-door stoner to refresh the place after complaints from vegan neighbors.

Chloe wondered if she would ever get to college at this rate. How was she going to make up for the time lost in school? Maybe they had a copy of *The Scarlet Letter* in the library somewhere. Maybe she could home-school herself. Apparently Kim did.

She started to open a door in a nearby hall, thinking

it was the kitchenette, but stopped cold when she realized what she was looking at. The room was large and mostly dark, lit by candles and oil lamps. The floor was made up of thick tiles of rough-hewn sandy stone, and in the back was sort of a stage, set higher than the floor. On this stage were two huge statues like the bookends she had seen in the library. The left one was a human with a lioness's head. On the right sat a giant black Egyptian stone cat, an earring in her right ear and a smile on her kitty lips. Separating the stage from the rest of the room was what could only be described as a moat, a thin rectangle of water stretching the width of the room.

Kim was kneeling at a little altar in front of those statues, her head down. She wore a rough, off-white robe and was murmuring quietly. Except for the three-dimensional perspective, it could have been a painting off an ancient Egyptian wall.

Chloe tried not to make any noise but accidentally scuffed her sneaker against the lintel. Kim's black cat ears flicked back in response to the noise, although the rest of her didn't move.

"Sorry," Chloe whispered.

Kim seemed to finish whatever she was doing and stood up.

"Didn't mean to disturb you . . ."

"No problem," Kim said easily. She slipped out of the robe and hung it on a rack near the door, where similar robes were hung, in different sizes. Under it she wore her usual outfit: jeans, a sweater, no socks or shoes.

"What's, uh, what's all that about?" Chloe asked as casually as she could, jerking her thumb at the two statues, afraid of the answer she would get.

"Those are our gods, Bastet and Sekhmet," Kim said seriously. "Two forms of the same goddess."

"Does, uh . . . everybody . . . ?" She tried to imagine Alyec kneeling in a white robe to ancient, foreign statues and couldn't.

"Not to the extent that I do."

Kim's ears twitched occasionally toward various noises in different rooms.

Chloe had to ask the question. *Well, I am a* cat, *after all, and curiosity hasn't killed me yet. . . .*

"Uh—I hope you don't mind me asking, but Sergei said you thought we all used to, uh, look like you, but how did you—?"

"I follow the path of the ancients," Kim responded, a little primly.

Chloe just raised her eyebrows and shook her head; it meant nothing to her.

"If you were to keep your claws out and your night vision constant for many years, you would look the same," the other girl responded, running a hand claw over one of her ears. "It takes a lot of concentration and meditation and prayer."

"O-kay." *Meditation? Prayer? What have I gotten myself into?*

Chloe's parents had never been particularly devout: her mother had been raised Episcopalian and her father Catholic, but they didn't take her to church on a regular basis. She had never really had to *think* about religion before, not apart from occasionally joining Amy for Passover or remembering to watch her mouth around Paul's more religious Baptist relatives. After her father left, Chloe's mom tried taking her to Anglican churches like she had gone to with her own more religious mother, but this was halfhearted and only lasted until Chloe put her foot down as a dissenting teenager.

Chloe focused back on the present and Kim, the weird girl before her with the cat aspect. What would her Episcopalian mother think now?

"I don't know if I can. . . ."

"Many have the same problem," Kim said soothingly. "They aren't accustomed to worshiping any god at all. But they are Mai and always choose a path. The way of Bastet is maternal love, the home, and physical, emotional, and spiritual nourishment." She pointed to the cat.

"Oh, like Olga?" Chloe remembered Sergei telling her. "How she takes care of everyone?"

Kim nodded. "Sekhmet is the side of war, disease, violence, protection." She pointed to the enthroned statue.

"Oh." Chloe thought uncomfortably of Sergei. "She's, uh . . . evil?"

"Neither goddess is *evil*," Kim said patiently. "They

just *are*. Sekhmet is the goddess of our soldiers, the kizekh, and she defends her young fiercely. Like a mother lion protects her cubs."

"Who else follows her? Besides Sergei and the 'kizekh,' I mean?" Chloe laughed uneasily, thinking of Alyec and unable to imagine him following either.

"That is a question you would do well to consider," Kim suggested. It would have sounded patronizing from anyone else, but with her alien, emotionless green eyes it sounded wise. "Before you make your own choice."

"Who do you follow?"

"Both. They are two sides of the same coin, a wholeness that is too often forgotten."

The lights in the room flickered. For just a moment it was as if a wind blew through the room, a zephyr from another, forgotten land. Chloe and Kim stood a few feet apart, and as their shadows seized and danced in the wavering light, Chloe noticed how frail the girl seemed, almost hollow. *An orphan, like me. Without even an adopted family.* No wonder she threw herself into these ancient rituals and history—it was a way of connecting herself with something, of fitting in with their people, even if it was only their past.

I may be a newcomer, but she's always been a loner.

"Huh. Hey, can you show me where the kitchen is? I got a little lost." Kim nodded and padded silently out before her, beckoning her to follow. "And can I ask you another question?"

"By all means."

"So there are very few of us left, we have these weird catlike characteristics, the Tenth Blade watches our every move. . . ."

Kim was nodding. She opened a door and Chloe filed after her into the small, linoleum-white room she had been looking for.

"Why don't the rich ones just pool resources and buy some frickin' huge tract of land somewhere—like, a hundred acres or whatever—and have everyone just move there and live happily ever after? Just a little independent Mai survivalist community where everyone can show their claws and hunt and use the litter pan or whatever?"

Kim ignored her last comment. "Some say it is our curse," she answered simply.

Chloe dumped the garbage in the can that was under the sink, then opened the fridge, looking for dessert. "What?"

"Our curse." In a fluid movement Kim leapt backward up onto the counter next to the sink and sat with her legs dangling down. It was one of the most human things Chloe had seen her do. "Five thousand years ago or so, the stories say that a Mai girl and human boy fell in love in the Upper Kingdom. *Egypt*," she added.

There was a lot of meat and cold cuts in the fridge. Good-looking stuff. Also weird pickled stuff, bottles and bottles of beets.

"Neither side was particularly thrilled with this, but

it wasn't unheard of—back then. One night, when the two lovers were supposed to meet, the girl, Neferet, was ambushed by friends of the boy's family and killed. Possibly raped and tortured," she added, almost as an afterthought. "In retaliation the Mai called upon their brethren and set out in the night, every night, until the moon was new again and disappeared from the sky, and killed *every human within a twenty-mile radius.*"

"Is this all true?"

Kim shrugged. "That is what is written. The gods cursed the Mai. Even Bastet and Sekhmet abandoned their own children. Never again would human and Mai be able to love, and the Mai would be driven from their homeland for thousands of years, unable to settle down until the wrong had been righted."

"And again I ask: Is this true?"

"It doesn't matter whether or not a thing is true if it is what people believe," Kim said philosophically. "Every time we seem to find a new home, something happens. Ugarit. Ur. Ashur. All destroyed, and we were forced to move on. The Diaspora from Abkhazia was only one of the latest examples. This particular pride used to have its headquarters in LA. Then our home was destroyed by the earthquake in '94. These *things* keep happening, to the point where even the skeptical become disheartened and draw the conclusion that we really aren't meant to live anywhere permanently until we have overcome our past."

Chloe was listening, but she also noticed an area of the fridge that was locked off, like a strongbox. She raised an eyebrow at Kim and pointed at it.

"It's where the adults keep the alcohol," she answered in the same even tone in which she had been telling the stories.

"I could really do with a beer," Chloe said wistfully.

"'Beer' in ancient Egyptian, as well as the old language of the Mai, is *henqet*," Kim said, a little pedantically. Then she raised her hand and extended her index finger, pointing her beautiful, thick black claw. She hopped off the counter and bent over to the fridge, inserting her claw into the lock. After fiddling with it for a moment, there was a *click* and the door swung open.

Inside were a bunch of frosty bottles of Rolling Rock as well as Michelob Ultras, Sam Adamses, and Anchor Steams.

Chloe took two out, offering one to Kim.

"To the Mai," she said, clinking a bottle.

"To Bastet and Sekhmet," Kim answered back, flipping the top off neatly with her thumb claw.

As Chloe downed the wheaty bubbles, she decided that she was beginning to really like this freaky girl.

Nine

On Wednesday, Paul was still thinking about what Amy had told him when he'd pulled his wallet out of his locker, ready to go across the street for comic day. Alyec had also been at his locker, down the hall. Paul had felt a wave of embarrassment, almost afraid that the other guy saw him. He had to do something about this.

As casually as he could, he strolled down the hallway toward the exit, past Alyec.

"Hey, Ruskie, you coming?" he called.

"Yeah, hang on." Alyec tossed his blond hair out of his face as he pulled his head out of the bottom of his locker, then slammed the door and joined Paul. "Did you read this month's *Wizard*? I think I might want to try *Heroes of the Adamantine Age.*"

Paul shrugged. "I really like the writer, but I can't *stand* Dave Applebee's art. It's so out of proportion. All muscles and tits and calves, like it's still 1982 or something."

"It's *nostalgic*!"

They walked out of school in silence. Paul had to walk slowly: Chloe's boyfriend was favoring one leg. Halfway to the store Alyec gave Paul a sideways look.

"Your girlfriend's a complete psycho," he said without malice.

"I know." Paul sighed, relieved that the other boy had brought it up first. "I'm sorry about that."

"Not your fault. She has a pretty wild imagination, though."

He should let it go. He *knew* it. He should follow his own advice. But he had to ask.

"Is Chloe safe? Just tell me that," he said quietly.

Alyec rolled his eyes. "You *too*? Are both of you crazy conspiracy freaks or something?"

Paul stopped and ticked off points with his fingers. "Weird stuff *has* been going on with Chloe since, you know, *you* and Chloe. She was fighting for her life on Friday, and suddenly you develop a limp at the same time. And you're her *boyfriend*, and you don't seem that concerned that she's been 'out sick' for the last three days. In fact, you don't seem very worried at all. . . . Which leads me to believe that you know something about what's going on and that she's okay."

Alyec was quiet a long moment.

"You're smarter than your girlfriend, too," he finally said.

"Nah," Paul said, smiling. "She's the über-PSAT girl. I just think *longer* than she does."

Alyec bit his lip—*Like a girl,* Paul thought—and tapped his hands against his sides in a near-silent drum solo, apparently weighing something carefully in his mind. Paul followed him, patiently waiting for an answer.

"She's fine," Alyec said at last. "She's *safe,*" he corrected himself, choosing more precise words, "from the man who was trying to kill her—and everything."

"That's all I needed to know," Paul murmured. "Thank you."

"Hmmph," Alyec said, a little annoyed at his admission.

"Could you—could you let her know that we miss her? And worry?"

"I think she knows already, but I'll get word to her. You're her best friends." They stopped in front of the comic shop and he frowned pensively, not really looking in the window but perhaps at something more distant. "I think," he said slowly, "Wonder Woman's breasts are pointing different directions in this poster—aren't they?"

Paul desperately hoped that if Chloe was involved in some international conspiracy/drug/gang/corporate espionage/murder thing, Alyec wasn't a key agent. He was nice enough, but he sure was lacking in the brains department.

Ten

"Hello?"

"Amy? It's Chloe."

She sucked in her breath, waiting for Amy to react. There was half a second when there was no noise from the other end.

"Ohmygod, Chloe! Where the *hell* are you?"

Chloe relaxed. This was the Amy she knew. Pissed as hell, but the same good ol' Amy.

Chloe was in her new room, sitting on the floor up against the wall by her bed. She figured if anyone caught her, she could just tell the truth: that she was telling her friends she was okay. No one had told her specifically not to call *them*. And she could always play the stupid-sullen-teenager routine if she had to.

Of course, why was she even worrying about that? These people, *her people*, had accepted her and protected her and taken her in with love and enthusiasm—no questions asked. She was even wearing really comfy yoga pants and a top that had been quietly provided for her—correct fit and all. Why was she suddenly worried about being *caught* or doing the wrong thing?

Chloe twisted a piece of her dark hair around her finger. It was time to get it cut soon—another thing she'd neglected with all the excitement of the past few weeks.

Unless it turns out I'm a shorthair. She almost laughed at her own joke.

"I'm with some people—they're protecting me from the people who want to kill me." Chloe flinched, realizing how stupid that sounded.

"What the hell are you talking about? I thought it was just that one guy! Was that mugger part of this, too? Are these gangs? Are you in a *gang*, Chloe?" Before Chloe could answer, Amy started shouting, sounding muffled, as if she was holding the phone to her chest. "It's Chloe! She says she's all right. I think she's been kidnapped. No, I'll tell her." The barely audible masculine voice that was answering back was definitely Paul. "Just get on the other phone!" Amy snapped.

He's over at her place. Late, Chloe realized.

There was a click, then Paul was on.

"Hey, Chloe." Calm as ever. She wondered, not for the first time, if anything ever ruffled his feathers. "You okay?"

"Yeah, I'm fine, Paul."

"Cool. We were worried about you, you know."

"I know." She smiled but felt a little strange. She was

glad that Paul seemed to accept her safety as a matter of fact and that he believed she could handle anything she was in the middle of right now. It was great that *some*one had that kind of confidence in her. But didn't he care enough to crack his cool exterior just a little? Shouldn't he be just a tiny bit more worried?

"Anyway, I have *not* been kidnapped. And it's not gangs—" Chloe thought about the Tenth Blade and the Mai. Strip down their history, legends, occult origins, and secret powers and, well, actually . . . "Okay, it's sort of like gangs. But it's also sort of international and stuff. . . ."

"I *knew* it!" Amy cried triumphantly. "Alyec's a spy for the KGB, isn't he?"

"Learn a little history, will you?" Chloe snapped, finding herself falling back into her old pattern with Amy instead of this being the I'm-okay-I-love-you call it was supposed to be. She took a deep breath. "This has nothing to do with the Cold War—" But then again, it sort of did. "Okay, there's these two groups—the Mai, who are basically related to me, and the Order of the Tenth Blade, who are sort of all about killing the Mai because . . ." *Think this one out, Chloe.* "Because the Mai were sort of a hunter-warrior caste who were . . . undeservedly reputed to be bloodthirsty and . . . animalistic. It's all really old and stuff. The important thing is that Alyec saved my life when that psycho from the Order tried to kill me." Well, that wasn't *exactly* true—he had held Brian at bay while she fought the Rogue, and the truth was that maybe Brian really *had* been trying to help her. . . . But if Alyec hadn't shown her the things he could do as a cat, she would have been slit from nose to navel immediately by the Rogue's daggers.

"He didn't," Amy said, obviously not wanting to believe her.

"He *did*," Chloe repeated firmly. "And more than that. These people are going to help me find out who my biological family is. They might have all been killed—" She thought about Kim with a faint gleam of hope, then wondered how she and Amy would get along. Chloe decided not to mention her potential sister just yet. "But they might still be alive. These people are dedicated to finding all of the people from Abkhazia, a country in the old Soviet Union, who were scattered and bringing them over here safely."

"Sounds like they brought trouble with them," Amy observed. Chloe opened her mouth to argue, but in a way, her friend was right.

"Come home," Paul suggested. It was *almost* a plea. "As soon as you can. I don't trust these 'people.' "

"Yeah, they probably tapped your line."

"Amy, this is a cell phone. . . ."

"Whatever! Don't be a douche. When are you coming *back*?"

It was a strange question. Chloe had only been at Firebird with the Mai for a week or so and it already felt like a completely new life. Sure, she missed her mom and Paul and Amy, but the thought of suddenly waking up tomorrow and going to school again was just weird.

She paused too long, trying to figure out how to answer it.

"So you mean you haven't even *considered* coming back," Amy said evenly.

"Not until it's safe," Chloe said, faltering.

"And when's that?" Paul asked. His voice was beyond cool. "When this Order thing has been completely wiped out? When they're all dead? How many of them are there? I mean, it sounds like a real gang war, from what you're saying."

She hadn't thought about it.

She *really* hadn't thought about any of it.

She thought about it now, though, sinking into her pillows. They kept saying—*Sergei* kept saying—she could go back "as soon as the danger had passed" and Chloe just accepted it, repeating it, making it the truth by repetition. What did she expect? That the Tenth Blade would just give up after a while? That they would grow bored with hunting the supposed killer of one of their Order? That there was some sort of statute of limitations on accidental death in the middle of a five-thousand-year blood feud?

Did she really believe that one day Sergei was going to come to her with an all-clear signal, hug her, let her go back home, and insist that she drop by once in a while? Now that she thought about it, no one ever acted like she was going to be leaving at any point. Alyec never said anything one way or the other. She had a *job*, for Christ's sake.

"I don't like the way this sounds, Chloe," Amy said grimly. "I want to see you. Myself. If these people are so great, they shouldn't mind letting you see your friends."

"Amy, now is not a good time. . . ."

"I mean it! Promise you'll meet us. Or I'll call in the cavalry. I call the police. *I'll tell your mother.*"

"All right, all right, I promise!" Chloe agreed.

"When?"

"I don't know! I'll call you again when I can, okay?" She looked at the battery meter. About a quarter left. She didn't have a charger with her and for some reason, once again, she didn't feel comfortable asking for one. Come to think about it, no one in the Pride knew about her phone except for Alyec—and now Igor and Valerie—so unless they told anyone, that was it. Why did that make her feel better somehow?"

"All right. Call me by Saturday or it's the cavalry. I mean it."

"All right! I'll see you later."

"'Bye!" Paul shouted.

Chloe flipped her phone closed and looked at it for a long time, sitting on the floor.

"Well, that's . . . weird . . . ," Paul said, distractedly arranging Amy's stuffed animals into extremely lewd positions.

"Stockholm syndrome," Amy answered promptly, pleased with herself. "She has begun sympathizing with her own kidnappers. She's beginning to really believe they are keeping her safe instead of just keeping her."

Paul looked up at her and narrowed his eyes. "Amy? What are you planning?" he asked evenly.

"Nothing," Amy said, crossing her arms. "Yet."

But they both knew it wasn't true.

Eleven

"Well, well, my own son wants to have dinner with me," Whit said, folding the painfully white linen napkin into his lap. "What an extraordinary honor."

Brian grimaced. Once again his father had managed to turn the tables so everything was to *his* advantage: Mr. Rezza had chosen the Ritz-Carlton's restaurant for dinner, much to Brian's dismay. It embodied everything that Brian did *not* want to get involved in during their discussion. Fussy place settings, crazy rich people, annoyingly perfect and subdued lighting, silent waiters, and worst of all, a dress code. *Technically* Brian wore the required "business attire," but he saw that the maitre d' was pissed at his Generation-Y interpretation: brown velvet pants, a leather suit-style jacket, and a Diesel shirt that he wore with a thrift store tie.

"Shall we start with a bottle of something? Maybe some Krug Grande Cuvée to celebrate the occasion?"

Brian had an almost overwhelming urge to point out

that he wasn't old enough to drink, but now was not the point in the conversation to start acting up.

"Whatever. You know I like reds."

"Oh, that's right." Whit looked at his son with something approaching fondness. "I remember: cabernets. A strange thing for a California boy, but I don't disapprove. I seem to remember they have some very nice native ones here. . . ." He took out a pair of reading glasses and buried his nose in the wine list.

Brian sighed. At least his father seemed a *little* nervous despite his posturing. It had been several months since they had really spent any time together outside the dusty walls of the Order's chapter house. The older man looked more or less the same, maybe a little tanner, maybe his jowls were just a little bit tighter. He had said something about taking up squash or tennis. He was a large man, imposing, with an utterly patrician face and a nose that was large enough to make him look regal but sharp enough so that he looked like he was something other than a hundred percent Italian. Only his easy olive tan betrayed a Mediterranean origin.

His outfit was impeccable, a several-thousand-dollar Armani suit that fit so well with the shirt, the cuff links, the tie, and the shoes that except for the slight paunch, Brian's dad could have been a model for some older men's magazine. Whitney Rezza was a living embodiment of taste and wealth well spent.

"Dad," Brian said, clearing his throat, "I think we should consider me leaving the Order."

His father looked over the wine list at him.

"Don't be absurd."

Brian had thought long and hard, and the best thing he could do for Chloe now was to cut all ties with the organization that was bent on killing her. Whatever happened between the two of them, he would be free of the Tenth Blade, and Chloe would feel confident that she could trust him.

But that was only partially it: this was also an opportunity for Brian to figure out what to do with his life. Which he knew, regardless of anything else, did not involve the Order of the Tenth Blade. At best it was a silly society of archaic rituals and secrecy; at worst it was a group of people devoted to killing other people. Either way, it was not going to be his life's work.

"I'm serious, Dad. I want a career, an education—I want a *life*." He ran his hand through his own thick dark hair, angry at his own nervousness.

"All of those things are possible while you remain in the Order," his father said, slowly setting the wine list down, "if that's what you really wish."

"I want to *concentrate* on 'those things.' I don't want to have to run out of a final because of some emergency meeting the way Dickless—uh, Dick did a couple of weeks ago."

"Richard is an extremely devoted young man,"

Whit said patronizingly. "He is an exemplar for the Order."

Then why don't you just adopt him and be done with it? His father's feelings toward Dick used to drive Brian up the wall; now he *wished* his dad was grooming the college student for eventual leadership. God knew he himself didn't want it.

Brian took a deep breath.

"Dad," he said patiently, "most people *choose* to join the Order. Even Edna—"

"That's *Mrs. Hilshire* to you, Brian."

"Even fucking *Mrs. Hilshire*—" He stopped when his father gave him a warning look. "Even *she* gave her kids the choice. Evelyn chose to join, and William and Maurice didn't."

"Well, I don't have the luxury of *three children* and the chances that *one* may follow in his father's footsteps. I only have *you*."

"It's not my fault you only have one kid," Brian snapped, his temper slowly getting the better of him.

"Oh, is this where you're about to blame me for the death of my own wife again?" his dad said, annoyingly lightly. "How if it hadn't been for me, she would still be alive? How I might have had three kids, and you would get out of your current predicament? You're right. Terribly selfish of me to let my *own wife die*. I didn't realize how it would inconvenience you."

Brian's foot began to shake under the table. He

forced himself to stop it, not wanting his dad to see how close he was to losing control.

"I'm not talking about that." *Though I should throw it in your goddamn face, you self-satisfied* . . . "I'm talking about my right to choose my own life."

"Sometimes we don't have those choices, son. Look at Prince Charles," Mr. Rezza said gravely. "Listen, I inherited this burden from your grandfather, just as he did from *his* father. Sometimes we just have to accept what we're given and bear it manfully."

Manfully? Brian almost cracked up. But it *was* interesting that his dad had phrased it that way. Was it possible that Whit Rezza had rebelled at some point? That his own father had shot him down? Brian's grandfather seemed like a gentle enough old man, but Brian knew there was a sharp and possibly evil mind behind his friendly exterior.

"I understand that, Dad," Brian said softly. "But these are different times. I have . . . individual rights, like the right to pursue my own path."

He knew as soon as he said "individual rights" that he had made a mistake. The almost-caring look his father had given him disappeared, replaced with a stony glare.

"Nonsense," he said with disgust. "Your generation has no sense of responsibility to a group, a calling higher than your own. You treat random friends like family and family like strangers. You want to dither your life away, pursuing one pleasure after another. That is not a *path*; that is a waste of life."

And that was that. Brian had tried to sail the choppy waters of his father's limited common sense—and failed. Mr. Rezza picked up the wine list again.

"Everybody in the Order has had their doubts at one time or another, Brian, even Edna. Even myself. It's an inevitable phase in the path to becoming a fully integrated member. You'll get over it." He paused, his eyes scanning the wine list. "What about a merlot?"

Twelve

Still sitting on the floor long after she'd hung up on her friends, Chloe picked up her jeans that were wadded in a pile. There was a wear spot threatening to tear into a rip. It was already tissue thin. She ran her finger over it and the harder nubbles of the denim around it. These were vintage Lees she had saved for herself at Pateena's.

"*I expect to see you back on Wednesday—if not, don't bother ever coming back.*" Her boss's words echoed in her memory.

Chloe sighed. Her job at the vintage store was just another thing her new screwy life had, well, screwed up. She had an overpowering urge to talk to Marisol, the owner and her friendly boss—if Marisol was still her boss, that is. The older woman always seemed to understand Chloe better than her mom ever did and sense her moods with an uncanny knack. Even if she couldn't tell her all her secrets, Chloe had always unburdened some of her feelings. Now, of course, that would be impossible.

Hi, Marisol. Sorry I flaked and didn't come to work after you gave me that last chance. I know I'm effectively fired, but there were good reasons. I can't really tell you why, but can I just vent for a while?

The sadness of a relationship ended fought for space in her head alongside her anger at the thought of Lania—her work nemesis—running the cash register all the time now.

Chloe prepared herself for a nice introspective and lonely sulk on her bed, but she was too nervous. Too energetic. Like that night that seemed so long ago, when she'd run out of the house and gone out to the club.

But then again, cats and lions weren't known for their mixed feelings or inaction. They just *did* things. She was upset, and she had to do something about it. Right then.

They wouldn't miss her for a *few* hours, right?

Waltzing through the front door was out of the question. But a glance out the window revealed a ledge and all sorts of nooks and crannies in the brick and stonework that were perfect for someone with claws. Using both her arms and a little force, Chloe raised the window until there was an opening high enough for her to get through. Cool, moist air entered the room. There were the scents of pine and mud and something so clear and snapping that she could only think it was like the moon.

How could Sergei spend all of his time in the old house? True, it was gorgeous and huge, but as a Mai, how could he resist the call of the outdoors?

She looked around one last time. Was she betraying the people who had let her in? Maybe she could talk to them and they could arrange some sort of escort for her so she could visit her mom safely, or Paul and Amy, or even Brian. . . . But she had to see her mom. *Now*. It hit her with an overwhelming urgency.

Without another thought, she pitched herself through the window and crouched on the sill, just barely touching her fingers to the wood for balance. Her feet itched inside her sneakers. Though the Sauconys' grip was great for running, Chloe suspected she would have an easier time climbing down with bare feet, her toes curling around the stones. She untied her sneakers and tossed them back into her room, under the bed. Her socks followed.

She wiggled her feet, now free, and was somehow unsurprised when claws extended out the tips of her toes, just like Kim's. She extended her hand claws and leapt, unsure what she was going to do as she fell but confident she would figure out something and positive that she would land safely.

And she did.

Chloe didn't even think about what she was doing as she shot down, as fast as she'd fallen off Coit Tower. She landed lightly on a lower gable. There was a quiet, high-pitched squeak of her foot claws against the stones. With only a moment's pause to grin at what she had done, Chloe scurried from curtained window ledge to curtained window ledge, one story at a time, letting her feet dangle and then drop down.

When she hit the lawn at last on the back side of the house, the grass was cool and wet and almost silver. With her night vision, she could see her own footsteps on the turf: slightly darker impressions where the balls of her feet dissolved the individual spheres of dew, causing them to blend together and sink into the ground. It was such a beautiful and fascinating discovery that Chloe had to force herself to look away and continue on with her journey.

No wonder you always catch cats staring at nothing for hours. I bet they see a billion little things.

She ran with her body against the walls of the house, trying to get to the woods as fast as possible. She tried a couple of test leaps as if she had four legs, stretching her arms in front of her and pushing off with her legs. Sort of like the way Gollum did it in *The Lord of the Rings* movies. It worked, but not too gracefully, and didn't seem to help her pick up speed. The Mai were one hundred percent upright walkers.

Which made her wonder about what Kim had said. Were they really a race created by ancient gods? Chloe still didn't quite believe it, but what if it were true?

Then again, what if the Order of the Tenth Blade was right? What if they weren't created by benevolent ancient gods, but by demons? What if they *were* demons of some sort?

But she had tried to help the Rogue after he tried to kill her. Chloe wasn't evil. Was she?

She let go of her thoughts and refocused on her present. She ran, and yards of ground disappeared under her strides. She felt herself slip into the shadow of the pines. No one could see her if she didn't want to be seen; she *knew* this. And if she had to, Chloe could easily live out of doors full time, in the trees, like a child's fantasy of freedom.

Her cat imaginings fell short as she ran along the edge of the driveway and came to the road. It didn't take more than a second to figure out how to scale the fence when the gatehouse guard had his back turned, but once she was on public streets again, she suddenly realized that even with her Mai speed, there was no way she could run all the way to her house, chat with her mom, tell her everything was okay, and get back in less than a few hours.

Feeling a little defeated, she took a bus over the Golden Gate, from the edge of Sausalito. She sat in the back, trying to keep herself from bouncing, only remembering to retract her claws at the last instant. No one took much notice of her bare feet; this was San Francisco, and with the wild look in her eyes and her barely contained energy, she easily passed for either a strung-out junkie or a riot grrl on the way to her next rally.

Chloe got off the bus when it crested around Golden Gate Park, preparing to run the rest of the way. She decided to take a somewhat circuitous route in case anyone was following but didn't go too out of her way because time was short.

In the end, it didn't matter.

She passed a surprisingly healthy looking street person—she would remember that later and curse herself for it. As Chloe gave him a wide berth, he turned to look at her. Their eyes locked, and she suddenly realized there was something far too sane and directed about him.

Just as she was about to move even farther away, he raised an ornate wooden club and smashed it down at her.

Chloe threw up her hands and claws to deflect it, but the club was moving so swiftly and the man who wielded it was so strong—and prepared—that she only managed to keep the tip from hitting her head.

It made a cracking noise as it hit her collarbone instead, but most of the impact was taken on the side of her neck.

Chloe fell down, pain and fear shooting through her at the same time. She tried to get to her feet, but the pain and feeling of *wrongness* in her neck kept her from moving properly.

Another person appeared over her.

He wasn't another "homeless guy": just a normal-enough man walking a tiny dog, distinguished only by his bright orange sweater.

"Help me!" Chloe cried, lifting her hand to him.

He reached for her, but then she saw that he held

something black and ropy that Chloe couldn't identify. As his sweater tugged up his arm, she saw the tattoo, the same one the Rogue had had : *Sodalitas Gladii Decimi.*

Chloe screamed. Her claws came out and she slashed at her captors wildly despite the overwhelming pain.

But both of her assailants were well trained, if slower than the Rogue. The one dressed as a bum put his knee on her chest, forcing all of her air out. He grabbed one of her arms while the guy in the sweater grabbed her other.

"Going to visit your *mommy*?" he asked nastily.

She kicked: this was something they were not prepared for. While Chloe couldn't reach the one crushing her ribs, the claws of her left foot shot out and neatly got sweater man dead in the stomach. He screamed as she felt his flesh gather up and tear beneath her claws. But she still couldn't breathe, and silver stars began twinkling at the edges of her vision.

Then somebody hissed—and it wasn't her.

Suddenly the weight was lifted off her chest. She sucked in as deeply as she could and was rewarded by a scorching pain that was so great it masked the pain from the wound on her neck. She could see again, although what was going on was mostly a blur: there seemed to be two other people, faster than the Tenth Bladers, attacking and pummeling them with an eerie silence.

Chloe sat up as best she could. They were Mai, of course, although she didn't recognize them. Their movements and their scent were unmistakable. They were *big*, too—which made their silence even scarier. Homeless guy landed with a thump next to her, his eyes blank with unconsciousness. Chloe lost her temper for just a moment, finding the urge to slash his face almost overwhelming. Instead she dug her foot claws into his crotch. When he woke up, he'd have something to remember her by.

Then she collapsed back on the pavement.

"I *knew* she was going to be trouble," one of her saviors sighed, walking toward Chloe. This was a woman; she was dusting off her pants. With a casual kick she stilled the "homeless" guy, who had begun to moan and twitch.

"Can't blame her. She's a kid," the other one, a man, said. It might have been Chloe's delirium, but the two looked very similar. "Besides, I haven't had this kind of fun since August."

The woman was scanning the night. Suddenly she dropped down, crouching with one hand for balance, the other pointing. "More coming."

"Bring 'em on!" the other said. Then he added, "I know, I know."

"You grab her legs—careful of the neck. It might be broken."

"Where's our glorious pride leader?" the man asked with heavy sarcasm. "*This* wouldn't even have cost him a life. Assuming he *has* more than one."

"Shhh! Keep it to yourself, Dima. The girl might still be conscious."

She is, Chloe thought, before fainting entirely.

Thirteen

They weren't traveling in the land of the warm sun anymore, of endless sky and sand. They were someplace colder and wetter, with incredible mountains and a very different sea, very close by. She walked through the streets of an ancient city. Stones of buildings centuries dead stuck out of the ground.

Few people paid attention to her. The markets were crowded with people from all over. One of her shadow companions sniffed the air disapprovingly, wrinkling her nose at the stink of the hordes. She smiled down at the four silent lions. "Let us find our orphans and move on from this place."

They turned a corner and a shadow fell over the five Mai; one whined as the stink of rotten eggs became overpowering in the wet heat of the afternoon sun. . . .

"Chloe?"

She opened her eyes. Sergei's face was uncomfortably

close to her own, and he looked concerned. His breath stank of garlic, which was not the smell in her dream at all but still made her sick.

Chloe was lying in her own bed at the mansion. There was cloth mounded tightly against her neck, wet with melting ice. She tried to turn her head—it was possible, but the pain was searing.

"Maybe you'll listen to me about visiting your mother next time?" he said gently, patting her on the hand. It was a little rough, the action of someone who wasn't used to showing affection. Chloe blushed and looked down, too embarrassed by her disobedience and its result to look him in the eye.

"I know you miss her," he continued, "but the Order wants you dead, Chloe girl. You took out one of their best—and craziest—soldiers. They knew you would try to go home at some point. Every exile does." His white-blue eyes looked beyond her for a moment, into the distance at something else.

He really does sort of look like a lion, Chloe reflected. *If his reddish-silver hair and beard were drawn back from his head—and just a little longer—it could be a mane.*

"All you're doing right now is endangering her. Give it time, let us help work things out, and we'll reunite the two of you eventually. Okay?" He patted her on the head.

"Okay," Chloe agreed, smiling despite herself. "I'm sorry."

"Don't be too sorry—Ellen and Dmitri had fun for the first time in a while. And neither of the criminals they took out will be causing any more trouble for a *long* time." He grinned, showing a mouth of teeth as short and square as himself. "Enjoy yourself, Chloe girl! You're a teenager who doesn't have to go to school for a while. At your age I would have loved such a thing."

She nodded, and he adjusted the sheets around her, tucking her in.

"Will I ever be able to go home?" she finally asked, sounding more pathetic than she meant to.

"Of *course* you will, Chloe," he said fondly. "We do not mean to keep you here forever—although, of course, I'd like to." He smiled and chucked her under the chin. His teeth were very carefully divided by the black lines separating them, Chloe noticed. It was a strange, perfect little grin.

"How is it ever going to be safe?"

"Ah. Well. Five ways," he said. He held out five fingers and counted them down. "One: Someone finds the Rogue. This is still possible—it takes a lot to kill one of those bastards and no one actually saw him hit the water. Two, and this is far less likely, we have a *true* détente and convince them of your innocence. They do not really consider us human—I mean, intelligent rational beings—and almost never agree to meet, but it has happened once in a great while. Three: We make things very difficult for them; tie their hands with other methods. Like a police investigation. Or, even worse, an IRS investigation. Or an accidental 'explosion' at one of their weapons factories."

"Weapons factories?"

"Yes. They skirt the law themselves a lot, these so-called protectors of the innocent. Four"—he coughed to show a sense of embarrassment where there wasn't really any—"we could threaten the family of one of the Order. I know," he said, putting up a hand and closing his eyes as Chloe started to say something, "this is an idea alien and horrible to your young, naive, human ears. But Chloe, they don't play by fair rules, either. Why else would they hunt an innocent teenage girl like yourself? Why would they send the Rogue after you to begin with?"

Actually, now that Chloe thought about it, why *had* they? She hadn't become a threat to anyone until *after* she'd had to defend herself from that psycho, when the Mai had sent Alyec to teach her how to defend herself. It was a chicken-and-egg situation.

"They sent someone after you because you were an easy target," Sergei said sadly. "You weren't part of a pride, you weren't part of a group who could protect you. It would have been an easy way for them to pick off a member of the Mai with no risk and few repercussions. They have done this before with other orphans like yourself—you should ask your friend Kim about it sometime. We found her hiding in an alley, living in a box in the garbage."

Chloe could see it, although she didn't want to. A little girl with black hair and bright green eyes, terrified, keeping to the shadows and hiding in piles of trash so the men hunting her wouldn't find her.

"Trust me, Chloe," Sergei said, a hard look coming into his face. "As someone who lived in a very dangerous part of Eastern Europe at a very dangerous time, survival is difficult and often unpleasant." His finger went up to a corner of his eye and scratched there, apparently of its own accord. Chloe had never noticed it before: part of his right eyebrow was especially kinked, and there was a very slight line where what looked like two different pieces of flesh had been sewn together to cover a wound.

"There was a fifth way," Chloe whispered. "You said there were five ways it could be safe for me."

"Ah. Yes." Sergei snapped himself out of his thoughts and looked at her both sternly and pragmatically. "That would be if one of us was killed by them in the next few weeks. Then we would be even." Chloe sucked in her breath.

With that, he left.

Chloe tried flexing her shoulder again. More pain, but still not so bad. Her neck wasn't broken, and neither was her collarbone. She noticed a glass of water on the night table next to the bed and a dish with two ibuprofen, which she immediately scarfed down. She grabbed the remote and fluffed up her pillows, preparing for a good afternoon of daytime TV. Then her hand hit something—her cell phone, which she had stashed there the night before, when she went out. She pushed the power button and saw that there was a message waiting from an unrecognized number. She called her voice mail as she began switching channels, looking for *Jerry Springer*.

"Chloe, it's Brian again. Listen to me—whatever you do, wherever you are, stay there for the next couple of days. The Order has blanketed the streets around your house with members looking to bring you in—one way or another. *Don't* try to visit your mom or your friends. I'll try to talk to you later."

Chloe checked the time the message had come in—8:12. Almost an hour before she had gone to try and visit her mom. If she had left her phone on, she would have gotten the call and avoided the fight.

Chloe thought about this, and Brian, for a while, looking up at the ceiling and finding little lion images playing in the knots and whorls of the wood there. They seemed to twist and jump, dancing like lions in the wild. . . .

Not ibuprofen, she realized, sinking into unconsciousness.

"I *told* her she was all fat and nasty—nobody would want her. I didn't know there were guys like Joey who liked *bleep* like that."

Currently there were four of the largest women

Chloe had ever seen on the TV. One woman didn't seem to have a neck at all, even when Chloe paused the TiVo to get a better look. Another had been to the hospital and had a fifty-pound tumor removed, without ever having realized it was there. Next to them were the men who loved them and across from them the siblings who reviled them. Now *this* was television.

When she had woken up, Chloe had been determined *not* to think about anything important or deep again for a while, but just to take advantage of being a sick little girl, recuperating in front of the TV.

Kim appeared at her door, silent as ever.

Chloe beckoned her in but held up a finger: the fat woman who had just been insulted was getting out of her chair and waddling over to try and hit her attacker.

"What's this?" Kim asked, coming over to her bedside and looking at the TV curiously.

"Jerry Springer," Chloe replied, shaking her head as it took four stagehands to pull the woman away from her sister.

"It seems sensationalist and distasteful," Kim said, wrinkling her nose. Chloe started to laugh, but then paused.

An ad came on and Chloe shut it off. "What's up?"

Even with Kim's alien features, it was easy to tell she was disappointed by something. She sat on the edge of Chloe's bed, gripping the covers with her foot claws for balance, and waved a manila folder of papers.

"I don't think we are related." She said it calmly, but Chloe could see her eyes flicker. "As far as the genealogical people have made out, you more closely resemble the Mai who fled to Turkey from Abkhazia in the nineteenth century. My family stayed in what is now Georgia."

Chloe didn't understand half of what she was saying. "You mean I'm Turkish, not Russian?"

Kim fixed her with a cool look. "You are Mai. Not 'Turkish' or anything else. There are no *human* nationals of any sort in your background."

Chloe had forgotten about that. She was a completely different race. Wonderful, colorful images of herself in scarves, black kohl eyeliner, and bangles, with belly-dancing music in the background—like at the restaurant her mom used to take her to—sadly faded.

"Is this my file?" she asked.

Kim shook her head. "No, it is a sort of general file with information on places we are all most recently from. I thought you would be interested. St. Petersburg, where Alyec is from." She passed Chloe pictures of an exotic city, with spires too long and thin to be mistaken for those of American churches. Onion domes dotted the skyline. Everything seemed to be covered in gold like a fairy-tale kingdom.

"What's this?" Chloe pointed to one of the other photographs, of a building with a wall of large white stone blocks. A woman was walking along it, a woman with long black hair. "It looks familiar. I saw it in a dream." She suddenly felt the crowded market street again, the shady, quiet alley with the horrible smell.

Kim looked at her strangely but turned the photograph over. "It is one of the old sulfur bath complexes in Sokhumi. This part of Abkhazia was a famous retreat with spas—the natural hot springs and mineral water there were supposed to have curative powers."

Sulfur . . . This is a little too weird.

"Does sulfur smell like rotten eggs?" she asked, afraid of the answer.

"Almost identically." Kim put the photograph down and looked Chloe in the eye. Her black velvety ears lay almost flat against her head, turned backward. Chloe couldn't tell if she was upset or listening for footsteps in the hall. "You dreamt that, too?"

"Yeah. It was humid, and there were people, and . . . it was kind of confusing. Modern and ancient at the same time. And it *stank*. But I remember that wall."

"Sokhumi is the city where our pride eventually settled after we left the Middle East for good. Only one of the Mai from that diaspora came *back* to Abkhazia—our previous pride leader. Her dream was to gather all of the scattered Mai in Eastern Europe and unite them somewhere, like the United States." She carefully put the photograph away and closed the folder. "But she was killed in a skirmish between the Abkhazians and the Georgians."

"There were other exiles, from all over, who rested and waited for her," Chloe murmured.

"What did you say?" Kim demanded, fixing her like a mouse with her eyes.

"In my dream I *was* the pride leader."

"That's . . . interesting," Kim said slowly.

"Do you think I could be related to her?"

Do you think she could be my mother?

Kim opened the notebook again and looked at the picture of the bathhouse in Sokhumi again. "It's possible. . . . But she had only one daughter that we know of, and she is dead. . . ." She sounded reticent, and somehow Chloe didn't think it had anything to do with the disappointment about the two of them not being related. There was something else. . . .

Maybe she was jealous of Chloe possibly being the daughter of the old pride leader. Maybe it meant something, like inheritance in an aristocracy. Maybe she would take over when Sergei's term was over. She wondered if that entailed anything besides running a real estate empire and tracking down lost and orphaned Mai.

What was it the two guards had said when they were rescuing her? *Where's our glorious Pride Leader? This wouldn't even have cost him a life. Assuming he* has *more than one.*

"Kim—before I went unconscious, one of the people who rescued me said something about the pride leader not risking losing 'one of his lives.' What did she mean by that?"

"Traditionally, in the past, the leader of the Pride is

also a true military leader, first into a battle or on the hunt, last to retreat—" One of her ears flicked. A moment later Chloe heard the noise, too: footsteps echoing loudly down the corridor. It sounded like Olga; she was probably coming to check up on Chloe.

Kim leaned close in, too close for a normal human. Kind of like Amy's cat, when he would push his nose and foul-smelling kitty mouth into Chloe's, smelling delicately around her face before withdrawing. "Listen to me, Chloe. *Do not tell anyone about your dream or what we spoke of,*" she hissed. "There are leaders, and there are *leaders*, Chloe King."

Fourteen

Paul might be complacent and all best buddies with Alyec, but Amy wasn't going to stand for it. If it were up to her stupid boyfriend, they would just sit back and do nothing until the world fell down. Which was exactly why she was skipping out of school early.

She'd given a half-assed excuse to her teacher about feeling sick and hadn't even bothered going to the nurse. Her brother's car was parked in the area of the lot reserved for seniors, and it had cost her an arm and a leg to borrow it: a guaranteed okay on any future favor of his choice. *It's not like he even needs it at Berkeley.* It was an ancient, all-black Chevy Malibu station wagon that he called the Batmobile. The Malibu was a pretty small car for its V6, though, so when she floored it, the car tore out of the school parking lot like a bat out of hell.

Amy zoomed through the streets and parked several blocks away from Chloe's house. She locked the car and went up to the front door, trying not to look around suspiciously, trying to make it look like she had every right to be there, pulling out Chloe's spare key and entering the house in the middle of the day when they both should have been in school.

Mrs. King usually came home around seven, and Amy had every intention of being out of there in an hour. Maybe she'd even go back to school. . . .

On second thought, who did she think she was kidding?

She had been planning this for several days and wore an appropriate outfit for breaking and entering (even if it was with a key): tight black jeans and a black tee, along with a black Emily sweatshirt whose hoodie had cat ears and sleeves that ended in gloves with claws. Perfect for a cat burglar. She had admired herself in the mirror for a while that morning. It was such a completely different look for her—all sleek and black. None of the crazy, bouncy, fringy, fluffy stuff she designed and wore. Her breasts stuck out a little bit; they almost looked as big as Chloe's in this outfit. What she really needed was a pair of long black leather boots à la Emma Peel and maybe to dye her hair black, but Paul didn't like it when she changed her hair color—he'd always liked the original shade.

She carefully closed the door behind her and listened for a minute. If anyone was staking out the place, there was no sign: everything looked fairly normal in the King household. No furniture was overturned, nor was there any other sign of violence. Just to be safe, however, Amy pushed herself up against the wall and slid toward the stairs, ducking when she got in front of windows, doing a crouching run up the staircase.

Which resulted in a very non-cat-burglar trip on the top step and a flying fall that nearly smashed her chin against the bathroom door. Most of Amy's life was spent trying to *get* noticed and stand out; this sneaking thing was entirely new to her. She pulled herself up into what she hoped looked like a shadow and tiptoed into Chloe's room.

Once again everything seemed normal, maybe a little dustier than usual but not noticeably changed. Chloe's computer was properly shut down. Amy turned it on, using the special black gloves so she wouldn't leave any fingerprints. She admired them while it booted up, then went online and logged onto Chloe's e-mail—her friend had had the same password for years: adopTED5.

Aha.

Chloe religiously purged her trash to keep her mailbox from going over its size limit, downloading and saving all of the particularly juicy letters in case her mother ever found her way on. She did *not*, however, empty her sent mail folder as often as she should—and was far too painstaking about adding names to her address book. After just a couple minutes of poking around, Amy found brian9@bitsy.net and, searching Chloe's "locked" Word documents, confirmed that it was *the* Brian that Chloe had been interested in.

Amy then signed off and switched Hotmail over to one of her own alias accounts—one that she used when she didn't want to be found, for contests and spam and mailing lists and stuff—and sent Brian an e-mail. Early on, Amy had decided to handle everything Chloe from foreign computers, not her own, in case someone was capturing her IP address.

Brian: This is from one of Chloe's friends. Where is she? Can you help us? Alyec seems to know something but won't tell. E-mail me ASAP.

Then she made sure it sent properly, deleted it out of the sent mail, and purged the trash. She checked it again to make sure it was really gone, cleared Explorer's cache for temporary files, and started to even defrag the hard drive—to *really* make sure all the information was gone—but looked at her watch and realized it would take twenty minutes. So Amy shut down, mission accomplished, and prepared to sneak back out.

Just like out of the movies, she was halfway down the stairs when the phone rang. Amy froze, flattening herself against the wall so hard that static electricity lifted her frizzy red ends straight up against the wallpaper and her shoulder almost dislodged a picture. She waited, frozen, knowing intellectually that it was okay to move but unable to make herself. She scanned the room until voice mail picked up, counting the seconds.

She noticed something that she wouldn't have if she had just snuck immediately back out. *Nothing in the house looks moved.* Like for a while. There was a stillness to it, and though there were no layers of dust, there was a palpably stale feeling about the place. It even smelled a little old, like the garbage had been sitting there for just a day or two too long; there was no tang of cleaners or soap or perfume or anything that connoted movement or life in a house of two women.

Shaken by this realization, Amy left the house less carefully than she'd entered—after all, she was only human, which was exactly what the people watching her exit the house wanted to be sure of.

Fifteen

A new loving family, a secret race of people like her, no more school ever again, and all Chloe could think about was how bored she was. Her "internship" at Firebird mainly involved stuffing envelopes, making copies, collating large stacks of contracts, and taking orders from the obnoxious Mai receptionist.

While she was waiting for a stack of . . . something, she wasn't sure what, from Igor, Chloe thought about her and Amy's dream of setting up a shop somewhere. Amy would design the clothes and Chloe would run the business. Assuming the two didn't kill each other, it would be a match made in heaven.

Igor must have seen the look on her face.

"You should become a full-time paralegal," he said, smiling.

"Wow. This for a living," Chloe said deadpan, tapping the stack he was adding to. "That would be just great. For my *entire* life."

"Remember, it is hard for people like us to integrate completely," Igor said seriously. "That's why it was so good for Sergei to set this up here." He was wearing khakis, a button-down with a fashionable tie, and suede shoes. The way he leaned back in his chair and clasped his hands behind his back made him look like any young professional: a little bit arrogant, but bright eyed and smart.

Pity about the name. Maybe assimilation would have been easier if the Mai hadn't named their kids after horror film characters. With just a slight tilt of her nose to the air Chloe could tell he was Mai. It wasn't a smell, exactly, but a feeling.

"Is this why he's pride leader?" she asked, waving her hand around the office.

"He is pride leader because when the previous one was killed, he bravely took up her mission of trying to reunite the Eastern European Pride." Chloe wanted to jump in and prove her knowledge to the older boy by saying yeah, yeah, the Abkhazian Diaspora, etc., but decided maybe it would be a good idea to pretend to know *less* than she did for once.

"He organized everyone after the Georgian violence, and when he immigrated, he began the process of bringing us all over. Sometimes legally, sometimes not so legally." His dark eyes were shining with admiration. "And he built all this—an *empire* of city real estate—from nothing, an immigrant! And a Mai. So in a way, yes, it's about all this but more, too."

"Seems pretty nice," Chloe said, meaning it. "So why does Alyec bitch about him not helping *his* family out?"

Igor chuckled. "Alyec is a whiner. Perhaps there is some prejudice—but the ones in St. Petersburg, Moscow, and even Kiev were better off than the Abkhazians. Sergei wanted to help out the most desperate first."

"Oh." She looked around for something to do now that their conversation was over. Her foot tapped spastically.

"I know what you need!" Igor said, suddenly popping up out of his chair and pointing at her. "You are all itchy and nervous and bored. You need a—" He suddenly looked around and trailed off. "A hike," he finished lamely.

"Oh. Boy. That will fix *everything*," Chloe answered with as much sarcasm as she could muster. Currently she was wearing a pair of expensive jeans—probably picked out by Olga or Valerie—that were a size too small around her crotch, so she had to leave them unbuttoned and wear a big, stupid, trendy wide leather belt around her waist. The sweater was light pink cashmere. She still had her Sauconys, but everything else wasn't hers and didn't feel like hers. Like her room, like her new family, like this crappy new part-time job—which didn't involve clothes *or* a cash register.

"Good," Igor said, taking her at face value.

Chloe wasn't sure if it was being Mai or Eastern European that prevented everyone there from getting sarcasm.

* * *

She had dinner that night with Sergei. It had become their little ritual on days that he worked late: she would come to his office and he would clear his desk. They would order Chinese, pizza, whatever they were in the mood for, and play a game of chess. Chloe never thought she would be good at it, but she was slowly learning. She treasured these evenings no matter how much she hated losing.

She wondered if her real father—her *adoptive* father—played chess. She couldn't even imagine thinking about her real, *real* father. . . .

"Igor told me I should go on a 'hike'; what does that mean?" she asked after moving a pawn.

"A hike? I haven't the slightest idea." Sergei blinked at her with surprisingly innocent eyes. In his emotions and movements, he seemed *very* childlike sometimes—maybe that came from being in his forties without a wife and children. "*Oh!* He means a hunt. Ah, that Igor, he is a smart one. I think they are organizing one for this Saturday. Do you know anything about raising wild-cats—bobcats, cheetahs? For pets?"

Chloe had no idea what this had to do with anything, so she shook her head. Sergei got up and came around to her side of the desk and sat on its edge, looking at her seriously, like he was giving her a very important father-daughter lecture. Chloe prepared to be bored, but it was sort of a nice new feeling.

"People up in Oregon and other places raise wild cats to sell. Some make great pets, like bobcats and lynxes, if they have been bred and raised properly by a loving family. But no matter how gentle, well behaved, and obedient a cat is, no matter how much regular cat food he can stomach—once a month the good breeders throw a live chicken into the pens and let what happens happen."

Chloe felt nausea rise as she imagined feathers and blood and screams.

"They have to do this, Chloe," he said gently, "because you cannot completely breed out a cat's basic nature. They need to hunt, they need to play with their prey, and they need to kill. We are no different. We have always been hunters. Nomads. We never grew our food; we went after it in the wild.

"If you feel anxious and trapped—if you have the urge to *run* at night and chase and follow—you need to give in to it once in a while. We cannot run free like we used to before the world grew civilized and the land was fenced off, but we must still obey the ancient instinct."

Chloe suddenly understood part of the Tenth Blade's credo. A Mai gone mad with hunt lust in a city or town probably *was* a dangerous thing. She decided to keep that thought to herself, however; somehow she suspected Sergei wouldn't share that conclusion.

"So we do this every month? Go hunting?"

Sergei laughed. "Not *every* month, Chloe. It has nothing to do with the moon, or your feminine things, or clockwork. Sometimes it's just . . . time to go."

* * *

Time to go.

Chloe thought about this while she waited by the Ford Explorer. It was dusk and they were on top of a hill somewhere near Muir Woods. It was a sharp hill, new and ridged, not like the older storybook rolling hills on the way there. A bright star shone in the south, although how Chloe knew the direction was south, she couldn't have said. Below, the land ran steeply down to a bowl of forest and scrub with smaller hills within it, like the bottom of a scenic snow globe. But instead of plastic flakes, darkness gathered at the bottom.

About a half-dozen Mai were there, speaking in low voices. They were all women. Olga and Valerie were there along with three she didn't recognize, one of whom she knew was Simone, the dancer who also lived at the mansion. Chloe never saw her in its halls.

Most of the women seemed to be in their thirties. They were all beautiful. They all had high cheekbones and thick, shiny hair; even with the different eye and hair color and body shape, it was easy to see a racial similarity once Chloe began to look for it.

One of the things they all had in common was how inhumanly they walked: standing mainly on their toes and moving with a careless precision that could have only been carefully choreographed by a human ballerina.

A dark-eyed woman Chloe didn't know began the evening with a chant, a strange hymn in a foreign tongue that went from low whispers to beseeching cries.

Her voice was good but alone and sometimes lost in the breeze—which made it even creepier. Chloe caught the name Sekhmet once or twice, but that was about it.

Afterward they were silent.

"I have a scent!" one of them hissed. She had yellow eyes, orange hair, and a round face that resembled Sergei's but a cool, high forehead and neck that could have easily gotten her on the cover of a fashion magazine. She wore a tank top and had tattoos of leopard spots ringing her upper arms.

They all cocked their heads, sniffing the air. Chloe did, too, and when the faintest breeze changed directions, she had it: a musky scent that made her think of herbivores, even though she wasn't sure she had ever precisely smelled anything like it before.

A deer. They were going to run down a deer.

The redhead who'd first caught the scent pointed and the rest began running, following the direction of her finger. Chloe paused, thinking about the mountain lion attack on a jogger that she and Brian had argued about just a few weeks before. He had insisted the lion should be put down for attacking a human; she had suggested the unfairness of humans moving in and destroying the lion's habitat.

Now she wondered if the attack had been by a lion at all.

The air tickled her nose again: the deer was farther away. *Getting away.*

She ran. Her companions were rarely visible: once they descended off the top of the hill and into the edge of the woods, the Mai darted in and out of shadows, keeping a more or less straight line along the scent of the deer but out of sight of anyone or anything that might be watching.

Clouds raced across the sky as fast the hunters beneath them. They slipped from the moon, and the blanketing shadows parted for just a few seconds: the bushes and trees went from gray and purple to white and silver-green, then faded back as the foggy curtain closed again. Chloe felt her legs pumping smoothly below her. Her arms moved at her sides as though they were pushing the air behind her to speed her up. Her lungs felt like bursting, but the air was light, inspiring her to run harder. Chloe leapt over a bush and laughed. *This is what it's supposed to be like.* Running with a purpose, running with her pride.

She paused for a moment to smell the air again and continued: they were catching up. Even though they were two-legged, they were running down a *deer*. A cat's growl sounded behind her. Chloe didn't answer. She went where her senses told her: to a clearing up ahead, a long field in the open. Chloe could feel the closeness of the brambles begin to give way to something that was open to the stars.

She came out suddenly, before she could stop herself. Momentum caused her to almost tumble over the rock she paused at—a beginner's mistake. She saw the deer. It, too, had paused and was flicking its long ears left and right. It seemed to look right at Chloe with big dark eyes, but she knew that if it actually *saw* her, it would have begun running again; the Mai were downwind from it. The deer was beautiful, and Chloe could barely wait for it to begin running again so they could resume the chase.

The deer must have heard something; it suddenly turned and leapt, a beautiful four-legged spring from a standstill that Chloe had only seen on nature programs. The smell of the terrified animal hit her nose with a slap, and before she knew it, Chloe was running again.

She saw her companions emerge from the bush and silently nodded at them in greeting as the pack drew up into a close formation, the redheaded girl taking up the rear. The deer flashed into darkness and the six women plunged after it into the woods, where Chloe could hear nothing but her own breathing and heartbeat, not a footstep of those around her.

They shot out into the bright moonlight again—the doe was only twenty feet in front of them. One woman pulled ahead with a series of springs and leaps that were so far from human that anyone watching would have been hard-pressed to recognize her as a form of sentient life.

Chloe suddenly realized what was going to happen.

They were on a *hunt*. There was the deer, there was the hunter.

She stopped running and turned her head, covering her eyes.

The girl before her let forth a cry—it was *Valerie,* Chloe realized, a little stunned. She put her hands over her ears and waited, unwilling to experience anything of what she knew had to come next. Her chase lust vanished.

"Hey, not a bad first hunt, eh?"

Chloe opened her eyes. One of the other women approached her, speaking gently. She was in her late thirties, as fit and taut as a circus performer. Her long hair, tied back for the chase, now swung freely to her waist. Her accent was pure Californian; she must have been here even before Sergei. "No rabbits, not a lot of blood—are you okay?"

"I'm just, uh . . ." Chloe wasn't sure what she wanted. "It's all a little, uh . . ."

"You feel better than you did before—the night you tried to sneak out?" She said this with a grin.

Chloe opened her mouth to snap back at her, but now that she thought about it, Chloe realized she really *was* a lot more relaxed. She still wanted to see her mom, but the insane urgency was gone.

"Yeah," she answered slowly.

"Here." Valerie came by with a bottle and handed it to Chloe. "To the hunt and your health!"

Chloe eyed the rim carefully, looking for bits of blood. Then she tipped it and took a huge swallow of the ice-cold, perfectly smooth vodka. The women's laughter rose on the smoke of the campfire up to the stars above them.

* * *

They returned to the mansion at seven or eight the next morning. It was like nothing Chloe had ever experienced before. The six of them spent the night laughing, talking, singing, passing around the vodka, and cooking deer steaks. It was like one of those New Age women-power touchy-feely weekend getaways she had seen in movies or in ads for antihistamines, completely unselfconscious and natural. She had tried a little bit of the deer—it was very different from the venison she'd once had at a restaurant her mom had taken her to, tougher and more gamey tasting. Nothing she would go out of her way to eat again, and now that the chase lust was gone, she couldn't help thinking about the doe's eyes and face right before they'd killed it. It made her feel a little sick or, at the very least, not so hungry.

Some stayed up all night and some—like Chloe—had dozed off. She should have been cold, but the campfire was warm, and she found she could just pull her arms into her shirt and retain her heat that way. She thought about the desert in her dream and how cold it must have been at night.

When she awoke, she had the feeling that there had been lions in her dream again, but she couldn't remember what had happened. There was just a vague lingering presence of a familiar warmth and coarse, honey-colored fur.

When they came in the next morning, Chloe felt achy but good, like she had hiked a mountain or had a really good workout. A couple of the women brought the rest of the deer into the back and finished butchering it or doing whatever it was they had to do, but Chloe went straight to the kitchen for coffee and a muffin—she was starving.

Kim was there, blowing delicately on a mug of green tea. Chloe wondered if there was *anything* the girl did that wasn't healthy, pure, or proper.

"How was the hunt?" the other girl asked politely.

"Great . . . I think," Chloe added. "I'm surprised you didn't come along—it seems right up your alley."

"I'm not sure what I think about it."

Chloe looked at her in surprise. The girl with the cat ears, slit eyes, and claws didn't know what to think about a *hunt*?

"I have given the matter a considerable amount of thought and prayer and meditation," the girl explained, seeing Chloe's expression. "We are hunters, yes—but the time of *needing* to hunt for food is over. Should we still do this and kill? Or would the gods consider it a waste?" Kim shook her head. "I don't have an answer yet." And she padded silently out of the room.

Chloe frowned, more confused than ever.

Sixteen

Amy and Paul were at his house, actually studying together for once. Amy sat on his tiny twin bed, Paul on the floor next to her, her legs often wrapped around his shoulders. Sometimes he would lean over to kiss her calf . . . and another half hour would disappear before they got back to work. But on the whole they were fairly productive. The room was quiet, much quieter than in Amy's household, and Mrs. Chun came up occasionally with a plate of cookies and to "make sure they weren't doing anything"—although she was obviously kind of hoping they were. Compared to his cousins, Paul was an extremely well-groomed, hygienic, cool dresser . . . and Mrs. Chun was a fanatic devotee of *Queer Eye for the Straight Guy*. She'd come to her own conclusions about her son, concerned that the divorce was somehow screwing him up.

Everything was still very neat in Paul's house but light: things were missing that Amy couldn't quite put her finger on, some essential furniture or spirit seemed to be gone. The Chuns were polite and amicable when it came to dividing up their possessions, but the whole place was a testament to their separation. Depressing.

Paul's iMac made some backward-sounding music noise, recognizable only to Amy as a tune by Siouxsie and the Banshees. "Mail for me!" she cried, leaping up and almost taking Paul's head off as her feet hit the ground.

"Who is this? You've been checking your mail all evening. You got another boyfriend or something?" Paul asked, straightening his shirt and looking back at his book. Amy clambered onto the stool in front of the two-by-three-foot wood board that passed for his desk, kept immaculately clear of the hundreds of books, records, and CDs that crowded the rest of the room. She hit enter twice: her account had no password on his computer; she had no secrets.

Her eyes widened when she saw the address of the sender.

"It's from *Brian*." She took her purple pen and wound it through her hair, sticking it down the middle of the knot to keep it all up off the back of her neck.

"Brian who?" Paul asked, not really interested. Then he looked up, realizing. "Brian *who*?"

"Chloe's Brian."

He couldn't see her face, but Amy flinched, waiting for the inevitable.

"Why is he e-mailing *you*?" He put his book down and got up to stand behind her and read over her shoulder.

Amy, you and Paul need to STAY OUT OF THIS. You're safer not knowing any more than you already do. Your lives could be endangered.

I don't know where Chloe is, but I've had word from her that she's safe.

Brian

P.S. Don't talk to Alyec about this anymore either.

"Where did you get his e-mail address?" Paul asked, wanting to solve that mystery before he tackled any of the other number of issues this missive brought up.

Amy sighed. "I cut out of school early on Wednesday and went over to Chloe's house. I broke into her computer. I also e-mailed him from there."

"You did *what*? *Why?*"

"Because Alyec won't talk, Chloe's still missing, and we still don't know *anything*!" she said, beginning to feel less defensive and more pissed off. Her blue eyes flashed and she stood, putting her hands on her hips. It would have been a far more effective gesture if the pen hadn't chosen that moment to pop out of her hair and fall to the ground.

"Besides that message from Chloe herself, two people have already told us she's safe—two people close to her. What more do you want?" Paul said, his voice also rising.

"What do you mean, 'two'?" Amy asked, frowning.

Already caught, Paul didn't have time to retreat into his blank look.

"What do you mean, *two*?" Amy repeated, pushing her face closer into his. "Brian and *who*?"

"I talked to Alyec," he finally admitted, "after you totally accused him of everything. I talked to him calmly and rationally, and he told me that she was fine, and he would tell her that we were worried about her."

"Oh, so *that's* how it is?" Amy shrieked. "You approach Alyec all man-to-man like after your hysterical girlfriend screws everything up and he just tells you everything?"

"It worked, didn't it?"

"Assuming he's even telling the truth. Why didn't you tell me?"

"Why didn't you tell me about your little breaking-and-entering routine?"

They both fell silent, staring each other angrily in the eyes. Then they both looked away. The answer to both the questions was the same: they were afraid the other was going to disapprove and freak out over it.

Which was exactly what had happened.

Then Paul laughed. "I can't believe you actually broke into the Kings' house."

"I know where the key is," Amy admitted sheepishly, also smiling.

They were quiet again, too full of their own thoughts

to say anything, for the second time that evening—and for the millionth time that week.

"When I was there? At Chloe's?" Amy began, quietly and more calmly. "It was weird—like it hadn't been lived in for a while. Nothing was messy, but it just had this *stale* feeling. A little dusty or something." She screwed up her eyes, trying to think about the last time she had been there, before they'd walked across the bridge, the last time they'd seen Chloe. "I don't think the glasses near the sink were washed," she hazarded, "but I'm not sure."

"Too bad they have voice mail," Paul said with a wry smile. "You could have seen if the answering machine light was blinking out of control with all the calls we left her. I don't suppose you have their password for *that*, do you?"

"No," she pouted. "If I did, there are a lot of messages I left over the years that I would have erased an hour later, when I calmed down."

Paul smiled and ran his hand up through her hair at the base of her neck. Amy closed her eyes and pushed her head back into his hand.

"Maybe it's time we called Mrs. King at work," he suggested quietly, picking up the phone.

Amy looked at him in surprise, then at her watch. "It's ten after five—she'll definitely be there."

He dialed and Amy pressed her head to the other side of the phone.

"Greenston and Associates," the receptionist said in a deep, interested, expensive-receptionist voice.

"Hello, can I speak with Anna King, please?" Paul spoke in an even voice. His tone might have been youthful, but the sound was polite and professional, something Amy never could have accomplished.

"No, I'm sorry, she's away on vacation this week. Can I help you or direct you to another lawyer?"

Amy and Paul looked at each other.

"Uh . . ." Paul cleared his throat. "Where did she go?"

"I'm afraid I can't divulge that kind of personal information," the receptionist said regretfully. "I hope it's someplace warm."

"When will she be back?"

"She has a *lot* of vacation time saved up, so I'm not exactly sure precisely which day—would you like her voice mail? She often checks it when she's away."

"Uh, thanks anyway. It's nothing urgent. I'll call back in a couple of weeks."

"Thanks for calling."

He slowly hung up the phone. Both of them stared at it.

"*Now* can we do something?" Amy finally demanded.

Seventeen

This was a different sort of dream, restless and real. It was daylight and silent; Chloe's feet made no sounds in the harsh grass beneath her feet. The broad blades cut into her soles, but it didn't matter. The only thing that mattered was the hunt. She saw her quarry on a rolling hill below her, a familiar doe who paused to watch a plane overhead. There was something wrong with that, but through her thickened mind Chloe couldn't figure it out.

With two powerful leaps she flew over yards of scrub, landing in the middle of the perfect road that separated her from the kill. The pavement was velvet black with solid yellow lines and seemed to focus all of the sun's heat on her. She prepared to leap again.

The deer turned toward her, as if it had known she was there all along.

"Chloe," it said, in an achingly familiar voice.

Chloe froze and screamed, but no sound came out.

* * *

She sat up suddenly in her bed—no, the couch. It was the middle of the night—no, she checked her clock and it was only seven thirty. *Another nap,* she realized. Chloe had drifted off to sleep again while she tried to plow through *The History of the Mai.* It was Bible thick and combined all of the confusing names of a Russian novel and the deadly dullness of a badly translated history text. She fell asleep fairly easily these days; if she was full, warm, and not immediately occupied, it seemed like sleep was the inevitable next step.

Chloe rubbed her temples with her knuckles. The doe in her dream had spoken with her mother's voice.

It was the scariest nightmare Chloe had ever had.

Just a few weeks ago she'd been fighting with her mom, making up, going to work, and hanging out with her friends. And now she was . . . *not.* She fingered the soft, richly colored velvet spread she had slept on. She squinched one eye shut, noticing how she could suddenly see all of the individual furry threads in different shades of ruby, like through a magnifying glass. Then they turned darker and matted down, sucked up into the weave of the fabric, as her tear was slowly absorbed by it.

She sat up again.

"I have to get out of here," she said aloud. "I want . . ." She couldn't quite figure out what she wanted. She ran a hand through her hair. A haircut? Some new vintage clothes? She leapt up and ran out of the room, suddenly terrified by the silence.

Out in the hall she slowed herself down, embarrassed by her behavior. Then she pulled her cell phone out of her back pocket and turned it on. Technically she didn't need to use it for *this* phone call—no one cared; in fact, they probably encouraged her speaking to Alyec. Only an eighth of a battery left and she had to talk to him *now*.

"'Alloo?" he asked, accented, as if he expected someone Russian to call.

"I need to go out," she said without preamble.

"Chloe!" She could hear the happy boyish grin on his face. Simple, just glad that she had called. "Didn't you just go out on a hunt?"

"I don't want . . . ," she growled, shaking her hands in frustration. If she couldn't make *Alyec* understand, she was doomed. "I just want to go out and do something *normal*. Fun. You know? *Fun?* Like a date?"

"I don't think Sergei will let you out alone with me. I'm a pretty strong boy, you know, but not a trained bodyguard."

"Okay, okay." Chloe thought furiously. "We'll make it a *group* date. He can't object to that, can he? A bunch of us—whatever goons he wants to send along with us—we'll *all* go out. To a *movie* together. How about that?"

She fell back against the wall and slid down until she was sitting on the floor. "I just want to go out," she said miserably. "I want to eat popcorn." *Not wild deer.* "I want to drink a blue slushy, watch stupid previews, and use a crappy public bathroom with ugly tiles and mirrors that show all my zits."

There was a long pause at the other end. She waited for Alyec to ask about that last thing—she wasn't sure why she had said it but remembered when she and Amy used to go in before and after a movie and make faces and put on lip gloss. Amy would complain about the size of her nose, wrinkling it, and Chloe would bitch about getting breasts too early.

He didn't let her down.

"I'll see what I can do. But your skin is perfect, Chloe. You have no zits."

Sergei said he couldn't refuse a thing to his adoptive daughter, which was how Chloe, Igor, Alyec, Valerie, a couple of the kizekh—the same ones from the other night—and Chloe wound up sitting around the lounge with the entertainment sections of different newspapers.

And Chloe was reminded how, no matter what your race was, whether you were human or Mai, trying to get more than three people in a group to decide on a movie was a royal pain in the ass.

"I would like to see *The Russian Ark*," Valerie said. "It's still playing at a couple of art houses."

The two guards nodded in approval.

"Kiss ass," Chloe muttered.

"Well, okay," Valerie admitted gamely. "I would rather see the new Hugh Grant movie."

"Is Julia Roberts in it?"

"No, but Reese Witherspoon plays his niece. . . ."

"No, thank you," Alyec said, sticking his tongue out in disgust.

"How about *Hills of the Dead*?" Igor asked.

"Yeah!" Alyec agreed, leaping, Mai-like, onto the back of Igor's chair and looking over his shoulder.

"Absolutely not," Valerie said, sticking out her jaw—a lot like Amy. "Horror movies freak me out."

"That's the point, dumbass," Alyec said. "I hear Raymond Salucci did the score," he added to Igor, who nodded excitedly.

"It's gonna suck," Chloe said hesitantly. Honestly, she didn't mind—but Valerie did look really upset.

"How about *The Return of the King*?" the other girl suggested, offering a compromise.

"I've seen it four times already," one of the guards replied, shaking his head. Chloe shot the scarred older man a look. He just shrugged. Although she was almost positive that he was one of the ones from the night she'd been ambushed by the Tenth Blade, the other kizekh, the woman, had called him "Dima," but tonight he had introduced himself as "Dmitri," and she was pretty sure that was the name Sergei had used, too. She didn't know what the woman's name was. *Living here is worse than being in a Russian novel.*

Chloe scanned the newspaper, hope dwindling. She didn't really give a rat's ass what they saw—as long as she was out, at a movie, with crowds of normal people around her. *Well*, she thought as she eyed the two guards, already standing protectively behind her, *somewhat farther around me*. The guards had their arms crossed like storm troopers.

"Hey!" She suddenly had an idea and flipped through the newspaper, looking for the right ad. "The Red Vic always shows *Star Wars* at midnight on the weekends."

"I thought it was *Rocky Horror*," Igor said.

"Theater one. Theater two always shows *Star Wars*." She finally found the ad, the sort of cheap, tiny five-line text-only ad that gave away the theater's independent nature. "Yep. Midnight tonight."

"Fine with me," Alyec said, still balancing on the back of Igor's chair.

"Okay," Valerie agreed.

"Absolutely!" Igor grinned, big, thick white teeth showing for the first time since . . . well, since Chloe had met the serious young man. Even the two *kizekh* nodded. Who, after all, could say no to *Star Wars*?

"Let's get ready and be back here in an hour," Igor said, looking at his watch. "An *hour*," he added, giving Alyec a look.

"That still gives me time to kick your ass in Soul Calibur," Alyec said with a sweet smile. Valerie rolled her eyes and gave Chloe a look. Chloe smiled back, sympathizing. But she felt pretty sure that *she* could kick Igor's ass at it, too.

"You're on," Igor agreed, suddenly leaping up so that his chair tipped backward because of Alyec's weight, sending the other boy flying. But he did a neat little flip in the air and landed on his toes and one hand—somehow reminding Chloe of Nightcrawler in *X-Men United. Who needs movies when you* are *a mutant?*

She went back to her room to brush her hair and grab her jacket. The only makeup Chloe had with her was cherry-tinted lip gloss. She put it on as thickly as she could and mourned the fading of her healthy skin to a pasty paleness from being inside for so long. She grabbed her cheeks and pinched them hard, remembering something out of *Gone with the Wind* or some other old movie. It gave her a little color; she hoped it would last.

Kim was padding silently upstairs as Chloe headed back to the lounge, reading a book she held before her with the deference of an ancient monk reading his hours. The brown tunic-length sweater with bell sleeves that she wore did nothing to detract from the image.

"Hey," Chloe called, catching up to her. "Want to go to a movie? A bunch of us are going."

Kim looked at her as if it was the strangest thing she had ever been asked.

"Thank you," she said slowly, "but I have some reading to do. . . ."

She said it unconvincingly.

"Come *on,*" Chloe said, exasperated. "It's a Friday night. You have exactly jack shit reading to do. I don't care *how* homeschooled you are; classes are over for the day, chiquita."

Kim looked her over again, curious about Chloe's strange energy and goodwill. *I certainly haven't displayed a lot of it since I came here,* Chloe realized.

"I haven't been to a movie in a long time," Kim hazarded, closing her book.

For some reason, Chloe couldn't imagine Kim *ever* going to a movie. "Great. Get your coat. Come on."

"Do the others know you're asking me?"

She said it in the same infuriatingly calm, even tone she always used—which kind of reminded Chloe of Paul—but there was a catch in her voice this time, the subtlest swallow. Her eyes were large, her pupils so wide that you almost couldn't tell they were slits.

The armor of the pious scholar had just cracked a little, and Chloe felt a rush of pity for the poor girl, aloof and alone. But if she did or said anything that was the slightest bit patronizing, it was all over.

"No, but I totally think there's enough space in the cars." She had no idea if this was true, but it was the *correct* answer. Kim looked relieved at Chloe's brashness, the assumption that everyone would just do what she said—and let Kim come—without question.

"I'll get my coat, then, and meet you in the lounge."

"Uh—what about your . . . ?" Chloe indicated her ears, not sure what to say. "I mean, is it going to be all right?"

Kim gave what was almost a smile through her teeth, pointy and sharp. "Yes. They always just think I'm some freaky goth kid."

Chloe smiled back. "Right on," she said, holding her fingers in a peace symbol.

Now that she thought of it, why *did* she just assume that the others would go along with whatever she said? Chloe wondered at her behavior as she went back to watch Alyec and Igor. Why would anyone disagree? Did people think Kim was that much of a freak and a pariah?

Alyec was jumping up and down, moving his body with the game pad, using his claws occasionally for a tight move. He threw his entire body into the game. Igor sat stock still, a serious look on his face, fingers barely moving across his own game pad. And he was royally kicking the other boy's ass. The two guards, looking almost like CIA agents, stood in the background, quietly waiting.

"Hey," Chloe said. She threw herself onto the couch with one leg over the side. "I just ran into Kim. She's gonna come with us."

"You're kidding," Igor said, but all his concentration was on the game.

Valerie came in, looking like a movie star. The cat was very strong in her, and even without Kim's eyes or ears, there was a barely contained power and sensuality beneath her features. Her eyes were heavy-lidded, like Sergei's, but with long lashes and a smoldering look. She slunk like a cat, too, smoothly and languidly. Her hair was lighter than Alyec's, an almost Marilyn Monroe blond. But natural.

Chloe tried to work up a little envy, but it was hard: she admired the other girl too much.

Of course, the fact that she had seen her take down a deer bare-handed might have something to do with the whole lack-of-envy thing.

"Ah, crap," Alyec said, throwing down the game pad as Igor executed his fatality. "You lucked out."

"No," Igor said easily, sliding back to put his hand on Valerie's knee, "you just suck."

"I'm ready," a voice said behind them.

Everyone in the room turned. Kim stood, all bundled up in a fake black fur coat that went down to her knees. A black baseball cap was pulled down over her ears. Giant black Doc Martens, several sizes too big to fit her foot claws, clunkily covered her feet. She looked a little defensive.

"That's a . . . very interesting outfit," Valerie said, as tactfully as she could manage.

Kim gave her a cold, dismissive look.

"I don't think we can fit everyone in the Explorer," one of the guards said.

"That's okay," Alyec said smugly, drawing on his leather jacket. "I have a car with me."

"Oh no," Chloe realized. "It's *not* . . ."

But he just grinned.

* * *

It *was*, in fact, the exact same hatchback he had stolen before from the senior running back at school. Igor and Valerie went with the two guards, muttering something about Alyec's proficiency at driving.

"This is your car?" Kim asked, getting into the backseat without being asked.

"Don't ask," Chloe recommended. "And buckle up."

"It's . . . very nice," she said doubtfully, unconsciously imitating Valerie's earlier comment.

Chloe checked the rearview mirror a couple of times to see how the girl was handling it, but Kim looked steady no matter how fiercely Alyec took the turns; she had one hand braced on each side of the car and swung between them, bouncing.

"This is great." Chloe sighed. "This is just what I need."

"I'm glad." Alyec leaned over and kissed her on the cheek. Except for their occasional sort-of dates, they had actually been far less physical in the last week than . . . well, ever. Sergei never said anything aloud about his feelings toward Alyec, but it was obvious there was a tension between them and some invisible line her boyfriend could not cross. But it didn't feel like a normal "don't date my daughter" scenario; Chloe got the feeling that if it were anyone besides Alyec, it might have been okay. She made a mental note to ask someone about that sometime—maybe Olga.

"Hey, Kim," Alyec yelled to the backseat, trying to be sociable. "You ever see *Star Wars*?"

"Of course I've seen *Star Wars*," she snapped; the *you idiot* was understood.

There was a long pause.

"Who's your favorite character?"

Chloe caught the girl's eyes widening.

"The . . . ah . . . furry one. Not only do his physical characteristics set him apart, but the . . . obvious subservient dynamic between him and the . . . uh, *protagonists* indicate his role as either a hero-ally or comic-mentor archetype."

"So what you're saying," Alyec said philosophically, squealing around a corner, "is that you've never seen *Star Wars*."

Kim glared at him. Chloe was glad their cat abilities didn't include anything like shooting lasers from their eyes. If they had, Alyec would have been fried.

"No. I have *not* seen *Star Wars*," Kim admitted, then looked out the window so she wouldn't have to look at them.

Chloe laughed.

In the theater she wound up sitting between Kim and Alyec, since he and Igor and Valerie all insisted that since *Chloe* had brought the other girl, she had to sit next to her. Actually, it wasn't so bad. Kim was inordinately pleased with the popcorn, another humanlike thing Chloe had a hard time comprehending. But the girl with the hidden cat ears relished every bite, using her claw to spear one kernel at a time and carefully deposit it on her tongue, never taking her wide, unblinking eyes off the screen.

Igor and Alyec shouted lines with the characters and other lines *at* the beloved heroes with the rest of the crowd. Valerie and their two guards watched it in silence. Chloe had to answer a lot of whispered questions from Kim but didn't mind; she knew the script by heart and found it kind of fun to initiate a newbie.

"What is that they are on?"

"A consular ship."

"*Space*ship?"

"Uh, yeah. Starship, really."

And:

"Why is everyone cheering? What is the significance of that being a space station and not a moon?"

And:

"Stupid Alyec. I was closer than I thought. This story taps perfectly into Western archetypes—from the hero to the quest to the tragic hero. It is right out of Joseph Campbell. In fact, there are even parallels between it and the Egyptian story *The Tale of the Shipwrecked Sailor*. . . ."

"So, in the other movies, do they reveal Darth Vader as being Luke's father?" Kim asked casually, picking up a flyer and looking at the upcoming releases.

Alyec's jaw dropped. "How did you know that?"

"It is pretty obvious, if you know anything about mythology and religious tales," she answered smugly. Chloe grinned, then noticed Igor trying to win a stuffed animal from one of the claw vending machines for Valerie. "Hey, win me a toy, huh?" she demanded, handing Alyec a dollar. Then she pulled Kim after her into the women's room.

"I don't have to go," Kim protested.

This is so not like Amy. Chloe sighed. She would just have to make the best of it. She pouted into the mirror and applied more lip gloss. Kim watched her without saying anything, taking off her baseball cap briefly so she could scratch her ears.

"Hey," Chloe suddenly said, remembering. "What was that you were going to tell me the other day? About the pride leader?"

Kim looked startled. She licked her lips and tried to speak didactically, but something was worrying her. "Um, just that the leader of the Pride has to be the first to charge in and the last out of battle. The leader has to stay to defend the weakest, run into a burning house to save the slow. The leader gives his or her life for the Pride. Up to nine times, if necessary."

Chloe laughed. "Like a cat, you mean? Like . . ." Then she suddenly noticed how grim the other girl looked. "You're *serious*," she realized.

"A true leader proves him or herself," Kim said quietly. "It comes out in battle. In war. In times of danger and catastrophe. Usually leadership runs in families. Sometimes a Pride gets lucky and several warrior family members rule together. But sometimes it does not;

sometimes a person rises up in a time of need when there is no one else. And is killed and rises again."

"Pride leaders have nine lives?" Chloe repeated slowly, to make sure she understood.

"Not all . . . *pride* leaders. But true ones do. It is what protects our race."

Coit Tower. Her fall. The dreams. The lions. "This *wouldn't have cost him a life. Assuming he even* has *more than one.*"

Chloe opened her mouth. "Are there . . . uh . . . others? Who can do that?"

"Well, there were," Kim said almost mournfully. "As I told you, the only daughter of our pride leader—the one before Sergei—was murdered before she had a chance to prove herself, and no one else of this generation has shown any signs. *Or* risked their lives to find out."

Kim was gazing steadily into her eyes. Chloe blushed and turned away. She couldn't deal with this now. *Pride leader?* But sooner or later, she was going to need to think about what Kim had said.

When they got home, Chloe went immediately to Sergei's office. It was very late, but he didn't have normal sleeping patterns, and she wanted to tell him what a great time they'd had . . . and maybe talk about finally getting to call or see her mom. She would have said something to announce her presence, but about four Twizzlers were crammed into her mouth. Alyec claimed he had won them from the prize machine at the movies. Twizzlers were definitely *not* one of the prizes—only cheap stuffed animals and plastic jewelry and stuff like that—but Valerie said that apparently Alyec had spent an additional five dollars to the one that Chloe had given him trying to get her something and had finally given up and gone to the concession stand. Chloe had laughed—that was definitely something lighthearted and stupid that someone like Brian would *never* do.

The older man was standing behind his desk, talking urgently to one of the upper-ranked Mai in his company and two of the kizekh.

"So we agree. She presents too many liabilities, I'm afraid. Something will have to be done to remove her—"

He suddenly noticed Chloe, his blue eyes fixing on hers without recognition—for just a second. Then he warmed up. "That's all for now, gentlemen. Thank you." All three nodded at him in a way that was practically a bow and almost backed out of the room facing him, as she had seen Olga and Kim do.

"What was all that about?" she asked, sliding into one of the enormous chairs that no one had been sitting in.

"Someone who is not working out at the company," Sergei said quickly, shuffling papers together on his desk and sitting down. "We will have to let her go."

"Why did the goons have to know about it?"

"They are not *goons*, Ms. King. They are highly trained warriors." He and his adoptive daughter locked eyes for a moment. Then he sighed. "It is not about an employee, you are right. It is about a member of the Order of the Tenth Blade we have to try to eliminate. I am not just the leader of a company that employees my people, Chloe: I am also pride leader of the Mai. There are ugly and distasteful things that go along with such responsibilities."

Chloe nodded, but her mind raced. She had never seen a female member of the Order. That didn't mean there weren't any, and she had certainly never seen any of its leaders, so maybe she was someone in charge. But usually someone used the term *liability*—at least in the movies—to mean someone on the *home* team. Like someone who has some good points who still has to be gotten rid of.

Not me, right? The thought flashed through her brain, and Chloe tried to hide her concern.

Chloe *did* present extra danger to the Mai, especially with her stupid stunt the other night. But no, there were too few of them left for the pride leader to just randomly go around and have them murdered.

"These are tough decisions," he went on, "things that hopefuls like Alyec don't understand. Things that make a man old before his time."

"Alyec?"

Sergei chuckled. "He is one of the ones 'in line' should something happen to me. Or at least that's what he thinks."

"Why not Igor? Hey . . . do you have any Sprites?"

"Perhaps Igor. There are many good qualities about him," Sergei said, reaching into the mini-fridge by his desk and taking out a couple of cans. He passed one to Chloe. "He is responsible and serious—but he is going to be married soon. Some would say he lacks a certain, ah, *aggression*. He is more of a president than a CEO, if you know what I mean."

Chloe nodded, concentrating on opening her can and making a Twizzler into a straw. There was too much new information to think about.

"I'm feeling a little hungry—what do you think about half sausage, half pepper?" he asked, punching the number for the pizza place on his phone. Chloe nodded again. Then he noticed her inserting the Twizzler into her Sprite. "Chloe, whatever are you doing?"

Sergei had enjoyed learning how to bite off both ends of a Twizzler to make it into a straw and laughed heartily about how you were really supposed to do it with cheap champagne. They'd had a nice game of chess—he'd beat her roundly, of course, but gently—and he'd told her all about growing up in the Communist Soviet Union, both the food lines and the amazing education and intellectualism that Chloe had only read about.

When they left, he gave her a bear hug good night, but as soon as she began heading back to her room, the uneasiness she'd had about the meeting she'd interrupted came back. For the first time ever, the term *cult* came to her mind. Not that there weren't actual reasons in this case: they were a different race, completely set apart. But that didn't change the suffocating totality of the Pride; even when Chloe was allowed to do normal things, like going to the movies, it was with other Mai. She was completely cut off from the rest of the world.

When she got back to her room, Chloe opened her phone and dialed. She had left too many people on the outside worried for too long. It was time to see her family and friends. But she would do it differently this time, intelligently. Far from her home and the watching eyes of the Tenth Bladers.

"Brian? I have to see you. . . ."

Eighteen

The next day Chloe was still thinking about her mom, Paul and Amy, even Brian.

"Hey." Chloe knocked on the temple door as she walked in. As expected, Kim was there in the corner, meditating or reading a book or something.

Kim must have detected something in her tone, because when she looked up, one of her eyebrows was already cocked and suspicious.

"Can you do me a favor? I want to go out and meet a friend—a human one. Would you mind providing an alibi? I'll tell Sergei you're, like, instructing me in the way of the Mai or our history or the twin goddesses or something." She tried to make it sound as casual as possible. "That way the goo—uh, kizekh won't follow me."

"You want me to *cover* for you," Kim said in her even, toneless voice.

"Yeah," Chloe said uncertainly; she had no idea what the other girl was feeling.

"All right," Kim agreed just as tonelessly; she flicked her ears once and went back to her book.

"Hey, thanks! I owe you one."

The other girl just grunted, not looking up again.

Chloe turned to go, not sure what to do, feeling like the interview was over.

"I really enjoyed last night," Kim suddenly said unexpectedly, eyes still glued to whatever she was reading. "Thank you for inviting me."

This was about as much joy as she was ever going to get out of Kim, Chloe realized. She smiled. "No problem. We should totally do it again."

She turned to go but couldn't. Chloe realized she had already asked way too much of Kim, but the question had been gnawing at her since the possibility had been raised.

"So, uh . . . did you find out any more? About my parents? If my mom, was, uh, the previous Pride leader? Because, you know . . ." Chloe trailed off.

That caused Kim to look up. She fixed Chloe with her eyes and closed her book.

"Your biological parents, whoever they were, are probably *dead*."

Chloe jumped at the harshness of these words; while they were most likely true, they were spoken completely emotionlessly. It was like she had been slapped.

"You should worry about your *human* parents now, Chloe. They are alive. And they are probably being watched and probably in danger."

Chloe thought about the Tenth Bladers who'd caught her when she'd tried to go home. Home was a trap. They were expecting her to return home at some point. But what about her mom, the bait?

"Okay, chill," Chloe said, getting angry. She didn't even feel like pointing out how she only had *one* "human" parent. Was Kim acting all pissy because she'd never had any real family at all and was *jealous* of her? "I just want to know, all right? Who gave birth to me?"

"I will let you know as soon as Olga's people have found something," Kim said, opening her book again. The conversation was officially over.

Chloe left, still confused by the other girl's seeming animosity. Maybe it wasn't jealousy—maybe Kim, the one friend she had actually made since coming here, was now keeping her distance because of the danger surrounding Chloe. The thought only fueled Chloe to get out of Firebird. Now.

On the roof of the Sony Metreon, lying on her back and looking up at the sky, Chloe felt freer than she had in months. Thick clumps of gray clouds sped across the heavens like dumplings until they massed into a heavy blanket on the far eastern horizon. As they passed over the downtown area, they glowed orange from below, only regaining more natural shadows and sky colors as they headed out over the bay away from streetlights, neon signs, and other illuminating pollution.

She thought about how easy it would be just to run from rooftop to rooftop, never returning to the Mai, never returning to her school, and never returning home. Just living in the night. Not a street person . . . a *skyline* person, like Batman without his cave or his mansion. She could probably survive with her Mai abilities—heck, she knew how to run down a deer now. How hard would it be to steal something from a convenience store?

A lone figure came walking across the roof toward her. She didn't move; she could tell by his walk, sounds, and smells that it was Brian. He almost tripped over her, she was so black and still, blending in with the harsh shadows of the buildings.

He was perfect, like a vampire, his dark hair and eyes barely distinguishable against the night sky. The wind picked up and played with his hair a little, and he turned his head to look out at San Francisco. Chloe got a perfect view of his profile, from shadowed brow to bitten lips. A scarf waved behind him like the tattered cape of a worn-out superhero.

He lay down next to her, also looking up at the sky.

"Beautiful night," he observed. "Feels like a storm is coming."

"I want to run into it," Chloe said. "I want to run away."

Brian didn't say anything.

"I have everything I ever wanted. A father figure. A *rich* father figure," she added with a chuckle. "A family.

Being told, once and for all, that I really am *special.*"

"I wish I was special," Brian said with a smile, quoting Radiohead. "You're so fucking special."

Chloe grinned sadly and sat up. She looked back down at him. The scarf that framed his head was soft chocolate brown and cashmere, knitted with intricate little cream diamonds in the pattern.

"You made this, didn't you?" she said, feeling the unbelievably downy ends and thinking about what had first brought them together, his funny homemade knit hat with the kitty cat ears.

"Yep. Had a lot of recent angst I needed to get out." He smiled ruefully. "You can always tell how upset I am by how crazy intricate the patterns are."

"You haven't . . . seen my mom, have you?" Chloe asked wistfully.

"No. My movements are kind of circumscribed these days. I got into a *load* of trouble after the whole bridge incident."

"Oh." She didn't say she was sorry. Chloe wasn't sure exactly what she did feel. An overwhelming sadness. A sense of loss or of having too much. "The Pride . . . I think it's like a cult."

There. She'd said it.

"Welcome to my world." Brian sighed, also sitting up. "You never hear the term used around the house, but there really is *no* line between 'cult' and certain 'secret orders'."

"Hey, you've got freckles," Chloe suddenly noticed, reaching over to touch his cheek. They were brown and added a lightheartedness to his features that wasn't normally there, without making him look too cute.

"I've been outside during the day a lot more recently. Since being, uh, dropped from your case. It's been kind of nice. I've been shadowing your friends some, making sure that they're okay, but it doesn't seem like either side is interested in them." He took her hand. "Thanks for trusting me, Chloe. For meeting me here. It means a lot to me."

"I'm beginning to think that no one's innocent of *anything*," Chloe answered with a lopsided smile. "But at least I think I know where you stand."

They were quiet for a moment. He didn't let go of her hand. She cuddled into him and looked up at the sky again. She thought about their first *real* date, when they'd gone to the zoo, and she'd bought him a stuffed monkey, and they'd talked about all sorts of important things.

"How did your mother die?" she asked softly.

Brian squeezed her hand and then dropped it. He played with some pebbles on the roof before answering. "My father's family has been in the Order since . . . well, since it was documented. All the way back to the *Mayflower* and England. Before that, actually. One time we were barons or princes or something in Italy. Royalty." Chloe could tell that he was being modest and knew exactly what they were and wasn't saying. "Italy . . .

Christendom . . . knights . . . the Crusades . . . I don't want to bore you with a history lesson.

"My mother's family comes from Klamath Falls, Oregon," he said with a smile. "My grandparents own a berry orchard.

"I guess like with any secret club, there are those who marry and *don't* tell their husbands and wives about it and those who marry and *do* tell their husbands and wives about it. But my father went beyond all that. He encouraged my mom to become a part of it *with* him.

"I don't think she really wanted to, but that may be my own subjective memory of it. I don't remember her getting involved much when I was little; I *do* remember her disappearing off with Dad later on, for long meetings and trips away, and practicing in the weapons room."

He threw a pebble down and stared at his empty hand. "She was killed on a mission. When I was twelve. They were raiding a Mai hideout in LA. She was shot in the head. Her face . . . It was a closed-casket funeral."

Chloe sucked in her breath. It explained a lot about Brian.

"One of . . ." What did she say? *Us? The Mai? Them?* "She was killed by a Mai?"

Brian laughed angrily. "That's what I thought for years. You've been living with them for a while now, Chloe. Have you ever seen someone with a weapon?"

She thought about the kizekh Ellen and Dmitri. She couldn't really remember what they carried.

"The Mai don't use guns," Brian hissed. "They almost never use any weapon with a blade, even. I didn't realize this; I mean I knew it, but I didn't put two and two together until a couple of years ago. My father let me believe it for *years*. . . . I finally found out the truth. She was killed by a random gang kid. He saw her gun, thought she was undercover or something, and let her have it."

Chloe shuddered. There were no clouds above at that moment, just a hazy sky with a few brave stars cutting through like diamond-tipped blades.

"She was killed for a cause she didn't even really believe in," Brian finished. "By someone who wasn't even involved."

Chloe struggled, looking for something to say. "Why did your father want her to join so much?"

"Because he's the head of the Order, Chloe."

A thousand things made sense now. Why Brian hated his dad. Why Brian, though he questioned and didn't approve of things the Order did, was still in it. He had been *raised* in the Order! It was all he had known his entire life. . . . Trying to leave it would be like Chloe leaving her mom and her friends and living an entirely new life, with new ideas and rules and people.

Yep. Exactly.

Chloe laughed quietly, a little crazily. Brian looked up at her, alarmed.

"My 'adoptive' father is the head of the Pride."

Brian blinked at her for a moment, then laughed himself.

"Great. Just *perfect*," he said. He put his arm around her and hugged her close to his side, a comforting gesture.

"Did you mean it before? On the phone?" Chloe asked softly. "Did you really mean you . . . ?"

"Yes." Brian closed his eyes, frowning. "I *love* you, Chloe." It was obviously hard for him to say, for a million different reasons. "Absolutely."

No one had ever said it to her before. Not outside of jokes, or out of friendship, or stupid grade school crushes. Not even Alyec; there was always humor around the word when he used it, like "love of my life"; inflated, expressive, hyperbolic, and not really serious at all.

It made her giddy.

But how did *she* feel?

She didn't want to think about it right then. It might spoil the moment.

"But we can't—"

"Your lips are poison, Chloe," he said with a smile, knowing exactly how dramatic it sounded. "Your tears, your tongue, your saliva, your sweat . . . they would all kill me with extended contact."

Chloe leaned back, putting her head on his shoulder and his arms around her waist. Surely that was safe.

"We should go soon," he whispered in her ear, not quite touching it. She shivered at the feeling. "If we want to meet your friends on time."

" 'We'?"

"I'm not leaving you alone until you're by yourself

on the way home again. Your friends . . . They mean well, but they leave a trail as wide as the Grand Canyon." Chloe smiled, thinking of Amy and Paul trying to be stealthy. "Amy even found my e-mail address somehow. I told her to stay away, that it was all dangerous for them."

"She won't listen," Chloe said dreamily, pushing herself up against him more. She kissed his shoulder. "Let's just stay another minute or two?" she pleaded. "It's such a pretty night out. This is . . . *perfect*."

Brian opened his mouth to say something: that there were a thousand reasons why this wasn't perfect, starting with the fact that she was being hunted and ending with the fact that their relationship was ultimately doomed. But he swallowed whatever he was about to say.

"All right," he said, holding her more tightly. When she shivered, he took the scarf from around his neck and wrapped it around hers.

Chloe smiled and closed her eyes, but a single tear leaked out down her cheek.

She was supposed to meet Amy and Paul in the street behind Café Eland, private but close enough to the public where there couldn't be an attack. Brian kept assuring Chloe that the Order of the Tenth Blade would never hurt a human, that they took oaths to *protect* them, but Chloe only knew one thing: These days, wherever she went, trouble followed.

Brian shadowed her silently. She only heard or saw evidence of his presence once or twice along the way: a scuffed pebble in an alley, a shadow above. He was almost as adept at hiding as the Mai, and Chloe had the sneaking suspicion that the few times she thought she detected him, he was letting her.

She quickly checked out the coffee shop: 10:05, the back door was just swinging shut. In the summer the café put a couple of chairs out on the delivery dock in the back for its regular customers who knew they were there. Chloe scaled the fire escape of a building nearby and looked down.

Amy and Paul were there, Amy underdressed for the weather as always, stomping her feet, with her arms wrapped around some gigantic pink puffy coat that looked like it should be warm but obviously wasn't. Paul was looking around, a drink in one hand and a cigarette in the other, nervously tapping ashes onto the pavement below.

Something pulled inside Chloe, seeing her two friends from above. It was like in a book: she was apart, beyond them, not part of their story and lives. Before she could think any more along those lines, she dropped down neatly out of the sky in front of them.

"Holy *shit*," Paul said. Chloe was gratified to see that he was actually capable of losing his cool: half of his hot chocolate went flying.

"Chloe!" Amy shrieked. Both Paul and Chloe gave

her looks. "I mean, *Chloe*!" she whispered, then threw her arms around her friend.

"Hey," Chloe said weakly, the air being pushed out of her. Paul ruffled her hair.

"What the hell, King," he said, his voice thick with barely contained emotion. "Where have you been?"

"And what are you *wearing*?" Amy asked, looking at the expensive jeans and long-sleeved black tee with *Paris* in gold grommets across it, the mismatched but beautiful scarf.

"Someone else's stuff." Chloe hopped back up on the rail that cordoned off the delivery area. The move was as smooth and graceful and impossible as when she'd landed in front of them.

"Uh," Paul said, clearing his throat, not sure what else to say.

"It's a long story. I only have a few minutes. Anybody get me a coffee?"

Amy managed to pull a venti out of one of the pockets in her pink coat; it hadn't spilled at all. Chloe took it, slipped down from the rail, and slugged back several swallows gratefully. "Russians," she began, "like really sweet and disgusting drinks."

Then Chloe took a deep breath. There really was no simple way to say it.

"Okay. Here goes. My people, the Mai, are actually an ancient race of cat warriors. The Order of the Tenth Blade is a Knights-Templar-style organization that has been trying to wipe them out for the last five thousand years or so."

Amy and Paul just looked at her.

"There is no Russian Mafia," Chloe went on. "At least, not in this case. It's a race war."

"Okay . . . ," Amy said carefully, trying not to look around her to see if other people heard.

"I believe you," Paul said in a tone that meant exactly the opposite.

Chloe knew her friends well enough to be pretty sure that they were trying to figure out the fastest, quietest way to get her to the psych ward at a hospital.

Chloe sighed and held up her hand.

"Okay, does *this* convince you?"

With a whisper-soft *sslting* noise, she extended her claws.

"Mother*fuck*," Amy said, eyes widening like those of an anime character.

Paul grabbed Chloe's hand and looked closely at the base of her claws, feeling around the tips of her fingers for prosthetics or a glove or something.

"I have foot claws, too," Chloe said casually, trying not to laugh at their reactions. "And I think my eyes go all slitty—like diamonds—when I'm in the dark. I can see at night, you know."

"I don't believe . . . ," Paul said, not dropping her hand.

"Believe," Chloe suggested sweetly. She pulled away from him and leapt straight up so that she landed standing on the rail. Then she bent over and stood on her hands, using her claws to clasp the metal. She did a couple of backflips.

"Okay, the über-nails thing I could question," Amy finally said. "But the Chloe King *I* know could barely touch her toes."

"This is completely fucked up," Paul muttered with grudging admiration. "You're just like Wolverine. It's so unfair. *I* read comic books and *you* get the superpowers."

Chloe sat down, took another slug of coffee, and told them *everything*. Starting from the personal: the night she beat up the mugger to the night Alyec took her to the Mai, with extra details on what happened after her friends left. "I *knew* we shouldn't have abandoned you," Amy said, hands on her hips. Then Chloe moved on to the historic and impersonal: as much as she knew about the Order of the Tenth Blade and the Mai and the history of the Mai (with many mental apologies to the book of the same name she'd never finished).

And she finally told the truth—all of the truths—about Alyec and Brian.

"I wish *I* had claws," Amy said wistfully, running her fingers over them. "It's like . . . your own personal defense system. You could go *any*where by yourself at night and not have to worry about rapists or muggers or anything."

"No," Chloe agreed, "only an entire organization whose sole purpose is to wipe out people like me."

"That's why they . . . your *Mai* . . . won't let you out to see us?"

"Yeah, I tried to sneak out to see my mom a couple

of weeks ago and was completely ambushed. I would have died if some of the kizekh hadn't been trailing me." Of course, now that she thought about it, she remembered that the man in the sweater had had handcuffs, not a garrote or daggers like the Rogue. Still, his intentions were obviously not good.

"So why don't they just send you out with a group of them in the open?" Paul asked suspiciously.

"They have to keep a low profile."

"Yeah? Or do they just want to cut you off from your past life? With your human friends and family?"

"They just want to keep me safe," Chloe said uncertainly. The words that came out of her friends' mouths were suspiciously similar to the ideas that had been forming in the back of her own head, in the murky area where the word *cult* had first caught her attention.

"It sounds like it all kind of sucks." Amy sighed. "But I *still* want claws. Was this the reason you wanted a manicure that day?"

"Sort of."

She told them about Xavier. How the night she'd fallen from the tower, she'd hooked up with a random guy and as a result, he'd almost died from where she'd clawed him on the back in the heat of passion. For some reason, it was far more difficult to talk about this to her two best friends than anything else. It was just sort of embarrassing. "So we can't, like, have sex or *do* anything with normal humans, 'cause it kills them."

"That doesn't make any sense," Paul said, thinking about it. "I'm sure you must have kissed someone, like in grade school, at a party, or as a joke or something."

Chloe shrugged. "It has to do with the spit itself, I guess. A peck on the cheek doesn't do anything. It's more like tongue to tongue. It just started around when, well"—Chloe shot an apologetic look at Paul—"I finally got my period. It's all about puberty, I guess."

Paul looked deeply uncomfortable, though he tried his best to hide it.

"And your mom doesn't know *any* of this?" Amy asked, amazed.

Chloe shrugged. "This has all been kinda recent, and it's all kinda hard to believe. I was thinking about maybe trying to sneak over to see my mom tonight after you guys," Chloe went on dully. "But smarter than last time. Not just, like, walking up to the front door."

"Oh. Uh." Amy and Paul exchanged another look. Paul cleared his throat again. "That's another reason we wanted to see you, Chloe."

"I think your mom's missing," Amy blurted. "I broke into your house about a week ago and it was like no one had been there for a while."

Chloe stared at her, mind numb.

"We were going to call the police," Paul began.

"I have to go home," Chloe whispered, and then, without another word, she turned and ran.

"Wait! Chloe!" Amy called out to the figure disappearing into the night.

"Chloe!" came a new voice, masculine, from somewhere above them. "Chloe! Don't go! It's a trap! Chloe . . . !"

Paul and Amy looked at each other, then ran after their friend.

Chloe ran until her lungs shrieked from the cold air and lack of oxygen, until her insides stung with heart attack pain. Even with her Mai strength and speed, she was pushing herself far harder than she ever had. When a car blocked her way, she leapt, sinking her hand claws into its roof and pulling herself over it like a pole vaulter, leaving the driver with a horrible tearing sound in his ears and the image of rabid dogs and werewolf movies in his mind. She stuck to the streets and lower levels, not wanting to waste any time with the sort of stunts she usually enjoyed on her nighttime runs. She felt her foot claws trying to come out, straining at the fabric in her sneakers. On one landing, they finally pushed through the soles of her Sauconys, grabbing the dirt below her to push her forward.

Chloe ignored the shadows around her. She was far too fast a moving target this time to worry about an ambush. She was only concentrating on one thing: the nightmare that had kept her awake since the whole thing began. Bringing the violence that was now part of her life home, onto her mom.

She ran up the steps and unlocked the door, slamming it open, and threw herself in.

"Mom?" she called.

A step in and she instantly knew something was wrong.

The air *was* stale, as Amy had suggested; there were no recent human movements, warmth, or smells in there except for her friend's. None of her mom's perfume, soap, or skin scent was less than a week old. And there was a rancid, rotting scent beneath everything, like the drain in the sink hadn't been cleaned in a while.

Chloe flipped on the lights. Everything looked exactly the same as it had the last afternoon she'd been there, except for a few glasses that were put near the sink. Maybe when her mom had come home from work and found that note of Chloe's—she looked around frantically. There it was, by the phone. Scribbled in her mom's handwriting on it was Keira's number under her name; Mrs. King had fully intended on checking up to see if her daughter really was where she said she was.

Hummus. Chloe realized what the sour smell was. She followed it to the fridge, where a clump of it trailed down the outside of the door. It was so unlike neat freak Anna King that Chloe felt her heart stop when she saw it. She opened the door and saw the open container of hummus, now molding.

On its surface, the word *help* had been sloppily inscribed.

Nineteen

I can't believe this.

The first coherent thoughts Anna King was able to form as the drug wore off were incredulous and disbelieving. She opened her eyes to confirm what she was *sure* couldn't be true.

She was tied to a chair. Just like out of the movies, she had come to, tied to a chair.

It was a very comfortable chair, more like a La-Z-Boy or lounger, and she wasn't tied to it *exactly* like in the movies, but still. Her arms were belted onto the tops of the armrests—the chair had been neatly altered specifically for this purpose. Her feet were connected to each other by some sort of hobble, rendering it impossible for her to walk, much less get up, but that did not prevent her from being able to switch to more comfortable sitting positions.

She closed her eyes again, still sluggish and sleepy.

The drug was thick in her mouth, like a morning-after-Nyquil hangover but a thousand times worse. They'd given it to her after they'd slipped her out of the house. As soon as she opened the door, she knew something suspicious was up. Years of living in the city first by herself, and then later as a single mom, had made her sensitive to vibes. They were polite and the woman in the group had asked if they could come in. When Anna had said no, they'd somehow wound up inside anyway. She'd pretended she wasn't scared, putting pieces of dinner away. They talked about her daughter, and the trouble Chloe might be in, and how they wanted to help. She'd written the word *help* in the hummus, inspired and terrified.

It was a good thing she'd done that, too, since a few minutes later she was trying to scream and they had a gag over her mouth and there was a big, sleek car like out of the movies and she was taken away into darkness.

"Mrs. King," someone was saying gently, trying to wake her up more.

"Anna," she corrected instantly, in lawyer mode. She blinked a few times before managing to keep her eyes open. Someone had thoughtfully taken her glasses when they kidnapped her and had put them on her when she was passed out.

The room came into focus after a couple of moments of blurriness. She was in an office or a library, nicely appointed with a thick wool rug and big mahogany desk. A man was leaning back on it, almost sitting, legs crossed. He was a large man, middle-aged and white, with a sleek patience in his eyes that Anna the lawyer instantly recognized as a direct result of having money and/or power. He was dressed in a suit without the jacket, his tie loosened.

"How are you feeling?" he asked politely.

She opened her mouth to tell him precisely how she was feeling, but nothing came out, like she had used up all her speech with her name before. *"Water,"* was all she managed to croak instead.

"Of course." He turned to look at someone blocked from her view by the side of her chair—she had begun to think of it as *her* chair—and made a little motion with his hands. Quiet footsteps went off to do his bidding, no questions asked. Money *and* power, she decided.

A moment later someone handed him a glass of ice water. He came forward, and just when Anna was afraid he was going to *feed* her, he unlatched her left arm and let her take the glass herself. She didn't drain it instantly; this was not a time to show weakness. Instead she took polite, demure little sips, as though she were at a dinner party.

"Is that better?" the man asked.

"Where's my daughter?" she countered.

"What?" the man said with wry amusement. "You don't think she's at her friend Keira's house?"

"What have you done with my daughter?" Anna repeated.

"*We* haven't done anything, Anna. Although Chloe *is* in a lot of trouble—she has fallen in with a bad crowd and has been involved in a murder."

The doubt that flashed through Anna King's mind registered nowhere on her face. "I don't think so," she said.

"Well, I'm afraid she has." The man sighed, crossing his arms. "One of my friends—one of my colleagues—is dead because of her."

"You keep *not* saying that she killed him," Anna noted, sounding exactly like the attorney that she was. " 'Involved in a murder' and 'dead because of.' "

The man laughed, and his full, jowly chin shook a little. His voice was rich and beautiful, and every time he used it, Chloe's mother hated him more. "You are absolutely correct, of course; this is not a black-and-white world. We have no actual proof that my friend is dead."

"Why am I here," Anna said wearily, "and where is Chloe?"

"Chloe is with her new friends, most likely. To make a long story as short as possible, Mrs. Ki—*Anna*—your daughter's biological family is from a long line of . . . well, I guess you could call them warriors of a sort, or maybe a hunting caste—more than anachronistic in this day and age. Anyway, her people want her back. We have reason to believe they contacted her about a month ago and are fairly certain she is with them now."

Anna stared at him for a long moment before speaking. Even though she was the one tied to a chair, with her blondish hair coming out in wisps around her cockeyed glasses, she didn't feel like *she* was the ridiculous one in the room.

"Do you mean to tell me that some crazy ancient Russian Mafia wants Chloe to join them like her parents did?"

"Something like that, yes."

"If you care so very much about my daughter's welfare, why aren't you talking to the police or to me on the phone instead of kidnapping me and tying me to a chair?"

"Well, that brings us to your first question, doesn't it?" The man uncrossed his legs and put his arms behind him, supporting himself on the desk. "*You* are here because the Mai are extremely dangerous. In situations that have occurred before, with adoptive children of American parents, they have been known to kill the parents to ensure complete loyalty of the child and to cut off all connections with the rest of the world."

"And again, why do you care?"

"The Mai don't play by normal rules—they are like a gang, but far worse. Very much like the mob you mentioned. My organization exists to protect the public from them. To limit their influence. Hopefully one day to destroy them completely."

"How charitable of you."

"My wife was killed trying to save someone from the

Mai," he said softly. "I don't want you or anyone else suffering the same fate."

Both were silent for a moment. The corners of the room were obscured in gloom, and there were no windows. She was someplace secret, dark, and impossible to find. Mrs. King felt like squirming, both from his gaze and from sitting still for so long, never mind how comfortable the chair was. She didn't, though. "Why am I"—she pulled at her right arm—"still tied to the chair if you're just trying to protect me?"

"Anna, if we had come to your house and told you what I just did, would you have come quietly along with us?"

He did have a point.

"It was imperative to get you out of your house *as soon as possible*, as quietly as possible. Any one of a number of things may happen next—someone, a hit man from the Mai, may be sent in to kill you—or Chloe herself might try to sneak out and visit you, encouraging them to have you killed, even if they hadn't decided to before. Remember, they want complete control of their members' lives. I'm sorry about any unpleasantness, but this really was the easiest way. Now we can keep you safe while seeing what can be done about Chloe."

"Will you release me?"

"Yes—but I'm afraid we're going to have to keep you confined for a time. In a much nicer room than this," he added quickly and apologetically. "The temptation for you to leave and try to find your daughter would be far too great."

So let me get this straight. The "good guys" are holding me captive so I can't get hurt seeing my daughter, who is being held captive by the bad guys who don't want her out seeing her mother.

"What *is* going to happen to Chloe? Can you"—*save* sounded too melodramatic—"get her?"

"Of course." But there was something in his face, a slightly surprised look, as though he had already dismissed Chloe and her fate. As though Anna herself and *her* safety were all that mattered now. *He probably considers her one of "them" now. Chloe will get no help here.*

"Who *are* you people?" she demanded, half sarcastically.

"I'm afraid I—"

"Can't tell me that either. Yeah, of course."

"You can call me Whit," the man offered.

Anna had every intention of escaping as soon as she saw a way. She might not return home; she agreed with her captor that would be a pretty dangerous thing to do. But she *would* go immediately to the police and call the cult hotline and tell them about *everyone*.

Twenty

Chloe was still sitting on the floor, head in her hands, when Brian came in.

"It's all my fault," she said miserably.

He knelt down and she buried her face in his shoulder. "It is *not* your fault."

She shook her head, trying to wipe the tears away.

"We should leave here soon," Brian said as calmly as he could. "I gave the members of the Order who were patrolling here false tips that you were seen at Pateena's. But it's only going to be a few minutes before they get there and figure out that it was a trick." She nodded and sniffed. He stood up and looked around. "Are you *sure* she's gone?"

Chloe nodded again, wiping her face and pointing to the bowl of hummus.

"O . . . kay . . . ," Brian said, raising his eyebrows. "Your mom is certainly a . . . resourceful woman."

Chloe tried to smile. She felt embarrassingly weak,

like a child who needed to be taken care of in a time of crisis, and here was savior Brian, rushing in to fulfill the role of hero. But she needed that right now.

"Ohmygod Chloe." Amy burst through the door, wheezing, bent over. Her hair was frizzing around her face like a solar flare, and several strands were plastered to her face with sweat. "Youreneversupposedtoreturn-tothesceneof—" She took a deep breath and noticed Brian. "Who the hell is *that*?"

"This is Brian. Brian, Amy," Chloe introduced formally, feeling a little ridiculous.

"*This* is Brian?" her friend said incredulously. She looked him over, up and down so carefully that he began to fidget under her gaze. "You are *way* hotter than Alyec."

Chloe shook her head with impatience. "Where's Paul?"

"He's coming. The, uh, you know"—she mimicked taking a drag from a cigarette—"slow him down."

"That and managing to skip every gym class since the dawn of time," Chloe muttered. Now was not the time to have people separated. The Tenth Blade "patrols" might have let them pass for now, but what if they were just waiting for more orders? And what if the Mai noticed she was missing and thought Brian was trying to abduct her? "We've got to find my mom."

"Absolutely," Amy agreed, still panting. "Where do you think she went?"

"Now, wait a moment . . . ," Brian began, putting his hand up to Chloe's friend.

"I don't think she *went* anywhere. I think she was taken." Chloe pointed to the bowl.

"Hey." Paul came in, trying not to huff, his face turning red as a result. For the first time ever, he actually looked healthy, with pink cheeks.

"*This* is Brian," Amy said, grabbing Paul's arm.

"Hey," Paul said again, waving and still trying to breathe normally. It was amazing, Chloe reflected. His clothes were still perfect. Of course, Puma originally made athletic gear, but still . . .

"Chloe's mom has definitely been kidnapped," Amy said, catching him up on things. "We're working out how to find her."

"*We* aren't doing any such thing," Brian said, exasperated. Suddenly he seemed a lot more than just a couple of years older than Chloe and her friends. "*You two* are now officially done with this part of the story. I thought I made that clear in my answer to that e-mail you so unwisely sent me."

"Oh, suddenly Mr. Studmuffin here is charge of everything," Amy snapped, putting her hands on her hips and sticking her chin out at him. "Where the hell did you come from, anyway? '*We two*' have been friends with her forever."

"I appreciate that," Brian said through clenched teeth, "but this is very. Dangerous. Stuff. Your friend has been involved in what might be considered a murder. A group of people are out for her blood. Another group of people are out to protect her at all costs. And now her mom is gone. Hello? Not the safest avenue for you two."

"I'm right *here*, people," Chloe muttered.

"What makes *you* so qualified for the role of detective and bodyguard?" Amy had come closer to Brian and, even though she was a head shorter, pressed her nose up as far as it would go. Paul was still trying to catch his breath, watching without saying anything.

"He is . . . was . . . is?" Chloe said, looking at Brian uncertainly. "A member of the Order of the Tenth Blade."

"The kooks who are trying to kill you?" Paul asked, amazed, finally able to speak.

"Yeah, but he saved me on the bridge. . . ."

"How do you know he's not a double agent or something?" Amy demanded.

"I'm not," Brian said.

"I don't," Chloe added.

"He doesn't seem like it," Paul offered.

"Well, *you've* taken a sudden switch," Amy said, rounding on her boyfriend. "I thought *Alyec* was the one you trusted."

"Okay, everyone, *stop*," Chloe finally said. Brian obviously knew what he was doing and had a pretty good idea of what was best for everyone, but it was also crystal clear that her friends weren't going to listen to him. "Arguing here, the four of us, from three different factions, isn't going to help anything. And it's just keeping all of us nice and neatly in the same spot for *someone* to come along and pick off."

"What faction are we?" Paul asked.

"Innocent," Chloe said, gritting her teeth. Amy started to say something, but Chloe interrupted her. "No, shut up, it's true. There's no reason to put your lives in danger. But from what I understand, the Tenth Blade won't hurt humans, and I don't think the Mai like attracting too much attention to themselves. You're in a perfect position to help on the detective side. Like the home base people." Amy and Paul looked at her blankly. "Like Oracle in *Batman*," she said desperately. "Like Willow in *Buffy*. Before the whole witch-powers thing. Like Pete in *Smallville*."

"Oh, cool," Paul said, relaxing and suddenly looking into it. Amy looked doubtful but nodded.

It is *kind of a lame-ass cop-out,* Chloe realized, but she hoped it sounded good and that her friends would accept it. She wasn't going to be responsible for more people she loved getting hurt because of her.

"We can do other things," Amy protested weakly.

"You aren't trained like the Order, and you don't have the abilities of the Mai," Brian pointed out. "If you got involved in an actual fight, you'd be seriously injured or killed. I hate to sound clichéd, but this isn't a game."

"Do a search of all of the newspapers for the last two

weeks," Chloe suggested quickly before Amy yelled at Brian again. *He has such a habit of coming off as well meaning but a little high and mighty.* She wondered if his father was like that and, if so, how he managed to retain control of his organization. "We need to see if there's anything, *anything* about a missing person, a body, someone in the hospital. . . ." She didn't *say* "the morgue," but Chloe could tell by the look on Amy's face that it was understood.

"Do we have any *idea* who kidnapped her?" Paul asked.

Chloe looked at Brian helplessly.

"It could be either the Mai or the Order at this point," he answered, shrugging. "Both have a motive."

"Why would it be the Mai?" Chloe demanded. "What would they want with my mother?"

"Chloe, she's your biggest connection to the world of humans." Brian *knew* this was a touchy thing to say in front of her two best friends, but he had to say it anyway. "If they thought you would completely go over to their side—"

"What do you mean, *over*? I live with them—they're my race and my family and want to get to know me and protect me from people—*humans*—who want to kill me!"

"I'm just saying we should keep it open as a possibility," Brian said as calmly as he could. "As you said, they are extremely *protective* of their race."

"But what you're saying still doesn't make sense,

Brian," Amy said unexpectedly, before Chloe could speak. "The Mai have no reason to *take* Mrs. King. What would they do with her? Why not just"—she glanced at Chloe, having a hard time saying it—"why not just have her turn up dead on the news? Then Chloe would have nowhere to turn, and she would have to stay with them."

"They would never do that," Chloe said slowly. "And they may want me to stay, but they've been nothing besides supportive and—" She didn't know what to call it.

There was something about having a guy like a father play chess with her and eat pizza, about having a group of people who she could just lounge with instantly accept her, not act pissed off or angry—or date her other best friend. They accepted her without conditions. Once she'd appeared, she was just there, part of the Mai, like she had always been and always would be.

Plus—and here was the bit she wasn't going to reveal to anyone present yet—the Mai made *perfect* bloodhounds. As soon as she got back, she planned on telling Sergei about what had happened. Even if he was reluctant, Chloe bet she could wheedle a couple of kizekh out of him to help track down her mom. And deal with her captors, if necessary.

"All right . . . ," Paul said, obviously not entirely convinced, but enough to not press it. Brian's face was carefully neutral. "She hasn't turned up dead yet, and whatever this was, it happened a while ago. But . . ." he paused. "There doesn't seem to be a logical reason for *either* side to delay your finding out about it. Is there anyone else we should know about? Someone else who might have taken your mother for some different reason? Who might not have anything to do with any of this at all?"

"Yeah, sure," Amy said, making a face. "Because *two* obvious secret organizations with hidden agendas aren't convincing enough for you, Paul?"

"Well, I mean, what if it was someone else close to you, Chloe—another interested party, with a totally different *x* factor?" Paul suggested.

"Like *who*?"

Amy's eyes suddenly widened with realization of who fit the bill perfectly. "Like . . . your dad, Chloe?"

"No way." Paul shook his head. "That's not what I meant at all. Why would he come back after all these years and do something like this? I don't remember him being that kind of psycho—and my parents don't talk about him that way."

"Yeah, I'm afraid I'm going to have to vote negatory on that, too, Ames," Chloe said, physically shaking her head free of all the different theories. She checked her cell phone. "Okay, look, I gotta go. I'm going to have to keep this off—it's got *no* juice left."

"Now, that's something I *can* help you with," Amy said, grinning. She dug into her enormous pink coat pocket and triumphantly pulled out a rugged but shiny techno-gadget. "And it has a charger. Here." She handed that over, too.

"What are you, Q from *James Bond*?" Chloe asked. "What *is* this?"

"A walkie-talkie," Amy explained proudly. "We've got one, too. Keep it on, and we'll always be in contact—untraceably."

"Wow. This must have been expensive. . . ."

"That's a nice model," Brian said approvingly, looking over her shoulder. "It's a newer one than my dad sells. Hey, doesn't it have—?"

Paul kicked him. Chloe blushed, wondering how much it must have cost her friends.

"Thanks, guys," she said, trying not to cry again. "You really *are* my support team. Even if," she added, with a grin at Amy, "you dress like a pimp."

Twenty-one

Chloe made Brian stop following her after they got to the other side of the bridge, not wanting to lead him to Sergei's house—although the way he didn't question where she'd gone made her wonder if maybe the Order of the Tenth Blade knew more about the Mai and their whereabouts than they were letting on. But Brian was a man of his word, and even though she paused often to scent the wind and listen for his footsteps, she found no trace of him. At one point she ran back and trailed *him* to see if her senses were correct, and they were: he had wandered back over the bridge. He'd stopped halfway across and looked back, maybe hoping for a sign of her. Finally he stuck his hands in his pockets and continued the rest of the way hunched over, looking at the ground. Not a silent, highly trained soldier of an elite order, but rather a failing hero—as though nothing good was going to happen if he wasn't there to protect her.

Something burned in the pit of her stomach when

she saw him like that. Chloe had to fight back an almost overwhelming urge to chase back after him and grab him. She could just see it: *He would hug her and lift her high off the ground. And when he put her down, he'd put his hand under her chin and kiss her*—But that was when the dream broke off.

That could never happen. That *would* never happen.

But watching him walk away from her toward San Francisco, she knew he could never be just a friend, either.

I love you, Chloe.

She let herself savor Brian's words one more time before heading back to Sergei's house.

Sergei was in his office with Igor, Olga, and some of the other higher-ranking Mai at Firebird.

"Sergei?" Chloe flashed an apologetic look to everyone else in the room, but it wasn't really heartfelt.

"Hello, Chloe," he said amicably. "We're a *little* busy right now. . . ."

"My mom is gone."

Everyone on the other side of the desk shifted and looked at each other in surprise. Sergei raised his eyebrows.

"I snuck out," Chloe said, coming farther into the room. She was slightly ashamed, but honesty really was the best policy in this case. Here was an army of people already on her side who could help her, trained with techniques and abilities specifically geared toward hunting and finding people. "I went to go see my friends,

Amy and Paul—they were worried about me." She tried not to look at Sergei's face, terrified of the disappointment she might find there. "They told me they thought she might be missing—our house didn't seem lived in, and she wasn't answering phone calls. So I went home—" There were some sharp intakes of breath from everyone around her. "She's obviously been taken, or kidnapped, or something. Days ago. Maybe right after I came here."

There were murmurs and low discussions. Olga gave her a sad look. Sergei bit his lip.

"I'm very sorry, Chloe." He sounded sad, but not surprised.

"We've got to *do* something," Chloe said, trying to ignore the sound of resignation she heard in his voice. "She might not be dead yet—we could track down whoever has her . . . like a hunt. . . ." She trailed off.

"I'm afraid we can't do that." Sergei looked down at his desk, as if he'd been expecting her to ask that, or this was the answer he had been forced to give others before. "Call the police if you want from one of our private phones, tip them off. But we cannot get involved."

"But this is my *mom*," Chloe said, desperately trying to think of some way of convincing him, of some point that he would accede to. "She raised me—and kept me safe until you found me."

"Chloe, we all feel terrible about this," Sergei said with feeling. "But I cannot risk the dwindling kizekh on such a mission. There are few enough of them as it is to protect *us*. And as for a *hunt* in the city—we cannot face that sort of exposure. *Ever.* The Order of the Tenth Blade would love nothing more than to see us out and around San Francisco; it would give them the excuse they need to attack in heavier forces. Not to mention if the police took notice. No, I'm sorry, Chloe, we cannot risk such a thing. Especially for a human."

The businesslike attitude with which he closed the discussion jarred Chloe even more than what he'd said.

"But this human . . . is my *mother*. . . ." She tried not to cry.

"I'm sorry, Chloe," he said again, a little more kindly. "There are so few of us. It is terrible that we have to so selfishly look to our own survival, but I'm afraid that is the way it is."

Chloe looked to the other Mai in the room, but most looked away or down at the floor. Only Olga met her gaze, with a sympathetic sadness.

Chloe thought about saying something sarcastic and final, about how they weren't a *real* true family, but realized that if she opened her mouth or even stayed half a second longer, she would begin to cry. She turned to leave, trying not to run.

Sergei sighed loudly behind her. "Someone have Ellen and Dmitri follow her again. She's going to look for trouble."

* * *

But she *didn't* go looking for trouble immediately.

First she called the Ilychovich household and left a message; that was all she could do—as far as she knew, Alyec didn't have a cell phone, and she should know, right? Then she wandered around aimlessly for a while, trying not to check her voice mail too often, miserably wishing he would somehow know to call or show up. She finally wound up in the library, which was dark, empty, and quiet; good for thinking. Chloe made her way over to a window seat and tucked herself up in it, looking outside.

It was a beautiful, surreally bright night, like something out of a painting or Narnia. The sky was a deep, rich blue, the moon a silver, detailed orb of shining white that made perfect beams when Chloe looked at it through her eyelashes. The great emerald lawn was a rich shade of black.

Chloe hadn't been outside in daylight for weeks, but it felt much longer—like a lifetime. She felt a strange, removed feeling. It reminded her of the clinking of glasses as her mom cleaned up dinner, like there was some order to the world that she wasn't quite part of. She couldn't help feeling a little stupid. Life wasn't like TV, and she had definitely *not* been whisked away to her Happily Ever After. No one could do that, she realized. Not even an ancient, hidden race of people with powers like lions who gathered in prides.

There were no real superheroes.

Why had she assumed that just because they had

these abilities, they would automatically come to the aid of the weak, defenseless, and—most of all—*innocent*? Rationally, she understood Sergei's reasons: there wasn't a huge population of Mai to begin with. Like pandas. Losing even one panda was a problem, too.

But forget helping to rescue her mom just for the sake of doing good; Sergei wouldn't do it for *her*. Didn't he . . . well, if he didn't *love* her, didn't he care about her? Didn't he care about saving the woman who was responsible for keeping Chloe—one of their kind—safe until she could join them? Couldn't he do Chloe this one favor?

The moon slowly glided across the sky, inching toward midnight, and Chloe watched the intricate shadows in the grass grow and change direction.

She was still at the window hours later when Kim came padding in, carrying a sheaf of papers and clippings and photographs. She wore a long black turtleneck sweater and a black skirt that went to the floor, making her look like an ancient priestess. A cat-eared female—and, Chloe noted wryly—a pretty sexy priestess.

"I have some pictures for you. Your relatives . . . I mean, they might be."

"I thought you didn't want to talk about it."

Kim sighed patiently, as if she had expected this response but didn't feel the need to apologize.

"How did you know I was here?"

Kim blinked once, then touched her nose.

"Of course." Chloe looked back out the window. "My mom's gone. You were right about my 'human parents' being in danger."

"I'm . . . sorry that I was right."

"Sergei and Olga and the others . . . they won't *do* anything. They won't help me. They won't risk the kizekh. . . ." She pounded her fist on the window sash. "And what can *I* do? If I try to go out, Sergei's goons will drag me back to make sure I'm 'safe.' If I manage to *get* out—and get anywhere near my home without an army, the Tenth Bladers will get me. . . ." She trailed off. "I guess I'll call the police, like Sergei said. It's the only thing I really can do."

"I'll help," Kim said simply.

"What?" Chloe looked at her; she hadn't really been talking *to* the other girl, just getting her thoughts out.

"I'll help. I'm the best tracker here anyway. We will return to the scene of the crime and look for clues." She said this in such even tones that Chloe worried she was joking. Not that Kim had a great sense of humor or anything.

"Really?" Chloe asked slowly.

Kim nodded. "I can evade the goons, too. So, do you want to see these pictures?"

It was like the conversation was over as far was Kim was concerned. She had made her choice, and that was that. Chloe stared at her a little more.

"I'm totally thrilled, but I have to ask—why are you helping me?"

"You're my friend," Kim said, shrugging. "And I believe that once you tell him, Alyec will come along, too. Unlike him, however, I will not be expecting physical rewards from you."

Chloe suddenly exploded with laughter—like she hadn't since Alyec had teased her into a good mood in the middle of the school hall. That felt like it has been ages ago. Her face relaxed into a smile. It felt good.

She held her hand out for the photos. "Let's see these."

"That woman in the background—and clearer, here: she is the former pride leader. The one who *might* be your mother."

Chloe took the picture from her. It was cracked and bent and had what looked like coffee rings in a corner. The woman in it was certainly not as pretty as Chloe, but there was a definite resemblance, with the high cheekbones and cupid's bow lips. Her eyes were also hazel but darker, or at least they seemed shadowed in the picture. Her forehead was wider. She was handsome and had thick black hair that came down over her shoulders and covered her breasts. She was laughing, and her whole body was involved: her head thrown back, her hands on her hips, her mouth wide open, exposing perfect white teeth. There were deep creases around her eyes, like she had seen more of the world than her age would seem to indicate.

"Both my moms spent their lives helping people," Chloe murmured.

"What do you mean?"

"My mother—my human mother—is a lawyer in a private firm, but she does a lot of work for legal aid. Mainly for a women's domestic abuse shelter in the Mission District."

"She sounds like a good person."

"She is." Chloe smiled weakly. "Thanks for not saying 'was.'"

Kim just blinked at her. Chloe wondered how much of the girl's slow transformation to something more cat than human had affected her mind.

"How did you know my mom might be in danger?" Chloe asked aloud.

Once again Kim looked uncomfortable. "It only stands to reason," she said slowly. "For one thing, she makes perfect bait for the Tenth Bladers to lure you out."

"And . . . ?"

"And if you are still asking the question, you are already familiar with the other possible answer." She bit the sentence off as she finished it. Chloe knew she wouldn't get more out of her about it. She continued flipping through the pictures.

"My friend Amy suggested that it might not have anything to do with the Mai or the Order of the Tenth Blade," she added casually. "My dad left when I was really young—my mom's story is that he went gradually psycho or something. It wasn't exactly an amicable breakup."

"I . . . don't think he's a likely suspect. Occam's Razor—the simplest explanation is usually the correct one."

"Yeah, that's what I think, too," Chloe said, sighing. "But it was kind of exciting thinking about him for a little while again, you know? I wonder what he's doing now. . . ." She shook her head. "I didn't know him very well. As a kid I thought he was a superhero, the best dad ever . . . and then an asshole for walking out on us. Of course, for a long time I blamed my mom for that." Chloe frowned, thinking about the fight they'd had the night she discovered her claws. "Then it turns out that one of the reasons they split up was because of *me*. . . . They had very different ideas on child raising. Apparently he was this super-strict jerk, all about not letting me go out or date or—" She stopped and looked away from the photos to Kim. "*Not letting me go*—he made my mom promise before he took off. To not let me date."

Kim came to the same conclusion she had. "Did your parents know what you are?"

"My mom doesn't," Chloe said, pretty sure of the fact. Things like claws and litter boxes had not been brought up during the tampons and Advil discussion. "But what if my father knew?"

"Then your mother's disappearance becomes even more complex. Aside from the Tenth Blade, I think I can say with some certainty that almost no humans know about us."

"It would be on the news instantly," Chloe agreed.

"Perhaps he was Mai," Kim wondered.

"Um, no? The whole sex thing? She'd be all, like, dead and stuff?"

"Oh. Of course," Kim said, blushing. She turned back to the manila envelope in her hand. "So you had no father growing up . . . ," the girl said, playing with the idea. "I can see why you would get attached to Sergei so quickly."

"What's *that* supposed to mean?" Chloe snapped.

"Nothing more than that he is a charismatic, charming, and powerful leader. A perfect father figure. A role he enjoys, I might add. There have been other . . . orphans he has attached himself to."

Was Kim trying to make her jealous? But that didn't make sense unless—*she* was one of those other orphans, who'd maybe gotten dumped when Chloe or someone else came along. Like Igor. He certainly looked to Sergei as a male role model. Maybe it was a warning?

"Did he take *you* under his wing?"

"Yes," Kim said hesitantly, "when I first came."

"What happened? You don't seem to like him very much."

"That was it. I never have." Kim shrugged. "There is very little room for personal choice among the Mai, especially if you're an orphan, being welcomed in by the only people who will—who *can*—take you. But something about him . . . I didn't like him from the beginning. So I was raised by everyone and no one."

Chloe thought about this, drumming her fingers on the photos. There was a lot of information in what the other girl had just told her, but she wasn't quite sure what to do with it yet. So Sergei liked to take the lonely under his wing—what was wrong with that? It was *nice*, in a sort of den-mother-at-the-orphanage kind of way. And Kim *was* kind of a freak—maybe she just resented authority figures. Maybe this was nothing more than a slight personality clash of two very different people. . . .

But she didn't rule out that it might be something more.

"Who's this?" Chloe asked, suddenly coming across a much more modern picture. In it a girl was grinning, standing with her arm around another girl, at the top of what was probably the Empire State Building. Old-fashioned quarter-operated binoculars, the kind that looked like giant silver robot heads, were blurry in the background, and there was something distinctly urban and gritty about the landscape beyond.

Kim leaned over, saw the picture, and cleared her throat.

"That's the girl who would have been your sister. If we are correct about your parentage."

"My *sister*?" Chloe held the picture closer. The girl was darker than Chloe and older; the date on the back indicated that it had been taken a few years ago, and she already looked like she was sixteen or seventeen. Her hair was the same as Chloe's, and there was a shape to her eyes that was similar; her nose was smaller, too. She had two fingers up in a V behind her friend's head.

Kim's exact words suddenly sank into her mind.

"What do you mean, 'would have been'?"

"She was the one I told you about who was killed by

the Tenth Blade. The pride leader's daughter. That would make you her sister," Kim said patiently, making Chloe feel like more of an idiot. "It happened several months ago. We think it was the Rogue."

"My *sister,*" Chloe said again, feeling it on her tongue. Again she felt nothing in particular when she looked at the photo, but the word brought a swirl of emotions.

"Why . . . ?" she began. Tears sprang up in her eyes. It wasn't *fair.* She'd wanted a brother or sister *all her life* and it turned out that she'd had one *all along* and she'd been taken from Chloe, scant months before they would have found each other. It was so wretchedly, horrifically unfair.

"I understand she was a lot like you, actually. Or you if you had been raised Mai," Kim added thoughtfully. "I heard that she went out a lot by herself, doing a lot of things strictly among humans, and after her mother was killed, she was sent to live with her relatives, who were members of the New England Pride."

"There's a pride in New England?" Chloe asked. She remembered Kim mentioning the Pride of New Orleans, but colonial houses, white Christmases, and freaky cat people roaming quaint cobblestoned streets struck Chloe as strange. *I guess that's all relative these days, though,* she thought.

Kim just nodded, without explaining further. "I didn't know her very well. She was killed by herself, far away from her home, at night."

"Picked off because she was by herself," Chloe said

grimly. But something seemed familiar about what Kim had said—almost déjà vu. A dream she'd had, maybe: something about a girl running, panicked, in dark city streets. Being caught and having her throat slit.

"Yes . . . although the fact that it might have been the Rogue lends an interesting spin to the whole thing," Kim said, looking at the picture again. "To send someone like that out after her means they were pretty serious about *getting* her, which means they somehow knew she was the daughter of a previous pride leader."

"Do you think they know about me?" Chloe asked in a small voice.

"We still have no actual proof you are who we think you are," Kim said carefully. "So I would assume they have even less of an idea."

She imagined the man who'd attacked her running after this other girl, in probably the same fashion, running her down—without an Alyec or Brian to help save her. Maybe without so much of a fighting instinct. Killed by whirring throwing stars and tiny silver daggers.

"Why are they called the Tenth Blade, anyway?" Chloe asked.

"Because a pride leader has nine lives," Kim answered. "It takes nine blades to kill the One. The *tenth* is for the Tenth Blader if he fails."

Twenty-two

After she and Kim had made some preliminary plans for searching her house the next night, Chloe finally crawled off to bed, a thousand different thoughts and ideas crowding themselves into her brain. She had just drifted off, the pictures of her possible mother and sister laid out on the quilt in front of her, when Alyec showed up.

"Pssst! Chloe?" He knocked lightly on the door as he opened it.

Chloe blinked awake, then immediately sat up. *"Where were you?"*

"What?" Alyec asked, the eagerness on his face changing to dismay.

"I've been trying to call you. I tried calling you at home—"

"I was at a party," he mumbled, a little shamefaced about having fun while she was stuck here.

"Why don't you have a cell phone?" Chloe snapped.

"I do. Have one. *Had* one. Too many people started

calling, so I don't use it much anymore," Alyec said defensively.

"My mom—she's been taken. Kidnapped. Killed, I don't know." She sank back on her bed, trying to hold back the quiver in her voice.

He came over and sat on the bed next to Chloe and put his arm around her. "I'm sure that's not true."

"It is," Chloe answered dully. "I went to meet Amy and Paul—" She knew she should have said *and Brian* but couldn't deal with it right then. "And they told me no one had been home in a while. I went, and there's no sign she's been there for at least a week. She must have disappeared right after I came here."

Alyec hugged her to him, waiting a careful moment before asking the potentially inflammatory: "You went back home? After the last time you were attacked?"

"What would you have done if it was *your* mom?"

"I would go to Sergei and we would instantly round up a posse and—"

"Sergei won't do anything. Because she's *human*."

"Oh." Alyec seemed surprised by this. "What a dickhead."

Maybe this racial hatred thing is generational, Chloe thought. She hoped it was so.

"Why didn't you take me along?" he asked quietly. "I would have gone with you. You know how much I love breaking rules."

"It was something I had to do myself." *And it would*

have been pretty uncool for you to tag along while I was seeing my other boyfriend. "Alyec," she said, sighing, "you get to go to school every day and do normal things with normal people in the outside world. I'm stuck here *all* day. *Every* day. Away from my mom and my friends and everything. I'm being . . . *cloistered* here." She gave herself points for the SAT word.

"Kim seems to be okay about it," Alyec said, a smile on his lips.

"I love her dearly, but she really is a bit of a freak, you know?" Chloe ran her hand through Alyec's thick blond hair. "She said she would go back to the house with me and look for evidence or something."

"I will go with you, too," he said, kissing her on the side of her head, above her ear. "Screw Sergei. She's your mom. Hey," he said brightly, suddenly sitting back and looking at her, "this is the most naked I've ever seen you!"

Chloe caught herself looking down, forgetting what she had on. It was *completely* unsexy: a pair of blue-striped boxers Olga swore were new and an oversized, comfy, Old Navy men's T-shirt. The neck was so big it hung off one of her shoulders. Except for that little bit of *Flashdance*, Chloe didn't think she looked very naked at all.

"You have *got* to be kidding me," she said, holding her hand against his head to stop him as he reached for her. "I look like a frump."

"A *sexy* frump. A college girl, taking a break from her studies," Alyec said, evading her hand and kissing Chloe on her belly. "A *librarian* at home. You don't have any glasses, do you?"

"Alyec, shut *up*. Stop it!" She tried not to giggle. Her mom was gone, she had two boyfriends, she couldn't trust anyone. . . . "We're being *serious*."

"As a good librarian should be. Chloe, tonight the area will be crawling with Tenth Bladers because you were probably seen. No—definitely seen. You, me, and the freak will go tomorrow night and figure out what happened. Okay?"

"Okay," she agreed grudgingly.

He lifted the shirt up over her belly and pulled her boxers just the slightest bit down. Chloe was zinging all over as he brought his lips to her skin, both fearing and expectantly awaiting of his next move.

Which was to suddenly suck down over her belly button like a fish and blow air out the sides, making a ridiculous *thirbrrrrty* sound.

"Alyec!" She cracked up, hitting him over the head with a pillow.

"Chloe," he said, more seriously, kissing her. "everything's going to be all right. I *promise*."

Then he *really* kissed her. It was even better than their little time-out in the janitor's closet. He pulled her closer to him, sliding his hand up under her shirt. She felt the tips of his claws come out and pressed back into him.

"Al-yec!" came a booming male voice, pronouncing the name as Russianly as possible. Sergei stood in the doorway, hands on his hips, a growl on his face. He looked extremely leonine. "Do I have to establish a curfew in my own home?"

"Hey, she's part of this, too," Alyec said mock whiningly, sliding up and away from her in one quick movement.

Chloe wasn't sure whether to scream, cry, or giggle. This was such a classic situation—one that she had never been in before. Besides being scary and embarrassing, it felt sort of warm and nostalgic.

"Get *out*, Alyec Ilychovich," Sergei said, raising an eyebrow. There was a little bit of tired amusement in his voice as well. Chloe got the feeling that this was somehow not as bad as the whole sneaking-out thing. It was *bad*, but not unexpected, and not out of the realm of the legal.

Alyec slunk out after giving a brave salute to Sergei and blowing a kiss to Chloe. When he was gone, Sergei let out a sigh, a breath he must have held the entire time.

"That boy is a menace," he said wearily.

Chloe covered her mouth, pretending to scratch her nose, desperately trying not to giggle.

"I just came by to apologize," the older man said more gently, coming in and sitting on the edge of her bed. "I truly *am* sorry we cannot help your mother more. We should do everything we can for the woman who adopted you and brought you up and helped make you the wonderful girl you are." He put his square, stubby hand somewhat clumsily on her own. "But these are tough times . . . and the Tenth Blade is in strange agitation over you. I do not wish to risk lives—there are so few of us. Do you understand?"

When he looked at her with those large, white-blue eyes and that childish, hopeful expression, Chloe just wanted to hug him and tell him everything was all right. She *wanted* everything to be all right. She *wanted* him to have her best interests at heart.

But . . . Kim doesn't like him. What are her reasons? Chloe once again wondered. Actually, Alyec didn't really like him either. Olga was carefully neutral on the subject. The only person Chloe knew who admired him completely was Igor, Sergei's sort-of protégé.

He's not my real father, Chloe reminded herself. *Where the hell was Sergei when I needed to learn how to ride my bike or couldn't figure out how to multiply fractions or when Scott Shannon turned me down for the dance and asked Tracy Lynn right in front of me?*

"I understand," she said, and it was sort of true. "I'm just sad. And I feel helpless."

"I know." He kissed Chloe on her forehead. "But remember, the Tenth Blade doesn't usually hurt humans. If they've taken her, she's probably fine, just a little shaken up. They're trying to lure you out, not hurt her."

She nodded, for some reason suddenly almost overcome with the urge to cry.

"Good." He patted her on the knee and stood up. "Are we on for a game of chess tomorrow? Lunch, maybe?"

"How about Scrabble?" Chloe suggested instead.

Sergei groaned. "Oh, good. A game designed for knowledge of English words. You just want to *win* for once, Chloe King. Okay, Scrabble it is." He grinned and left, his surprisingly thick and stubby legs rocking him out of the room. From the back he almost looked like some sort of alien from *Star Trek*.

As Chloe settled back down into her covers, she suddenly noticed the photos that she had left out on her bed. Had Sergei seen them? Would he care? Should she be worried?

Questions kept her awake for a long time before she finally fell asleep.

Twenty-three

As a kid, Brian had known there were secret rooms in the Order of the Tenth Blade's chapter house. As he grew older and advanced in the Order, some were revealed to him.

But he knew there had to be more.

And if the Tenth Blade was in fact holding Chloe's mom, they would probably keep her in some area Brian didn't know about.

As a kid, he had made incredible drawings and plans of where he thought the other rooms might be. While many of these floor plans were lost or had been destroyed by his father, a few had survived, stuffed into boxes of memorabilia and report cards. As soon as he got home from Chloe's house, he dug them out and pored over them, trying to remember what he could, picturing the old Victorian with eyes closed, estimating area and distance. When he had done as much as possible, he paid a visit to the house.

Mrs. Chung let him in, smiling and kind and looking exactly the way she always had from the first day he had been there. She was tiny but perfectly erect, grandmotherly but formally dressed, like the maitre d' at a fancy Chinese restaurant, her hair always up in elaborate pins. Whit Rezza might own a security company that constantly invented and sold the latest computerized systems, but in the end, few things could beat the watchful eyes of a *human* doorkeeper, one who was polite but firm with strangers, friendly with guests, and much better equipped than a computer to pick up the emotions of those who came in.

"Is everything okay, Brian?" she asked, looking as though she still wanted to pinch his cheeks.

"I'm having a sort of crisis of faith, Mrs. Chung," he sighed, telling her part of the truth. It was easier—and made it less likely that she would detect what he was up to—than an outright lie.

"Oh, I don't know about all that, but I'm sure it will be fine." She always claimed not to know what went on in the house whenever anyone—even members—tried to talk to her about it. She stood by the line that it was a private club. Brian doubted that she was really quite so innocent.

"Thanks, Mrs. Chung," he said as she took off his coat and went to hang it up somewhere.

Brian was well aware that cameras and monitors might be anywhere—he even knew where a few were. So he made his movements random—first to the library, where he said his hellos to a few of the older members who were sitting around reading or napping. He flipped through the latest *Sports Illustrated*—besides the dedication to violence, it really was, after all, an ordinary private club—and eventually rose, asking if anyone wanted tea or coffee. No one did.

He went to the kitchen, counting his steps, and poured himself a full cup of coffee to give himself an excuse for walking *very slowly*. Then he proceeded down the hallway to the stairs, counting his steps and trying to determine the length of the staircase.

While Brian did all this, he tried not to think of Chloe, partly because he was afraid it would affect what he was doing. And partly because it was too complicated to think about.

Five, six, seven, eight . . . About eight and a half paces to the stairway.

He had first been assigned to track her over a year ago; because of her adoption records, they had suspected that she was a Mai. He had tracked others before her, ones who already knew their heritage, and while it was never up to him to kill them—or decide to kill them—they always seemed different enough, alien enough for him to think of them as not quite human. Even discounting their greater strength and agility, they *moved* strangely, for one thing. Sometimes they cocked their heads when smelling for something, which made them look entirely animal. Late at night Brian had once caught a flash of a female Mai's face as she raced through a pool of streetlight and saw the catlike slits in her yellow eyes.

Chloe was just a normal high-school girl. Well, not quite normal. She was on the edge of the social crowds but never resentful of them. She had an amazing attitude toward work—Brian had seldom seen someone her age so committed to a crappy job. At least half the time Chloe showed up early at Pateena's and often stayed late to help the manager close up, without complaining or demanding overtime.

The Tenth Blade ordered him to get closer, to get a better reading on her and how close she was to discovering her background. He did as he was told.

He'd arranged their first "accidental" meeting at Pateena, the place where she worked. Liking her instantly was unavoidable: Chloe was funny, passionate, gorgeous, and had a spark of something else Brian couldn't put his finger on. Energy, verve, *something* that made him want to go everywhere with her, do whatever she was doing, not be left out in case he missed something great.

But he'd never counted on her liking him back.

Or having to decide how much to tell her. Or having to choose between betraying her or his father and the way he had been brought up, all the people he had known since he was a kid, the way of life he had always lived. In the end, he'd made a half-assed decision to come to her rescue at the bridge when she was fighting the Rogue without telling her anything beforehand. Not that she'd really needed his help.

And he'd screwed it all up again anyway. While there *were* Tenth Bladers waiting in the Marin Headlands for her to go running by, he hadn't *really* had to throw the shuriken so hard into Alyec's leg to stop them from going that way.

He *knew* that Alyec really wasn't the cause of the trouble—that one way or another Chloe would have realized she was different and, even worse, if she'd done it alone, the Order of the Tenth Blade would have simply killed her.

But the other boy could kiss her.

While Brian was forced to walk a strange tightrope with Chloe between friendship and something more, Alyec had no such difficulties. He was free to pursue any level of relationship with her, without having to worry about dying from it.

Brian was on the third floor, in a small complex of secret rooms where the *real* library was and where he was pretty certain there were *more* secret rooms, ones he didn't know about. He did a few quick calculations in his head and noticed how the decorative architecture was confusing, with excessive paneling and wainscoting, bookshelves set up in mazelike arrangements, lots of extra crown molding, cornices, and other random decorations.

A flash of something on the floor caught his eye. Brian bent over and picked up what could have been a gum wrapper. It was actually a silver earring. It looked expensive, patterned, and faux ethnic—and far too modern for anything Edna Hilshire would wear.

Brian quickly thought about all the other female members of the San Francisco chapter. Only two of them had access to this room besides Edna. Sarah-Ann never wore jewelry, except for a *Sodalitas Gladii Decimi* pendant, and Tyler always had a pair of simple diamond or pearl studs.

"What are you doing here?"

Of course. Of course Dickless would see me come in and follow me here. He was probably monitoring the security cameras.

Brian didn't turn around immediately, pretending to continue looking for a book.

The excuse he'd originally been going to use was that he had lost a knitting needle somewhere—his hobby amused some chapter members and annoyed some others, who thought it was unbecoming and housewifeish for a member of the Order of the Tenth Blade. Like flash camouflage, his answer would probably amuse or annoy an interloper, completely disarming any suspicion.

But Richard had a real grudge against him and still thought that the two were competing for Whit's affection and eventual leadership of the Order.

"Richard," Brian said formally, only turning around after he pretended to be done with whatever he was doing. "How are things going for you?"

"What are you doing here?" Richard repeated. His

eyes were black and intense, and his hair was black and intense, too. He sneered so much, it looked like he was constantly trying to stop a runny nose.

He was also smaller than Brian, which suited Brian just fine. Brian walked up to him as close as possible without making it an actual insult, looming over him.

"Not that it's any of your business, but I am experiencing a crisis of faith," Brian said, with just a touch of excitement in his voice to make it seem more real. "I wanted to read through the Sidereal Codex again and think about the vows."

"Don't you think it's a little late for that?" Richard demanded, retaining his sneer but obviously accepting the excuse.

"Remind me to tell the others that you're the go-to guy for spiritual support," Brian said, rolling his eyes and walking away.

"You can't just *leave* the Order," the other boy spat after him in a final attempt at ruffling his feathers. "*Nobody* just 'leaves the Order.' It's for *life*."

"Whatever," Brian called back.

"Even your father knows that, Brian. He understands the rules and lives by them. He'll do what's right. For all of us," he added.

Brian kept walking, but the smile he could hear in Richard's voice left him feeling cold.

Twenty-four

"Get anything yet?" Alyec needled.

"It would be a lot easier to 'get' a scent if you weren't wearing so much cheap cologne," Kim growled.

"It's not cheap! It's Eternity, by Calvin Klein!"

Chloe winced, fingering one of her mom's rings that lay next to the sink. The whole thing would have been funny if her mom's life wasn't at stake. Alyec seemed to rub *all* of Chloe's female friends the wrong way, not just Amy.

The three had escaped the mansion with little attempt at covering up their trail; with Kim's superior hearing and smell, they'd managed to eventually evade the two kizekh who had followed them. Alyec had crowed in triumph, but Chloe wasn't so sure it really had been just that easy; perhaps Sergei thought it was safe enough for her with Alyec and Kim.

Closer to Chloe's house Kim had detected two seemingly random people who, on closer inspection, were making fairly regular circuits of the area around the house. The three Mai simply waited until there was a break and dashed in.

"This is where you live?" Kim asked. Normally the girl was immediately down to business, but she seemed genuinely interested in Chloe's life before the Mai. She moved her head back and forth, taking in *everything* in the living room and kitchen, eyes wide at the coffeemaker, the little TV on the counter, the garbage cans, the books on the coffee table. . . .

"Yeah. Pretty sweet, huh?" Alyec threw himself down on the couch, making it clear that *he* had been there first and was much more familiar with the territory.

"This is where I found the . . . uh, 'clue.'" Chloe opened the fridge and showed her the hummus. Kim came forward to smell it, then buried her nose in her hand.

That had been fifteen minutes ago.

While Alyec made the occasional derisive comment and Chloe looked around for other, obvious out-of-place things that only she would be able to notice, Kim moved around the rooms, sometimes upright, sometimes on all fours, trying to catch a scent. She spent an inordinate amount of time with her nose close to, but not touching, objects, sniffing them—and Chloe couldn't quite watch. It was too inhuman.

"Here," Chloe said, slipping in between Kim and Alyec, who were glaring at each other. *I'm glad I have such great, supportive, helpful friends,* Chloe made herself think. *But maybe I should have brought only one of them.* She reached into a cabinet over the sink and pulled out a full bag of gourmet coffee beans—another sign her mother hadn't been there in a while. Normally she would have been through a "tasting"-size bag like that in about a week. She broke open the seal and held it under Kim's nose.

"What's this for?" Kim said doubtfully.

"They have little dishes of coffee beans out in fancy perfume stores and things like that," Chloe said, shrugging. "To clear your head of all the previous scents. I thought maybe you could use it for the same thing."

Kim looked at her without blinking but took a deep whiff. Then she wrinkled her nose and did the cutest little wheezy sneeze Chloe had ever seen a human—*Um, almost human*—do. She put her nose to the air again.

"Huh, it works," Kim said in wonder, and got back to work, taking the bag with her and glaring at Alyec.

"Hey," Chloe said, remembering something. "How come the night you were teaching me how to do all those things you reeked of gasoline, not CK?"

"Sometimes the Tenth Bladers use dogs," he said, making little ears on the sides of his head with his hands. "Gas covers the scent. Also to keep you from recognizing me. No one knew if you were going to freak out over everything. Like if you would suddenly start talking about all of this to your mom or the press or whatever—my name wouldn't be part of it."

"Well, I guess you guys lucked out about me, huh?" Chloe said dryly.

She watched Kim continue to sniff around the apartment. She wished she could do the same sort of thing—she had tried, but the overwhelming familiarity of the house doused all other scents. Kim would occasionally point to an area or a section of a door or something, but all Chloe got was a strange unfamiliar smell, mammalian, but she couldn't identify or distinguish it.

She wished she could do *something*. *Any*thing.

From the fight at the bridge to here, back home, a few things had changed. This time it wasn't Chloe who was in danger, but someone close to her. Last time she had been kicking a *trained assassin's* ass, feeling every blow bring her closer to victory. This time she was just standing here, uselessly watching someone else do the only thing she could think of.

Finally Kim stood up and shrugged. "There were two human males here and a woman who wasn't your mother. There are traces of fear and a chemical smell that I don't really recognize. . . ."

"O-kay," Chloe said. "But what does this mean?"

"It means that your mom was probably kidnapped, but the kidnappers didn't kill her. The chemical smell—it means they used something to make her pass out," Alyec said, leaping up and coming over to the two girls with a big grin. "It means that everyone's probably right about the Tenth Blade taking her to lure you out."

Kim nodded slow, grudging agreement.

"Well . . . now what?"

"Now we should go outside and see what else we can learn," Kim said, looking worriedly out at the street.

"You shouldn't worry about the two Gerbers out there," Alyec said, grinning. "I'll lure them away and get back here ASAP."

"Don't," Chloe said as he went to the door, even though she knew it was the best thing he could do.

"You think this is the *first* time I've done this?" He blew her a kiss and went out the back door, closing it silently as he went.

"We'll wait ten minutes and go," Kim suggested.

They were both quiet, watching the microwave clock.

"I'm gonna run upstairs and get some of my own, you know, undies," Chloe said after a moment.

"Can I come?" Kim asked shyly. "I'd like to see your room."

"Sure." Chloe shrugged. "C'mon."

She went upstairs, pushing her hands against the wall—something her mom hated—while Kim followed delicately behind. *If this was an actual friend-coming-over scenario, there'd be snacks on the table or popcorn in the microwave,* she thought dizzily. Here she was in her own house, late at night, her mom having "disappeared," toting a cat-eared girl who seemed as anxious as a freshman to see how the cool kids lived.

Chloe went to her dresser and began to look through its drawers, trying to disturb things as little as possible.

Out of the corner of her eye she saw Kim looking around, eyes wide, paws spread as if she would like very much to *touch* something. Chloe wondered what the other girl's room looked like: probably bare and ascetic, like its owner. Not covered in posters of Ani DiFranco and Kurt Cobain and Coldplay, not filled with IKEA furniture, not strewn about with Mardi Gras beads and scarves and other useless sparkly crap.

Chloe had found Monday, Tuesday, Wednesday, Friday, and Sunday of her Paul Frank panty-a-day collection when she heard a slight hiss from her friend.

She turned just in time to see Kim dive with a speed and movement completely unrecognizable as human.

When the girl stood up again, she had a mouse between her thumb and forefinger.

"It looks like the vermin have already taken over in your absence," she noted, holding the mouse above her head and eyeing it critically.

"That's Mus-mus," Chloe said, putting out her hand, claws extended, and gently but firmly taking the terrified mouse from her. "He used to be my pet."

Kim let it go, fascinated.

Chloe cupped her hand around the mouse with her claws so he couldn't get out. He was obviously terrified. Any hope that his fear of her was temporary disappeared. When she'd developed claws and her other Mai attributes, he'd become as scared of her as he would be of any cat.

"A cat with a mouse as a pet," Kim said, almost sounding delighted. "Weird, but kind of ironic."

"I thought we were lions," Chloe said, crouching and letting him go again under her bed. She fished in his old drawer for some more Cheerios to leave out for him. At least he had decided to stick around. She should be grateful for that much.

"Well, then there's that fable about the mouse who begged the lion who caught him to let him go."

Chloe vaguely remembered the story but not the details. She tried to concentrate on it so she wouldn't cry again over Mus-mus.

"The lion let him go, and later, when he had a thorn in his paw, the mouse pulled it out. They became friends after that."

"What's the moral?"

"Do kindness to even the least significant creatures—it may wind up helping you far more than you imagine sometime down the line."

"Sounds a little self-serving," Chloe said, finally turning around and jamming the undies into her pockets.

"Perhaps." Kim cocked her head at her. "Who knows what thorn of yours Mus-mus may pull out?"

"I think we can probably go now," Chloe said, suddenly uncomfortable. Kim nodded and waited politely for Chloe to exit first, following her silently downstairs, through the house, and out the back door.

Once outside, Kim crouched down in what would

have looked like an impossible position to balance in if Chloe hadn't known herself what it was like to be a Mai. The other girl tracked the sky and then the ground like a werewolf out of a very, *very* bad movie. Black against the dim light of the street she was skinny and beautiful, and for a moment Chloe felt a pang of envy.

The Kings' and their neighbors' tiny patches of "yard" were separated by a fence and dwarf privet trees that grew out of brown, unhealthy-looking dirt.

Chloe's mom did not exactly have a green thumb with outdoor plants. Whenever she came across a pretty landscape in a magazine that might work with their minimal space, she would hold it out to Chloe, who would look at it and grunt. Sometimes there would be a trip to Home Depot or a nursery, things brought back, and diggings begun, but then Anna would take on an especially heavy caseload and would recede from the project, muttering something about hiring someone to do it.

Chloe suddenly grew depressed when she saw a bottle cap and some gum wrappers stuck to the ground under the trees. Her house was empty; without its two occupants—its soul—it was nothing more than a monument to crappy urban living. She had to resist the urge to bolt.

Kim had come crawling back to her, looking irritated and confused.

"Well, it was definitely cased before they came in—I got a perfect scent trail of the two male humans."

"And?"

Kim carefully cleaned off her claws, polishing them with the edge of her jeans. As prim and feline as it looked, it was as obvious as if a human were doing it that she was trying to delay an answer.

"And?"

"There were Mai. Two of them. Slightly younger trail. *After* the humans, but not by much."

"Oh." Chloe thought about this. "I guess Sergei sent them to guard my mom, without telling me, to keep me from getting upset."

"If Sergei had sent two Mai to guard your mom and three humans showed up, your mother would still be okay, safe in her house, even now. The humans would be dead or incapacitated," Kim said. It was obvious she had already come to her own conclusion, and its implications darkened her brow.

"What are you *saying*?" Chloe grabbed the girl's shoulders, wanting to shake her out of her neat little world of logic and puzzles. "That they were sent to *kill* her?"

"It wouldn't be the first time. . . ." Kim trailed off.

Chloe fell back on her heels. "No!"

"There is no real evidence, but—"

"Why haven't you told me this before?" Chloe demanded.

"Because everything is *watched* at the house and *every*one listens!" Kim hissed. "I have tried to tell you that a *thousand* times!"

"Does everyone hate humans that much?" Chloe asked dully as her universe shifted.

"It is not about hating humans—it's about control and keeping the Pride together. The Path of Bastet involves doing it with connection, love, nurturing, and purity. The Path of Sekhmet means doing it through war and violence, by any means possible."

"And the current leader is a follower of Sekhmet," Chloe realized, thinking about what Sergei had told her.

"Once your mother is gone, you have no more connections to the outside world."

Chloe smiled weakly. "That's what Brian said."

"Who's Brian?"

"He's my—" Chloe stopped, unsure of how much to reveal. "He's a friend of mine in the Tenth Blade who saved me, sort of, when I was fighting the Rogue and then when Alyec and I ran away. . . ."

It was Kim's turn to stare in incredulousness.

"Your life," she observed finally, "is very complicated. And extraordinarily dangerous."

"Tell me about it." Chloe looked at the blank eyes of the house, its dead windows. "So—you think my mom is dead?"

Kim shook her head. "If she was killed by the Mai, there would be signs. We aren't perfectly neat killers. Ironically, it may be a good thing that the Order of the Tenth Blade—or whoever—got to her first."

"Hey, guys, stop with the chatting!" Alyec poked his

head into the bushes where they sat. "We have about five minutes before they figure out I led them on a wild-goose chase."

He put out his hands and helped the two girls up. Chloe was surprised that Kim didn't object, but the girl still seemed a little stunned by the evidence and their discussion. As they walked back, just three normal-seeming teenagers, Kim filled Alyec in on what she had found.

"So we think she's been kidnapped by the bastards?" Alyec asked excitedly.

"She's probably still being held somewhere by them, yes. Assuming it is the Tenth Blade and not someone else, for some different reason," Kim said. "If it *is* them, your little diversion with their guards tonight may have bought us some time—it proves to them that Chloe is interested, or *someone* is interested, in coming back to this house. Which means they have a reason to keep her mom alive."

"Excellent," Alyec said, rubbing his hands together. "We can have a real raid! I'll bet Sergei knows where their HQ is. . . . This is going to be great! There hasn't been any real action in years!"

"I hardly think the leader is going to sacrifice a troupe of us and the kizekh to attack the home base of the Order of the Tenth Blade to save a woman it looks like he was meaning to have killed."

"Maybe we can embarrass him into it," Alyec posited.

"Pride leaders don't embarrass that easily, Alyec,"

Kim objected, with the faintest gleam in her eye. "I think we should look to volunteers. There are enough who think we've been too intimidated by the Order for years and are just itching for some payback."

"I wonder how many we can get."

"I wonder how we can avoid too much death and injury."

As her two friends animatedly discussed and formed plans, Chloe remained silent. In the streetlights, their three shadows climbed the empty street before them, doubled, and then receded into the light of the next to be reborn slowly again behind them. They could have been Amy, Paul, and Chloe for all the detail their gross shades gave them. Just turned away from a party or something, planning great revenge, or discussing their dreams, filled with the sort of energy only walking on the streets at night can give you.

Instead of making war counsel.

"Hey, are you all right?" Alyec asked when they got back. Chloe still hadn't said a word.

"Yeah. I'm just a little . . . tired." She couldn't even smile weakly at him. "It's a lot to think about, you know? I thought Sergei was like—"

"Your dad?" Kim prompted quietly.

"And now it looks like he was just going to kill—"

"All the fun, if he catches the three of us skulking around," Kim interrupted what Chloe was about to say, looking obviously around with her eyes. Chloe understood immediately. No more talking. *Not here*.

"I should get home, anyway." Alyec kissed her sweetly on the lips. "I'll come back tomorrow after school and we'll talk about this more, okay? What to do about your mom, I mean," he added pointedly. While Alyec had seemed a little aghast at what Kim had accused Sergei of, he, too, didn't seem particularly surprised. Between the family enmity and his desire to maybe take over someday, the boy was all gung ho about disobeying the leader—and possibly punishing the older man somehow.

Chloe waved good night to him and Kim and went upstairs.

Hours later she was still awake. The photos were once again spread over her quilt as she sat huddled against the headboard, knees drawn up to her chin. Sometimes Chloe would pick up a picture, like the one of her sister, and hold it in front of her face for a long time, staring at it like she was trying to see the 3-D image in one of those trick posters. She tried to *feel* the other girl through her face, tried to pick up some sort of impression or thought across the void. Then she would put the picture carefully back down in the exact same place it had been.

Her photo quilt was missing quite a few panes: there should have been pictures of her mom, Amy and Paul,

Marisol from the shop. All the people she hadn't really been related to but who felt like family had been slowly replaced with people whom she was probably related to but knew little about. Kim and Olga. Igor and Valerie. Even Sergei. And what about Brian and Alyec? If things continued the way they seemed to be going, Brian and Alyec might be literally facing off in a few days.

She thought about her mom, who hadn't known what she was getting into when she'd decided to raise Chloe on her own.

Amy's walkie-talkie buzzed.

"Hello?" she asked distractedly, still staring at the pictures.

"It's Brian. Look . . . I can't talk much now." He was panting as though he were running, and Chloe could hear street sounds in the background. "Listen, I was just over at the . . . Order's place and found an earring. Does your mom wear big blocky silver things with patterns and black in the etchings. . . ?"

"John Hardy," Chloe said calmly, both shocked and unsurprised. "Does it kind of look like animal plating? Like of a snake? Or like spheres that have been squished flat, almost into polygons?"

"Bingo. I don't think anyone in the Order wears anything like them."

"Can you . . . can you get her out?"

"I don't even know exactly where she *is*, Chloe. And people are becoming suspicious of me over there.

If we tell the police, it will amount to nothing—my dad's *very* experienced in avoiding that kind of trouble." There was a long pause. "Chloe, if you are planning some kind of raid, you should know—it's going to be a bloodbath."

Chloe didn't say anything.

"Some people have been waiting years for this kind of direct confrontation. And while the Mai may not carry weapons, we do."

Chloe felt trapped and uncertain. "Have you told Amy and Paul?"

"Not yet. I'm meeting them in a few minutes to give them back their walkie-talkie—they're very possessive about it. Maybe the three of us together actually *can* think of some way of extricating your mom secretly. Anyway, three heads are better than one. And your friend Amy seems pretty experienced at the whole hacking and breaking-and-entering thing."

She smiled at that. "All right. Thanks. Keep me posted."

"Will do!"

Chloe hung up and put the picture of the Mai woman back on the bed with the others. Then she flipped open the phone again, dialed Brian's home number, and waited.

"Hi, this is Brian Rezza—if you're looking for Whit Rezza, you can reach him on his cell at 415-555-1412. Leave a message. Thanks!"

She hung up. Then she dialed again, carefully remembering the number.

"Hello?" A rich, masculine voice answered the phone.

"Hello, Mr. Rezza. It's Chloe King." She paused for a long moment, working up the courage to speak her next sentence. "I want to talk to you about a trade. Me for my mom."

Twenty-five

Chloe waited on a rock in the middle of the Presidio, obviously by herself and open to attack.

This was one of the most central, hidden areas in the mazelike complex of abandoned army buildings, a long-empty row of houses that were small and neat and as kept up as a suburban dream—but completely empty. The grass was trimmed on the little shared green the houses all looked out on, and the rock on which Chloe sat had obviously been moved there from somewhere else. Lucasfilm was moving its headquarters or something there at some point; for now, the area at dusk was as weird and perfect and lonesome as a Tim Burton set.

Chloe sang a little song to keep up her spirits, but all she could think of was "New York, New York." It still had a lot of 9/11 connotations to it, patriotic and stirring—fitting for her current mood in the empty military base. But her voice was reedy and got lost in the wind;

she kicked her heels like a little girl and waited for something to happen.

As the breeze changed direction, she caught a scent. *Human*. A few of them. And something familiar—a warm scent, a comforting skin smell.

"You can come out here," Chloe called carelessly. "I'm all alone." She tried not to get too excited, but they really *had* brought her mother with them. The exchange would happen. And no one would get hurt. Except for maybe herself.

Whit Rezza stepped out of the shadows. He wore a long, flowing raincoat that made it look like he was about to get on a plane for Europe, not negotiate for the release of a captive. Following him was a younger man in khakis and a black leather jacket, propelling her mom forward with a gun to her head.

"Chloe!" her mother said, trying to cut the sob of relief into a direct order. "Get out of here. These people are insane."

"No can do," Chloe said cheerfully. "It's my fault that all of this stuff is happening, and I'm going to fix it."

"Chloe, leave this *instant*," her mother said again, standing up straight and looking over her glasses at her.

"None of this would have happened if you hadn't adopted me," Chloe said.

Her mom rolled her eyes and almost stamped her foot. "Chloe, would you *shut up*? I *love you* and I'm *your mother* and I'm *telling you* to run away while you still can!"

"How much did he tell you?" Chloe demanded. "What did he tell you about me?"

"I told her the truth," Whit said. "Well, up to what she could handle."

"He told me that there's some sort of Russian Mafia connected with your biological family and they're involved in . . . I don't know, bad crimes or something, and that they had lured you in. And that they needed to protect me from them—that they would come after me. And that you had been involved in a murder. Whatever the story, this gentleman has a *gun* to my head, so I'm guessing that the truth is a bit skewed."

"You never believed anything we were telling you?" Whit asked, a little surprised.

"Piss off," Chloe's mother spat.

Her daughter couldn't help grinning. "Don't worry, Mom, it's for the best."

"You would do well to listen to your daughter," Whit suggested mildly. "For a member of the Mai, she is surprisingly logical."

"Yet you're *still* going to kill me," Chloe said, rolling her eyes.

"You killed a member of our Order."

"I did *not*. I tried to *save* him," Chloe said, leaping down from the rock, frustrated.

"Yes, that's what my son keeps saying."

"That's because it's the *truth*!" Brian stepped out from around a building, throwing stars ready in his hands.

"Brian?" Chloe said, surprised.

"Brian?" his father said, confused.

"Brian," Richard spat. "I should have known you were going to try to save the cat bitch."

"Don't talk to my son that way," Mr. Rezza snapped, surprising everyone.

"Since when does the Order start carrying guns, you coward?" Brian demanded, coming closer, eyes locked on the other young man's.

"How did you know I was here?" Chloe asked, relief washing over her. She still had every intention of saving her mom and keeping the bloodshed to a minimum, offering herself up as a sacrifice—but she was also extremely grateful that there suddenly might be options other than her possibly being killed.

"I didn't. Once I was pretty sure that they had your mother, I kept an eye on my dad and followed him and Dickless here."

Brian didn't look like the brooding, complicated man she knew; he strode forward confidently, never taking his eyes off the gun, every inch the hero she wanted him to be. The wind blew his thick dark hair back, and his face was livid with anger.

"I *saw* her reach her hand down to try to save Alexander when he slipped—with my own two eyes!"

"But *why* would she do that?" his father asked, sounding genuinely confused and a little exasperated.

"Because she's a *good person*, Dad."

"You saw that when you were at the bridge *helping* her," Richard said, jerking his chin in Chloe's direction. "I'll bet."

"Yeah. That's right," Brian spat. "Sue me for trying to help an innocent girl you sent a *psycho killer* after."

"So the betrayal is complete," Mr. Rezza said wonderingly. "Of the Order, your forefathers, your own father, your mother—"

"Don't you *dare* bring Mom into this," Brian yelled, aiming one of the shuriken at his dad.

"I cannot—will not—protect you from whatever action the Order takes against you," his father said levelly, not looking at the weapon targeted on him. "Or random acts of revenge." He said this to Brian, but his eyes flicked toward Richard.

"Will you *listen* to yourselves?" Chloe said, suddenly weary. She had watched the whole fight between father and son in silence and finally couldn't take it anymore. "Kidnapping innocent people . . . hired assassins . . . revenge and protection and betrayal and weird secret societies that go from generation to generation. It's insane! Both you *and* the Mai. This is America in the third millennium. *AD.* Leave all that other shit back in Europe and the Dark Ages where it belongs. You think of yourselves as self-appointed protectors of the human race, but you're nothing but a group of barely restrained vigilantes waging a war on people who never did anything to you!"

"The Mai killed my wife," Whit began, with great emotion.

"No, they didn't. Brian told me. She was killed on a raid that *you* sent her out on."

Chloe's mom turned to look at Whit. "You lied even about that? That's *sick*!"

"She wouldn't have *been* killed if a human hadn't been attacked and killed by the Mai, forcing us to call the raid—"

"Okay, just stop," Chloe said, throwing up her hand. "Each side can claim a million random violences done back and forth on them—"

"Since the Slaughter five thousand years ago, when you wiped out an entire country of humans," Whit interrupted. "And I will *not* be talked to by a teenage girl, Mai *or* human, like that. As for 'random violences,' Miss King . . ." He stepped forward as he spoke, glaring at her. "While luring you out of hiding was important, we've done this to *protect your mother*—who was as good as dead the moment you took up with Sergei."

Chloe's eyes widened.

"Oh yes," Whit chuckled, "I know Sergei. And his habits . . . Did you know that male lions, when they take over a pride, often kill all the cubs fathered by other cats?"

That gave Chloe pause.

"We kidnapped your mother for her *own* sake. To keep her safe."

"It's amazing the lies you continue to tell." Sergei

came tapping up the previously empty road, his expensive shoes echoing against the pavement. Behind him were seven deadly looking Mai, all trained kizekh. Unlike a troop of humans, they didn't march in unison: they prowled and sniffed the wind and kept their unblinking slit eyes on the enemy.

"There are four more hidden behind the house and two over there," one of them hissed to Sergei. "They reek of machine oil. . . . They must all have weapons, guns, except for the two behind that bush."

"I suppose this was inevitable, wasn't it, Sergei?" Whit said easily, turning from Chloe as if she were dismissed. Richard tightened his grip on Mrs. King.

"Nothing is inevitable," Sergei replied crisply. He cocked his head, and two of the Mai disappeared into the shadows to take care of whoever they found there. "Since when has the Order stooped to kidnapping innocent women?"

"As soon as you sent out assassins to kill her, you murdering animal!" Brian's dad began to lose his cool; black anger shone in his eyes.

A gunshot went off, muffled, somewhere among the houses. No one jumped except for Chloe. There was a thump and a growl somewhere else—like they were in the middle of a horror movie, with horrible things happening all around them in the dark.

"Um, was this little secret meeting of mine secret to *any*one?" Chloe asked, partly of the world, partly of

Brian. Mostly it was a failing attempt to lighten the situation. She had tried to fix everything herself and avoid a fight—and what she'd done was bring the opposing parties together, armed, at an out-of-the-way place where no one would have any idea what was going on.

Young, feminine screaming—and a not-so-feminine male shriek—came from the bushes.

"Wait! We're not sworders—uh, Bladers—don't hurt us!"

"Amy?" Chloe said, recognizing the confused voice. Two of the kizekh slunk into the open, one with an iron grip around Amy and Paul.

"They're with me," Kim said, stepping out of the darkness. Alyec was next to her, cursing in Russian and wiping blood off his arm.

"How did you . . . ?" Chloe looked at them in wonderment. *Everyone* really was here.

"I am the best tracker in the Pride," Kim said, drawing herself up straight.

"And the walkie-talkie I gave you?" Amy said, stepping carefully away from the scary-looking soldier with his mouth open and canines bared. "It's got GPS."

"We knew where you were every minute. We tracked you on it." Paul was camo-chic, in army pants and a tight-fitting camouflage windbreaker.

Chloe had a thousand questions: How had they all gotten to know each other? How had they gotten together? How had Amy and Paul reacted to Kim? How were Kim and Alyec getting along?

But most of all, she felt like sobbing in relief. All of her closest friends had come to help her out. To save her.

"Paul, Amy, go *home*!" Mrs. King ordered. "You too, Chloe. I don't know what the hell is going on, but you need to get out of here."

"The deal was Chloe for you," Whit said, pulling his attention away from the four new teenagers and back to Sergei. "We are prepared to let that deal continue, no questions asked, no blood, everyone goes home safely."

"You're trading a woman's life for that of her own *daughter*?" Brian said bitterly. "I guess I should have seen that coming. After Mom . . . I should have known."

"You shut up, Brian. I've had just about enough of your lip about your mother for this lifetime," his dad growled. "You're unworthy to even speak her name."

"Ah, father and son." Sergei sighed. "I do so love the warmth in human families."

"What would you know about that?" Richard demanded, jamming his gun into the side of Anna's face for emphasis. "Don't cats screw anything that moves and then move on?"

"You'd better muzzle the child, Whitney. Don't let him start what you can't finish," Sergei said, waving his hand in the air. It was clawed. Chloe wasn't sure if Brian's dad understood what that meant: that he was just about ready to attack.

"*Finish?* Like when you *finished off* entire villages—"

"That was five thousand years ago," Kim pointed

out as calmly as possible. She and Alyec had slowly put themselves in between Amy and Paul and the rest of the people there. Amy bobbed her head around so she could watch what was going on; Paul just looked confused.

"Um, yeah." Chloe cleared her throat and spoke up. Just to let people know that she was still there. Wasn't *she* the reason everyone was here tonight? *No, I'm just an excuse,* she realized, looking at the fanatical faces around her. Both sides were itching for a fight, a real one, after years of uneasy sort-of truce in this country. Led by two middle-aged leaders who felt they had something to prove.

"Maybe we can talk about this," Chloe's mother suggested, also as calmly as she could. "There seems to be a long-standing dispute between your two groups here."

Chloe was horrified to see tears running down her mother's cheeks—of fear or pain as the gun was jabbed into her temple, she wasn't sure. *My mother.* Something inside Chloe finally snapped.

"Sir! Ramirez is down!" A young man wearing an outfit similar to Richard's came running forward with a gun, four neat lines of blood across his face. "We were attacked from behind—he's bleeding badly, sir. But we got one of them *good.*"

"A preemptive strike, Sergei?" Whit demanded, pulling a short, curved sword out of his coat.

With a snarl, the female kizekh who had been arguing with Kim leapt at the soldier.

Ellen, her name is Ellen. Chloe had watched *Star Wars* with her just a few evenings before. She was completely Mai now, eyes slit and fangs bared and tearing into the young man like he was paper.

From then on everything happened in slow motion.

Silently, Richard took the gun from the side of Chloe's mom's head and pointed it at the lion woman. Almost in aftereffect, muffled blasts afflicted Chloe's ears, three bangs, one after the other.

Brian immediately made for Richard, a look of raw hatred on his face.

Amy and Paul looked at each other, confused, then Amy screamed ever so slowly; Chloe couldn't make out the words, but she and Paul began to run.

More Tenth Bladers came out of the night. Chloe was stunned by their numbers—at least a dozen; far more than the kizekh had thought. They must have been hiding downwind. Why had Brian's dad brought them all? It was just supposed to be her and him. Even the dickhead holding the gun to her mom's head was a surprise. . . .

As in a bizarre instructional film about reproduction, each Tenth Blader found a Mai, each Mai found a Tenth Blader, and they all began throwing weapons or struggling in the dust. Even Kim and Alyec. The look on Kim's face—white-eyed horror turning to rage as someone attacked her, as if she couldn't quite believe it. Alyec tried to shove her out of the way. . . .

Chloe didn't know what to do.

She had come here to save her mother. And now what? What *could* she do?

No one was attacking her; the struggle was going on inches from her feet, the very one she'd been trying to prevent.

Sergei neatly avoided Whit's attack with the knife, moving far more agilely than a man of his age should have been able to. Before Brian could reach Richard, Sergei brought his square hand full of claws down like it was a giant paw and cuffed him squarely on the side of the face; Richard fell down instantly, and Sergei neatly retrieved the gun as he did.

"Nobody move!" Sergei demanded, spinning around and leveling the gun at Mrs. King. "Call off your men, Whit, or I'll shoot your captive."

Chloe couldn't quite believe what was happening. It made sense—the Tenth Bladers would do anything to protect a human, but still . . . was he serious?

Paul and Amy froze; Mrs. King did, too.

Suddenly Chloe had a path, a thing to do.

She ran, sprinting for her mom. That was why she was there.

"No!" Brian screamed, and made for Sergei. "Leave her alone!"

And Sergei fired.

It could have been meant for Brian, or it could have been meant for her mom. Chloe would never know. All she was sure of was that this was her fault, her doing. She dug a claw into the ground and pushed herself forward.

There was very little pain when the bullet first entered her flesh.

But when it hit her heart, it was like her entire body caught on fire.

"Chloe! No!"

She had no idea who was screaming: it could have been male, female, or a number of people.

She crumpled to the ground.

Her heart was very loud in her ears, and the ground was very cold under her head. The rest of her was on fire, as though she were being burned alive.

She listened interestedly to the muted sounds around her and the slow thumping of her heart.

After a few more beats, it stopped entirely.

Twenty-six

Blackness. Echoes.

The sounds of something distant that might have been water dropping, but thicker. Wind howled somewhere, but no breeze touched her face.

Chloe recognized where she was even before she opened her eyes.

She was farther back from the edge of the cliff than the first time, when she had come to this place after falling off Coit Tower. Far below was what looked like a pool of mercury that bubbled and rippled uncertainly.

She noticed things she hadn't before: directly overhead there were millions and millions of stars and galaxies and strange planets she couldn't have named, far more terrifying than the emptiness she had thought was there. It was like she was at the end of the universe, the end of everything.

Something screamed, low and insistent. When she squinted, Chloe could just make out shadowy forms flickering in and out of sight, just beyond her vision, impossible to hold for more than a second. Like they weren't there—or like they were an optical illusion.

Chloe backed away to the edge of the cliff, putting as much distance between them and her as she could.

"Chloe. *Saht.*"

It was a whisper, a purr, and a growl all combined.

One shadow hovered closer than the rest, lingering.

"Daughter."

"M-mom?" Chloe asked, quavering. The shade had no recognizable form, slipping back and forth from something vaguely bestial to something upright.

"*Now you know your destiny.* Go back."

"But wait—what is this?" Chloe asked desperately, trying to grasp at things she knew in her heart were fleeting and impermanent. "Where am I? What happened to you?"

The shadow wavered and shifted, like there was extremely hot air between them.

"Return to your living mother. She is reality now—as I am, in your past."

Chloe didn't understand. She opened her mouth to ask something more, but a rush of hot air hit her on the chest like a fist. Chloe flew backward off the cliff, into the darkness below.

Life, when she returned to it, was pain. She reached into her chest with her claw and with an agonized groan pulled out the bullet that was lodged there. Blood poured down her front and slowed to a trickle as she watched. Soon it stopped entirely, and she felt an itching where the skin and sinew began to knit.

Sounds began to make sense around her, not that she cared. Murmurs of, "She is the One!" and, "Why isn't she dead?" and just, "Chloe!" from the people who simply loved her. The fighting seemed to have stopped; several of the Mai were on their knees before her.

Her mother was beside her, making sure she was okay.

No, wait—her mother had carefully angled herself *between* Chloe and the Tenth Bladers, shielding her daughter with her body. Whit's men shifted hesitantly on their feet, starting to raise their guns and then dropping them, unsure what to do.

Shakily Chloe got to one knee and then rose from there. It hurt every part of her, but she stood.

"*Any*one," she said, loudly and evenly so everyone could hear her, "human *or* Mai ever touches my mother again, I'll *kill* you. I will hunt you down and kill you. And I have seven lives left to do it in."

Chloe put her hand to her side, which still burned. She leaned over a little to ease the pain, facing Whit and his remaining Tenth Bladers. "Listen to me: I did *not* kill the Rogue. He fell off the bridge when I was *trying to help him back up*. I have never hurt *any*one. Neither has Alyec or Kim, or Paul or Amy. *Or my mom*. You can all leave us out of your little war."

Amy and Alyec ran forward when she began to sway,

each throwing one of her arms over their shoulders. Paul and Kim followed.

"As for the Mai . . ." She looked directly at Sergei. There was no proof that he'd actually sent assassins after her mother, but he was the second person that evening to train a gun on her. "Home isn't Mai or human. Home is home. And I'm going home *now*."

She put out her hand and her mom took it.

Clasped, unnoticed in her other hand, was her mother's silver earring, the one Brian had found. She looked back at those they left, the wounded, the dead, the respectful Mai, and the confused humans.

Brian was not among them.

Chloe, her four friends, and her mother walked quietly out into the night.

Twenty-seven

Two Mai and two human teenagers sat in a booth at the Washington Diner, silently drinking coffee or hot chocolate, picking at a large order of cold, greasy fries topped with thick bright ketchup that reminded everyone there too much of blood. The fluorescent lights made everything harsh and lifeless. The late-night waitstaff was grumpy and standoffish, which was fine for the four gathered, who had no urge to socialize with strangers.

Alyec, Kim, Paul, and Amy sat uncomfortably, like distant cousins long separated at a family reunion told to go make friends with other kids their age. Kim had borrowed a scarf from Amy and wrapped her head with it like a babushka, hiding her ears. The waitress had just rolled her eyes—she was used to the late-night freaks who came in.

"So . . . ," Paul said, playing with a fry. "What does this whole . . . being-the-One thing mean?"

Kim had her paws wrapped around a mug of hot

chocolate and was staring into the depths, looking spacey even for her.

"It means she is the natural leader of this pride. That her mother was probably the previous leader and that she, like her mother, fulfills all of the traditional requirements: loyalty, bravery, compassion, fair-mindedness, and a willingness to come up with solutions to seemingly impossible situations." Kim pulled herself together a bit, falling into her usual didactic role. "It means that her ka is true and noble and that she would do anything to defend her friends and family. It means she has nine lives—or seven now, as she said. And other . . . less definable traits."

Paul and Amy nodded mutely, and even Alyec seemed interested in the subject, like it was news to him.

"It means Alyec is no longer next in line to be leader," Kim said carefully.

"That's okay; too much responsibility," Alyec said, trying to be humorous—but it came off sounding bleak. Even he wasn't untouched by the events of the night.

"From what you've said, it sounds like that Sergei guy should no longer be the leader," Paul said slowly. "That it really should be Chloe."

Kim nodded mutely and looked back down at her hot chocolate.

"Did you see those two old freaks?" Amy spoke up, voice wavering. "It was like Mr. Rezza and Sergei were off in their own little world. . . . Did you see how he treated Brian? Like either *one* of them is likely to give up power. *Ever.*"

"I have never seen violence like that before," Kim said into her mug, then looked up, wide-eyed and shocked, like a child. "I've seen fights and duels, but . . ."

Alyec nodded, leaning on his hand. "I know. I thought it would be *fun* or something."

Paul and Amy looked at each other. Paul reached out his hand and squeezed hers.

"We didn't end up doing *anything* to help her," Amy finally said, frustrated. "We were supposed to be doing all this detective legwork crap, and none of it mattered. . . ."

"If it wasn't for your idea with the walkie-talkie, we never would have found her," Alyec pointed out.

"We were there." Kim looked up at all of them. "Supporting her. I think that sometimes, that's enough."

"One thing's for certain," Alyec added, stirring his coffee with a claw. "Her life is going to get even more complicated and a lot more dangerous from now on. . . ."

Twenty-eight

Chloe and her mom sat on the couch, mostly silent. It had taken over an hour just for Chloe to tell her mother the story and another hour for Mrs. King to ask the inevitable questions.

Mrs. King got out some expensive scotch and downed a shot. She offered Chloe some, but Chloe declined, wanting cocoa instead. Mrs. King made it for her, going through the movements robotically.

"Oh, here's your earring," Chloe remembered, taking it out of her pocket. It gleamed dully in the light. She turned it over in her fingers, staring at it. "It's so random. . . . Such a tiny chance that it fell, and that Brian found it."

"Give your mother a *little* credit," the older woman said with a wry smile, indicating how *both* of her ears were bare. "Every time they moved me, I dropped another piece of jewelry or whatever, hoping it might provide *someone* a clue as to where I was. I think I'm out about three thousand dollars' worth of the stuff." She handed Chloe her cocoa and shook her head.

Chloe smiled—it was still too soon to grin. *I really do have the coolest mother.* She couldn't imagine Mrs. Chun or Amy's mom thinking to do something like that. But her face darkened again as she thought about moms and the other thing she had to tell hers.

"I saw my biological mother," she said after they had been silent for a while. "When I was, uh, dead."

Mrs. King looked up at her through slightly glazed eyes—dim from the evening, not the drink. There were bruises and scrapes on the side of her head where the gun had been jammed against it. Her usually pixie-perfect hair was tousled, and her glasses were bent. Chloe wished she didn't have to see her mother this way—she might have thought her mom was a perfectionist bitch sometimes, but seeing her like this was almost unbearable.

"What did she say?" her mother asked after a moment.

"She said that she was proud of me and that I should go back and rescue you—that you were my real mother, too."

It was a difficult thing to say, but Chloe was glad she had.

Even when her mom began to cry and hug her.

They finally said good night, somehow both knowing it was safe for now. Chloe had meant every word she had said about killing whoever tried to attack her home again, and the Mai seemed to respect her now. And the Tenth Blade had something to think about.

She wearily climbed the stairs to her room, wanting desperately the hot, cleansing water of a bath but too exhausted to seriously consider the effort of running the water or waiting for it to fill.

Chloe sat on her bed, empty of all thought, trying to kick off her sneakers without bending over to untie them.

She was startled by a tap at the window.

Brian was there, his frame obscuring a surprisingly clear night full of stars. Chloe felt her stomach lurch for a moment when she saw him. There was blood on his face and hands; where he tapped, an ugly dark blotch remained.

Chloe leapt up and pushed open the window.

"Brian!" she cried. He was holding his shoulder, like there was a wound there.

A bullet wound, she realized, catching a faint odor of metal and powder. It smelled like poison to her, like death.

"Hey." He smiled weakly. "I'm all right. Nothing too serious."

"Come in—I can get some bandages. . . ." He was balanced on the outside of the sill as neatly as if he were Mai, and she was afraid he would fall if he lost too much blood.

He shook his head. "I can't. I just came to say goodbye."

She didn't understand; it was all over. The good guys had won—and he was a good guy.

"Why? What's the—?"

"I'm a dead man," he said wearily. "Richard is basically calling a fatwa on me—as a traitor to the Order. And my father refuses to protect me. You never quit the Order while you're alive."

"But you had no choice! You told me! Your father made you."

He shrugged. "It doesn't matter. I said my vows when I was fourteen—and now I'm a wanted man. I have to disappear."

Finally Chloe began to cry, streams of silent tears coursing their way down her cheeks.

"Brian, it's not *fair*. You were just trying to *help* me. It's all my fault. . . ."

"*Nothing* is your fault, Chloe." He reached in and grabbed her hand, squeezing it. "Nothing is your fault. You're good, kind, and smart. . . . I have no doubt that you'll make a great leader to your people." He looked her seriously in the eye. "But you know that you're a top to-kill on the Order's list, right?"

"I know," she said sadly.

"My hanging out here would only put you in more danger, Chloe." He took his hands off hers and began to stand. "I love you," he said, and kissed the glass near her face.

She leaned forward and kissed him back, the cold glass between them keeping him safe from her.

Then he fell into the night, disappearing into the city.

Chloe covered her face with her hands and wept.

Epilogue

Sergei sat at his desk, hands clasped under his chin as though he were praying. He had run a claw through his hair, fixing it, but there was blood on his cuffs from when he had taken down one of the younger members of the Order, pulling at the tendons in the boy's neck while closing his fingers.

It had been a long time since Sergei had personally gotten involved in a fight. He had missed it—there was something incredibly stirring and visceral about protecting your people with your own body. That was one of the signs of a real leader.

A real leader knew what to do during peacetime as well, knew how to manage a modern bureaucracy to gather his people safely, to work the system and reunite families and keep them all employed and safe and hidden. He had done exactly that for the past fifteen years or so. *I am a leader,* he told himself, *and no one is going to take that away. Certainly not some little girl from San Francisco.*

He opened a drawer, using his claw to undo the lock, and took out a small, nondescript gray cell phone. He dialed a number with his thumb, claws receding.

"Hello, Alexander? First, let me offer my condolences," he said with a chuckle, "since everyone seems to believe that you are dead.

"In other business, I thought we could help each other out again. Remember the pride leader's daughter? The one you, ah, *took care of* with my . . . *assistance*? It turns out she has a sister, Chloe King. Yes, you've met—Yes, she's the One. . . .

"And I can help you find her. So you can take care of *her* as well."

THE CHOSEN

For Gg Re and Billy, love and congratulations.

One

"Hey, King, how you *feeling?*"

Chloe closed her eyes and sighed, resisting the urge to rest her head against the locker behind her. She knew Scott was just being friendly—he wasn't even making a joke—but the reality of Chloe's situation was exhausting. All her life she had been content to surf the shallow waters of the pond of high-school popularity, reveling in her basic anonymity.

Of course, all that was over now.

"I'm still a little tired," she said, turning around with a wan smile. "But mostly better. Thanks."

"Dude, that shit is *serious.* My cousin got it and he had to be homeschooled over the summer, he was so far behind." Scott adjusted his headphones and made a gunlike gesture at her. "Peace out."

Why did it have to be mono? she wondered for the fiftieth time that day. Coming down with Epstein-Barr was the fake excuse Sergei had fed the school's administrators about Chloe's long absence, and even now that the dust had settled, Chloe didn't think sharing the real reason for her absence would go over too well.

Sorry about the whole not-showing-up-at-school-for-a-few-weeks thing, Chloe pictured herself saying to the principal. *You see, I'm a* cat person *and had to hide with others of my kind in a gigantic mansion called Firebird that also houses a real estate firm while this ancient Masonic-like cult tried to hunt me down because they think I killed one of their assassins. Oh, also, I have nine lives and am apparently the spiritual leader of my people, who believe they were created by ancient Egyptian goddesses.*

Nope. Chloe couldn't imagine it would fly.

"But couldn't it at least have been a brain tumor? Or even a nose job?" she wondered aloud. She watched Scott walk down the hall, slapping hands with actual friends. He was only someone that Chloe knew vaguely before, but at least his reaction was better than most. Keira Henderson, for instance, kept telling everyone how there should be a special health class devoted just to STDs and Chloe.

Of all the things Sergei had done to her, the mono/"kissing disease" lie was up there with the worst. Well, of the things she could actually *prove* he'd done, that is. It was hard to pin down exactly when keeping her safe from assassins had turned into just plain keeping her. And while the Order of the Tenth Blade was an organization whose sole purpose was to wipe out the

Mai cat people, they had kidnapped Chloe's mom, insisting it was for her own protection. At the showdown in the Presidio their leader swore that Sergei would stop at nothing to cut Chloe's ties to her human friends and families, and even though Chloe had come to see Sergei as sort of a surrogate dad over the previous few weeks, she found herself wondering if it might be true.

Chloe had really hoped life would get back to normal when she left the Mai, returned home, and went back to school. *No such luck.* Not yet, anyway. The Order was reasonably quiet now that Chloe had given up one of her lives to save her mom and everyone realized she was "the One." Plus—and Chloe wasn't even really talking to anyone at Firebird right now—her feelings toward Sergei were still unresolved, Brian was missing, and, well, she was still torn between him and Alyec. *And everyone thinks I have mono. Great.*

Chloe pulled out her cell phone and called Brian, but it clicked immediately over to voice mail, like it had the last twenty times she'd tried. And his voice mail was full. She hadn't heard anything from him since the night she'd died and come back saving her mom from the crossfire between the Mai and the Order. Brian, the *son* of the Order's leader, had come out on her side—and vengeance was promised by the rest of the Bladers. He had said his goodbyes at her window, where they'd shared a kiss through the glass pane, and then he'd disappeared into the dark city.

"Hey, Selina, what up?" Paul asked, going up to his own locker. He had taken to calling her that since she had told him and Amy about her true nature. Selina was Catwoman's alter ego, and, she suspected, his way of dealing with the fact that *she* had superpowers while he, the comic geek, remained a normal human. *Whatever helps him cope,* thought Chloe.

"So, besides being tired all the time and getting mocked by the general school population, are there any other symptoms of mono I should know about?" Chloe asked.

"I know you can't go to some countries in Africa because Epstein-Barr interacts with some weird fungus and can kill you," Paul said diplomatically.

"No African countries, no weird fungi. Check and check." She thought vaguely of the Pride in New Orleans, made up primarily of Mai who had chosen to stay in Africa after they were forced to leave Egypt and had eventually migrated to Louisiana.

"How you doing, dealing with being back and all?"

Chloe sighed and leaned against the lockers, hands behind her head. "Let's see. Three weeks of extratricky trig to catch up on, I somehow managed to miss the Civil War Reconstruction, and I have to figure out oxidation-reduction reactions on my own in the lab after school. Oh," she said, snapping her fingers, "*and Moby-Dick*. The entire thing, whale meat, peg legs, and all, by next Tuesday."

"That, uh, sucks," Paul said.

"I don't think they have invented a word beyond *sucks* yet that adequately describes my academic situation," Chloe reported. They started walking down the hall together, Chloe dragging her feet to phys ed, seriously bummed. She still hadn't decided between blowing Mr. Parmalee's mind by suddenly slam dunking something or pulling a *Smallville* and trying to hide her secret powers by acting like a normal, physically inept slacker.

"What about, you know." Paul searched for his words awkwardly, something he rarely did. He made a little clawing gesture.

"Fitting in with you monkeys like a normal human being?" Chloe said dryly. "It's really not that big a deal, Paul. I've done it my whole life."

He nodded, but Paul's expressive caterpillar eyebrows were drawn together a little, like an anime character miming worry. Paul swished down the hallway in his hipster DJ track pants and Chloe realized she hadn't seen him in khakis since . . . well, before she discovered who she really was and fell in with the Mai. As she pushed her way into the locker room, a thought occurred to her: *I wonder what else I missed.*

When she went over to Amy's that evening to study, her friend's already cloth-covered and messy bedroom looked like a costume factory had exploded—a sure sign that Halloween was on its way. There were Styrofoam coffee cups filled with sequins, beads, buttons, and other shiny things dotting every free surface. Bits of lace and pieces of velvet were strewn everywhere. A glue gun and scissors and needles and a sewing machine all perched precariously in one corner, as if afraid of falling into the chaos below and being incorporated into an outfit. Amy's previous triumphs were hung on hangers, looking strangely organized against the chaos of the rest of the room. She was already playing her Halloween music: *Buffy: The Musical* blasted through her old-school wood speakers that were hidden under the craft crap.

"I'm thinking seventeenth century," Amy said, a finger to her lips. "You know, by way of the undead. Zombie, not vampire."

"Yeah. Vampires are *so* passé," Chloe muttered, erasing the math problem she was working on and starting over again. She had managed to carve herself a little nest on one end of her friend's bed and was using a bolt of muslin as a lap desk. In front of her, Chloe's notebook teetered unevenly on her math book, covered with sines and cosines and bits of equations.

Amy took her friend's comment at face value. "I *know!* Isn't it ridiculous? But this will be great. I'll use real boning in the corset this time—you know that place Dark Garden? They said they'd sell me scraps of their two-way coil boning and tips to go over them."

"Amy, I'm trying to not get held back here," Chloe said, raising her math book so she could see it. "No offense, but I really have to knuckle down."

"Oh yeah, sorry, no problem." Amy squinched her nose and Chloe tried not to laugh. Her friend's dark hair was frizzing out all around her face, exploding out of the strip of cloth she'd tried to tie it back with. There were giant, baby-diaper-sized safety pins lined up neatly on her T-shirt's shoulder, and a measuring tape hung around her neck. "I am *all* about schoolish things these days." She leapt and crash-sat on the bed, causing Chloe to hug the textbook to her chest and grab her calculator for its safety. "Look at this!"

Amy pulled a pamphlet out of the back of her jeans. She had been wearing pants a lot more often these days, ones that were—for her—surprisingly tight and shapely. *She used to, um, eschew them as being banal and pedestrian,* Chloe thought carefully, trying to use her SAT words. She took the brochure and began reading.

"*'Fit'?* What the hell is that, a new diet?"

"No, it's *F-I-T,* the Fashion Institute of Technology. In New York. It's like, the best clothing design college in the country. *Very* prestigious."

Chloe looked at the photos: people dressed weirdly—like Amy—sitting in classrooms, walking happily down the street, pinning things up on mannequins, designing jewelry on computers.

"Cool. Looks great," Chloe said, handing the pamphlet

back. "But, uh, you've got a ways to go yet, you know? We're sophomores, remember?"

"Yeah." Amy blushed and looked down. "I'm, uh, kind of thinking about graduating a year early."

"What?" Chloe demanded, putting her book aside.

"Chloe, I'm *done* here," Amy said, sighing. "I'm already taking one AP course—with just three more by next summer I'll have fulfilled all my requirements."

"I . . . shit," Chloe said, unsure what to say. The only other person she knew who'd graduated early was Halley's older brother, a certified genius who went immediately to MIT, not FIT. It wasn't the sort of thing people like *them*—her and Amy and Paul—did.

One more year and suddenly Amy would be gone from her life.

"Actually, you—I mean, what's happened with you—was a big part of my decision," Amy said shyly, her blue eyes round and big. "You know, the last month when you weren't really here, when you were doing that whole Mai thing and none of us knew what was going on—you had this whole other life going on. You're, like, a cat person, and leader of your people and dealing with feuds that go back hundreds of years and you're, like, sixteen. And still going to school. I want a cool life, too."

They were both silent for a moment.

"I'm not 'the leader of my people,'" Chloe finally mumbled, opening up her math book again.

For the next few hours they interacted normally:

Amy interrupted Chloe's studying, constantly asking what she thought of a particular fabric or lace, and Chloe responded by throwing things at her. They took a break at eight thirty and Mrs. Scotkin made them espresso and s'mores over the flames on her stove. At ten the two friends stopped working and watched *The Daily Show with John Stewart.*

On the drive home, as Amy chatted excitedly about FIT and her plans for next year, she kept looking askance at Chloe. *She's been wanting to tell me this for a while,* Chloe realized. *She's been working herself up to it.*

When they pulled up the driveway, Chloe's mom was already looking out the kitchen window for her. Amy waved. Chloe sighed and gritted her teeth. Anna King never used to do that, and if she *was* waiting up, she always made it look like she was doing something else, like watching TV or reading. Her philosophy was to respect her teenage daughter and trust her—something her ex-husband hadn't agreed with. Although Chloe hardly remembered him, her adoptive dad had had been very overprotective. He'd even told her mom that Chloe shouldn't date. Ever. Chloe wondered if it was possible that he had known who she was all along—a Mai, a lion person—and that any human she was intimate with would die.

Chloe waited as long as she could, waving at Amy until the black Malibu faded into the black night, its red taillights growing smaller like a match going out. Finally it was time to go in.

"Hey . . ." Chloe stepped inside the warm house.

"Hey, Chloe. How was your day?" Her mom sounded casual and was washing something in the sink. For just a moment, Anna King looked like a suburban housewife, not a single mom who lawyered by day and had to deal with her adopted freaky lion girl at night. Even though things had basically turned out all right, Chloe still couldn't forgive herself for her mom's kidnapping.

"All right. I got most of my math done at Amy's—if I can get through fifty pages of the *Dick* tonight, I'll be golden."

"I really wish you wouldn't call it that," Anna said, giving a smirk that was—just for a second—all lawyer and old mom. "Do you want anything to eat?"

There had suddenly been a lot of extra meat in the fridge, and while Chloe wished her mom would stop trying to be so subtly and awkwardly supportive, she was secretly grateful. She hadn't gone totally Atkins since her claws first came out, but she definitely found more of a preference for things salty and red these days.

Vampires are so passé, she thought. *Cats are in now.*

"I'll grab something in a little while. I really want to get this done." She began to head up the stairs to her room.

"Chloe?"

She stopped, cringing at the openness in her mom's voice.

"I'm really proud of you." Her mother's pixie-cut

hair was pulled back flat and into two tiny pigtails on the back of her head, but she still managed to look maternal and older in that instant. "Not just because of . . . everything you've been through, but how you're really working hard to get back to where you were in school. I think you're doing a great job."

"Thanks," Chloe said. She wasn't sure if she was supposed to say anything else, but her mom just nodded and went back to doing the dishes.

After the showdown at the Presidio, the two of them had had a big ol' heart-to-heart about a lot of things. Chloe told her all about her secret powers, the Mai, the Tenth Bladers who kidnapped her, how when she was dead, she saw her biological mom. Her mom had sipped scotch and listened. Finally they both cried and hugged, and that was that.

But things *had* changed between them, and she was uncomfortable even thinking about it. There was no getting around the fact that she had saved her mom's life by taking a bullet and dying, losing one of her eight remaining lives. That was a big, heavy thing for a mother to accept, a mother who still thought of herself as protector and guardian.

And Chloe didn't like the walking on eggshells her mom was doing while trying to figure out the best way to deal with her superhero teenage daughter. *I should do something bad and get grounded,* she half decided. *That would set things normal real fast.*

Her cell phone rang—or rather, Amy's cell phone, the one with the GPS that had allowed Chloe's friends to track her down when she was trying to trade herself for her mom with the Tenth Bladers, rang. Chloe hadn't given it back yet, another loose thread from the whole incident. *But not the loosest one.*

"Hey," she said, recognizing Alyec's number.

"Hello, Chloe girl! Guess where I'm calling you from?"

"The All-State after party?" she guessed.

"Absolutely! Can you believe it? There's no beer!"

"Amazing. And in our state's capital, too." Chloe smiled tiredly, dropping her books. "How was the concert?"

"Not too bad. But I'm beginning to think that the flute is for losers. I'm going to learn piccolo—at first I thought it was totally gay, but those guys get *all* of the chicks after their solos."

"Nice, Alyec."

"Hey, I gotta go, but I'll see you tomorrow, okay?"

"Yeah, see you tomorrow," Chloe said, kissing into the phone. He kissed back and she hung up.

She drew *Moby-Dick* out of her bag and leaned back on her bed, slowly turning to the page where she left off.

Okay. It's eleven fifteen. Two good hours and I'll be in the black.

But her eyes soon glazed over. The fact that it was all about the fatty part of the whale called *sperm* didn't even amuse her. She put her finger down to mark the page and looked out her window.

A round, misshapen moon rose, too white to really be called a harvest moon. Amy would be so disappointed—it wouldn't be full at Halloween but past it, already waning. Something she never would have known or noticed before becoming fully Mai. Mist or fog or smog blurred the bottom part of it and winked out the stars in the lower half of the sky.

Brian was somewhere out there. The last missing thread of the fight. All of the other key players were accounted for.

Chloe looked outside for another moment, then finally turned back to her book.

Two

She was having that dream again.

She knew it was a dream, but there was no way to stop what was about to happen: His arms had curlicues of ink and scar tissue spelling out the words *Sodalitas Gladii Decimi.* He dressed in matte black, like a shadow. His eyes were blue with something crazy in them.

Wait, there was something familiar about that. . . .

And then she ran.

She ran into an alley, even though she knew that was the wrong thing to do. In the nightmare, it was the only thing she *could* do. The darkness swallowed her whole and before she could be spat out into the other end of the alley, a barbwire-topped gate loomed above her.

His first throwing star hit her in the leg. A second caught her wrist. She fell down and he was above her, brandishing the silver dagger that would end each of her eight lives. He smiled, almost sadly, and cut her throat.

Chloe sat up in bed, covered in sweat. "*Seven* lives," she told herself aloud. "I have *seven*. That was my sister, not me."

The dreams were always about her sister, the other possible Chosen One, who had been murdered earlier that year. Once in a great while they were about her biological mother and her quest to unite all of the Eastern European Mai twenty years ago. But Chloe never had any dreams about the brother she'd been told she might have—did that mean he was still alive? Did she only relive memories of the dead at night?

Her clock radio said 4:17. It was still dark out, and the stars shone in the coldest part of the night. Chloe got up and opened the window, letting the freezing air cool her down. There was no way she was going to be able to get back to sleep anytime soon.

With one last glance toward her bed, Chloe leapt up to the sill and down onto the ground, disappearing into the darkness.

Three

"Chloe? Chloe?"

A familiar, nagging voice was . . . well, nagging her into awakeness. Chloe dizzily swam toward consciousness, suddenly aware that her left arm was asleep, crushed against the desktop.

"Maybe you really *do* have mono," Paul said, kicking her chair to rouse her. "Trig is over, buddy. The good news is that Abercrombie dashed out to make a phone call."

"Gnnerrrrhh," Chloe said, trying to make her mouth work.

"What's going on with you? Burning the midnight oil? It's only a few weeks to catch up on."

"Yeah, I'm having a hard time getting a hold on this stuff. You know, like you can't train cats to do tricks? Like that. I'm a dumb cat." She stretched and, because no one was around, let her claws out. Paul still wasn't entirely used to it, and his eyes widened. *Lying to them again. What a great way to start over.*

"Yeah, that's why you're in superadvanced math. Because you're *stupid,*" Paul said dryly.

Chloe shrugged, choosing not to answer. "Kim's going to help me out later with French."

"Kim can speak French?"

"Flawlessly. It's kind of eerie." Of course, watching the Mai girl with the big cat ears and slit eyes and fangs do *anything* normal was eerie, but for some reason conjugating verbs and reading aloud from *Les Liaisons Dangereuses* was particularly disturbing.

"Are you going . . . uh . . . there?" Paul asked, meaning to Firebird. She suspected that if he ever actually used the word *Mai,* he would whisper it, the way her grandmother said the word *homosexual.*

"No, I don't think so. We're going to get a cup of tea or coffee," Chloe said, shoving her notebook into her book bag and putting the pen behind her ear.

"You don't like going back there, do you?" Paul asked.

He was absolutely right. When Chloe was first taken there, it seemed like such a haven—not only were they protecting her from the Tenth Blade assassins, but Alyec, Olga, and Sergei introduced her to a whole new world. They helped find out who her biological mother was. They supported her and took her in . . .

. . . and kept her there. Everything she did, she had to do with them. She couldn't even leave by herself "for her own protection." It was only toward the end that she began to think of them as a cult.

Individual members were fine, like Alyec and Kim, one of her newest, closest friends. And Igor and Valerie were harmless, even if they bought into the whole philosophy of the place.

It was Sergei she didn't want to think about.

There was no *proof* that he'd sent members of the Mai's warrior class, the kizekh, to kill her mom. On Chloe's one real escape from Firebird, while they were "protecting" her from the Tenth Blade, Amy and Paul had told her that they thought something weird was going on at her house—like that her mom was never there anymore. As soon as Chloe realized her mom had been kidnapped, Kim had volunteered her particularly feline talents to search Chloe's house for clues. The girl with the cat ears had not only sniffed out traces of humans from the Order—but also the presence of Mai. What had they been doing there? If it was just to watch and protect her mom, surely Sergei would have told her . . . wouldn't he?

Kim had darkly hinted that Chloe wasn't the first Mai raised by humans whose human parents had "disappeared" in order for the orphan to be brought back into the fold. But even if Sergei hadn't been planning to actually kill her mom, he also refused to rescue her from the Tenth Bladers. When Chloe finally decided to "fix" everything by offering to trade herself for her mom, both sides showed up at the Presidio—along with Kim, Alyec, Paul, and Brian—for a royal showdown that ended in Chloe losing one of her lives.

Sergei had let out a shot, but Chloe still wasn't sure who the bullet had been meant for. Had it been really aimed at Brian and not her mom? Could it have been meant for Chloe? Sergei had taken her in and treated her like a daughter, lecturing her, playing chess with her, eating dinner with her, and doing other dad things that she had never gotten from her real father *or* the adopted one who took off when she was little. And there was the whole being-the-One thing she didn't want to deal with, either. It would effectively mean usurping Sergei's leadership of the Mai, which wasn't something Chloe particularly wanted to do or even talk about.

"Yeah, I'm a little off the whole kitty-kennel thing right now," she admitted.

"I don't blame you. Hey, did I tell you I'm going to audition to spin at the fall formal?" He held up some twelve-inch records and waved them excitedly.

"You're going to make them dig up a turntable?" Chloe asked dryly. They started toward *The Lantern*'s office, the school newspaper Paul sort-of worked on so he could get access to their office and computers.

"What? No. They're totally not that hip. I just bought these off of Justin. I'm using my iPod and a computer."

"Wow. That's *so* old school."

"Piss off, King. At least we'll get to hear some good stuff this year."

"Yes, but can we dance to it?"

"I'm *counting* on you to help fill the floor until things

pick up," Paul said earnestly. "I even promised Amy and some of her gothier friends that I'd play some Switchblade Symphony and New Order in the first set."

"You know, you should actually write something for the paper sometime," Chloe said as Paul unlocked the office door to *The Lantern*'s office. She didn't actually work on the school newspaper herself but often took advantage of the couch and computers that her friend had access to because of his position as editor. "Put your vast musical knowledge to use. Write a 'just released' column or something. Get some college application points."

"Huh." He paused, considering it. "Sure would beat editing the crappy freshman editorials. Well, that's why you're the brains of the operation."

"Nah, just the brawn. *And* the claws." Chloe shuffled in after he opened the door for her, prepared to throw her backpack onto the couch like she always did before throwing herself onto it, but she stopped herself midswing, just in time to keep from throwing the ten-pound bag onto Amy's head. She was flipping through a copy of *The Nation,* her legs primly crossed, pretending not to have realized she'd surprised Chloe and Paul.

"Hey, guys," Amy said casually. "What's up?"

"Not much—how'd you get in here?" Paul didn't sound as thrilled as he probably should have been—his girlfriend had decided to surprise him by suddenly appearing in a semiprivate room. Once Chloe left, it would probably mean a major snogging session—what gave?

"Carson let me in." Amy jerked her thumb over her shoulder. Somewhere in the supplies closet, someone was rummaging.

"I can take off . . . ," Chloe suggested. She would have to find someplace else to nap—maybe under the bleachers at gym? The only people to find her would be janitors or dealers, and neither would show up until after school.

"Nah, it's okay," Amy said, putting the magazine down.

"Good." Chloe heaved a sigh of relief and fell down next to Amy, immediately curling up and putting her head on one of the well-worn and slightly grimy pillows.

Carson came out of the supply closet and glared at the three of them. "Paul, you're an editor. You *work* here—you can't just keep using this place as your private club room."

"Actually, I'm a columnist now," Paul said with an evil grin.

"I've got an idea," Chloe called sleepily from the couch. "You shut up about us being here, and we won't tell Keira that you made the hot and heavy with Halley last night."

Carson didn't even try to deny it; he just huffed and spun on his heel back into the supply closet.

"And *how* do we know that?" Amy asked, looking at Chloe.

Paul pointed at his nose and made a little cat-clawing motion with his hand.

"Oh, right. Nice work, Chlo."

But Chloe was already fast asleep.

Alyec actually took her out to dinner that evening—a diner, but at least it wasn't McDonald's—and gossiped about the band trip. He was as bad as a girl, his eyes lighting up delightedly as he related the exploits and disasters of various hookups that had occurred. No wonder he didn't mind the cultish aspects of Firebird: it was just one big soap opera to him.

The lighting in the diner was dismally fluorescent and the decor was faded plastic aqua, all the way from the scratched-up bar to the bench seat Chloe's ass was sticking to. Outside giant pane windows, the blackness was solid except for the lights of an occasional passing bus—kind of like that famous painting by Edward Hopper. It was a far cry from Firebird, with its velvet curtains and mahogany desks.

It was the same place where Alyec, Kim, Paul, and Amy had eaten after the fight at the Presidio, wondering what was going to happen next. Chloe had gone home with her mom and had the big talk about everything she had been hiding for the past couple of months: the claws, the Mai, *everything.* Afterward Brian had said goodbye to Chloe through her bedroom window.

She probably shouldn't have been thinking about

him while she was at dinner with Alyec, but it was hard not to. She nodded when it seemed appropriate and grunted at regular intervals.

"... and then I shot flaming chickens out of my ass," Alyec finished, biting off the end of a fry that was speared on his fork.

"Uh, what? Sorry," Chloe said when she realized exactly what he had said.

"You're not listening! They're talking about actually having a *king* and *queen* of the formal—like out of some cheesy old movie or something."

"Oh. Bizarre." She stared out the window, looking at the darkness, concentrating on not letting her eyes go slitty. She could feel the muscles tensing.

"Is there something you want to talk about, Chloe King?" He mock-frowned when he said it, but Chloe could see the worry in his eyes.

This was her chance to be honest, to let him know how confused she was about him and Brian, even though Brian was nowhere to be found.

Nope. Not yet. She just couldn't.

"Remember when we were eating Chinese," she said instead, "and you told me that it was hard for you sometimes to relate to normal humans and normal human life?"

"Yes. We had chicken and ten-vegetable lo mein," he recalled fondly.

"How do you do it?" Chloe asked earnestly.

He raised his eyebrows, surprised by the directness of her question.

"I don't know. . . ." He squirmed uncomfortably, like a completely normal human teenage male. A lock of thick blond hair fell into his eyes. "I have fun with everyone at school, but I'm not really that *close* to them, you know. They think it's because I'm Russian or supercool or something. And . . ." He frowned, thinking about it. "And I've got my mom, and my dad when he bothers to come home, and everyone else—I grew up Mai, you know? Surrounded by them. It's easy to be 'normal' in the day if you can relax with others like you at night."

"Oh. Right," Chloe said glumly, picturing her own mother and house in the evening. Not exactly relaxing. She suspected that if there was a book called *Dealing with Your Adopted Mai Child,* her mom would have already read it and decided to make sure Chloe was appreciating her native culture. *Difficult when my ethnicity is a big ol' secret and my people can—and do—take down running deer with their bare claws.*

"And . . . you're *different,* Chloe," he continued gently. "Even from us. You're our spiritual leader—you have nine lives. Chloe, you *died* and came back to life. *Twice.* That makes you different from *everyone.*"

Chloe began to suck noisily on her chocolate milk shake, not wanting to hear about it. There were big issues—death, the afterlife, the goddesses of the Mai, God in general—concepts of thousands of years and infinities, and she wasn't really prepared to think about them right now. Maybe never. Dying and coming back to life *was* weird. And she didn't want it to have anything to do with her current ennui at school.

"I'm sorry," Alyec said instantly, seeing her look. He brushed her cheek with his hand. "We don't have to talk about this. But you asked. I think maybe readjusting to your old life is going to be . . . difficult, Chloe."

"*So* not the answer I wanted," she growled.

"Okay, how about this: If you have sex with me—like actual sex—I promise it will fix everything. Including your acne."

Chloe cracked up. *That* was what she needed right now—to laugh, even if it only put off thinking about the inevitable for a little while.

"Wait," she said, suddenly sobering. "What acne?"

Four

"Il faut que *nous parlous,*" Kim repeated patiently.

"Il faut que nous parlous," Chloe said, trying to copy the sounds exactly.

"Better. Now can you give me *all* of the present subjunctive of *parler?*"

They sat on the roof of Café Eland, Chloe with a latte and Kim with her green tea. While the other Mai girl was growing more and more curious about Chloe's daily life in San Francisco proper and what "normal" teenagers did, she was still too shy to ask. It had taken a *lot* of pleading from Chloe—as well as personal coaching on how the buses and BART worked—to get Kim to agree to meet in the city instead of at Firebird.

"Parle, parles, parle, parlous, parliez, parlient . . ."

"Par*lent,*" Kim corrected. Then one of her ears flicked back and for just a moment her eyes narrowed. "Your friends are here—in the café below us. They just came in."

"Amy and Paul? I'm not meeting them tonight," Chloe said, intrigued. And willing to do almost anything other than conjugate verbs.

"Perhaps they're on a date," Kim said mildly.

"Maybe." Chloe crawled over to the heating vent and put her ear up next to it. Her hearing was nowhere near as good as Kim's, but it was still several times better than a normal human's. It took her a moment to sort through the extraneous noise: chairs scraping against the floor, the cash register ringing, other people talking, before she was able to single out her friends.

"Yeah, she kind of freaked when I told her." That was Amy, settling herself into one of the big, comfy chairs. Chloe could imagine her friend tucking her long legs up underneath her, looking like a little girl in a big chair. *Affected, but cute.*

"Well, it's big news." That was Paul, stirring even more sugar into his hot chocolate.

"*You* didn't freak out."

"I want whatever's best for you." There was a pause and some wooden-sounding noises, like someone was pushing around them to get by.

"You up to a long-distance relationship?" Amy said this perkily, but there was something in her voice, something strained. Something *testing*—like this was a question on which many other things were balanced.

Paul let out a sigh, which he tried to cover by blowing on his drink.

"Amy, I'm not sure we're up to a *close-distance* relationship," he finally said.

There was a long, frosty pause. Even Chloe stopped breathing.

"What's that supposed to mean?"

"I . . . We . . . It hasn't been . . . You haven't felt anything weird recently?"

"Well, yeah." Amy probably had that angry-sarcastic look on her face, where she scrunched up her nose. "What with saving Chloe and the cat-people thingy and Halloween coming up and all . . . What are you *saying,* Paul Chun?"

"I don't know. With Chloe back, it's kind of like the old days. Maybe this—*us*—is just sort of an aberration. A *nice* one," he added quickly. "But maybe we were trying to make too big a thing out of some sexual tension and all the other weird things going on."

"It's *not* the old days, dipshit," Amy snapped. Usually she used that word endearingly, but there was very little warmth in her voice this time. "Chloe's a freaking *cat person.* Who lived with other *cat people.* Who are hunted by other *crazy people.*"

Chloe's stomach sank into a little ball. Amy wasn't actually saying anything *bad* about her, but hearing about herself and her recent life put that way was . . . cold. Kim looked away, pretending not to have heard.

"And if there's a problem between us, it's between *us,*" Amy went on to say. "Leave Chloe out of it."

There was another moment's silence that must have been horribly awkward between her two friends. When Amy spoke again, there were tears in her voice.

"I—*I've* been pretty happy recently," she said weakly, talking in quick sips, the way you do when you're trying not to cry. "I know I've been busy. . . . What's *wrong?*"

Chloe moved her head away from the vent, not wanting to hear any more. She felt a little disgusted with herself for having heard that much. If it had been anyone else in the world or just *one* of her friends with someone else, she wouldn't have minded at all. She probably would have kept listening. But this was way, *way* too close.

"They're breaking up," she said tonelessly, crawling back over to Kim. "Or Paul's dumping her, I guess."

Kim didn't say anything, just watched her with large, unblinking green cat eyes.

"I should have realized something was going on," Chloe continued. "I should have noticed—they haven't been spending as much time together lately, and Paul doesn't seem to want her around much."

"What was her big news?" Kim asked, then suddenly remembered she had been pretending not to listen. She looked around herself uncertainly but didn't blush. *Just like a cat,* Chloe thought, smiling inside a little.

"She's graduating from high school a year early. It *did* freak me out." She sighed. "She never talked about this before—I don't know, it was just kind of sudden."

"It seems that the three of you are each beginning to head down very different paths," Kim said slowly.

"I hope you're not going to start talking to me about this whole being-the-One crap again," Chloe said, more harshly than she meant.

Kim lowered her eyes back to the French textbook. "I meant exactly what I said. But you *will* find it more difficult to escape your . . . heritage than you think." Chloe was glad that she hadn't used the word *destiny,* but she still didn't like it.

"I'm sick of people telling me that!" Chloe stood up. "I am *sixteen.* I have spent my *entire life* as a 'normal human.' It can't all suddenly change. I want to get good grades, go out and party, go to the dance, go to college. Which is hard enough with the weeks I lost! I don't have time for this, or Amy and Paul suddenly calling it quits, or my mom acting all weird around me. . . ."

"You want to go back to the old days."

"Yes, I . . . Shut up."

"What do you intend to do after we finish here?" Kim asked her.

That threw Chloe off. "What?"

"When we finish your French lesson here, what will you do?"

"I'm going to, uh . . ." *Go home, read some, and go to sleep.* These words had been well prepared, rehearsed, and used many times since she had returned from Firebird. But she couldn't lie into Kim's big cat eyes.

Chloe thought about what Amy had said about her and wondered if she was actually fooling anyone. "Go running," she finished lamely, sure that Kim would know what she meant.

Kim leaned over and, in a rare move, actually *touched* Chloe, wrapping her hand with her clawed paw.

"Whatever you decide to do," she said levelly, "don't lie to *yourself,* Chloe."

Chloe thought about Kim's words as she raced across the skyline, leaping and tumbling over rooftops and electric poles. She couldn't ignore the fact that she was cheating by coming out here at night, that she was stealing time from schoolwork and lying to people. Before—weeks ago—she had been able to ignore all that and just enjoy the freedom of the night. And now she couldn't.

Chloe.

She stopped suddenly. There was a whisper, an almost-voice that sounded like it was calling her name. The wind had picked up and was whistling through the old dead antennas that still decorated some rooftops like cactus spines. Chloe put her nose to the air and turned her head, trying to focus her ears on the sound.

"Mirao."

Without thinking, she turned and followed the sound, leaping across a gap to the roof of the house beyond. There, sitting primly in front of the round chimney of an oil furnace, was a little black cat. Its whiskers and chest were white, matched by little white socks. A *dairy* cat, her mom would have called him. The kind that hung around dairy barns, catching rats and in return being given bowls of fresh milk.

What's it doing up here? Chloe wondered. As she looked around for a door or skylight that was left open, the cat demurely picked up a paw and began licking it, like it had all the time in the world. Like it wasn't a little tiny cat on a cold rooftop in a big city with winter coming on.

"Hey, little guy." Chloe figured that being Mai, she should be able to speak cat or something—but apparently not. It paused, its licking for a moment, then went back to work.

"You shouldn't be up here. Are you lost?"

Chloe crept closer to it, making the *tchk tchk* noises that Amy's cat always came running to. She crouched down and started to extend her hand, but the little cat leapt up to the top of the chimney, out of her reach.

"Mirao!" it said again, louder.

"Come on, easy now." Chloe dug her toe claws into the brick and prepared to push herself up. "You might be able to outrun a normal human, but I'm afraid—" She swiped her hand up, but the little cat jumped down and ran faster than Chloe's claws could come out, scrabbling its feet like a cartoon. "Kitty!" Chloe called, beginning to get annoyed.

She ran across the roof after it, but it leapt over the side of the building.

"No!" Chloe looked down to the street. She couldn't see into the darkness below, even with her cat eyesight.

"Mirao!"

Chloe looked up: the cat was on the roof of the far building, patiently waiting for her. It must have dived down to a window ledge and then climbed back up again. "Mir-ao!"

"I get it now. You want to play, is that it? We're playing tag?" It wasn't a lost little kitty—it was an alley cat, or a *sky cat,* more like. This was its world, and it just wanted to play with a newcomer. "Okay!"

Chloe grinned and leapt. The cat waited a moment, as if giving her a fair start, then took off—pausing now and then to make sure she was following.

This is great. I should totally get a cat, Chloe decided. And it wasn't as if her mom could really object to having one in the house anymore.

Whenever she got too close, Chloe made herself slow down; neither she nor her playmate wanted the game to end too soon. She smiled, wondering what they might look like to a random bystander: a witch and her familiar flying across the upper stories of the city? A large cat hunting a smaller one? *Maybe they would just dismiss it.* Halloween was just around the corner; anything supernatural seemed possible.

Suddenly the dairy cat veered to the left, down to the top of a fire escape.

"Ha! Getting tired?" Chloe taunted.

The cat gave her what she could have sworn was a nasty look.

"Okay, but I can't play too much on the streets with you," she warned. "I can't let other people see me."

"Mirao!" The cat turned and slipped down the metal stairs like a black Slinky.

"Is this your home? Are you showing me your—?" Suddenly Chloe stopped, forgetting the cat entirely. The fire escape led down into a dark dead-end alley, apparently unused except for garbage collection. Most of the pavement was pocked and puddled with slick black flats of shiny city water.

There was an ominous outline that cut into the oily reflections, large and organic and shaped suspiciously like a body.

And there was a smell . . . a familiar smell . . .

Chloe leapt straight down the last two floors, landing in a crouch just inches away from the edge of the shape. She crawled over closer and as her eyes adjusted saw what was indeed a human body, unmoving and broken looking.

It was Brian.

Five

"Oh my God—"

Chloe put a hand to his neck, carefully retracting her claws. There was a pulse—but it was sluggish. His skin was cold and clammy, as if his body could no longer fight the chilly environment around him.

"Chloe?" Brian croaked.

Chloe ran her hands over his body, trying to see and feel what was wrong. He moaned and struggled a little—it didn't look like his neck or back were broken.

He held his hands over the top of his stomach, just under his chest. When Chloe pushed them aside, warm, syrupy blood seeped out. His entire shirt was soaked, and slow rivers of it ran down his sides and congealed in the water. A knife wound. Of course it was a knife wound. While the Order of the Tenth Blade used nine daggers to kill all nine lives of a Pride Leader, it took only one dagger to kill a member of the Order who betrayed them.

"You were supposed to run away—to disappear!" Chloe cried, trying not to panic.

Brian tried to say something, but nothing came out. He took a deep breath and opened his eyes. For a moment he saw her clearly—or at least the shape of her, since it was too dark for human vision—and smiled. Then he passed out again.

"Fuck," Chloe swore. Where could she take him? If she brought him to a public hospital, he'd be a sitting duck for the Order to finish the job. She couldn't protect him twenty-four/seven and had no idea how to go about hiring a bodyguard—especially one that didn't work for Brian's dad's security company.

There was home, where she had taken Alyec after Brian wounded *him* by the bridge. But as much as that thought appealed to her, Chloe had made a firm decision not to put her mom at risk again with her strange life. The Tenth Blade had already broken into their home once to kidnap Chloe's mom; bringing a man there they wanted dead was just asking for trouble. Which left only one option: the Firebird mansion. The home base of the Mai.

"Holy ironic justice, Batman," she muttered as she knelt down to gather Brian up in her arms.

Once again the similarities between Chloe and a real superhero ended when she realized that carrying him all the way to Sausalito would not only be impractical, it would be really slow. And there was no way she was going to be able to get a cab that would be willing to pick up a girl with her bloody, injured boyfriend. Of course, the bus was out, too.

She resorted to the only superweapon she had: her cell phone. She punched the numbers quickly. Alyec had a car, but only when he stole it. Which left . . .

"'Sup?" Amy's cheery voice came over the other end.

"Amy, I need you—it's an emergency. I found Brian—bleeding to death in an alley. I need to get him help."

"Ohmygod. Where are you?"

"Somewhere near Chinatown." She looked around, but the alley had no name. "Track me on your phone." Amy had the other matching GPS cell phone so they could track each other; the only downside was that its screen wasn't very big, and Amy had to look at it while driving.

"I'll be there ASAP."

With the little bubble of normal conversation over, Chloe became more aware of the loneliness of the alley and the silence of Brian. She couldn't remember much of junior high first aid and hoped she was doing the right thing by tearing off the sleeves of her shirt and tying them around his wound. Apart from that and trying to keep him from rolling through the puddles—though even the dry part of the cobblestone lane wasn't a particularly sterile environment—there was little Chloe could do besides comfort him and wait.

"What's going on here?"

Chloe turned to look at the owner of the new voice. A pair of boys, too healthy to be street people, too confident to be scared of a lonely alley. Both were muscled. Asian. All in black . . . *gang* members.

"You got a problem?" the other asked, smiling. Take away the attitude and the tattoos and it was obvious they were barely twenty. And actually pretty good-looking.

This could go two ways, Chloe realized. One of which was that they could turn out to be reasonably decent local guys who just wanted to help. But Chloe wasn't going to wait around to see if it was the other—more likely—possibility.

With a frightful hiss she leapt up, extending her hand and foot claws, making sure her slit eyes flashed in the light. In two springs she was a foot from them, yowling and swiping her claws.

"Li Shou!" one of them cried. Then they turned around and fled.

"Almost too easy," Chloe murmured. She retracted her claws and walked back to Brian, who suddenly looked a little too still. She knelt beside him and began stroking his hair. "Stay awake—you've got to stay awake. . . ."

He groaned in response, but his mouth was moving like he was trying to say something.

"Leave me," he whispered. *"They'll be back. It's over. . . ."*

"Not on your life, sweetie," she said with a forced grin. "Help's on the way."

"Chloe . . ." His lips moved more, but nothing came

out. Chloe leaned closer. Then he fell back, unconscious.

"Brian, no," she whispered, her eyes filling with tears.

Ten minutes later Amy arrived in her brother's old black station wagon. Chloe took most of Brian's weight because of her superior strength but needed Amy to hold him straight and steady in case there *was* actually something wrong with his back.

"Holy shit," was all her friend said. They carefully laid him down in the backseat and, completely unconscious, he didn't even groan. His skin was deathly white.

"Sorry," Chloe said, taking the driver's seat. "The hideout's kind of a secret, and you're going to have to blindfold yourself somehow. . . ."

Amy looked a little piqued, but only for an instant. "No problem. As the loyal sidekick, I should expect to be put into ridiculous situations." She leapt into shotgun and pulled a jacket over her head.

Chloe burned rubber pulling out, and as she turned onto the street, a man-shaped shadow hugged the wall near the entrance to the alley, watching the car go. But *one* person couldn't have done this to Brian. . . . It looked like he had been beaten from all sides at once. And it wasn't like the Tenth Blade to skulk in the shadows: if they knew a Mai was there, they would have come out and tried to kill Chloe, too.

She didn't begin breathing normally until they were going over the bridge, shooting past the National

Guard, who had been on her ass after the big duke-out with the Rogue.

Ignoring the niceties of *road* and *right-of-way,* Chloe took the car off road the moment they turned onto the street that led to Firebird.

"My brother's going to *kill me . . . ,*" Amy muttered from under the jacket.

Chloe drove around to the back of the estate and honked the horn, shouting, "It's me!" as she barreled up to the gate, which the guard opened just in time for the car *not* to crash into it. On the old TV show the Batmobile came roaring through a discreetly hidden tunnel into Wayne Manor; Batman didn't need Alfred to let him in.

Must do something about that.

She pulled up to the kitchen, or back entrance, door and jumped out. By the time she had jumped out, someone was already opening the door, curious about the late-night intrusion. When she saw who it was, the female Mai bowed her head. "You have come back, Leader."

"I need to get him into a bed or something," Chloe ordered. "*Help* me."

The woman opened her eyes and sniffed the air. "But he—and she—are *human!*"

"Can I take this off yet?" Amy asked, still in the front seat under the jacket.

"Please! I'm begging you!" Chloe cried, frustrated.

"The One doesn't need to beg," the woman murmured. She called behind her in either Russian or Mai; Chloe wasn't listening enough to be able to tell the difference.

That's Eleni, Chloe thought distractedly as the woman hurried back over to the car to help her with Brian. Eleni was one of the Mai who had most recently come from Turkey, like Chloe's biological family. "Just two more minutes," Chloe told Amy.

Among the other Mai who showed up—some bleary-eyed, some wide awake—was Ellen, the kizekh who used to be Chloe's sort-of bodyguard when she had lived with them full-time, just a short time ago. Her partner, Dmitry, wasn't with her, which was unusual. She grinned at Chloe before giving a slight bow, genuinely glad to see her back. Everyone else bowed deeply and politely eased Chloe out of the way while carrying Brian in.

"Where are you taking him?" Chloe asked.

"The emergency ward, Honored One." Ellen winked. "Don't worry—we'll have him fixed up good as new." The Mai disappeared down the halls of the house at a trot.

"Emergency ward? We have an *emergency* ward?" Chloe wondered as she took Amy by the hand and followed them. *There really is a whole little world inside these walls.*

This was obviously one of the oldest parts of the mansion. She hadn't been here before and was struck by the narrow stone hallways and cold, damp smell—like there was a well or a cellar nearby. Something caught inside

Chloe: this was an old house, like right out of something on PBS, and she had full non-museum-pass access. She could even *live* here if she wanted.

They wound up in a dark room whose lights came on a second after they got there, switched by a female Mai rubbing her eyes and pulling on a white lab coat. There were two hospital-style beds, what looked suspiciously like a gleaming, stainless-steel operating table in the middle of the floor, and antique metal cabinets full of medical equipment. The floor was old wood, completely clashing with the sterile nature of everything else.

Ellen and the other Mai carrying Brian carefully put him on the operating table.

"A *human?*" The doctor was a tiny woman with a body like Tinkerbell and huge, dark hazel—almost brown—eyes, a color unusual among the Mai. She was probably in her late thirties, but it was hard to tell.

Ellen quietly jerked her head at Chloe.

"Oh." She bowed her head and spread her hands, palms up, a curt but heartfelt gesture of respect. Then she immediately began examining Brian, who made pathetic little sounds as she prodded him.

"Why does the other human have a jacket over her head?" Ellen whispered to Chloe.

"I was trying to keep the location of Firebird secret," Chloe whispered back, not wanting to tear her eyes from Brian. The doctor was ripping off Chloe's make-do bandages and probing the wound. Instead of normal medical instruments she used her claws, with amazing precision.

"Someone clean this guy up with sterile towels while I work on him," the doctor snapped. "The rest of you"—she looked up, managing to fix everyone with the same look—*"get out!"*

"Please, Honored One," she added to Chloe after a moment.

Chloe paced in the small study outside that served as a waiting room. Everyone else went to bed, bowing obeisances and backing away from her just like she had seen them do with Sergei. The gestures seemed a little more extreme, a little more heartfelt than the ones for him, though. Ellen had brought the back of Chloe's hand to her forehead as she bowed, like something a knight would do in the Dark Ages, swearing fealty. It was all a little uncomfortable.

Chloe had expected many things if she ever returned to the mansion or the Mai: disappointment about Chloe's decision to leave them, anger over Chloe's love for humans, sadness that they had "lost" someone to the outside world. Cold shoulders, at least. And maybe, from the slicker ones who wanted her back in the fold, hugs and kisses and smothering love. But certainly not worship.

It looks like they would do anything for me, she mused distractedly. Their immediate agreement to help Brian was unbelievable. Not only was he a human, not only was he once a member of the Tenth Blade, but he was the *son* of the *head* of the Order. The enemy was in their camp and they'd welcomed him with open arms. Well, sort of.

"So wait, what was that you were saying before? That I'm the hero and you're my *sidekick?*" she finally asked, trying to distract herself with her and Amy's previous conversation in the car.

"Yeah, like Batman and Robin. Xena and Gabrielle," came the voice under the jacket.

"Um, we're not gay. At least not me. And what about Paul? Who's he?"

Silence.

"Arch-villain, maybe," Amy countered. "Nemesis, perhaps. He's already jealous of your powers. Right now he could be plotting your doom."

"You, uh, you want to talk about something?" Chloe ventured. It was a strange way to have this conversation: while she was nervous about Brian, at Firebird, with her friend, who had a jacket over her head. Yet it seemed as good a time as any.

There was a pause. "No," Amy said stubbornly, but she didn't sound certain.

"I heard you and Paul talking at the coffee shop earlier. I wasn't spying on you," Chloe added quickly, reacting to the face she knew her friend was making. "I was practicing verb forms with Kim on the roof."

"He wants to break up," Amy said softly.

"And you . . . ?"

"I thought it was pretty good. . . . I mean, it wasn't perfect—he's a little hard to get through to sometimes. But it's a *real* relationship. Not like any of the other guys I dated . . . We were doing it right. Friends *first,* you know?"

"Yeah, but . . ." Chloe bit her lip, unsure how to say it. "Philosophy aside, do you *like* him?"

"Yes," Amy said, a catch in her throat. "When he isn't being a *douche bag!*"

"Did he start acting like this before or after you told him about graduating a year early?"

"Why?" her friend demanded.

"Well . . . it's a big thing, Amy. Kind of out of the blue." Chloe realized she was no longer talking about Paul. "I mean, it wasn't like you were planning it all along. . . ."

"Well, your *turning into a cat* kind of came out of nowhere, too!" Amy snapped indignantly.

Chloe took a deep breath, forcing herself not to respond to that. It was hard.

"Yeah, but you're going to be leaving us. Permanently—the beginning of the end, you know? It's hard for me to imagine losing you. And I'll bet it's harder for Paul, who's in the middle of losing his family. His parents have barely spoken since the divorce began."

Amy grew silent and seemed to pull into herself a little, as if she was actually thinking about this.

Just then Kim came calmly padding into the room. "Hello, Chloe. Hello, Amy." Once again, the girl with the giant cat ears was unfazed by anything; it was like she had been expecting them.

"Hi, Kim," said Amy from underneath the jacket, like Cousin It.

"I think you can take off the blindfold now, if that's what that is." Kim didn't smile, but Chloe was beginning to get used to the other girl's extremely dry sense of humor.

She pulled Amy's jacket off as gently as possible. Her friend's frizzy hair staticked anyway, billowing around her head like a goth clown's.

"How'd you know it was me?" Amy asked, running her hands back over her hair, trying to do something with it and failing.

"Your smell," Kim answered primly.

"Yeah?" Amy wrinkled her nose, also sniffing. "Speaking of, it *definitely* smells a lot like cat here. . . ."

Kim looked startled and slightly mortified.

"So this is the Cat Cave, huh? The secret hideout?" Amy looked around eagerly.

"I'll give you the tour later," Chloe promised.

"What happened?" Kim asked.

"I found Brian left half dead on the street. I think the Tenth Blade probably thought they finished him off, or maybe some people came by and interrupted their 'business. . . .' "

"And you brought him here." It was a statement, a wry question, an accusation, all in one.

"What else was I supposed to do?" Chloe demanded. "I know it's weird and I'm sorry—I could promise it will never happen again, but I don't think I can promise anything anymore. I'll make it up somehow. . . ." She sat on the couch, head in her hands. "No one really seemed to mind that much," she added, to the floor.

"That is because you are the One, Chloe," Kim said gently, sinking gracefully onto the couch next to her. Amy took a plush chair across from them. "They would die for you if you commanded it."

"That's ridiculous," Chloe muttered.

"It's the truth. I know this is hard, but you are our spiritual leader. You always have been. It's not so much your destiny as your birthright."

"But some of these people are too young to have ever even had a . . . uh, *the One* before! Why should they just suddenly accept me as their new leader?"

"Chloe, *the One* is not an inherited position, like a king or certain Republican presidents," Kim said with the faintest smile and Chloe got her joke. "Just because someone is Kemnet'r doesn't mean that his or her child will be. The One must be *different:* not only pure of heart, strong, determined, and willing to do good, but chosen and blessed by the Twin Goddesses with the abilities to make things so. Nine lives, to lead her people to battle again and again if need be. *Connection* with the past, previous Chosen Ones. Connection with the present, her Pride, in a way that is beyond metaphysical."

Chloe looked at her.

"I don't know about the last two." Then she remembered a presence at death, a feeling of her mother being there. Comforting like a powerful protector, powerful as anything that could defeat death. "Okay, just the last one."

"You stopped a battle between your Pride and the Tenth Blade single-handedly," Amy pointed out.

"I *died*, remember? *That's* what put the kibosh on things."

"Even so," Kim said, nodding.

Chloe sat back, feeling somehow defeated in the face of the eternally calm—and serene—girl next to her. "*You* don't worship me, though, right?" she said in a small voice. "You're, like, my only real friend here."

Kim cocked her head, thinking about it for a moment. "I . . . revere the position of the One and her sacred duties," she said slowly. "And no leader is ever perfect, even ones gifted with the divine. You, like every Kemnet'r before you—you could definitely use an adviser."

"Hey," Chloe said, annoyed but amused. "I said *friend*, not adviser."

Kim turned her paws up, shrugging, but there was a wry smile on her lips. "I think you may find you need both in the upcoming days."

"I'll be the friend," Amy said diplomatically. "You can be the adviser."

"I never said I was going to take this on," Chloe

pointed out. "I'm from a culture of choices, you know. Not destinies."

"As the old man said in that movie you took me to, 'You must of course do what you think is right,'" Kim said, referring to the night they had all gone to see *Star Wars*. "But whatever choice you make as the One, it can only *be* right."

"No pressure, though," Chloe muttered sarcastically. First Amy offered to be Jet Girl to her Tank; now Kim wanted to be Obi-Wan to her Luke. It was kind of bizarre.

The door to the emergency room opened and the doctor came out with her hands shoved deep in her pockets, just like on TV. She even bowed that way. Even though being bowed to all the time was weird, it *was* pretty good for the ego. Like the cute waiters at a Japanese restaurant. *Of course, I'll have to put a stop to it.*

"Okay, your friend is pretty badly banged up. Not only has he lost a lot of blood, but there's an injury to the back of his head that looks serious. His right arm is broken, five of his ribs are cracked, his left leg is broken, and some of his toes have been crushed."

She waited a moment, a questioning look in her eye. Chloe didn't say anything, unsure what she wanted.

"Can I ask . . . ?" the doctor finally prompted.

"He sort of quit the Tenth Blade, something I guess you just don't do. And he did it when we were all duking it out at the Presidio, trying to save me and my mom from the Bladers when he should have been fighting *with* them. So they made him number one on their hit list. Even though he's like Order of the Tenth Blade royalty or something," she added.

"*That's* Brian Rezza? Son of Whitney, the head of the Order?" The doctor gave a low whistle. "And his own people did this to him?"

"They are obviously not his people anymore," Kim said dryly.

"And they call *us* feral." She sighed. "I'm going to be honest with you: I don't know the extent of the damage to the head yet and if he *does* recover, it's going to be a long, painful process. You don't know his blood type, do you? Regardless, someone will need to get a couple of quarts of it."

As hard as she tried to stop it, Chloe's eyes filled with tears. *Real leaders don't cry so easy.* Just more proof of her point.

"I'll fix what I can here, but if you don't want to take him to a real hospital, a lot of his healing is going to depend on his own body." She ran a hand, claws now safely sheathed, through her shoulder-length brown hair. "We've never been introduced, I don't think. I'm Doctor Calie Lovsky." She put out her hand and Chloe extended hers, thinking that they were going to do that special "secret" Mai handshake Igor had taught her: slight extension of the claws to graze the other's palm. Instead, like Ellen, she took the back of Chloe's hand and put it on her forehead. Unlike Ellen, she didn't bow.

"Is, uh, everyone going to keep doing this?" Chloe asked, turning to Kim.

"The kizekh will. For everyone else, it's only the first time they are formally introduced to you."

"I'm so glad you're here," Dr. Lovsky said, putting her hands back in her pockets. "We really need you."

Her easy switch from doctor to worshipful servant gave Chloe emotional whiplash. The woman was older than she, *waaaay* better educated, and a doctor besides. *What the hell is she doing looking up to* me?

"Can I go see him?" she finally asked.

"Yeah, but as the old platitude goes, don't stay too long; he needs his rest."

Chloe started to walk past her into the room, then stopped. "I'm—I'm really sorry about bringing a human here."

"Whatever the One wills," the doctor said, shrugging.

They had moved Brian to a bed and replaced his clothes with a simple cotton hospital tunic. He had also been bathed; most of the dried and sticky blood was gone. As were two of his teeth, Chloe noted with a shiver of horror. Like someone had kicked him in the mouth when he was down. There was a white bandage around his head and another around his chest. A clean white sheet was pulled up to his neck.

"Hey," Chloe said softly. "How you doing?"

A disturbing gurgle came from the back of Brian's throat. He coughed a couple of times, trying to clear the blood out, but then winced because of the pain in his chest. His crusted eyes flicked halfway open. When he saw her, he smiled. Chloe touched his cheek.

"You're going to be all right," she whispered.

Brian tried to say something, but it came out like the dry rattle of an old man. She leaned closer to listen.

Using all his remaining strength, Brian pushed himself up another inch.

And kissed her.

He held it as long as he could before he fell back to the bed again, passing out.

Chloe froze, refusing to believe what just happened.

He had *kissed* her.

It was a death sentence for a human. Man and Mai had not been able to love each other since the war between them first began, thousands of years ago.

Chloe knew it all too well: she had accidentally killed or almost killed—she still didn't know—a guy she hooked up with at a club before she knew any of this. The last time she had seen Xavier, he was covered in sores and his face was swollen beyond recognition. She had called 911 and fled.

And now, because Brian was convinced he was going to die anyway, he didn't think it would matter.

Six

Chloe managed to sneak back in to her house just as the clock turned five thirty. *Great, a whole two hours of sleep.* She stripped down and fell into a deep slumber almost before she hit the pillow.

She was barely awake two hours later when she came stumbling downstairs. There was her mom, with doughnuts and coffee for breakfast. She dumped them onto the table, attaché case still slung over her shoulder, and beamed at Chloe.

"They had that chocolate kreme-with-a-*k* you like so much this morning . . . ," Anna started. "Wait, you look *terrible.* What happened?"

"Thanks," Chloe grumbled. That was the humorous part; now came the difficult one. Would she start the whole avalanche of lies all over again? *I'm just really stressed out about my makeup trig exam tomorrow. I could barely sleep.* Two sentences, fourteen—no, fifteen words, and her mom would let the whole thing drop. And if she told the truth? *Hey, Mom, my human boy, uh, friend, well, I found him half dead on the street last night when I was prowling around at 2 a.m., so I took him to the people who sort of held me captive for several weeks.*

She and her mom looked each other in the eye, and each paused too long.

"Well, some coffee will make you feel better," her mom finally said, turning her head quickly away.

Chloe came the rest of the way down the stairs, feeling both infinitely relieved and extremely disturbed. Uncomfortable. *You're not supposed to feel uncomfortable with your mom.* That was for best friends you betrayed with gossip, guys who said they didn't like you back that way, and guidance counselors who were pretty sure you had weed in your locker. You could be *mad* at her . . . but *uncomfortable?* It just didn't seem right.

"Thanks," Chloe said, stuffing her mouth with as much of the doughnut as she could cram in, like she did when she was little. "Hey, shpeaking of . . ." It was hard to form the words around the delicious, thick, totally fake nondairy kreme. "Could you help me study tonight? I want to run some practice proofs."

Chloe meant it as a sort of peace offering to her mom, and it turned out to be exactly the thing to say: Mrs. King smiled, almost as broadly as she had before and tucked a stray wisp of her hair behind her ear. "Absolutely! We'll get Chinese and make a girls' night out of it."

"Girls' night with trig," Chloe said flatly, raising an eyebrow. *Uh-oh, I'm beginning to sound like Kim.*

Her mom leaned over and kissed her on top of her head.

"Girls' night with trig. Gotta run, don't forget to—"

"Lock up, yeah, yeah. Got it."

Chloe watched as her mom grabbed her purse and her glasses and whirlwinded out the door, a dust devil of Ferragamos and Anne Klein. Then she looked down at the rest of her doughnut and sighed.

At school Chloe walked in a daze through the halls, watching the early-morning bustle of students making what use they could of the few free minutes before the day began. The National Honor Society kids were putting up posters about some volunteer thing or other they wanted to get people involved in. The geeks were in a huddle, avidly discussing last night's episode of *Stargate.* The cheerleaders were trying to sell Halloween candygrams to everyone who passed. For a dollar you could send a piece of candy with a note to anyone in the school and have it delivered to his or her homeroom on Halloween morning. In middle school, they had been cheap hard suckers. Now they were little wrapped Godivas.

Every year on Valentine's Day, Easter, Halloween, and Christmas/Hanukkah/Kwanzaa/Diwali, Amy and Chloe had sent each other mysterious notes from "secret admirers," with the sitcom philosophy that boys would see how many candygrams they each got and assume that Amy and Chloe were popular and desirable. Never worked, of course. Not that Amy had even needed them the last few years. *I wonder if she's going to be sending one to Paul?*

"Candygram?" a television-perfect little cheerleader suggested in a peppy voice. Her body was tiny and she wore the home-game uniform, complete with tiny red-and-white skirt. She stood on her toes a little, bouncing.

But Chloe couldn't even work up the energy to hate her; she just shook her head and pushed on. In the open area in the middle of the *X* where the math-science and English-history wings crossed, students were standing on chairs, hanging up autumn-leaf-colored bunting around a giant—and surprisingly tasteful—poster that read *Something Wicked This Way Comes—Get your tickets to the fall formal at lunch! $60/couple, $35/single.*

"What do you think?" Alyec asked, swooping in behind her and kissing Chloe on the cheek.

"I think they're sticking it to people who can't get a date again," Chloe said, hooking her thumbs in her backpack straps.

"Yeah, well, who can't get a date?"

"People who aren't foreign, sexy, and drop-dead gorgeous," she said, kissing him back on the cheek. It was strange: normally they would kiss on the lips if there weren't any of the more monastic teachers or hall monitors about. But right now it just didn't seem right.

Especially after what happened last night. As soon as she had gotten to school, Chloe had called to find out about Brian, but the doctor said he was in the same state, possibly doing a little better than before. No other, "new" symptoms, even when Chloe questioned her carefully. She had to resist calling back every five minutes for an update to make sure the kiss they'd shared wasn't killing him.

"Well, we can't all be lucky." He put his arm around Chloe's shoulders and turned so they could both admire the poster. "I put Hannah Ellington in charge of signage and programs."

"*You* put? I thought you were just on the music committee."

"They all needed some . . . help." It appeared that Alyec was using his powers for good, though: already the event looked like it was going to be better than last year's, less like a stupid high-school dance and more like a college, well, *formal.*

"Did you hear what happened last night?" Chloe asked as they turned and began walking to history. Alyec shook his head. She told him, omitting the part about Brian kissing her. ". . . and if *that* isn't bad enough, I'm having a real hard time wrapping my head around this whole 'being the One' thing. You're supposed to bow to me, you know," she added, elbowing him in the stomach.

"I think the Chosen One's chosen one gets a break," he said, shrugging.

"But you'll still worship me, right?"

"Haven't I always?" He ran his hand back through her hair—like she had done to Brian the night before—and smiled fondly at her. It was a rare moment for him: there was no lust or teasing—just *fondness.*

They walked together to American civ, passing one of the few windows in the hall, which looked out on the strip of dying grass and fence that separated the school from the rest of the world.

Something wasn't quite right. Chloe turned back to look again, but all she saw was what might have been the remains of a footprint in the grass, quickly disappearing as the tough, yellowed stalks sprang back up.

"Hey—did you just see something?" she asked, pulling at Alyec's sleeve and pointing outside.

He frowned. "No—why?"

"I don't know, I just . . ." She shrugged. "I've been getting super creeped out recently. I keep thinking I see someone or someone's following me."

"Nerves. You know what'll fix that?"

"Sex. Yes, I know," Chloe said, laughing.

They sat down at desks next to each other. When they had started dating, he had moved to sit closer to her—a rare thing so late in the term. Chloe was just thinking she might get through the day *normally,* without having to deal with anything really Mai related, when her phone rang. She didn't recognize the number.

"Hello?" she answered it.

"Chloe? It's Sergei."

Chloe's heart sank, her stomach quickly following. Here was another very loose thread from the night of the fight. Yes, Sergei had taken her in and treated her like a daughter, acting like the father she never had, but he might *also* have sent assassins to kill her mom and cut off Chloe from all human contact. And while she was beginning to find that people were a little more complicated than she ever realized before, she still had no desire or ability to deal with the mess that was her relationship with Sergei. Chloe had gotten along recently by forcing herself not to think about the Pride Leader.

"Sergei," she said, feeling her belly twist into ulcerous knots. Alyec raised his eyebrows, listening in.

"You sound well, Chloe."

"I am, thanks. More or less."

"I see you brought us a little visitor last night. . . ." *Here it comes.* Ms. Barker was erasing the board in preparation for class and shooting nasty looks at everyone who was talking on cell phones. Leader of an ancient race of lion people aside, Chloe didn't want to be one of those obnoxious jerks who put a hand up for the teacher to "wait a minute" while finishing a call. She was in enough academic trouble as it was.

". . . I think you and I, and maybe Olga, should get together and have a little chat about things."

"Yeah, uh, sure." She tried to sound upbeat and lighthearted, like that was a great idea.

"When you come to visit your friend today, then?" It wasn't really a question.

"All right."

"Good, I look forward to seeing you later. Good luck in school."

Click.

Chloe slowly closed the phone.

Let's make a deal, she sent a mental message to the Fates or the Twin Goddesses or her biological mom or whoever was casting the dice for her life. *Can you at least switch off crisis weeks? Like, one for school, the next for Amy and Paul, and the next for everything else? Does it all have to happen at once?*

Something hit Chloe's head with a small but pointed *thunk* and snapped her out of her thoughts. Lying on the ground next to her desk was a slightly squished Godiva chocolate. Alyec was grinning wickedly; he must have stolen or sweet-talked it away from the cheerleaders.

Chloe smiled back and whispered a thanks, unwrapping it immediately and popping it in her mouth.

God really does work in mysterious ways, she reflected.

Lunch was a chilly affair that almost made her wish school would hurry up and end so she could face her next set of crap. Chloe sat across from Paul and Amy, who were obviously trying to interact normally—without even touching each other or making eye contact—until the bell rang and Paul gave Amy a perfunctory kiss goodbye. There wasn't so much *tension* at the table as there was a complete freeze on normal, casual behavior. *I knew this would happen,* Chloe thought. When Amy first told her she and Paul had hooked up, it was obvious that, unless they kept dating until college, it could only end in tears for the trio of friends.

She stayed after for an hour to work on one of the many chem labs she'd missed, called "Forming Ionic Compounds." Mrs. Mentavicci was *much* more laid back in these sessions, and when she wasn't grading something—or playing solitaire—she actually helped. Chloe began to see the lure of being tutored. Without the tenseness of a forty-five-minute time limit and having to deal with a lab partner, she was able to work slowly and methodically and actually *understand* what she was doing.

Afterward she took a bus over to Sausalito. Chloe didn't want a car to come pick her up—while luxurious, it was also incredibly disempowering; she felt completely in the Mai's control. It was a good place to think, under the shaky fluorescent bus lights that made everything clearer and more real. Every rivet in the floor, every grommet on the ugly matted upholstery of the seats stood out.

But she could only focus on one thing: There was a chance that Brian could be dead or dying by the time she got to Firebird.

It hadn't been immediate with Xavier, the guy she'd

kissed at the club. When Chloe found him lying on the floor in his apartment a few days later, he was covered in sores and unable to breathe properly—but still alive. Barely. A few more hours—maybe minutes—and he wouldn't have been. She had never followed up on what happened to him. Now was definitely the time to open up that line of inquiry again.

When the bus stopped, Chloe was the only one to get off. The sky was overcast, the clouds high in the atmosphere. Chloe drew as far into her hoodie as she could as a cold wind cut through tree branches and telephone poles. She let her feet slap the ground, willing herself to make ugly, human noises, to challenge the sky and the wind and the graceful lion woman within her. She kicked rocks and pebbles and wished she was thirteen again. Or at least fifteen, before everything had changed.

She reached the gate and realized how tiny she must look against it: a wastrel teenager in a faded sweatshirt and jeans, under a guardhouse that protected one of the largest real estate firms in San Francisco—as well as a dying race of ancient feline warriors.

"Oh, Miss King—would you like me to send a car down to you?"

"No thanks, I'll walk," she said, slipping through the tiny invisible pedestrian "door" that cracked open out of the imposing double gates and led up the long gravel driveway. Chloe couldn't help notice the trees and the topiaries and the bushes and all sorts of beautiful garden things she had never explored while she lived there. She had stayed inside, except for when she escaped to see her friends.

Chloe chose to go around the back, avoiding the lobby and the receptionist and the crowd of people who would be there. Staring at her. Bowing to her. Directing her to Sergei.

Though she didn't remember exactly where the hospital room was, she pieced it together through memory and smell. Chloe tentatively knocked on the door before opening it and going in, as quietly as she had through the gate.

"Hey." Dr. Lovsky was there, checking off something on Brian's chart. She gave a little bow.

Brian was in a slightly different position from when she saw him last and had all sorts of tubes and wires on him. A drip in his arm. Something in his nose. He looked fragile and was the pale color of chicken fat. *Small.*

"How's he doing?" Chloe whispered.

"Talk as loud as you want. He's on so many painkillers, it would take an earthquake to wake him," Dr. Lovsky said, hanging the chart back on the end of his bed. "Stabilized—I'm going to take a closer look at his head today. He's pretty resilient for a human."

"Speaking of human . . ." Chloe closed her eyes and ground her teeth. *A leader isn't afraid to tell the truth.* Think of Washington and the cherry tree. Or Honest Abe. ". . . I probably should have told you this before, but when he thought he was going to die, he, um . . . he kissed me."

Lovsky's clipboard slipped perilously until it was hanging from just one of her claws.

"H-how hard?" she managed to stutter.

"Uh, pretty hard, I guess." Chloe fidgeted. "A teensy bit of tongue," she added, flushing furiously.

"Why didn't you tell me this before?" the doctor shrieked, running a clawed hand over her head. "Honored One."

"Because I thought you would just give up on him—assume he was going to die."

Strangely, Dr. Lovsky didn't argue with that. She seemed to be one of those rare people who didn't protest when they knew the other person was right. "I kissed another boy before I knew who I was, too. . . ."

The other woman just tapped a tooth with her claw.

Chloe cleared her throat. "Is he going to be okay? Can you do something for him?"

The doctor shook her head. "I was . . . involved in a case years ago with a Mai and a human who had only kissed. He died. The hospital couldn't do anything—and it was a damn sight better than anything *here*."

Chloe was cowed into silence—there was definitely a story behind and beyond what she had said.

Calie then frowned, looking puzzled. "But . . . I have seen no evidence of toxic shock or anything even *like* that. *Yet*. It's kind of odd. . . . I'll keep an eye out and prepare some ephedrine." The doctor stomped out, shaking her head and muttering under her breath.

And now, to my doom.

As Chloe made her way upstairs, she played a mental game with herself, trying to decide what she would rather do than meet with Sergei. Pull a hangnail, definitely. Deal with a yeast infection, possibly. Clean her room, almost certainly. Work a midnight sale at Pateena's, absolutely. Spend the afternoon at Aunt Isabel's? Maybe. That was a close one.

Working at Pateena's, much less working midnight sales, weren't really an option anymore, though. Since the owner of the vintage clothing store had told Chloe to not bother coming back at all if she didn't show up on that Wednesday weeks ago, Chloe had given up her job as a complete loss.

She tried to slip past the cheaply dressed receptionist who sat alone at her island of mahogany and dark wood in the middle of the lobby. The only thing keeping her company was a giant vase of expensive flowers.

"He's waiting for you in his office," she said without looking up. *"Honored One."*

Was there the slightest bit of sarcasm in her voice?

Chloe sighed and slunk over to Sergei's door and knocked. The door seemed to open of its own accord, and Olga let her in. Her dark eyes lit up a little when she saw Chloe—but she also looked worried.

"Chloe! Honored One! Come in!" She gave Chloe a

squeeze on the shoulder, not quite a hug. Sergei's right hand was a direct, uncomplicated, and genuine woman; Chloe was pretty sure she knew where she stood with her at all times.

Sergei stood up from behind his desk and gave Chloe a very proper, angular bow. It should have been amusing, considering how short and square he was, but with his heels together and his perfectly trimmed beard he gave the impression of a foreign dignitary. The door clicked shut behind her. *Well, here we go,* Chloe thought, sinking into a chair next to Olga. *If I really am the One, why don't I feel like it?*

"Chloe," Sergei said, sitting back in his chair, "let me begin by saying how glad we are to see you again. We missed you while you were away."

"While I was *home,*" Chloe found herself correcting him. She wished she hadn't. The Fine Art of Making Friends and Influencing People*, not by Chloe King.*

"Yes, while you were home," Sergei said easily, as if it wasn't a concern. "So I take it you're not back for the long haul, as it were?"

There it was. *Wheeeeeeeeee* plop! Like a lit firecracker half dud that lay unexploded between your feet. *Do you pick it up or run?*

"I don't know what my eventual plans are," Chloe said carefully. *Jesus Christ, I'm a sixteen-year-old kid! I shouldn't be having to make decisions about the rest of my life or speak so carefully—politically—to someone three times my age and ten times better at it! I should be dating, fighting with my mom, popping zits in front of the mirror.* "For now, I'm going to live with my mom."

"You gave us a bit of a surprise at the Presidio, leaving with your friends like that," the older man said, eyes flicking briefly to the ground and back up to her as if it were a painful memory. "It really . . . *hurt* me," he added softly.

Chloe felt like vomiting. Right there and then. Was he the greatest actor in the world and *completely* evil—which she sort of preferred at this point—or just a man who had thought he'd found a daughter figure and whose heart had been broken?

"I—I'm sorry. I just . . ."

"It was difficult for you, we understand," Olga said, reaching out to pat her hand. "All the violence must have been a shock."

"But we were there for you, Chloe. You know that, right?" Sergei sort-of pleaded.

There. A little tiny spark of anger. *Grab it, Chlo; follow it down to the source.* It was the only "power" she felt she had right then.

"I *just died,* for Christ's sake! *Again!*" she exploded. "*Tell* me you wouldn't want your mom after something like that."

"Still," Sergei said, crossing his legs and trying a different tactic, "fleeing for a while is completely understandable, as Olga has said. We will always be here, waiting for you. *But bringing a human into our complex?*"

He didn't raise his voice, but it was *cold,* each word ending in sharp silence.

She had been waiting for this, and she was still completely unprepared to answer it.

Chloe opened her mouth, but just then there was a soft click as the door opened behind her. Kim padded silently into the room, as calm and tranquil as a breeze on a sun-soaked oasis. She bowed to Chloe and Sergei and pulled up a chair.

"Kim, this is a private meeting," Sergei said, both baffled and stern.

The girl with the giant black cat ears nodded, smoothing some unseen wrinkle on the front of her long, priest-like black dress. "You are discussing the transition of leadership to the One, correct?" she asked coolly.

"Correct," Sergei answered through gritted teeth.

"I too must cede my power—I no longer represent the spiritual body of this Pride. Chloe is now the high priestess. This must be discussed as well." She sat down, and that was the end of the story.

THANK YOU! Chloe thought at Kim. *A thousand times, thank you.* If the other girl noticed Chloe looking at her, she ignored it, as if it was all just business as usual. But there was the slightest gleam in her eye that the two adults didn't notice.

Now, if being the One came with cat ears and a tail or something else visually freaky, I'd be able to pull stunts like that without batting an eyelash, too, Chloe thought a little jealously. Kim got away with a *lot* because of her ingrained weirdness.

The leader of the Pride let out a large sigh, as if he was giving up, changing his previous stance. "Chloe, this is just really hard. For a number of reasons," he said frankly, "besides the personal ones—I *really do* want you back here. I *like* our little chess games and chats and . . . having you around," he added quickly, as if he was a little embarrassed. Whatever else was true about him, the lion-haired middle-aged man really did like her, but did he like her so much that he had tried to kill her mom to keep her?

"And think of me," he went on, gesturing to the walls around him. "I spent my *entire life* and millions of dollars building this little safe haven for us, this little real estate empire, and bringing our people over. It's a little strange to suddenly have to hand it all over to a young girl."

"I don't think Chloe needs to involve herself with the business part of our Pride," Kim suggested in a tone that made it sound more like a statement of the obvious. "At least not yet. It's not really part of her 'job description' anyway. She is our *spiritual* leader, leader in all things having to do with the Mai. Not humans."

"What does that mean?" Olga asked bluntly.

"Well, in ancient days, she would have led us in the rites and rituals of the Twin Goddesses," Kim said thoughtfully. "Or led us to war against out enemies. Or led the Hunt. Sacrificed herself, if need be, for the continued survival of the Pride. Now it means leading the Pride in whatever direction it needs to survive—and thrive—*today* in the modern era, in this new world."

Olga, Sergei, and Kim looked expectantly at Chloe, who still had no idea what that meant. What *would* she suggest they do to become "more modern"? *Get an MP3-player hooked up to the speaker system in the lounge, maybe?*

"The first thing I think we should do is hold an all-Pride gathering," Sergei decided. "A meeting where we introduce you to everyone properly. There are those who won't believe you're the One until they've seen you in person. Kim, you should give her a crash course in our spirituality and the rites of the Twin Goddesses. I'll fill you in on how we've been more or less governing ourselves for the past few decades." He gave Chloe a weak smile. "As well as the traditions of leadership and the kizekh. We could order pizza . . . ?"

A peace offering. He really did want her back—if only part time.

"Okay," Chloe said, nodding, trying to look like it was no big deal.

"Good—can we meet this Friday?" Chloe shrugged. Sounded fine. "And we should have the gathering soon thereafter." He flipped a page on his desk calendar. "Tuesday, maybe."

"Shouldn't you check everyone's schedules first?"

Chloe found herself saying. Even Kim had difficulty not rolling her eyes.

"Chloe King," Sergei said mock-sternly, "the first thing you should know about the Pride is that this is *not* a democracy."

Not a democracy. As Chloe followed Kim back to the sanctuary where the cat gods Bastet and Sekhmet were worshiped, those words repeated themselves over and over in her mind.

Okay, let's play this game. Pretend I'm leader of this entire group of felines. What do I think is best for them? Chloe asked herself.

Integrate more, was the immediate and loudest answer. There must be a way to survive racially and socially and not resort to holing up in a mansion on the outskirts of town like vampires. Play video games. Go to the movies. Make everyone go to college.

"Kim, I have no idea what these people expect me to do as the One or even what I *should* do," she admitted aloud, sitting down on a bench as Kim bowed and said a little prayer to each of the goddesses: Bastet, house cat with the gentle smile and the earring; Sekhmet, with her teeth bared. The only sound in the room was the "moat" that separated the goddesses' dais from the rest of the room, a gentle trickle of water meant to remind worshipers of the Nile.

"What you should do will come with time," Kim said,

shrugging. "You are only sixteen and the world is much more complicated than it was in the days of hunting and gathering. As for the expectations of others, the wise will understand. Everyone else will have to be patient."

"What am I supposed to do in the meantime? If you asked me what I would do *today,* I would say breathe some fucking *air* and light into this place. Uh . . . not the temple, I mean Firebird," she added quickly as Kim frowned. " 'Sergei was right: the Mai *shouldn't* be trapped here. They should be free to interact with the rest of the world and control their own destinies instead of being bound to some five-thousand-year-old curse. *And* a boring real estate company."

Kim watched her curiously, listening without judgment.

"If it were up to me," Chloe said slowly, thinking of Xavier and Brian, "I would do everything possible to get rid of the curse. That would be my number-one goal. It's not fair to us *or* the humans we might accidentally wind up with. And besides that, it really adds to the whole cultish aspect of the Pride. No mixing with humans means a lot of dating at home and—well, pressure to keep it in the family. Having the place where you live for only a few years destroyed so you're forced to move on makes everyone clingy, to a leader as well as each other. Lions roam free over hundreds of miles, going where and with whom they please . . . staying in their pride because they want to, not because they're forced, you know?"

Actually, Chloe didn't know if that last part was true, but it sounded good. In the dreams she had there was a sense of power and freedom that was definitely missing from her own close Pride. Kim nodded, looking almost hungry for that freedom.

"But let's say we do that, huh?" Chloe said, slumping. "We somehow get rid of the curse, Mai and humans can interact again, everyone goes off and lives happily ever after on their own. The freedom of the Mai means their eventual integration and disappearance. I mean, there are six billion humans to meet and fall in love with and have babies with. The Mai would cease to exist in a couple of generations—is *that* the right thing? How can you have complete individual freedom and still maintain the culture of the Mai?"

A small smile curled at the edge of her friend's lips, and her ears dipped a little. "Chloe, I think maybe you have answered your original question. Perhaps a *spiritual* guide who keeps us all connected is what is called for in this age."

Chloe blinked.

"Anyway, you still have that five-thousand–year-old curse to lift, people to win over, and French to pass, so your plate's pretty full right now, as they say," Kim added, lighting a candle and picking up a handful of sand to continue her benedictions.

"Yeah, thanks for helping me," Chloe said a little glumly, brought back from her philosophical daydreams about the future to the reality of schoolwork. "And thanks for crashing the meeting, too, by the way. Things with Sergei were getting a little tense."

"No problem." It was strange hearing modern phrases come out of Kim's mouth with her little fangs showing.

"But of course he's going to be a little weird about just handing over leadership of this Pride to a sixteen-year-old, right?" Chloe looked to her friend expectantly. "I mean, who wouldn't be?"

Kim paused in her ritual and stared at Chloe unblinkingly, for a long enough time that Chloe actually began to feel uncomfortable.

"Hey, drink up," Alyec said, toasting her and tipping back a frosty mug of India Pale Ale.

Chloe looked around the library, realizing how much she'd missed the Thursday night cocktail parties at Firebird. Everyone was dressed up and taking drinks that were served on silver trays. The older Mai who had grown up in Abkhazia or Russia or Georgia had straight champagne and expensive shots of vodka in glasses made of ice.

Igor, Valerie, Alyec, and the other younger members of the Pride tended to drink beer, but Chloe was enamored of the sophisticated drinks she could never afford, the ones that they talked about in magazines and *Sex and the City:* pink cosmopolitans, three-olive dirty martinis, Bellinis with champagne and peach nectar.

When she'd lived there, Sergei had always watched

Chloe carefully and never let her have more than one. So she sipped slowly.

I'm the One now, though. Doesn't that mean I'm old enough to drink?

It was pretty amazing, she thought as she sat on a velvet love seat among the younger members. Here she was in a library out of a mystery novel that was full of lion people—her *own* people—a secret feline race living among humans and all of them gorgeous.

"I want a full veil," Valerie announced, throwing a much-thumbed *Martha Stewart Weddings* magazine down onto the coffee table for all to see.

So much for the cool, sexy, secret stuff. Chloe sighed, but she looked at the page interestedly.

"That's a patriarchal tradition for this day and age," said Simone. She was the beautiful, red-haired dancer Chloe met at the hunt. When she moved—even casually—it was hard for anyone, male or female, to take eyes off her. "Though the lace is pretty."

"Patriarchal, whatever, bah. This is what I want."

"Whatever you want, it shall be yours," Igor said, kissing her on the forehead.

Alyec and Chloe smiled at each other, rolling their eyes.

"Kim suggested adding some traditional Mai stuff," Simone pressed. "You going to do that?"

The couple looked at each other, lips pursed in thinking expressions. "I think it's a good idea," Igor finally said. Valerie nodded.

Chloe had just sat through one group "service" that Kim led—it was always a personal religion, the cat-eared girl had emphasized, but a surprising number of Mai showed up. Instead of psalmbooks there were scrolls in languages Chloe couldn't read. Some of the service was in English, but most was in Russian and Mai. Kim had poured out little measures of dried meat—it looked suspiciously like cat food—and honey and wine at the base of each statue. Kind of interesting, from an anthropological perspective, but not something Chloe really felt she could get worked up about.

"But you have to throw a bouquet," one of the other girls said. "That way one of us unmarried girls can catch it."

"Agreed." Valerie laughed.

"Are you going to have your father bring you down the aisle?" Chloe asked, thinking about other possible "patriarchal" aspects of the service.

"I don't know who my father is," Valerie said, shrugging. "He's probably dead."

"Oh," Chloe said. "I don't know mine either."

The other girl nodded, as if it were obvious.

"It's funny . . . ," Chloe said slowly, thinking about it. "Everyone is all concerned about finding out who my biological *mom* is, but no one has said anything about my dad."

"Uh, Honored One." Simone coughed delicately.

"Lineage in the Mai is always determined through the *mother* because you always know who your mother is."

"Yeah, but—"

Alyec cut in. "What she is trying to say, Chloe, is that in the past your husband was not always the father of all your children."

She knew it was impolite, but Chloe couldn't help gaping. Was this a cat-legacy thing? Or was it just a result of the violence and chaos in Eastern Europe?

Somehow Chloe didn't think it was the latter. The implications were . . . not nice images.

"So, have you and Alyec talked at all?" Valerie asked, changing the subject. "You know, about this?"

Alyec began to choke on his beer.

"I'm sixteen!" Chloe said, stunned at the implications of the woman's question.

"Oh, I didn't mean *now,*" she said, laughing heartily. "But do you, you know . . . have any plans? Going steady?"

Everyone was staring at her and Alyec interestedly, even Igor. Her boyfriend was completely silent for once and seriously blushing.

Suddenly Chloe got it. There were fewer Mai than Rhode Islanders—probably fewer than the Amish. Every couple was a pair of potential breeders.

"Oh, look at the time! Gotta go," she said without attempting to disguise the lame excuse.

"Yeah, I've got to go find my mom. Uh, early night," Alyec said instantly, also getting up.

"Oh, Chloe, you are so funny," Valerie said. "You too, Alyec. You're a *perfect* couple."

The perfect couple left as quickly as possible without knocking furniture over or books off their shelves.

"Well, uh, good night," Alyec said when they were outside.

"Uh, yeah." Chloe kissed him, but it was short and sort of perfunctory. He didn't hold it either. When they finally looked into each other's eyes, they laughed nervously.

Seven

A = 33 degrees, B = 95 degrees, a = 6 cm
What is the length of *b*?

In the last couple of months, Chloe had grown claws, fought an assassin, died twice, and become the leader of her people. It just didn't seem fair that she had to deal with *this* as well.

She took a deep breath, thinking about the late-night study session she'd had with her mom. *Law of sines.*

$$a/\sin A = b/\sin B$$
$$6/\sin 33 = b/\sin 95$$
$$6/0.5446 = b/0.9962$$
$$b = \sim 10.97$$

That seemed right.

Chloe heaved a deep sigh and peeled the exam off her desktop, where it had stuck from the pressure and hand sweat. Maybe elbow sweat, too.

She handed it to Mr. Hyde, the calculus and computer teacher who had been quietly waiting for her at his desk, solving a puzzle in *Scientific American.* He took the test from her as if he had forgotten she was there, faintly surprised and pleased. He was ascetically thin and all Vulcan, except for the ears and the sense of humor. All arching eyebrows and flawless logic.

"Listen," he said, a little louder than his usual soft-spoken self. "I was kind of thinking of having you as an alternate on the math team next marking period, after Christmas."

Chloe almost dropped her books again. *Her?* She wasn't a geek—just kind of good at math. Or at least better than a lot of other sophomores.

"I don't know. . . . I've never been much of a joiner."

"Just think about it, okay?" he begged. "I'd really like you on the team. You'd be a great role model to younger girls."

"Uh, sure. See ya." Chloe got out of the classroom as quickly as she could, waving her hand behind her. *Her* on the math team? *If one more thing gets freaky in my life, just* one more thing, *I swear I'm gonna—*

"Hey, Chloe. You look like you've seen a ghost," Paul called out to her. He was flipping through the comic books that he had just bought, brown bag under his arm.

"Jekyll and Hyde just basically asked me to join the math team. As an alternate," she added quickly.

"I didn't know trig was one of your superpowers. Speaking of, how are things over at the cathouse?"

"They want me to be their leader." Chloe leaned against the wall and slid down it until she was sitting on the floor. Paul followed suit. She dug through her bag, hoping for a candy bar or something, but only found an old cough drop. It was a little dusty from being at the bottom of her bag, but she unwrapped it and popped it into her mouth anyway. Cherry. Her favorite. "You?"

"My dad has a girlfriend," he said, staring at the floor with large, unblinking eyes.

Okay. That was officially "it." The last freaky thing.

"How long?" she asked, also staring at the floor. Paul got embarrassed easily and he looked dangerously close to freaking out, so it seemed the safest thing to do.

"I . . . I don't know. I think they knew each other—I know they knew each other—she's the daughter of some friends of my parents."

Daughter!

"Korean?"

"Yeah. A lot more . . . traditional than my mom. *And* a lot younger," he added with an angry smile. "She's my dad's new secretary."

"Oh, you are *shitting* me," Chloe sympathized.

Some of the anger drained out of his smile and it became broader, if sadder. "I don't think they actually had an affair before my parents began the divorce—I don't even know if they're sleeping together now. She still lives at home with her parents—she's thirty-*two.*"

They sat quietly for a moment, side by side. That seemed like all Paul really wanted: someone to listen and understand and not react. Chloe understood the feeling all too well.

"Would—would you do me a favor?" he asked, sniffing a little.

She nodded.

"Don't tell Amy?"

Chloe felt her stomach freeze. This was the beginning of a whole new "it."

"I'll tell her myself, but not yet—I just found out, and . . ."

Of course it made sense: things were already weird between her two best friends. Now was not the time for further complications, sympathy, or anger. But he had made Chloe his confidante—once again the three of them were split two to one, but this time Amy was the odd man out.

And if she ever finds out I knew about this before her and didn't tell, I'm toast.

"Yeah, whatever. Sure," Chloe said.

They sat there for a few minutes, not speaking. Chloe looked down the empty hall of the math wing, so silent, it was almost like it had already been evacuated for the summer or Christmas vacation. Long rows of green and blue lockers, recently repainted, reflected glossily in the tiles of the floor, extending their length six feet into a blurrier universe. Doors were left open here and there and the very slightest hint of fresh air managed to tunnel through the ancient smells of paste, dirt, textbooks, and copy paper.

Very soon, Chloe realized, this would all be a memory. Whatever happened with the rest of her life, as a cat or as a human, less than three quick years would pass and all that would remain of these turbulent days were memories, like this silent, still image of her and Paul on the floor.

A bell rang and there was a school-wide shuffling and shifting as those who stayed late or were in detention finally got to go free. Chloe rose to her feet and pulled Paul with her with the ease of her Mai strength.

"I dare you to give me a piggyback ride," he said weakly.

"Don't tempt me." Chloe smiled. "You know, I could have your dad's girlfriend killed," she said brightly as they began to walk down the hall together. "I know an entire organization of assassins now. Two organizations, actually."

"As much as I don't want to sound like a sensitive New Age boy," Paul said with a sigh, "I *think* my dad might have something to do with this as well. You know?"

When they got to the lobby, Amy saw them and waved; she had something that looked suspiciously like a giant portfolio under her arm.

"Hey, guys. How are things?" It sounded forced. Even for Amy.

"Not too shabby," Chloe answered, shrugging.

"How's Brian?"

Chloe tapped her tooth, remembering at the last moment to keep her claws sheathed. It was really much more satisfying the other way, but they were in public. Finally she decided. If she had no control over the rest of her life, at least she could keep things clear with her friends.

"He kissed me."

Both of her friends' jaws dropped, and Chloe wished they could see themselves. They actually made a pretty good couple. It sucked that they were breaking up, considering Chloe was just getting used to them as an item.

"He's not dead," she said shakily, hoping it was still true. It had been at least two hours since she last called Dr. Lovsky. "And he hasn't shown any symptoms yet, either. They've got him pretty closely monitored, so if he goes into anaphylactic shock, at least they'll be able to catch it. He was a *dumbass,*" she added before Amy could open her mouth. "I guess he thought he was going to die—he was so out of it from the blood loss."

"Holy cow," Paul said, shocked beyond the realm of swear words. "*Sooo* glad I didn't wind up with you for two minutes in the closet at Amy's thirteenth birthday party."

"Life sucks," Chloe said, letting the misery descend on her for one brief moment, in the safety of her friends. Then she shook her head. "I've got to find out what happened to Xavier."

Amy shrugged. "I've been checking the newspapers and public police records online every day since you asked a couple of weeks ago—nothing has come up about him yet. There was one obituary for a Xavier Constantine, but he was eighty-seven."

"Well, that's good news, I guess. Not for the old guy, I mean."

"Are you going to check out his apartment? See if he's even still there?" Paul asked.

She shook her head. "Not tonight. I'm . . . kind of exhausted. I'm just going to go home." Chloe wasn't sure she would be able to deal with it if she found out Xavier was dead—one of the reasons she had been putting it off for so long.

"Oh, you're busy tonight," Amy said, a little too quickly. She turned to Paul. "You want to hang, maybe? Watch the *Star Trek* marathon?"

As clichéd as it was, Chloe realized this was a train wreck she could only watch. She kept hoping her friends would not say the inevitable. *Superhuman strength, night vision, and no way to salvage the next minute of conversation.* She sighed.

Paul shifted uncomfortably. "Not tonight."

That's one. . . .

"Other plans?" Amy pushed, still trying to sound bright.

That's two. . . .

"No, I just . . . I don't think it's a good idea right now."

That's three!

Between Amy's constant pressure and Paul's stupidly excessive honesty at the wrong time, it was amazing they hadn't spontaneously combusted earlier. Chloe found herself actually closing her eyes and wincing.

"Oh," Amy said, color rushing to her cheeks.

"Well, I gotta get going," Paul said, pretending to ignore everything that had just happened. He reshouldered his messenger bag—this one said *Aladdin Sane* on it—and went through the emergency exit that hadn't been hooked to an alarm system since the seventies, when students started toking up in the alley. *Exit the cowardly hero, stage left.*

"I have to go to the dance meeting," Amy said shakily, too shocked and upset to react yet.

"*You?* You're on the fall formal committee?" Chloe asked with more surprise than was strictly necessary, trying to get her friend to smile.

"Alyec bet me I couldn't do a better job than Mrs. Dinan. . . ."

"I'll go with you," Chloe volunteered, thinking about what a smart guy her boyfriend was.

The gym was decorated with little dots of students in socks and bare feet—*No Street Shoes*—with charts and clipboards, pointing at this set of bleachers and that basketball net, joined by the art teacher, who waved her arm around like she was painting the ceiling. A pile of fake ravens was thrown into a corner, bags of little evil glowing plastic spiders and caterpillars next to it. Probably favors or something. It was the only time Chloe had actually seen anyone excited about anything in the gym. But through the windows and skylights she could see that the sky was bleakly heading toward sunset, the layers of white clouds like dryer lint after a load of whites. This was the downside of fall—Halloween, leaves, apples, cider, and the beginning of the party season aside, this was a little bit of the autumn that set in before Thanksgiving and lasted through Christmas: dark and drear, cold and snowless.

Chloe led her friend to the closest set of risers, where she could cry in relative peace.

"We haven't—he hasn't *said* anything definite . . . ," Amy murmured, the tears finally coming.

"Sounds like he pretty much just did," Chloe said as gently as she could. But sometimes her friend got so wrapped up in her own emotions, she wasn't able to clearly see what was actually going on around her.

"Hey, pretty ladies." Alyec neatly vaulted straight up over the side and onto the step where they sat, with an ease and grace that was completely inhuman. No one in the gym was watching. Amy sniffed back a tear; Chloe knew she liked being let in on the Mai's secret lives, that even *Alyec* trusted her with it. But she still quickly lifted her bright green scarf to cover her face and blot her eyes.

"Hey, we're waiting for you."

"I still can't believe you're doing this . . . ," Chloe muttered.

Amy was still blowing her nose and trying to hide her tears; Alyec answered for her. "Yup, she's helping with the overall installation. The gestalt, if you will. Putting the 'Wicked' in 'Something Wicked This Way Comes.'" There was an extraloud sniff behind the scarf. "Hey, what's wrong?" Alyec asked nonchalantly. "And where's your little friend?"

Chloe whacked him with the back of her hand.

"What, he finally came out of the closet?" Alyec asked, faking concern.

"He's not *gay,*" Amy protested, blowing her nose and crumpling the napkin up. "It would be easier if he was," she added weakly.

"Well, he does have a bit of the mama's boy," Alyec said. "I mean, he's nice and all, but not exactly a *stud.* Oh, come *on.*" He grabbed the tasseled ends of Amy's scarf and tugged them a little. "I'll bet he never really got your juices going, someone like *you. . . .*" He pulled Amy in and suddenly dipped her so low that her frizzy hair was inches away from the wooden benches, his face inches from hers.

"What are you *doing?*" Amy demanded, the sadness momentarily banished from her face.

"Cheering you up. I could kiss your tears away if you wanted, but that would be fatal—wouldn't it?"

The two were frozen there for a long moment.

Neither Alyec nor Amy blinked or looked away. Tension crackled.

Chloe found herself staring, too. And then she found herself getting *really annoyed.*

"Let me up, douche bag," Amy finally snapped, breaking the spell.

"As madam commands; I live to serve." With one fluid curve of his arm he pulled her upright, then brought it below his stomach for a formal bow.

"Thanks for, uh, staying with me," Amy said, turning to Chloe. "And for the little lesson about how *all* men suck," she added with a glare at Alyec, then marched off toward the art teacher, who now looked like she was conducting an invisible orchestra with a large paint-brush she had found somewhere.

Chloe watched her friend go; as angry as her steps were, she still fidgeted nervously with her scarf and the places where Alyec had touched her.

"WHAT THE HELL WAS THAT?" Chloe demanded, turning back to him.

"I was cheering her up, like I said." He sat down on the step above her and picked up a flyer that someone had left there, as though the incident was almost completely forgotten.

"Alyec." Chloe tore the paper out of his hand so hard that her claws threatened to come out.

"I wasn't really going to kiss her," he said innocently. "I don't want her dead."

"You weren't really *joking* about kissing her either, were you?"

The silence between them was as deep and long as the one between him and Amy—but for very different reasons.

"Chloe," he said with a smile, "you knew I was a flirt. You've *always* known I'm a flirt. It came free with purchase."

Chloe glowered. She knew what he said was true, but still . . . It was one thing when it was Keira and Halley and whoever else. He'd *told* her he didn't really feel anything for them—besides the unavoidable fact that they were human. But her best friend? And *right in front of her?*

"And what if you *could?*" she demanded, thinking of Brian and Xavier and her talk with Kim. "Would you have?"

"Chloe, why are you getting so pissed?" he asked, frowning. "Nothing happened—I really was just cheering your friend up."

But she didn't believe it. There was definitely something different between him and Amy than the other girls. For one thing, she hated him. And for another, the opposite of love isn't hate. It's indifference.

"I just—" She couldn't put it into words. She was just pissed. That was all—she didn't like what she had seen and it had pissed her off and he was her *boyfriend,* for chrissake.

"I didn't realize you were so jealous," he said, a little

coolly. "Do you really think you have a right—what about that sick human lover of yours?"

It hit her like a slap; he had never spoken to her that way before. But from the day she first saw her claws, the afternoon when she was on the phone with Brian and IM'ing with Alyec, she knew this moment was coming. It was all fun and games with two boyfriends, two different races, one in love with her and one, well, in "fun" with her, but now was the moment of reckoning.

"Fair enough," she said, swallowing and choking back tears, the same way Amy had just a few minutes earlier with Paul.

"I know the way you feel about him," Alyec continued quietly. She had finally gotten beneath his carefree, joking exterior, and *this* was how. *Happy now, Chlo?* "I keep hoping you'll change your mind. But whatever we have, even if it's just for kicks, it would be nice if you kept the same rules for everyone."

Run away.

It was a powerful instinct; she hurt and didn't know what to do or say. She fought it; she was the One, right? She had faced down psycho-killer assassins before.

"Fine," Chloe said through a clenched jaw. "You're right." She stood up and shouldered her bag. "I have to think about this. I'm going home now."

"Chloe," Alyec said, a little more gently, a lot more uncertainly. "I didn't mean for us to fight about this—"

"No, you're right. I shouldn't keep the two of you

dangling. It's wrong. I'm going home, good night," she said with finality, and walked off to the bus stop.

Chloe had only gone for the bus to put some literal space between her and Alyec, but she got off after a couple of stops. The only time she had to think anymore was when in transit, and she wanted to make it last as long as possible. In the cold dusk air, by herself, the irrational passion drained away. True, the whole Alyec-Brian thing would have to be worked out sometime, eventually, but that wasn't the real issue of the fight.

The real issue was how she *couldn't* have a relationship with Brian. The real issue was a stupid curse because she was Mai and because of things that people had done five millennia ago. Chloe was suddenly overcome with panic and she froze: she really could be responsible for the deaths of Xavier and Brian. They could really die or already be dead.

She shook herself and ran a hand over her face and scratched her scalp, extending her claws, trying to snap herself out of it. *This had all better—*

Chloe stopped, suddenly aware of an almost-noise. Something so slight it could have been missed even by her Mai hearing or dismissed as some random night noise—a mouse, a rat, a can being blown—but it ended too sharply. Like the moment she noticed it. A very slight crunching of gravel, a . . .

She started walking again, picking up the pace. If it was a mugger or rapist or whatever, she had no doubt she could handle herself. But those were monsters of the past; the things she feared now were more complicated and dangerous. She shook her head and kept walking.

What I really need is a vacation. Yeah, that was it. The sort of place inspired by sequined flip-flops, flowery beach bags, expensive sunblock, and fruity drinks. She and her mom could go somewhere fun for Thanksgiving instead of Grandma and crazy Aunt Isabel's; maybe bring a lot of good, crappy books, lie out on the beach, *swim*. . . .

There it was again.

Perfectly matched with her own footsteps.

"Okay, come on out!" she yelled, planting her feet and resting her thumbs around her backpack straps. "You *sure* picked the wrong day to screw with me!"

A low wind hit her coldly in the shins and made ripping noises as it tore through fenders, hydrants, and other metal obstacles. Pebbles eddied around Chloe's feet like they were caught in an invisible wave. A man rode slowly past on a Vespa, staring at the crazy teen in the street. His headlight had no power against the gray in the air and lit up nothing besides itself.

"I *warned* you! We have a truce," she shouted. The wind shifted direction and threw the words back into her own face; her voice couldn't have carried more than a few feet.

No one appeared or owned up to making any noises.

"This sucks," Chloe muttered. "I am *out* of here."

And *then* she turned and ran.

Eight

"Hey, Mom," Chloe said wearily, closing the door behind her. It was only half an act. She threw her book bag onto the counter and went over to the fridge, looking for something easy, filling, and comforting.

"Bag off the counter," her mom said without looking up from the magazine she was reading on the couch—*Utne Reader.* "I have some risotto from Lixia's we can nuke and a salad, so don't spoil your appetite."

Carbs. Nice, warm, comforting carbs. Just what Chloe wanted. She grabbed a Diet Coke with lime and wandered over to the couch, where she plopped down, head in her mom's lap and feet propped up on the armrest.

Anna King looked over the magazine at her daughter. "Hard day at work? How was your exam?"

"Oh, that was *fine.* It's everything else that sucks." Chloe ticked off things on her fingers. "Paul and Amy are breaking up. I think Alyec might like Amy. Paul's dad is already dating his secretary. I have two boyfriends, both of whom are kind of . . . burdens right now. Mr. Hyde—not even my own *teacher,* mind you—wants me to be on the math team. And according to Kim, I'm supposed to lead my lion people into a new age of spiritual enlightenment."

"Paul's dad is dating his *secretary?*" Chloe's mom said excitedly, leaning forward and putting her magazine down.

"Mom . . ."

"I know, honey. It's just . . ." Her mother's eyes unfocused, trying to imagine. "*That* little piece of fluff? She's like an anime character. One of the evil ones."

"While I appreciate the teen-appeal metaphor, can we please get back to me now?"

"Being on the math team will look *great* on your applications." Anna began to play with her daughter's hair, twirling a stray lock with her finger and trying to fix it to the top of her head under another lock.

"So would being the leader of a clandestine race of human feline warriors," Chloe growled.

"I suppose . . . ," her mother said carefully, "if we couched it in different terms, like that girl did in her speech for *Whale Rider.* Actually, that would be a *great* essay—how you looked for your biological roots as a teen and found far more than you ever expected. . . ."

"Mom." Chloe sat up and looked her mother right in the eye. "They really want me to *lead* them. You know, *lead?*"

There was a long pause. Her mother opened her mouth and blinked a few times, stalling—something Chloe had never seen her do before. Attorney Anna King was almost never at a loss for words. Even when she was the victim of kidnapping.

"Better make sure you get into Berkeley, then," she finally said with a faint smile. Then she squared her jaw and her look turned serious. "Chloe, I know I don't understand everything that's going on with you and the other . . . *Mai,* or even have anything to do with it. It's more than obvious what some of your other . . . *friends* and people think of me, your *human* mother. But whatever you decide to do, do it educated. Foreign kings and royalty have always sent their children, princes and princesses and whatever, here for college. You would make a much better leader of your people with a university degree."

Chloe thought about this, sinking back into the couch. "I don't think Sergei would mind keeping a heavier hand in until I'm ready."

"He's the one with the red hair and the gun?"

"Uh, just a gun that one time. Usually it's claws."

"It looked like he was trying to shoot me. Or Brian. Or that other boy," her mother said levelly.

"At least he didn't kidnap you," Chloe countered weakly. "Are you going to try to press charges? Against the Order of the Tenth Blade?"

Her mother made a nasty face. "Who would I have

for witnesses? Are your Mai going to stand up for me in court? And Brian—who seems to be the only decent one of the lot—has disappeared."

Chloe winced guiltily. All cat business aside, if she revealed to her mother that "the only decent one of the lot"—and sort of her boyfriend—had been beaten half to death by his own friends . . . Well, it would just confuse the whole dating issue more, and that would definitely make Chloe's life even more complicated.

"I can't believe you're just going to drop it."

"I didn't say I was going to drop it," her mother answered, almost absently. "I just have to . . . figure out the right strategy."

For the first time in the last few months, Chloe suddenly wondered if her mother was hiding something from *her.* Something strange, illegal, or awful. *Parents with secrets* . . . Not a comforting thought. Which reminded her.

"Hey, do you think Dad knew anything about what I am?"

Anna King was knocked out of her reverie. "No, I don't think—" Then she stopped, shifting on the couch uncomfortably. "All of our fights about how to raise you—he even wanted to give you back to your own people at one point. I just thought he meant the Russians," she said slowly. "He was so . . . adamant about certain things. Way, *way* too overprotective—"

"And then he disappeared. So there's a chance,"

Chloe interrupted with more bitterness than she'd intended. Maybe her dad had skipped town to avoid the assassinations, the kidnappings, and the general craziness of being caught between the Tenth Bladers and the Mai. Or maybe he was just trying to protect Chloe—the man who knew too much getting out so she could live a more normal life. *Maybe he thought Mom was safer not knowing about anything.*

Suddenly Chloe was exhausted. She fell back into her mom's lap again. "Did I mention Paul and Amy are breaking up?"

"A little too weirdly timed, with his parents and all, don't you think?"

Her mom reached over for the cup of coffee she had been sipping from. Unlike many things in the house, it was old and the handle had broken off and been glued carefully back on almost ten years ago. It was a dark aqua, kind of out in household furnishings since the early eighties, and clashed with all of the jade- and turquoise-themed pieces that fit into Mrs. King's New Southwest style.

Out of place, old, and infinitely comforting. Her mom had used that mug since before Chloe could remember. She closed her eyes, squidging her butt more comfortably into the couch.

"So they're not going to the fall formal together?" her mother continued, after a loud sip. "Maybe he'll take you. Or all three of you could go together or something. I went to my junior prom with my best friends. We pretended we were Charlie's Angels, undercover. With potato pellet guns."

"Oh, those wacky seventies." Chloe tried not to think of Alyec. She and Paul and Amy only ever went to dances when Amy dragged them. If Brian lived—*when Brian got better*—she would really have to decide what to do about him. Them. *Us.* Things had gotten too serious. Of course, there was still the question of Mai and humans and toxic kisses; just because Brian hadn't died immediately didn't mean there weren't long-term effects.

Chloe sighed.

It was time to visit Xavier.

She didn't have to scramble around her messy room desperately looking for his address this time; whether it was another Mai ability or something she'd always had and never used, Chloe had no problem remembering exactly where the apartment was—by landmark and general direction, though, not street names and house numbers.

She went immediately after school the next day; no makeup classes that afternoon. It was nice to get away from everything. *I really do need a little more "me" time,* Chloe reflected unironically as she skipped up the steps to the old house. *And not just running at night across the skyline.* She needed a good book or a hobby or to get out on the mountain bike her mom had given her for her sixteenth birthday.

Chloe rang the doorbell, her scarf unfurling behind her in the October breeze. Then, without even asking who she was, Xavier—or someone—clicked the thing that unlocked the door and Chloe went in.

Just three floors until I find out if Xavier is alive or dead.

She rushed up the stairs two at a time, trying to make as much headway as she could before her nerves failed her. Once again the old-house smell of wood and lemony cleaner made her ache to live in a beautiful house like this, even if it was just an apartment. She *hated* her house—it looked like every other piece of two-story urban ranch mediocrity out there. One of the things that first drew her to living with the Mai at Firebird was waking up in an old gabled nook with perilously warped wood plank floors and the dusty quietude only an old house could have.

When she got to the right landing, Xavier's door was already open a crack. She knocked anyway, not wanting to just walk in. Not like last time.

"It's open . . ., " came a voice from inside. The voice was male—but she couldn't tell if it was Xavier's or not. It was hard to hear anything right now over the fast and heavy heartbeats that drummed in her chest—and the only words they'd exchanged had been shouted at the top of their lungs in the club and whispered outside in the parking lot.

The apartment looked almost exactly like it had the night she had come upon him rolling on the floor, dying. A few extra magazines were scattered around, a new candle placed on a windowsill. Still spare, expensive, casual, and Euro-bachelor-y. From the scraping sound of a pan and a spatula, Chloe decided he was probably in the middle of cooking something. . . . But was it him?

"Oh." Xavier came in from the kitchen, dish towel under his chin and pan in one hand, spatula in the other.

Chloe almost threw up with relief. He was alive. And okay.

More than okay, actually. Chloe was shocked by how good-looking he was even in daylight: raven black hair, lovely tan skin, and eyes an incredibly, amazingly light brown. Very exotic. He wore jeans and an impossibly crisp white T-shirt, like he was just preparing for a "casual" model shoot.

"Chloe—right?" he said, raising his perfectly formed eyebrows. "The girl from the club?"

She was floored that he could remember. As far as she knew, he was just a rich foreign college student who was into picking up random American high-school girls. Her heart was finally calming down; for a moment there it was fifty-fifty she was going to pass out.

"Uh, yeah." Chloe had had no actual plan for when she actually met him, if he was still alive. Now that she had seen him, all she wanted to do was rush back and see Brian. There was hope.

"Have you eaten yet?"

Eaten yet? It was two thirty. Lunch? Tea? Elevensies?

"Uh, I'm fine, thanks," she said awkwardly. Her hands itched for her cell phone.

"So." He put the pan carefully down on a coffee table. "I haven't seen you at The Bank, but then again, I haven't been there much recently myself," he said, referring to the club where she met him on the eve of her sixteenth birthday.

"You've been sick," Chloe said as neutrally as she could, making it sound like both a question and a statement.

"How did you know?" He looked up at her sharply.

"I . . . came here a couple of nights after we met," Chloe admitted. "Your door was open and I found you lying on the floor, all . . . suffocating and covered in hives and stuff. I called 911."

"That was *you?* I would have died if you hadn't come. I was all alone here." He shivered. It was weird seeing the sexy guy from the club—the one she almost had sex with. "They said I was in shock, the whole deal. My body just started attacking itself and they couldn't figure out why."

"But they were able to treat you," she said, again neutrally, trying to sound like she wasn't digging for information.

He shook his head, his beautiful black hair staying neatly put. "They couldn't do anything. I went into a coma . . . and then one day I just suddenly got better. I woke up and it was all over. They said it was like my body was all of sudden able to heal itself or something. No explanation. I just woke up, on October 19."

"Well, I'm glad you're okay. I just came back to see how you were." Chloe turned to go, feeling it was a good time to exit.

He put a hand out to stop her. "But they said no one was in the apartment when the ambulance came."

"I freaked and ran away. Sorry about that," Chloe apologized with a small smile. Why was it easier to tell a stranger the whole truth than her friends and family? "If my mom found out I was in some strange guy's apartment at night—even if it wound up saving his life—*my* life would be over."

Xavier laughed, an open, clear-eyed laugh that held none of the seducer's smile from the night at the club.

"In fact, I should probably get going," she added. *Okay, you're not dead. This is where the Xavier-Chloe story ends. Goodbye and good luck. No more complications.* "Like I said, I just wanted to make sure you were okay."

"I mean it, I owe you, Chloe," he said standing up with her, wiping his mouth with the back of his hand in an extremely sexy, masculine way. "I would have died. If there's anything you want or need, name it. Even, like, help moving in somewhere," he added with a grin of teeth as white as the plastered wall on the postcard of Santorini that hung on Chloe's fridge.

"Uh, I'll keep that in mind." Although the idea of a

rich young Euro playboy who owed her was an intriguing concept—visions of a free vacation in Greece came to mind—Chloe was pretty sure she was never going to see him again.

"Hey," he called as she walked out. "Maybe I'll see you at The Bank sometime?"

"Maybe!" Chloe shouted back. But she was already two flights down.

Nine

Xavier was alive.

Chloe repeated this over and over to herself as she rode the bus to Sausalito, her foot impatiently marking the seconds as she tapped it against the seat in front of her.

There still remained the mystery of how he "just woke up," but it seemed like her kiss wasn't fatal—this time, at least. Maybe it wouldn't be for Brian either. Maybe the curse was losing its power as the centuries wore on, remaining overhyped as something to scare the kids with. Maybe everything was going to be okay.

A bubble of hope grew out of control in the back of Chloe's head, threatening to explode and drench her spirit with joy. She tried to rein it in, not wanting to be disappointed later if reality went south on her. Instead she channeled it into movement, leaping off the bus as soon as it stopped and running all the way to Firebird.

No going in the back way this time. Chloe was the *leader of this Pride,* for chrissake. She didn't need to go slinking around into her own den, embarrassed by the presence of her human boyfriend and intimidated by Sergei. Chloe walked right up to the front door and strode in breezily past the receptionist.

"I'll tell Sergei you are in," the sharp-angled woman said with the slightest of bows.

"Tell him I'll be right there," Chloe said, trying not to snap, not looking over her shoulder. "There's something I have to do."

How did a leader speak to her subjects? Not that she was, really—but she wasn't going to be treated as a helpless teenage girl by Sergei and his employees anymore. Until she found a middle ground, it was going to be tricky.

And as much as she wanted—*needed*—to see Brian, there was another person Chloe had to talk to first.

She went straight to the sanctuary, knocking on the door lightly before cracking it open and stepping silently in. Surprisingly, Kim wasn't there, though the lingering traces of incense indicated her recent presence. There was another Mai woman there—Valerie, Igor's fiancée. She was bent over on the floor before the statues of the twins Bastet and Sekhmet, murmuring something plaintively. She was beautiful, a perfect devoted servant of the Twin Goddesses, and might have been taken right off an Egyptian wall painting had it not been for her bright lavender suit and stiletto heels.

Chloe backed up quietly until she was out, not clicking

the door completely closed, afraid of disturbing the woman. What was she praying for? Her marriage? A baby? Or was her visit just something routine—like going to mass every Sunday? Chloe wasn't sure she could show that much devotion to the goddesses she supposedly received her power from; in the same way that Buddhism sounded neat, she was just too Western, Judeo-Christian monotheistically raised to be able to treat ancient deities with much belief or reverence.

Valerie had taken down a deer with her bare hands—and claws—on the Hunt that Chloe had attended. Another thing Chloe was also pretty sure she couldn't do. *They should have chosen* her, she thought sadly. *Or Kim.* People who actually deserved leadership of the Mai.

She headed upstairs to the library, the other obvious place Kim would be, though she checked the dining room and the little Firebird kitchenette first. All empty. *Except for the usual coffee-swilling real estate drones.*

Chloe kicked herself mentally. A lot of these people would have died for an opportunity to live in America and be—mostly—left alone with their Mai habits to work for a Mai company and be fairly well paid to do so. She would really have to stop judging people so much if she was actually going to be a leader.

Bingo.

Her friend stood at the end of a long bookshelf, silently turning the pages of a monstrous leather-bound volume. The long windows were shaded and draped by equally long velvet curtains; motes of dust hung silently in the air, unsparkled by any stray beam of sun. It was to protect the ancient and rare books, Chloe understood, but the darkness made the whole place also kind of reek of doom.

Kim looked up directly at her, even though Chloe could have sworn she hadn't made any noise.

"Hello," the girl with the black, velvety cat ears said in a normal voice, strangely out of place in a room that demanded whispering.

"Hey, Kim—I have a question for you."

Kim's ears flicked back and her green slit eyes focused, waiting.

"Is there a chance . . ." Chloe bit her lip. She was calling into question all this other girl believed in. She sucked it up. "Is there a chance that the whole human-and-Mai curse thing could be a little, well, overblown?"

Kim blinked her heavy eyelashes. "Which part? The feud? The story of the Mai girl who was killed?"

"No, the, uh, biological particulars. Could it be a complete fib that humans and Mai can't interact?"

"Chloe, unlike many of the Mai, I believe that you are free to choose your relationships however you wish, but I cannot advise testing that theory on any human you particularly like."

"No, no." Chloe sighed and sat down on the edge of a table—something she would have been screamed at for in any other library in the world. Kim merely raised an eyebrow. Chloe couldn't help noticing the Ethernet ports and wireless broadband antennas that stuck out of the center of the table, incongruous against the old wood and tarnished brass printers' lamps. The Mai were such a strange mix of boldly going modern and completely hung up on the past. "Look, I've already kissed two humans—uh, boys."

Kim's eyebrows climbed even higher than Dr. Lovsky's had. "The one at the club . . . Olga mentioned it," Kim said.

"Yeah, I checked up on him. He's *fine* now."

Kim stood in way that implied that had she a tail, it would have been swishing back and forth. "And who else? Paul, maybe?"

Chloe started. "What? I don't know, maybe as a kid. No, I meant *Brian*. Right before he conked out." Didn't Kim realize how much she liked him? And what did Paul have to do with anything? "And Dr. Lovsky says he's recovering normally."

The two girls looked at each other for a long moment.

"It sounds like our curse is somehow being lifted or fading," Kim said slowly, thinking. "How exactly did the boy from the club 'recover'?"

"I don't know. He said he just sort of woke up; they told him that he suddenly just 'got better.' "

"And when exactly did this happen?"

"Uh, October 19th."

Kim's eyes widened. "That's the night you died—at the Presidio, with everyone."

"Yeah, so . . . ?" Chloe hadn't made the connection and still didn't see what it had to do with anything.

"You're lifting the curse!" her friend practically shouted, scaring Chloe with her intensity.

"Um . . . what?"

"You died *saving a human!*"

"She's my *mom,* Kim. . . ."

"Yes, but listen—we were cursed because we killed whole villages of humans!" Kim said excitedly, her fangs gleaming and her eyes a little crazy. "Maybe because you died saving one, it mitigates our burden. And Brian? How is he?"

"I'm going downstairs to see him now, but the doctor said that so far he hasn't shown any signs of anything."

Kim glowed with excitement. "I must research this further," she said, disappearing back into the stacks. "I'll call you later if I find an answer!"

As she headed downstairs to the hospital room, Chloe smiled to herself at the idea of *her* lifting an ancient curse. Besides it meaning that everyone would be okay . . . how cool was that? It finally sounded like something a real leader would do.

Brian was still unconscious on the bed, IVs and tubes sticking in and out of his body. There was almost no discernable change from the other day, except that maybe his wounds looked a little scabbier, like they were beginning to heal around the edges. Maybe. No signs of death or toxic shock.

"Hey," Chloe said softly, taking his hand. Without her realizing it, her claws came out, slowly and delicately. She used them to comb back his hair.

"Oh." Dr. Lovsky stopped short when she came in and saw the two of them together. "I, uh, I'll just leave the two of you alone. . . ."

"No, it's okay. Has he shown any signs of—has he—?" Chloe didn't know how to say it.

"There has been no sign of any of the traditional symptoms associated with humans who have . . . closely interacted with Mai," the doctor answered, shaking her head. "I even went back and looked up in our oldest documents any description of what happens. Boils. Fever. Strange bruises and scratches." She ticked them off on her clawed fingers. "Inability to breathe. Eyes sealed shut. Blood from the pores. *Nothing.* Zero. Zip. Nada. Aside from being severely beaten, Brian is fine."

Chloe's bubble of hope grew a little bigger.

"I don't understand it at all. I'm completely thrilled for my patient, but . . . I've *seen* what happens when a Mai kisses a human," Dr. Lovsky said helplessly. "Anyway, the best thing for him now is rest—and lots of antibiotics—to let his body get on with the process of healing."

"Why antibiotics?"

Dr. Lovsky narrowed her eyes at Chloe as if she were an idiot and raised one eyebrow to further illustrate her feelings. "You *found* him *injured* on the *street* in a *puddle.* Would you like me to list all the sorts of buggies an already-stressed body can be taken up with?"

"Uh, no, that's okay," Chloe said, quickly holding up her hand. "I get it. Thanks for everything."

Dr. Lovsky left and Chloe turned back to Brian.

He rustled in the bedclothes—though his leg in the cast was eerily still. "Chloe?" he whispered hoarsely.

"I'm here," she whispered back, kissing his cheek as lightly as possible. While it might not have mattered, there was no reason to tempt the Fates.

"Where am I?" After a few tries he managed to open his crusted eyes. Chloe swallowed her sadness at the damage done to another human being, the ravaging of his good looks. Brian's eyes were red and there was a pool of blood or something covering half of his left one; his right was sunk in a swollen mass of purple flesh.

What a stupid, stupid *thing!* was all she could think.

"You're safe," she said, deciding that was the easiest answer.

He snorted. Then he coughed, a long, rasping fit.

"No," he croaked. "Really." His dull eyes managed to twinkle just a little.

Chloe sighed.

"You're in the emergency room of Mai HQ. Can't reveal the location; it's a secret."

"I'm—" He hacked some more. Spittle came out of his mouth and ran down his chin. No blood this time, Chloe was relieved to see. Before she even thought about it, she took the edge of her shirt and wiped his face with it. "I'm *where?*"

"Well, where *else* was I supposed to take you?" she snapped with feigned annoyance. She was just relieved he was able to speak this coherently.

"That doctor . . . lady . . . ?" A weak finger pointed at the door.

"Mai."

Brian took so long to answer that she was afraid he had fallen asleep with his eyes open.

"Holy crap," he finally said, groaning. "Irony . . ."

"Shhh. Rest."

"Not . . . dead . . ." he suddenly realized, eyes flaring. He turned his head and tried to move his shoulders so he could look at her. "I *kissed* you! Not dead . . . How?"

Chloe shook her head. "I don't know. . . . Kim thinks the curse might be lifting because I saved a human life—my mom's." She decided *not* to burden him, once again, with the details of Xavier. Later. When he was feeling better.

"Kiss me," he ordered.

So she did.

He pulled her partly onto the bed with him, and except for one bad moment when her elbow dug into what was probably a cracked rib, they remained that way for a while. . . .

Chloe was so distracted by the fact that Kim seemed to be right—the curse did seem to be lifted—that when she finally left to go see Sergei, she forgot to be nervous or worried.

"Hey," she said. Olga and Sergei were bent over his desk together, looking at a newspaper or a contract or something. Her short platinum hair and his natural tweedy orange clashed so badly that Chloe almost had to look away.

When Olga looked up and saw her, she smiled with genuine affection and dipped her head.

"Yes, Chloe." Sergei also smiled, but Chloe saw something else in his blue-water eyes: fear, mistrust, eagerness; she couldn't tell. "Oh, and we're confirmed for Tuesday, October 28. Your introduction to the Pride."

"Oh, great. I have to check my class schedule and talk with Mom, but I don't see why not." All Chloe could picture was Sergei onstage in a giant auditorium, speaking at a blue-draped podium with Chloe sitting in a folding chair beside him, waiting to be introduced. All of the eyes she could see beyond the foot- and spotlights were slit, and there were occasional hisses from the audience.

"Has Kim fitted you with a robe yet?" Olga asked, jotting something down on the PalmPilot she carried.

If only that woman knew how ridiculous those words sounded coming out of her mouth. Chloe could just see it on her college application: Math team, AP French, and two years of mostly dead ancient-Egyptian-related language and religion. Well, at least Brown would be interested.

"Robe?"

"You have to start learning the Precepts of the Mai and at least some of our language before the ritual."

"Ritual?" The scene in Chloe's head switched from a high-school assembly to a cross between a bat mitzvah and something she might have seen on *Buffy*.

"Chloe, you have to start taking this seriously," Sergei said sternly. "It is not all about fun and power."

She opened her mouth to tell him Kim's theory about the curse and her possible lifting of it—but something made her stop. Something her cat-eared friend had told her weeks ago, when she first came to the mansion, about not always revealing everything she knew.

Sergei misinterpreted the look in her eyes and sighed. "I'm just trying. . . . There's a lot more to being a leader than just, well, 'leading,' Chloe. You really need to understand the soul of our people. And while you were born with a better *natural* insight of our ways and religion, you are still without a connection to those who live it every day."

"Yeah, I know, you're right," Chloe admitted.

"Even those of us who have had many years of experience can still make horrible mistakes. . . . I feel terrible about what happened to your mother, Chloe," he said out of nowhere and stiffly, as if he wasn't used to apologizing. "My previous decision to not risk Mai life for the mother of the Chosen—of *any* Mai—was shortsighted and foolish and almost led to great harm. Anything could have happened once the Order kidnapped her—and I would have been partially to blame."

Where is he going with this? Chloe wondered.

"I know how important your human friends and family are to you. At least I do now." He tapped a manila folder on his desk. "Consider this a peace offering, not a bribe. I've set our human resources department the task of finding your adoptive father."

Of all the things Chloe was expecting him to say, this definitely wasn't one of them. She felt like she had been hit on the forehead with a shovel, too stunned to speak.

"My dad?" She stared at the folder, wanting and not wanting to reach for it.

"We don't have anything yet," Olga said gently. "But we've tackled tougher cases—nameless orphan Mai half a world away. We will find him," she added.

"Oh." Chloe shifted her weight from one foot to another. "Thanks." She got up and turned to leave, unsure what else to do. "I guess I'll see you. . . ."

"Chloe—," Sergei called. She looked back. He had a pained expression on his face, like he was really trying to get through to her but didn't know how. "Olga and I are here for you, for whatever you need. *Anything.*"

"Thanks," Chloe said, maybe actually meaning it this time.

She closed the door behind her and stood there a moment in the lobby, trying to take in what had just happened. He was going to help find her dad. Her *human* dad. It was obviously Sergei's way of apologizing.

"Honored One," Igor greeted her coldly, approaching Sergei's office. His eyes never looked more feline as the light caught his irises and made them almost red.

"Igor," Chloe said uncomfortably.

There was no trace of the former friendliness he had shown her when she had interned briefly at Firebird. "I heard about the big meeting—where you will take over," he hissed. "Sergei has devoted his *entire life* to the Pride, you know."

So much for automatic acceptance of their divinely gifted spiritual leader, she thought glumly. There didn't seem to be an upside to any of this.

"I'm not trying to take it away from him. This is the way I was *born,*" Chloe said, a little desperately.

"Yes. Just remember, while you were being raised by *humans,* Sergei was helping to save the *Mai.*" And he strode off—*Rather cowardly,* Chloe thought—not giving her a chance to reply.

"This just keeps getting better and better," she muttered.

Things seemed to be finally getting back to normal that evening. After homework, Chloe treated herself to watching some dorky reality show and flipping through the latest *Vogue.* It was the first mindless, enjoyable downtime she'd had in weeks.

"Hey." Her mom suddenly appeared next to her, kneeling by the couch with an expectant look on her face. For the second time that day Chloe was pretty sure she didn't like where things were about to go.

"Yeah?" Chloe said suspiciously.

"I was just thinking about Paul and Amy, and you and all the stress you're under, and your, uh, other friends . . . Alyec, and the one with the ears. . . ."

"Yes?" Chloe said, still suspicious.

"Well." Her mother brushed a wispy lock of ash blond hair behind her ear, once again pixie perfect. Her earrings—replacements for the ones she'd dropped at the Order's hideout when she was kidnapped—swung, hypnotic dark silver crescent pendulums. "Whatever happens, I really need to be more informed about your life and get to know your friends better." While this was said lightly, there was a look in Anna King's eyes that allowed no defiance. This was a Mother Decision.

Chloe braced herself.

"I was thinking about throwing a little pizza party for all of you," her mom said with a brilliantly white grin.

The surprise party that she had thrown for Chloe's sixteenth birthday was actually pretty swank and fun. But this . . .

"Awww, Mom! Come *on,*" Chloe said desperately. "That was cool when I was, like, *ten. . . .*"

"It's still fun," her mom insisted. "We can do make-your-own pizzas—maybe even get the dough from

Carlucci's. Different toppings—it will be totally retro. Like a little pre-Halloween party."

"This is *not* a good idea," Chloe pleaded.

"I'd really like to meet your friends," her mom said through gritted teeth. "Since they came to help rescue you and me."

"You know how, like, *Angel* and *Buffy* used to do crossovers? Like, Willow showing up on *Angel* and Angel appearing in the last episode of *Buffy?*" Chloe said, trying not to sound whiny. "Well, *Smallville* and *The O.C.* don't—and this is like that. Paul and Amy are breaking up. Amy and Alyec . . . something weird is going on there. And *Kim?* Mom, you don't even know her—she's a freak. I love her, but she's not exactly a party animal and she doesn't like Alyec, either. . . . I just can't really deal with this whole worlds-colliding idea."

"I want. To meet. Your friends."

The Mai had a thing or two to learn about intimidation from this woman who had normal, round pupils, Chloe decided.

She sank woefully back into the couch. No good could come of this.

Ten

"Hello, Mrs. King."

Chloe's mom opened the door for Kim, then stared at her. She wore a black felt hat pulled tightly down to cover her ears and loose black jeans with a frumpy black sweater, like she was trying to disguise her whole body, not just her head. Round Lennon-style sunglasses with thick red lenses hid her slitted eyes. She stuck a *gloved* hand out and presented Anna King with a bouquet of flowers. "Here. I hope this is an acceptable hostess gift. Thank you for inviting me to the party. I've never been to one before."

Chloe closed her eyes in horror and exhaustion. Amy tried not to giggle, for the first time ever not the weirdest and most socially inept person at a party.

"You can take all that off," Chloe said, trying to sound lighthearted and polite. "Mom saw you at the Presidio, and anyway, she knows who you are."

"These are *lovely* flowers, Kim, thank you." Chloe's

mom had her game face on, but she was genuinely touched by the gesture. She rummaged for just the right vase in the cabinets. Kim took off her gloves distastefully and removed her hat.

"Here, I think this will do." Anna King turned around with the flowers nicely arranged in a cobalt blue crystal thing just in time to see Kim running her clawed hands through her hair, scratching at the base of her unfolding, velvet black ears. "Ah," she said, trying not to look surprised, trying desperately for the politically correct you-can't-shock-me look she usually reserved for transsexuals or the severely deformed.

"I've never interacted with humans like this before—undressed, I mean," Kim said, a little uncomfortably.

"Hey, have a drink," Amy suggested, waving at a little platter of virgin coladas with grenadine "blood" dripping down the sides of the glasses. Sometimes Chloe wished she had a younger sister just so her mom would have someone else to get all Martha Stewart on.

Kim picked up a plastic glass suspiciously and her tongue darted out, taking the smallest lick from the top. Apparently it was acceptable; her eyes widened and she took a sip.

"He's such a douche bag," Amy said, turning to Chloe and continuing their conversation from before as if nothing had happened. Kim nodded wisely as if she knew what was going on. "He just fucking gave back the CDs I gave him, like I was just loaning them or something. 'Oh, uh, Amy, I think these are yours,'" Amy said, standing on her toes and imitating him. "What's up with *that?*"

"Paul and Amy are definitely breaking up," Chloe told Kim, feeling the need to let her in on it. Also, it gave her something else to do. It was easy to console Amy when the boy involved was someone Chloe barely knew; with previous boyfriends she had joined in with a happy chorus of "he can go to hell" and wishing various poxes on his genitalia.

She didn't really want to say anything bad about Paul—although he really *was* being a douche about this, Chloe reflected. But he had his own shit to deal with. . . . She really didn't know *what* to say or do now.

"Is this a bad thing?" Kim asked with all the innocence of a vaguely interested psychotherapist.

"He . . . I . . . ," Amy began and stopped. "He's just being a total douche bag about it!"

"Do you want to stay together?" Kim said, in a tone that was like she was just repeating the previous question.

"I don't know. Not if he's going to be like this all the time."

Chloe marveled at how well Amy and Kim seemed to be getting along. They seemed to have bonded even more since the night at the diner; Amy was spilling her guts to the girl she normally would have been dead jealous of—beautiful, exotic, and far more outré than herself. "I don't know *how* to break up," Amy finally admitted, pulling one of her dark locks straight. "I don't know if we can go back—if *I* can go back to just being friends again." She paused, chewing her lip uncertainly. "We were intimate, you know? We—"

"Stop," Chloe suggested, deciding it was time she entered the conversation again. "Please."

The three of them were silent, sipping their drinks for a moment.

"He wasn't very good," Amy couldn't help saying.

"Stop," both Kim and Chloe said at the same time.

"Your necklace," Kim began, trying to change the conversation, "is fascinating—it's one of our Twin Goddesses."

"Bastet, yeah. What do you mean Twin Goddesses?" Amy asked, fingering the little cat charm she had worn every day since her bat mitzvah.

"Bastet and Sekhmet, the goddesses of the Mai. Whose divine blood runs in our veins and whom we worship."

"Get out!" Amy said, excited. "You all are like *Egyptian* and polytheistic and stuff?"

Chloe shook her head as the two girls spoke animatedly about religion. *Even Amy would make a better Mai priestess than me.* Aside from being Jewish, her best friend was always the one into Wicca stuff, and Buddhism, and ancient pantheons and things like that.

Just when Chloe began to relax, Paul and Alyec

arrived—together. Which was weird for a number of reasons, not the least of which that the latter had been dissing the former pretty badly just a couple of days before.

"Hey, Mrs. King," Paul said. He came bearing a Greek salad.

"Nice to meet you, Chloe's mom," Alyec said, both charming and breezy, polite and insouciant. *That's Alyec.* She hadn't really talked to her mom much about him or Brian since being caught dating both of them—when she wasn't originally allowed to date anyone at all. That would require talking about Brian, and that was still a subject best left alone until he had fully recovered.

Alyec also brought her mom flowers but presented them with more of a flourish than Kim. Once again Chloe wondered if some of the stranger habits of her new family were a result of being Mai or Eastern European.

"*Two* bouquets in one day," her mom said, instantly smitten with Alyec like every other female on the planet. "I haven't gotten that many even on Valentine's Day."

"Chloe." Alyec came over and kissed her on the cheek, a safe bet. Paul and her mom exchanged pleasantries, then Paul suddenly found himself deeply interested in a bowl of wasabi peas.

"Hey," Chloe said uncertainly.

"I'm sorry—," Alyec began. Somehow she suspected it was something he wasn't used to saying.

"No, you're completely right," Chloe said, stopping him. "I . . . wasn't treating you fairly."

Amy had discreetly removed herself a few feet, looking at their CD collection, eventually wandering over to Paul. Chloe's mom had managed to corner Kim and was questioning her as politely as she could without reverting to lawyer mode.

"So, you've lived with your, uh, *Pride* your entire life?" her mom was asking Kim interestedly, popping a chip into her mouth. "Never went to school or anything?"

It was supposed to sound neutral, a casual question, like Anna King was talking to another adult. But Chloe could hear the tone in her voice, see the look on her face: maternal concern was beginning to manifest. Chloe thought about her biological sister, the one whom she had only found out about recently, the one who had been murdered—probably by the Rogue—before they ever had a chance to meet. She had told her mom about the other Mai girl but wondered what would happen if she had brought her home. What would Anna King do?

Throw a party, came the obvious answer.

"So," Amy said, turning back to Alyec. "How's the music for the prom coming along, prom boy?"

She cocked her head and sat down. Amy's latest new look involved shorts almost like knickers, tights, leg warmers, and a cardigan over a T-shirt on top. Long used to looking at the outfits while carefully erasing her friend from the picture, Chloe could see it was a look that might actually grace a runway. Amy, while pretty in her own way, never really made a good model for the clothes she designed. Her looks were complicated, second-look beauty; she should have worn simpler outfits.

And if Chloe didn't know better, she would have thought Amy was interacting almost humanly with Alyec for once.

"It's not a prom," Alyec said haughtily. "It's a *fall formal.* And *I* managed to help snag Xtian Blu to spin for an hour."

"No *way!*" Paul said, his jaw dropping as he joined the conversation.

"Yep," Alyec said smugly. Amy and Chloe rolled their eyes, having no idea who the DJ was.

"Doesn't anyone ever hire bands anymore?" Chloe's mom asked plaintively. "Even jazz?"

"Who played at your prom?" Paul asked politely.

"Formal," Alyec corrected.

Anna King sighed in happy memory. "The Creepy Sheep."

Chloe wasn't the only one staring at her. Even Kim's eyes widened. "It was the seventies. It was *punk,*" Anna protested.

"This is a dance?" Kim asked. She finished her virgin colada down to its dregs, sticking her inhumanly long and narrow tongue into the core to scrape up the bits. Her fangy canines made little clicking noises against the glass. Chloe's mom tried not to stare.

"The theme is 'Something Wicked This Way Comes,' Mrs. King," Alyec said, not really answering her. "We're getting a drama geek to do the lighting—make it look all like trees and stuff. The disco ball," he said with great wisdom, "is the *moon.*"

"Are all the DJ slots filled?" Paul asked casually, tracing the lip of his cup. Still full, Chloe noted, of virgin colada-y goodness.

"There's still nine to ten, for people who show up early. Do you want to take it?"

"Sure," he said, trying not to grin.

"I've never been to a dance before," Kim said, to no one in particular.

The comment hung in the air. Even Chloe's mom seemed like an awkward teenager, not knowing what to say.

"Is it fun?" she demanded.

"No . . ."

"Not really . . ."

"They're actually kind of a drag."

"Totally boring . . ."

"But you're all going," Kim noted.

Again the silence.

"You." Paul coughed. "You, uh, want to go?"

"I'd love to. Thanks," Kim said promptly. She tried to make it sound as toneless as everything else, but she couldn't hide the delight in her face.

"Uh, 'scuse me, I gotta go use the euphemism," Chloe said, trying to cover her giggles.

Alyec extended his hand with a little flourish to help her out of the deep couch. She took it and pulled herself up, as effortlessly and gracefully as someone who wasn't human. Someone Mai. Alyec showed no strain or effort; the tips of his fingers barely moved. For some reason, this little thing, this private moment that took less than five seconds to pass imprinted itself with crystal permanence in Chloe's mind. *She was not human. He was not human.* According to ancient myth, they could not have sex with humans—only each other. The rest of the Pride already approved of the Chosen and Alyec as a lifelong couple.

Tears sprang to her eyes.

"I don't *want* this," she whispered, then headed for the bathroom, already crying.

"I'll go check on her," Alyec said before Amy could. Their voices were muffled through the door—which she slammed shut. The cool tiles and porcelain in the bathroom were overwhelmingly appealing; Chloe sat down on the side of the tub and put her head in her hands.

"Chloe?" Alyec knocked lightly on the door with his knuckle. "Are you . . . okay?"

She began to sob, rocking back and forth.

"Chloe," Alyec said softly, opening the door and sitting down next to her.

"I don't want, I mean, I want"—she tried to say in between tears—"I want my *old* life again. I want my friends acting normal. I want my mom acting normal—this party is the craziest thing she's done yet. *I don't want to be leader of the Pride,*" she cried viciously. "I *don't.* It's not *fair.* They expect me to just pick up and rotate my life a full one-eighty—to stop being a high-school student and start leading them into glory."

"No one thinks—," Alyec began.

"Yes, they *do-oo!*" Chloe sobbed. "Everyone keeps saying I can have a normal life and go to Berkeley or whatever, but I have to do all these other things—rituals and stuff I don't even believe in. I can't lead anyone. I can't lead myself. I *suck.*" It all came out, loud. Everything that had been growing in the back of her head, whispered cynicisms and sly doubts, finally burst forth. "I've been mean to you, I don't deserve you, you shouldn't be here. . . ."

"You're not mean to me," Alyec said softly, with a faint smile. "You may be confused about a lot of things right now, Chloe King, but I can tell you that you are not *mean.* Except maybe to yourself."

Chloe kept crying.

"I want to start the year over," she moaned. "I want—this all—to stop."

"Shhh." Alyec finally put his arms around Chloe and began to rock her.

"Paul is taking Kim to the prom—*dance,* excuse me. Amy obviously wants to go with you. She totally does. Brian can't go because he's sort of almost dead. I couldn't go anyway because I'm going to be *really* busy learning dead languages and leading the Pride and being on the math team and it's not like I'm even part of *high* school anymore. . . ."

She wiped her face with the back of her hand, eyes burning from the tears and nose definitely swollen. *I probably look like shit.* But most of the crying seemed to be over; Chloe was just angry.

"It must be really confusing for you right now," Alyec said, giving her shoulders a squeeze. "I wish I could help."

"Mai relationships are a lot less . . . *complicated* than human ones, aren't they?" she asked, sighing.

"I think they're a lot more *immediate,*" Alyec said with a grin. "Instead of getting upset or running away, if you had been raised Mai and didn't like seeing me with Amy, you probably would have let your claws out."

Chloe smiled a little at that.

"I like that you care enough to be jealous," he said gently, squeezing her arm. They sat quietly for a few minutes, Chloe resting her head up against his shoulder.

It was nice, but if she was going to lead anyone anywhere, it had to begin with the truth. *And here's a good place to start.*

"Alyec, I think . . ." She took a deep breath. "I don't think this is exactly what I want right now."

He looked a little upset but nodded. "I've been a little freaked out since the whole thing about marriages in the library. . . ." He struggled for words. "It's a lot of pressure, and to be suddenly dating the One . . ." He trailed off for a second. "It's not that I don't think someday, maybe—and this wasn't just all fun or anything—I didn't think at the beginning anyone would be looking at it to be permanent. We're *dating,* for chrissake. One thing about the Mai . . . our options for even dating are limited," he said a little sadly.

To her embarrassment, Chloe hadn't thought about any of this from his perspective before; suddenly he wasn't just fooling around with a new member of their community—he was going out with the Chosen One. In a lot of the older people's minds they were probably already engaged, with children, and leading the Mai together into a whole new era of peace and prosperity. She breathed a deep sigh of relief and held herself back from telling him that the curse might be lifting and that maybe they really could date other people—it just didn't seem like the right time.

Paul's favorite episode of *Star Trek* came to her mind: *"I found I did not wish to be married to a legend. . . ."*

Alyec as her consort. It just didn't work.

"Is there anything else you want to get off your chest?" Alyec asked gently.

"Let's see," Chloe said, wiping the last of her tears away. "I have just been made leader to a people I know almost nothing about. People aren't exactly rooting for me, you know. I'm still behind at school, and my relationship with my mom has been all fucked up since I've, um, fully become a Mai. I don't belong anywhere, and my *friends*"—she indicated the kitchen with her thumb—"have their own things going on. Oh, *and* there's someone following me."

"What are you talking about?" Alyec asked, meaning her last point. "The Rogue is dead; you sort of forced an uneasy truce on both us *and* the Tenth Blade. And no matter what Igor or anyone who supports Sergei really thinks, no Mai would ever dare lay a hand on you."

"I just have this feeling that someone is following me—I know it. What about that guy who hates Brian? Rick or Dick or whatever, who was with Whitney Rezza the night at the Presidio . . ."

"I hardly think he could sneak up on *you;* he's just a human and not even as good as the Rogue."

The streetlamp outside glowed through the frosted window, making everything in the bathroom bleak and soft at the same time, well defined but gray. Individual tiles stood out against old grout; larger things like the mirror and the sink seemed to fade into a matte painting of a bathroom. A car went by, breaking the silence for a few moments.

"Do you know who tried to kill Brian?" Alyec asked softly.

"No, I haven't asked." She pulled some toilet paper off the roll, wadded it up, and daubed her nose. "I guess I should."

"I wouldn't worry too much." He put his hands around her shoulders and gave her a squeeze. "You can take on whatever they dish out," he added, brushing her cheek with his hand and pushing back a stray lock of her dark hair. "Why don't we go back to the party?"

She nodded, sniffing. He tore off some toilet paper

for her to blow her nose on and they returned to the living room, Chloe hoping desperately she didn't look like an idiot.

"Everything okay?" Amy murmured.

"Yep," Chloe said, wiping her nose again and knowing what a liar her red and puffy face made her out to be. Kim looked alarmed. "I just—I had a little bit of a breakdown."

Her mother was stationed behind the kitchen island, clasping the sides like it was the wheel of a ship. Her knuckles were white.

"I'm, uh, a little overstressed right now," she added with faint smile. "It just kind of all got to me."

Chloe felt like she was eleven again, when she'd run to her room crying during her birthday party. All the boys had decided to play football in the street and Jason Pellerin told her that *she* couldn't because she was in a dress. Chloe had stayed in her room a good long time, weeping. By the time she finally came out, the party was sort of stilted and over.

"You know what you need?" Paul asked, breaking the silence. *"Marriage wanna."*

"Paul," her mom said warningly.

"How about a *Matrix* marathon?" Amy asked, digging through her voluminous pink purse, whose trim matched the fringe on her leg warmers. "I was just going to lend these to someone. . . ."

"That sounds . . . *excellent,*" Chloe said, breathing a

deep sigh of relief. Suddenly the whole tension of the party was broken. *TV—the ultimate party solution.* Paul and Alyec were obviously interested, and Kim took the DVDs, turning them over curiously in her hand. Her mother went back to chopping pepperoni.

"I've never actually seen the third one," she said, without looking up from her cutting board and chef's knife.

"It *sucked,*" Alyec, Paul, Amy, and Chloe all said at the same time.

"Like the dance," Kim said wryly. "And like the dance, we are going to watch it anyway."

"*Now* you're getting it," Paul said, clapping her on the back.

Chloe wiped her face but wasn't embarrassed about it anymore. The boys took over the seemingly difficult process of putting in the DVDs and setting up the TV, and Amy made kettle corn in the microwave.

"Are you feeling better?" Kim asked quietly.

Chloe nodded and smiled. "I just needed to—I needed the cry." Waves of endorphins and relief were still washing over her. Like it was all going to be all right now. "What did you all do while I was gone?"

"Not much," Kim admitted. "I thought I heard someone approaching the house; that was exciting for a moment. But no one was there."

Chloe felt her waves break. But before she could question her further, Kim turned abruptly to Paul. "Are you going to drink that?" she asked, pointing to his glass.

"Huh?" Paul reluctantly dragged his attention away from wide-screen and Dolby digital options. Alyec grabbed the remote while he looked, distracted, at his still-full but slowly melting virgin colada. "Um, well." He looked at Chloe's mom, trying to decide what to do. "No," he finally said.

Kim reached over and took it with both hands, then began lapping at it greedily. "This," she pronounced, licking the slightest bit of foam off her lips, "is a good party."

Eleven

It will be *okay,* Chloe told herself the next morning, sort of believing it this time. Her mom seemed satisfied—or possibly horrified—and likely to drop the whole needing-to-be-more-in-her-life thing for a while. After sitting through all six hours of the *Matrix* with Amy snoring through the first hour of *Revolutions,* Kim pausing the videos every few minutes to ask questions, and Alyec and Paul fighting during the middle of *Reloaded* about why Jet Li didn't wind up being in it, Chloe's mom was feeling pretty well acquainted with her friends.

And her Mai friends were apparently not outside the range of normal teenage behavior; even Kim with her ears and slit eyes and claws.

"She's a little bit of a geek," was all her mom had said about her after the guests had gone.

Chloe had laughed. "Yeah, the Mai think so, too."

And now here she was, a normal high-school girl

going to high school. She was almost caught up with her homework and exams and had sorted stuff out with Alyec, and Brian was recovering. It even looked like she and Brian could hook up without fatal consequences. Amy and Paul—well, they weren't really her problem. After last night her two best friends seemed to realize the amount of stress she was under and lowered the weirdness meter a bit. No longer chanting the *I will be the cool best friend* mantra, Chloe told herself instead, *They got to work their own shit out.*

After her last makeup French quiz, Chloe was so glad it was over and confident of her grade that she signed her test with a flourish and a fleur-de-lis. She handed it in with a little bow and *merci beaucoup.* Mme. Sassoon already had her car keys in her hand. Thanks to Kim, Chloe was pretty sure she would get an A.

She checked her voice mail: two messages. One from Alyec, asking how she was doing, and one from Sergei.

"Chloe, we found something on your dad. I have to look at this property near your school." Sergei described exactly where it was and how to get there. *"It's an old theater. If you meet me there at four, we can talk."*

"Sacre bleu," Chloe muttered, snapping her phone shut. He had kept his word—he was really trying. Of course she would meet him.

Speaking of French, where *had* Kim learned to speak it so well? She had never been to France, as far as Chloe knew. Many of the Mai had never been to San Francisco proper, much less Canada, much less France. *Do they dream of doing other things?* A few of the Mai had broken out, like Simone the dancer, but it was rare. It was a self-imposed ghetto. She wasn't sure how much Sergei actually had to do to keep them there.

What about her own dreams, while she was at it? Running a retail clothing empire. Would she just substitute her slavery for Sergei's; would the Mai insist on working for her?

And, uh, speaking of retail empires, remember how you promised to go see Marisol . . . ?

Chloe had been putting it off for a long time, too smothered by guilt to even think about it. Now she was finally in a good enough mood that she could force herself through it and take whatever was thrown at her, whatever she deserved. She had already chalked up her relationship with the shop owner as over, so at the worst this wouldn't change anything.

She hadn't even been by Pateena's since coming back from Firebird. Once it was her safe haven, her home away from home and school. An entirely different set of people and problems and the first real hard work she had ever had to do. There was nothing to make you appreciate the weekends more than a La-Z-Boy-sized pile of jeans that needed to have their cuffs artfully ripped. Chloe's short internship at Firebird had just been boring and strenuous.

She stood outside the windows and looked at them

for a moment. They had put up a Halloween display—probably Marisol's doing. She was far more artistic than she had much of a chance to express. One mannequin hung upside down, wearing a leather jacket, like a bat; another wore all orange, like a pumpkin. A third had earmuffs redone as ears and long black Lee Press-On Nails for claws.

A cat, Chloe realized.

Marveling at the irony, she took a deep breath and went in.

"Well, look who's back," Lania said immediately. Of course she had to be there. Of course. Chloe's quest for redemption—and subsequent humiliation—wouldn't have been complete without it. Though a menace to retail, snotty to the customers, and still not able to understand how to void a credit card sale, the girl had been allowed to work the cash register just because she was a couple of years older than Chloe. And there she was, now assistant manager.

"Coming to get your things?" Lania pressed, hands on her hips and a smug grin on her face. She looked like an afternoon cartoon—the kind that targeted girls and involved teenagers doing shallow things to each other at malls. Chloe couldn't even work up any contempt; it would have been like dissing a clown.

"Excuse me," Chloe said instead, carefully walking around her to the back.

"She don't want to talk to you!" Lania shrieked in

the fake homegirl accent she sometimes put on. Lania was from La Jolla—her parents owned a horse ranch.

Chloe took another deep breath, pausing before the metal double doors left over from when the place had been a diner. Then she pushed her way in and sat in the folding chair in front of Marisol's desk.

Marisol was on the phone. She looked over at Chloe and then stared at her, as if she didn't trust her not to steal anything.

"Baby, I gotta call you back. Something's come up. Just wait."

The little woman was older than she looked: thick, beautiful waist-long hair went a long way to making her look like an art student. But there was a hardness in her eyes and tiny wrinkles that formed around her lips when she pursed them.

Chloe cleared her throat, suddenly not sure where to begin.

"Why did you even come back here?" the woman demanded. "To apologize? I *told* you that if you didn't show up on that Wednesday, you were gone for good. What happened, you break up with one of your two boyfriends? You get pregnant? Honey, unless someone *died,* I don't even want to hear about it."

"Well," Chloe said slowly, "a number of people actually *have* died."

Marisol's eyes widened.

Chloe thought of the Rogue and the fight at the

Presidio—one of the Tenth Bladers hadn't gotten up when it was over. And of course if you counted *her,* that was two deaths right there.

"My mom was kidnapped by these weird cultists. And they . . . sent this crazy serial murderer after me. And then I was sort of being held captive by these people who are kind of related to me. . . . It's kind of a long story. You can call my mom and ask her if you want, though."

There was a long moment while Marisol stared into her eyes.

"No," she finally said. "I . . . believe you." She didn't look happy, though, like she didn't *want* to believe it. She had to try one last test. "And no one missed you at school?"

"They were told I had mono. My mom's law firm was told she was on vacation."

"Are you . . . okay?"

"I'm alive." Chloe shrugged.

There was another silence between them, as Marisol was obviously trying to work out what was polite to ask about and what would be prying, what was concern and what was curiosity.

This was where Chloe could tell her. This was where she could come clean, demonstrate the claws. Show Marisol just how far from the ordinary her life had been recently; as far from work and her and vintage clothes and receipts and hems and even Lania as it could get. She *used* to tell her boss things she never would have told her mom—it was like having a much older sister or aunt with objective, slightly less "mom" views on her life.

"How are your two boyfriends?" Marisol finally asked.

The moment was over.

"Only one now. He's lying in a hospital bed recovering from having the shit kicked out of him trying to save me." Chloe decided to cut the next awkward silence short by standing up again. "Well, that's really all," she said, shrugging. "I came by to apologize and let you know that my going AWOL wasn't really without a reason."

Marisol's face softened into the look she used to have when Chloe would sometimes cry about her mom or school. "Why didn't you at least call?"

"I . . . I was feeling really guilty," Chloe admitted. But now that she thought about it, now that she was standing before the woman she was terrified of ever seeing again, it was kind of ridiculous. "You told me not to come back and all, so I figured you'd be mad at me and never want to talk to me again. You said that this was a business, not babysitting for flaky teenagers."

"Oh, Chloe, you *imbécile,*" Marisol said, smiling sadly. "I didn't know your mother was kidnapped and whatever else. I just thought you were having boyfriend problems. You could have—you *should* have called me. You should always feel you can do that, no matter what."

"Thanks," Chloe said. *Remember this,* she told herself. Not that Marisol was nice enough to forgive her, but that some things transcended personal guilt. She had to understand what was really important and what were her own screwed-up feelings and the difference between the two.

"I—I just hired this other girl," Marisol said hesitantly. "I can't give you back your old hours."

Chloe put up her hand. "Don't worry about it. Believe me, there's so much on my plate right now I'd flake on you *again,* something I'd rather avoid. And according to my biological family, I'm sort of a princess or priest or something."

Marisol looked skeptical. "Do you get a crown?"

Chloe laughed. *If only.* "No, just a whole lot of shit to learn about the people I come from."

"That doesn't sound so good. There should at least be jewels. All right, well, if you want to work some hours, call me. Andy's no worker like you. But she gets along okay with Lania."

Chloe rolled her eyes. Marisol barked with laughter.

She tried to avoid both Lania and the new girl on the way out, the latter of whom was chatting merrily on her cell phone while rearranging racks that the customers had gotten out of order. She had black goth hair, but her attitude was all wrong, kind of like a flightier version of Amy. Chloe sighed and left, unable to resist throwing one smug, calm smile in Lania's direction—the girl had obviously been trying to listen in on her and Marisol's conversation.

She wandered over to where she was supposed to

meet Sergei, correctly expecting him to be a few minutes late. Everything else about Firebird Properties ran like clockwork, but some of the older Eastern European employees, even Sergei himself, seemed to have trouble getting anywhere on time.

The theater was disappointing: there wasn't even a cool marquee or anything like that left outside, just empty frames where posters had once hung. With the ticket booth all smashed in and graffiti on its brick walls, the building looked a little *beyond* abandoned and well on its way to condemned.

If I ran Firebird, I would do something cool with this, Chloe thought. The possibilities were endless—really great apartments, an awesome bar, maybe even a theater again. For repertory movies *and* local theater, or maybe her own version of the coffeehouse in *Smallville*. Hey, Lana was like sixteen and she ran it—Chloe was sixteen, leader of her people and a cat person besides. She should have *no trouble* with just managing a coffee shop.

"Chloe."

She jumped; even without actively paying attention with her improved Mai hearing, Chloe should have been able to hear him walking up. Sergei was fairly square and . . . heavy and tended to wear shoes that clicked when he walked. But there he was, barely two feet away, a light smile on his face, hands behind his back.

He was dressed more casually than usual, and Chloe had to admit that it immediately made him a lot more likable. Even in just his polo shirt and khakis he looked less imposing, more human.

"I can't believe I startled you," he said, chuckling. "You've been living with humans for too long."

"Yeah, funny," Chloe said, instantly on the defensive again.

"Oh, I'm sorry," the older man said, instantly sighing and putting his hand to his face. "I shouldn't have said that. It's not funny. I just meant it as a joke, to lighten the tension."

Chloe relaxed a little. "I'm kind of sensitive about my mom these days."

"Completely understandable. Here, shall we go inside as we talk?" Sergei gestured for her to go first, getting a big ring of keys out of his pocket. "The fool owner couldn't meet us here; he had another prospective client for a penthouse restaurant, and this is small potatoes compared."

"That's kind of rude." Chloe was *dying* to know what Sergei found out about where her dad was or what he was up to, but she reminded herself to remain patient.

Sergei shrugged. "It's business. You have to learn, Chloe, that often nothing is personal. You can't take it to heart. You'll get ulcers. Ah, here." He found a big old-fashioned key and put it first to the locked metal bar that went through all of the metal door handles in the front. Then he took a smaller, bronze key out and opened the farthest door to the left.

"It's like a video game," Chloe ventured.

"You know, I've never played one—here, let me go first in case there's anyone in here squatting or something," he said, as if people like that were rats. He pushed his way in and shouted, *"Hellloooooo,"* then waited to hear if there was any movement or scuttling. He nodded. "Just a whole lot of roaches. It's safe."

Chloe realized with distaste that *she* could hear the bugs, too, dozens of them, little feet making little noises as they rushed away from the light. She noticed with amusement that Sergei didn't do the thing they did in the movies, or on TV, or in real life: he didn't take out a flashlight and wave it around in the darkness, swinging its pale yellow beam over walls and doors and floors. He just walked in, waiting a moment for his eyes to adjust to almost complete darkness. If he were facing her, Chloe knew she would have seen his eyes become slits and then wide, like a cat's eyes in the dark, barely any iris showing.

The lobby didn't look all that derelict; once her own eyes adjusted, Chloe saw that the red carpet was only dusty and worn, not ripped up and moldering away. The concession counters had their glass smashed in a couple of places, and the popcorn machines were gone. A pity—she always wanted one. It would have been a fun thing to take home. There was still one napkin dispenser with napkins in it and a fake crystal chandelier that was missing some of its glass festoons and garlands.

"What are you going to do with this place?" Chloe asked, already redecorating it in her mind.

"Haven't decided yet," Sergei said, shrugging. "I know this may disappoint you, but unless the structure is really intact and we can find something to do with it, we may just raze the whole thing. The plot of land it's on is worth more for apartments. Or a parking garage—that's where the real money is."

Chloe sighed. Weren't Russians—okay, he was Abkhazian—supposed to be better educated and more artistic and intellectual than Americans? How could he miss all the decaying grandeur, the shabby beauty of this place?

"So how are you and Kim getting along with learning Mai?" he asked sort of casually, peeking over one of the counters to peer at what remained of the slushy machines.

"Uh, we haven't really started yet," Chloe admitted. "But I've just finished all my makeup work and I'm a pretty fast learner." Well, okay, that wasn't really true about languages—but she was pretty sure it was just going to be memorization. She didn't have *time* to learn all the conjugations or whatever ancient Egyptian she'd have to know for tomorrow.

"Just remember your audience," Sergei said, suggesting more than chastising. Chloe wished her mom was a little more like that sometimes. "You're kind of like a second coming to them—so you'd better not disappoint."

Chloe sighed again. Here it came. The second unavoidable conversation of the day. She leapt up onto the ticket taker's podium and sat there balancing on its four-inch-wide top, an impossible position for any human except maybe Jackie Chan or Jet Li.

"Sergei, I never wanted this," she admitted with all of her heart behind it. "I think I wanted to finish high school, go to college, and maybe start my own retail clothing empire. Nothing I ever wished for involved claws, paws, or leading the Mai."

"But you are who you are," Sergei said, pausing in his inspections to fix her with his slit eyes. He cocked his head like a cat. "You cannot change anything."

"What I meant was"—Chloe took a deep breath—"I don't *want* to take the Pride from you." *Unless of course it turns out that you really did send people to kill my mom.* But then Chloe would have chosen anyone else to lead besides her. Igor or Olga or someone.

"Chloe, that's very sweet," Sergei said, meaning it. "But you're not really taking it from me. You are the One, anyway—that is your right."

"Isn't it," Chloe said hesitantly, "isn't it a little weird in this day and age to have *inherited* leaders? I mean, just because I was born with certain abilities, does that really make me fit to rule?"

"It is archaic, *I* agree—even if no one else does. It's not exactly a merit-based position. I built Firebird from the ground up and love running it, but that counts for nothing. Our previous Pride Leader, everything else aside, really tried to *do* something. Her goal was to unite all of the scattered Mai in Eastern Europe, and she worked very hard to accomplish that."

Everything else aside? What did that mean?

"But Eastern Europe was—still is—a very dangerous place to be and our time there was over. Too many wars, too much prejudice, too much random violence. It was always my goal to get us out of there. To go west. Run ahead of ourselves, start over in new land. Maybe escape the old curse," he said, a little sadly. "I worked very hard to bring them here, to build Firebird, to make a safe place for all of us to live. Don't you think that makes me a leader?"

"Sure," Chloe said, not sure what else to say.

Sergei sighed. "Too bad no one else agrees with you. I wonder if there's anything actually left in the main theater—usually they tear out all the seats and sell them in auctions. After you." He opened the door for her and gave a little bow as she went in.

The darkness inside was absolute, but Chloe could feel the vastness of space around her. A good place to be scared in. She felt all floaty, like she was going to start drifting into the air.

"Hey, where are the lights?" Chloe asked.

"I'm sorry we don't have our little discussions anymore," Sergei said, his voice suddenly coming a dozen feet from her, completely unplaceable in the shadows. "And our chess games, too."

"Me too," Chloe also admitted. "Is the power out or something?" She put her hands out to find the closest wall, suddenly nervous.

"I'm going to miss having lunch with you."

"They don't have to stop just because I'm not living there anymore." Was she just being a wimp in the dark, or was there something ominous about the way he said that?

"I'm afraid that won't be possible," the older man said with regret. "Not because you're the One or anything . . ."

Suddenly all the houselights came on, full power. The theater was flooded with bright yellow light and Chloe was blinded, throwing her arms over her face a second too late.

". . . but because you'll be *dead.*"

Chloe forced her eyes open, blinking painfully as the muscles in them contracted her pupil faster and smaller than they ever had.

Before her stood the Rogue.

Twelve

The first thing she thought was, *Oh my God, he's alive.*

Alexander Smith, aka the Rogue, the psycho assassin of the Order of the Tenth Blade, should have been dead.

When Chloe fought him on the Golden Gate Bridge, she had seen him plummet to his death, or so she had thought. When the Tenth Blade found out, they sent an *army* of assassins to scour the city, looking for her to avenge his death. And the truth of the matter was, at the last minute she had extended her hand—to help *save* him, for reasons she could never really put into words more than "it seemed like the right thing to do."

He was tall, muscled, maybe a little thinner than the last time she saw him, with the same dumb white-blond ponytail over his shoulder, the same crazy eyes, the same neoprene-ish black suit that no doubt held the same innumerable daggers, blades, shuriken, and other assorted traditional weapons of the Tenth Blade.

"Chloe King," the Rogue said, with a bit of a smile.

"You're looking well," Chloe said before she could stop herself. Now was *not* the time to be funny. *And it's not like the Rogue really has a sense of humor.* "What's going on?" she demanded, swinging around to face Sergei.

"I'm . . . afraid . . . your time with us is over, Honored One," Sergei said with a little mock bow. "Sorry you'll miss the meeting tomorrow."

"Why are you doing this?" Chloe asked, knowing the answer anyway.

"Weren't you listening to *anything* I was saying?" Sergei said, exasperated. "The Pride is just going to toss me aside now that you're here. Thirty years of hard work—of my *life*—gone, just like that. I am hardly going to let a teenage upstart who was brought up with *humans* take everything away from me, whatever her lineage may be."

"Lineage . . . ?" Chloe asked, confused.

"Your mother was our previous Pride Leader." As Sergei spoke, the Rogue remained as still as a statue, only smiling occasionally at certain points. "Your sister could have been the next leader—she was older than you, you know, and required all nine blades. Had she lived, we would have had *two* 'the Ones.'" He chuckled. "That hasn't happened in a very long time."

Chloe felt something in the pit of her stomach. Imagine—a sister who could also die and come back, who could take some of this burden from her, who had been actually raised Mai and could show her the way. *Wait*—two *"the Ones"?* What about the third, the brother Kim had suggested there might be? Sergei didn't seem to know about him. . . . Chloe shoved that thought to the back of her head.

"This gentleman here"—Sergei twirled his hand at the Rogue—"took care of her. Poor girl, she shouldn't have gone wandering city streets at night by herself. . . ."

Chloe had a flash of her recurring dream—the one about her sister's death. She shuddered but refocused her attention on the present. Chloe still didn't understand. She looked back and forth between the two of them. The Rogue was *devoted* to wiping out the Mai—it was his whole life. And he and Sergei, the head of this Pride, were working *together?*

"We had tried tracking you down for a while," Sergei said, turning back to Chloe. "Finally we assumed you died in the violence between the Georgians and the Abkhazians. Imagine my surprise when you turned up *here,* right under my nose!"

"You two are working together to kill everyone who might be a real Pride Leader?"

"I really don't like that phrase," Sergei said with a pinched look. The Rogue just smiled. "But yes. For this one thing our purposes crossed paths—the Tenth Blade doesn't want any mystic, powerful leaders of the Mai who could unite them and lead them to victory—or whatever it is they think you're going to do—and I rather enjoy my current position."

"You're working with a man who wants to wipe us

out," Chloe said, the thing in her stomach becoming rage as her confusion dissipated. "With someone who has *killed* Mai! If you really love them so much, how can you murder them—us? You've told me how few there are left!" Chloe said desperately, trying to understand.

"Strange bedfellows, I know," Sergei said, nodding. "The loss of you two girls is a shame genetically, but it's a small sacrifice to prevent complete chaos in the Pride—which was working just *fine* before you came along, Miss King."

Chloe opened her mouth but didn't know what to say. The Rogue was still, but who knew how long it was going to be before he attacked? Her time was running out.

"Did you send people to kill my mother?" she finally asked quietly.

"Which one?"

Chloe's eyes narrowed. "My adoptive one." But now that she thought about it . . .

"Yes," Sergei answered promptly. "But that was before we all found out you were 'the One.' You were another Mai we welcomed into the fold, only you didn't seem to be ready yet to leave your past behind. We were just hurrying that process up a little."

"You would have had to kill more than my mom to get me into your fold completely," Chloe said hotly. "You would have had to kill Paul and Amy and Brian. . . ."

"I do what needs to be done," Sergei said, shrugging again. "Don't flatter yourself in thinking you were the first Mai to be raised by humans. There are six billion of them and only a thousand of us, Chloe. They don't need you. *We* do. Well," he added apologetically, "not *you*, obviously, but in general."

The Rogue finally seemed to be tensing a little, bored with the conversation.

"Did you even look for my dad at all?" But she already knew the answer.

Sergei put the big set of keys back in his pocket, getting ready to go. "I don't know. Olga might have since I mentioned it in front of her. I really will miss our time together," he said with a sigh. "In any other circumstances, I would be proud to be your father."

"I'm tired of listening to this," the Rogue finally growled. "Prepare to die, Mai whore." He started to cross his arms over his chest, reaching under each sleeve for a blade.

"Don't call her that," Sergei snapped, annoyed. "Just do your job."

"I'm tired of you too, Demon," the Rogue said tonelessly, and neatly whipped a shuriken at him.

Before Chloe could react, the star ended its flight buried in Sergei's throat. It stuck beneath his neat, short beard, neat, long, dark red ribbons streaming from it.

"You—," Sergei gurgled, ripping the star out of his throat. His claws came out and he launched himself at the Rogue.

Alexander leapt easily out of the way, though not so

far as to avoid one of Sergei's fat, square paws raking five bloody troughs in his arm. He spun around and buried a long knife into Sergei's back, causing him to let out something between a groan and a scream that was completely inhuman.

"You're Mai, too, Sergei Shaddar," the Rogue whispered as he held Sergei to drive the blade farther in. "You mean nothing to me."

Sergei let out a last bubbling groan and died.

Thirteen

Chloe gaped at the scene in front of her. She felt disconnected, like it was all happening on TV. There was just too much to take in.

Sergei and the Rogue had been working together. *And now the relationship seems to be, uh, over.* Sergei had helped kill her sister and lead Chloe to this theater to have the Rogue kill her, too.

Who was the better person? The assassin or the traitor to his race?

Hey, Chloe. RUN.

She shook herself out of her thoughts just as Alexander let Sergei's body drop to the floor with an ungraceful *thump.* And unlike Chloe, Sergei showed no signs of returning to life anytime soon.

"Well, what do you know," the Rogue said with little surprise, "he really wasn't the true Pride Leader."

The assassin standing before her probably knew *way* more about the Mai than she did, Chloe realized.

"Even for a Mai, he was traitorous filth," the Rogue continued, pulling out his blade and wiping it off. Then he turned to face her. "You, on the other hand . . ."

Should she stay and fight or run? The part of Chloe that had snapped her out of her thoughts before still urged the whole fleeing thing, but somehow she didn't think that would be a wise move. *No exposing the back—especially to someone who has range weapons.*

"Me, on the other hand . . . ?" she prompted, tensing, preparing herself to go into fight mode, sidestepping a few feet to the left.

"You would make a truly great leader; your false gods chose well. Too bad you're not human." He gave her a little bow. "Which is why," he added apologetically, "I *really* have to do this."

"You don't *really* have to do anything," Chloe pointed out. She moved so her back was to the theater door, Sergei's head pointing at her feet. "I've never done anything to hurt anyone—for chrissake, I even tried to save *you* from falling."

"I know." For just a moment the Rogue's cool expression broke and he looked puzzled. Then the moment was over and he gave her a grim smile, drawing out twin blades. One was still stained with Sergei's blood. "Probably comes from being raised by humans. It would be an interesting experiment—if you weren't the Chosen One, I mean—to see how you'd turn out. To see which side you'd choose."

"There. Are. No. *Sides.*" Chloe leapt just as he threw one of his long daggers at her; she went straight up and it passed beneath her to bury itself in the velvet-covered wall behind.

"There is good and evil, us and you," the Rogue said, circling to where she was, keeping his eyes locked on her.

"No, there is sane and fucking *nuts,*" Chloe corrected. "Or in your case, fucking nuts and *really* fucking nuts."

At some point he had pulled out a second knife to replace the one he had thrown; Chloe was dismayed to realize she hadn't noticed it. He had also managed to force her away from the doors so they were behind her—she was now at the worst-possible angle to escape.

"And what about Brian?" she pushed, continuing clockwise around Sergei's body. His head pointed at the doors. "Was it 'good' what the Order did to him?"

The Rogue frowned. "What Richard did was inexcusable, treating a human and one of our *own* like that. There would have been other ways to deal with Whitney's son."

His hands moved so fast they blurred and suddenly there were daggers spinning toward her.

Chloe hissed and threw herself up into the air and backward.

Her claws extended and she grasped the back of a seat, knowing it would be there. Her legs came down and her foot claws came out, grabbing a seat in the next row. Suddenly she was terrified and powerful, hunted but in control.

She knelt on the narrow seat back, barely using her claw tips to balance.

"Ah, the animal comes out. This makes it easier," Alexander said, grinning. He threw a screaming silver dagger at her. He, too, was as he should be: the hunter.

Chloe turned and sprang from seat back to seat back, down to the front of the theater.

Keep it under control, she told herself. But it felt *so good* to be moving.

"Your sister was hard to kill," the Rogue taunted, running down the aisle to keep up with her.

My sister.

By the time Chloe found out she even had one, the girl was already dead. Thanks to Sergei. And the Rogue.

Rage exploded in her heart, burning her limbs. She took a last wild leap from the first row to the proscenium, twisting in the air so she landed facing the Rogue. Now she had higher ground: a distinct advantage.

"One last question," she growled. "Was it *you* following me all this time?"

"Unless there was someone else, yes," he said, jumping from the floor to the first row of seats. He ran along their backs as nimbly as a Mai. "But you're almost always surrounded by humans. We had to get you alone."

The Rogue launched himself forward, vaulting up onto the stage and landing neatly in a crouch.

Chloe threw herself at him before he was completely down, growling. It took all of her effort to resist instinct, which told her to just get him in the chest or the stomach, disemboweling him the way a cat would. But she could see that under his neoprene he had Kevlar armor rippling over his arms and chest.

She reached out with her claws, aiming for his throat, right above his matte black armor, his only exposed and vulnerable place.

The Rogue brought his arms together and up, holding a dagger diagonally down against his wrist to protect his throat. Her left claws clanged against metal, sending shivers up her arm like a nail bent backward. But her right claws got something; as she pushed herself off him there was blood, but she couldn't tell if it was on his hand or ear. The Rogue didn't scream; he just sucked in a choking lungful of air.

She flipped backward twice and landed fifteen feet away. Her hands came up, protecting her own throat, and she waited for him to react. If she turned her back and tried to run, even for a second, Chloe knew she'd have a dagger between her vertebrae.

This theater could easily become her mausoleum.

And she would wake up with him leaning over her, waiting, and he would take his little silver dagger and drag it across her throat. Seven times. Until she didn't wake up again.

Chloe panicked for a moment, filled with memories that weren't hers. A girl, running through the dark. A city at night. An alley. The dream she had—a tattoo on an arm. *Sodalitas Gladii Decimi. Her sister.*

The Rogue stood up, a little shakily, but he already had a shuriken in the hand that didn't have the dagger.

She had lost her concentration.

"FREEZE!"

Both of them turned.

The doors of the theater crashed open and a policeman stood there, his .45 drawn and aimed. It was hard to tell which one of them it was aimed *at.* It didn't matter; another appeared by his side and also clicked her safety off. A third came forward, saw the body, and ran forward to kneel by him.

"Both of you. PUT YOUR WEAPONS DOWN," the first policeman shouted.

For a split second Chloe and the Rogue shared a moment, looking at each other. Then at the same time—without a signal—they both began running in opposite directions. Chloe made for the emergency exit on the right side of the screen.

"I SAID FREEZE!" the policeman bellowed again.

She leapt forward off the stage, putting all of her strength into her arms and crouching into a cannonball. She crashed into the door, forcing it open as the first shot went off. It was *loud.* Louder than she could have believed from TV.

Chloe barreled through the door and rolled onto the pavement outside, just ducking and pulling her legs in before it swung hard shut behind her. Her knuckles were bloody and raw from protecting the top of her head.

She took off, running and leaping and jumping from hydrant to awning to fire escape to roof, grabbing and swinging until she was back on the skyline, where she could travel quickly and safely, where she belonged.

Fourteen

What now?

Chloe kept running but forced herself to *think*—something her cat instincts didn't like.

She had spent the last several weeks at home, recovering from a previous attempt on her life, integrating the relatively sudden manifestation of her new abilities, two death-resurrections, and the Order of the Tenth Blade, the Mai, and their relationship for the past thousand years into her normal teenage life.

But what *hadn't* she done?

"Prepare, make a safe room, dig out a Cat Cave," Chloe answered to the night air as she leapt across the gaps between buildings, ignoring the hundred-foot drops below. "Actually train myself in fighting. Come up with some sort of defensive strategy. Initiate an emergency or panic routine for me, Amy, and Paul to follow. And Kim. And Alyec. COME UP WITH A PLAN."

She cursed herself for not having done it sooner. *Complete denial mode does not save lives,* Chloe thought.

"A little late, Chlo," she muttered.

At least the Rogue probably wasn't following her. As strong and skilled as he was, Alexander was still human and couldn't make the sort of jumps or move at the pace she could. For a moment Chloe allowed herself to picture him in a Rogue-mobile, with an evil grinning face on the front like a blond Joker. Even if he did have a car, he was probably driving it as fast as possible away from the police without any regard for her.

"Thank God for the police," Chloe muttered, for once without irony. How did they know what was going on? How did they know that anyone was there?

She made for the tallest point on the local horizon before her, a large satellite dish that was screwed solidly but inexpertly to the top of a chimney. If anyone was coming after her—the police or the Rogue or whomever—she would see them coming.

Once carefully balanced on top, one claw wrapped around the rim of the dish, she pulled out the one weapon she had available to her.

Her cell phone.

First she dialed Firebird.

"'Allo, Firebird LLC," the receptionist's voice came over. *Someone should really tell her to cut the Russian accent on outside calls,* Chloe thought. She *knew* Alexandra could speak almost perfect English; at this point anything else was an affectation.

"It's Chloe. Get me Olga."

"She's out at the moment—can I take a message?"

"No. Get me Igor."

"Honored One, he is in a meeting," she responded deferentially but promptly.

"Get him out," Chloe said, rolling her eyes at the strange incongruity of the other woman's words. "It's *very* important."

"Yes, Honored One," Alexandra said, putting her on hold. Chloe was still amazed; the other girl obviously hadn't liked her from the beginning, and now she did whatever Chloe asked without hesitation and only a little sarcasm.

After a surprisingly short wait, Igor got on.

"Hello?" He sounded a little irritated and snappish. *Not so much into the whole spiritual leader thing.* Which was going to make what she had to say next that much worse.

"Igor, Sergei's dead."

There was a pause, as if he was wondering if he had heard right. Igor's English wasn't perfect, so that was understandable. "What are you talking about?" he finally said.

"The Rogue just killed Sergei. I was with him at the theater you guys are looking at." Later she would burden him with the details about how she was there so that Sergei could have her *killed;* for now she just wanted the news out.

"Wait, wait. The Rogue is still alive? I thought you killed him."

"No, in fact, I tried to *save*—oh, never mind." Chloe sighed. Someday she would straighten that story out, too. "Apparently he did *not* die falling from the Golden Gate Bridge. Somehow he lived. And he just killed Sergei at the theater."

"What theater?" Igor demanded, his voice rising.

"The theater you guys were thinking about buying and tearing down for apartments or something or other," Chloe said, exasperated he had chosen to fix on that particular point.

"We weren't about to buy any theater. . . . I don't know what you're talking about."

Chloe sat back on the rim of the dish, stunned. It was bad enough that Sergei had been trying to kill her, but the lengths he had gone to plan it . . . Having keys to a property that no one at Firebird knew about just to have a convenient place for Chloe to be killed. Having Olga look for Chloe's dad to give her a reason to meet them there. Was there anything Sergei didn't lie about—or anyone in the Pride he didn't lie to?

"Where is this theater?" Igor prodded. "I'll get there right away—"

"No," Chloe cut him off. "The place is crawling with police. They showed up right after the Rogue and I began going at it. Stay away—tell *everyone* to stay away, even the kizekh. We can't risk the exposure."

She couldn't believe she was talking like this.

"Are you sure he's dead?" Igor said in almost a whisper.

"I'm pretty sure, Igor," she said as gently as she could. "If there's any chance he's alive, they'll bring him to a hospital. But he looked pretty gone. I'm sorry."

There was a long pause.

"Did you kill the Rogue?" Igor finally asked with a deadly calm to his voice.

"What? No," Chloe said, knowing it was a mistake as the words came out of her mouth. "In front of all those police?"

"Did you pursue him at all?"

"No, Igor, I fled the scene. Did I *mention* the cops? With the guns?" She tried to sound equally calm and directed, not cowardly, like he probably thought she was. "Listen, I'll explain it all to you later, okay? There is a *lot* to explain. I'll come over tonight. But I have to go now." She hung up. *Why couldn't it have been Olga?* She was terrified, adrenalized, and now she felt like cowardly shit just because of Mr. Sergei's ultratestosterone Padawan.

Who was out there who would *sympathize* with her? Not accuse or question?

As she dialed, a police car sped by a hundred feet below her, its siren howling. Chloe turned to watch, but it didn't stop.

"Chloe!" Amy chirped on the other end. "What's up?"

"Remember Sergei? The old guy who was trading insults with the other old guy at the Presidio . . . ?"

"The leader of your Pride, yeah," her friend answered. Sounding smug that she knew all that.

"He's dead. Killed by that assassin who tried to kill me on the bridge."

"Oh my God!"

"But he was actually trying to have *me* killed by the Rogue; it was kind of a setup—"

"Holy shit," Amy interrupted. "What are you going to do?"

"I think . . ." Chloe thought about it. She had no desire to go over to Firebird immediately; it was probably a mess. And in the interest of full disclosure—since she was probably going to see it on the news anyway—it was probably best to come clean to her mother. "I think I'm actually going to go home. If anything weird is going to happen, I want to be able to protect her."

"Good thinking. Paul and I will go over, too. We might as well be all together since everyone already knows about us."

"I—okay, yeah, good idea."

"Absolutely. See you in a little while."

And now the last call. It was even set for speed dial.

"Hello?"

"Alyec." She took a deep breath. "Sergei's dead. The Rogue killed him."

"Oh my God! Are you okay?"

"I'm fine. I'm going home to make sure Mom's okay and everything. Don't know *what's* going to happen next."

"Do you need me? I'm kind of in the middle of band practice—but I'll drop everything and come if you want. . . ."

"No." Chloe smiled and shook her head, forgetting he couldn't see it. "I'm fine. Call me when you're out."

"Okay. Be safe, Chloe."

"I will."

Chloe clicked her phone off and shoved it back in her pocket. When she first was hunted by the Rogue and had developed her powers, she always took circuitous routes home to confuse anyone who might be following her. Since her mom's kidnapping it was obvious that *everyone* knew where she lived—now it was just important that she get there first. She took one last long look around, enjoying the view and the moment's respite from the horrors of what was to come next.

Then she leapt down to the rooftop and hurried home through alleys and back ways, invisible to everyone—including the police.

When she heard her mom jingling her keys at the door, she opened it but forgot to retract her claws and Anna started at the sight. Chloe had spent the hour before her mom got home from work patrolling the house, making sure the windows and doors were locked, and listening for the sounds of an intruder. Amy sat in front of the TV, flipping between *CNN Headline News* and local channels (and reruns of *Invader Zim*). Paul wasn't there yet.

"Not dipping into the catnip, are you?" Anna King asked a little nervously as she came in and put her attaché case on the counter.

"Not exactly," Chloe said with a wry smile.

"Hey—it's on again!" Amy called from the couch.

Mother and daughter moved farther into the living room. A grim-faced young newsman talked while the words *Local Businessman Murdered* lit up the corner of the screen in red, yellow, and blue.

"Local real estate magnate Sergei Shaddar was found dead today in an abandoned theater. Connie Brammeier in Inner Sunset has the story."

The camera switched to a female reporter, younger and serious, on the scene. Things were going on behind her, but it was hard to tell what exactly. There were policemen, a tired-looking detective who frowned over her clipboard, and flashes going off.

"Earlier today police were alerted by a local about suspicious activity in the condemned building. Inside they found the body of Sergei Shaddar, owner of Firebird Properties LLC, gruesomely—and possibly ritually—covered in stab wounds."

"Covered? There was only one," Chloe said before she stopped herself.

". . . his throat also cut. Whether this was some sort of gang-related activity or a random attack remains unknown. Shaddar was a reclusive but popular businessman who donated ten thousand dollars every Christmas to local charities."

That's news to me, Chloe thought. Like inverse variables and people who liked Avril Lavigne, it was hard to wrap her mind around someone who was so absolutely evil—*and* gave to the poor.

"Investigators say there is no trace of the two suspects who fled the scene, but police are looking into it. Anyone with information on this crime is encouraged to call the number at the bottom of the screen. All tips are kept anonymous. Bob?"

"Why do I get the feeling that one of the 'suspects' is *you,* Chloe?" her mom asked in what was dangerously close to a growl. Amy turned down the volume.

Chloe took a deep breath. "Sergei told me to meet him at that theater because he had information on Dad." Her mom's eyes widened. "He was setting me up to be killed by the Rogue, who was also there waiting for me."

"I thought that person—the Rogue—fell from the bridge," her mother said slowly.

"Two percent of suicides survive the fall every year," Amy said, not tearing her eyes from the television.

"Anyway, he's still alive," Chloe continued as her mom frowned. "He and Sergei were working together to kill any potential 'Chosen Ones'—for different reasons, obviously. They're the ones who killed my biological sister a few months ago. But the Rogue turned on Sergei and killed him before attacking me—just another Mai he wanted dead."

Anna King looked at her daughter for a long moment, unblinking, just like Kim. Her eyes were much harder and flintier than the cat girl's, and her blond hair wasn't as wispy as she usually kept it. When she finally spoke, it was as calmly as Igor.

"That's it. We're moving."

Chloe had to replay what she said several times before accepting it.

"What?"

"We're moving. San Francisco is way too dangerous. It's ridiculous." Anna King took her glasses off and turned away, getting a notepad. "I shouldn't have any trouble finding a job in Seattle or New York. . . ."

"Mom, what are you talking about?" Chloe followed her around. Amy sort of wilted back onto the couch, just peeping over the top.

"In the last few months, there have been *two* attempts on your life." Her mother ticked things off on her fingers. "*I've* been held hostage, *you've* been basically held hostage, I have personally witnessed a gang war, no matter what you want to call it."

"We can't just run away—the Mai have looked for me for so long—they won't just give up. And the Rogue will, too!" Chloe protested.

"Then we'll go into hiding. I'll tell the authorities about what happened to me and we'll go into a federal protection something or other. Start over. I don't care."

"I can't just *leave* everyone!" Chloe wailed, wishing she sounded less teenage-y.

"And *I* can't just let you die!" her mother shouted back. Her eyes blazed; her jaw was set with frustration.

Suddenly Chloe understood. Her mom felt helpless that she couldn't protect her daughter. She felt ignorant and left out; her daughter's life was suddenly flooded with ancient cults and mythological races and Anna was angry because she had no control. And that was one thing she treasured more than almost anything else.

Of course, the whole situation really *was* out of control: Sergei was dead, the Rogue was still on the loose, Brian was probably still on the Order's hit list, the Mai were leaderless and lost, and, Chloe slowly realized, there was only one person who could fix it.

She squared her shoulders and kept her voice calm. "Mom, I know this is all upsetting, but running away really won't fix anything. The Mai can track me like bloodhounds. And . . . I *can't* leave them. I'm their only leader now." When her mom opened her mouth, Chloe gently cut her off. "*You* saw me die and rise from the dead. You see my claws. This isn't just a high-school varsity club or something—this is serious. And I'm the only one who can stop this cycle of violence," Chloe found herself saying. *Wow, do I really believe that?* When she thought about it, she realized it *wasn't* a "belief"; it was a truth. She *had* to be the one who stopped it. Or else it would keep on going. Forever.

Or until everyone involved was dead.

"And *I* can't let you keep on being involved," her mother said shakily. But Chloe could hear her resolve cracking.

"Neither you *nor* I have that choice," Chloe said. "If I don't go to them, they'll come to us. And I swore you would never get hurt again."

"Why can't I swear that about my own daughter?" Anna whispered, putting her fingers to her temple. She wasn't crying, not quite, but it was obvious she was holding it back.

Then someone knocked on the door, causing everyone to jump.

"Hey," Paul yelled cheerily through the glass, holding up a bag of Krispy Kremes. Then he saw the looks on everyone's faces. "Did I come at a bad time?"

Her mom insisted on driving if she couldn't forbid or direct. Paul and Amy sat in the backseat, stuffing themselves with doughnuts to get through the tension.

Almost like old times, Chloe thought wistfully. Something about being in the passenger seat made her feel like she was ten again. Her mother's jaw was still clenched, teeth gritted; even her earrings swung determinedly from her ears.

Chloe sighed, tracing the little bits of rain that built up on the window before marching their way down to the side and bottom, held up against the glass by wind. Someone once said something about a leader being only as good as the friends and advisers she surrounded herself with. *Maybe I should give Paul and Amy a little more credit.*

When they arrived at Masa—the restaurant was as neutral a meeting ground as any—they were led discreetly to the back, where Olga, Igor, and Kim were already waiting. Her mother's eyes bulged when they all said, "Welcome home, Honored One," and bowed. Chloe gave her mom a weak grin and shrugged.

It was a rectangular table and Chloe immediately made for one of the long sides, next to Olga, but her mother nudged her and shook her head the slightest bit, indicating the head of the table with her eyes.

"If you really want to stop the violence and lead your people, you have to *lead* them," she murmured. "*Take* control, Chloe. No one's going to take it for you."

Chloe nodded, seeing something in Anna King's eyes that she'd never really paid attention to before. Something that involved a high-powered job and politics. Something about being a woman and a partner at a major firm. *I'll have to ask her about that someday,* Chloe thought, slipping into the chair, sinking into its soft leather. She tried to concentrate on the impression the ass of the previous person had made on the seat to avoid the nervous feeling in her stomach.

Igor and Olga were obviously surprised and uncomfortable with the unscheduled presence of the humans.

"Igor, Olga, this is my mom, Anna King." Chloe indicated with her hand. Olga got over whatever shock she felt and shook hands warmly.

"It is so nice to meet you," she said in her thick accent—which got noticeably thicker whenever she was stressed.

"Hello," Igor said curtly.

"My friends, Paul and Amy."

The two Mai nodded at the two human teenagers; neither Olga nor Igor had been at the fight at the Presidio. *They were busy getting actual work done,* she thought with a mental snort. Not playing power games like the two old men who ruled both sides.

"This is Olga and Igor, the Mai's top two, uh, officials," Chloe said.

"Nice to meet you," her mom said, a little coldly.

"Paul, Amy." Olga nodded in their direction. "Mrs. King."

Kim just gave a little wave—somehow completely adorable with her cat paws.

"You *know* these people?" Igor asked her, astounded.

"They're my friends," Kim said nonchalantly

"I'm sorry if I compromised security," Chloe said, indicating that the other Mai should sit down, too, as well as her mom. All three did, looking at each other a little distrustfully. "I . . . wasn't sure what was going to happen next and I wanted to keep them safe."

"Of course," Olga said promptly. "They helped save you, yes? They are certainly welcome with us."

Igor didn't say anything.

"Before we go any further with anything . . ." Chloe took a deep breath. "You should know that Sergei was trying to have me killed when this happened."

Kim's eyes widened until they looked like they were going to pop out of their sockets. Olga slowly shook her head.

"That's ridiculous," Igor said.

"Unfortunately, it's not." She told them the whole story, as accurately and in as much detail as she could remember it. Especially Sergei's exact words.

"So basically Sergei and the Rogue had been working together to find and kill all other possible Chosen Ones, including *my sister.*"

"There's no reason," Igor scoffed.

"He wanted to keep power, and he was afraid of it being taken away."

"But you are the One," Olga said helplessly. "Why would he do that?"

"I *just* told you," Chloe said, trying not to lose patience. Her mom gave the slightest shake of her head: *Calm down, Chloe.*

"I don't believe it," Igor said again, taking a gulp of his coffee.

"Okay, believe it or don't; the fact is that he's *dead*

and the police are making an investigation. What do we do now?"

Everyone around the table was quiet. Olga delicately sipped tea the waiter had brought. "We'll talk about it at the meeting with you and all of the Pride tomorrow night," she said.

"I'll teach you the main opening prayer phrase; I think that will be enough for now," Kim volunteered.

"*Prayer . . . ?*" Chloe's mom turned to glare at the cat girl. Kim's ears flattened and she shrank under the older woman's look.

"More of an—an invocation," she stuttered, "a traditional opening to a speech."

Chloe tried not to smile.

"Let me be entirely clear on one thing: I don't entirely approve of all this," Anna King said firmly, "though I respect the needs and beliefs of Chloe's native people. But if *anything* happens to Chloe, just remember: unlike you and the Order, I have nothing against guns."

Igor started to roll his eyes, but Olga kicked him under the table. Chloe imagined her mom posed with an automatic, screaming and waving the weapon back and forth, firing round after round at unseen enemies. In Chloe's vision she still had her reading glasses on and her swinging silver earrings.

"What do we tell everyone right now? About why you're not there with them?" Igor demanded.

"You tell them the truth." *Dipshit,* Chloe almost

added. "That it's really dangerous right now, that the Rogue is hot on my tail—that I'll see all of them tomorrow back at the Cat Cave."

"What?" Olga asked, startled.

Whoops. It's only funny to me, Chloe realized. "Uh—Firebird." But Paul and Amy were smiling. "You *also* tell them that there is to be *no retaliation.* Not from individuals, not from the kizekh."

"But loyal Mai will insist," Igor sputtered. "If I myself had the skills . . ."

"You—tell—them—there—will—be *no retaliation,*" Chloe said again slowly. "No one is to do anything until after the big speechifying tomorrow night. Everyone's eager for blood—and the Tenth Blade will be prepared and waiting once they see the news. They'll be *expecting* an attack." She hoped this sounded reasonable.

"She's right," Olga said. Chloe was still stunned at the older woman's absolute faith in her as the Chosen One. She had been just as loyal to Sergei as Igor but had no problem accepting what the new, teen spiritual leader of the Mai said, no matter how far-fetched.

And it's a good thing, too, considering the dagger eyes Igor's giving me. . . .

"I believe we have a few hours lull before the storm," Kim added. "It would be a good time to take stock and make plans."

"Isn't the investigation of Sergei going to lead the police back to you guys?" Paul asked. "I mean, they're going to look at Firebird and all of his business associates and disgruntled employees. . . ."

"That's right," Chloe's mom said. "Do you guys even *have* a plan for that kind of investigation?"

Igor and Olga looked at each other, then at Chloe.

Apparently *not.*

Fifteen

The next morning Chloe realized it was a Tuesday. But instead of going to school, she stayed in bed for a while and decided that with everything that was going on around her, one more day wouldn't be the end of the world. She couldn't deal with anything else right now. No after school makeups, no seeing anyone, no nothing. Nothing until seven o'clock that night, when she had to address the tiny tribe of homeless, leaderless Mai, over a hundred people she didn't know, slit-eyed faces upturned to her, looking for hope.

Chloe decided to treat it like an oral report and not worry about it until later. She stretched and sat up, letting her claws emerge for just a moment from the tips of her fingers and toes. Her pajamas were an old pair of boxers and a giant Tide T-shirt her mom had gotten free at Target or something. Big. Orange. Ugly.

Alyec liked her in frumpy, oversized nightclothes, she remembered a little sadly.

Chloe shook her head. She had made peace with him last week along with her homework. She had made peace with Marisol. *And Sergei is, uh, at peace.* Now she needed a day of peace and quiet for herself, before the shit started going down again that evening.

I need to go on a bike ride.

She showered off the night ick and pulled on clean jeans, a T-shirt, and a Patagonia fuzzy she rarely wore to school for fear of Amy accusing her of being crunchy. Her mom was downstairs at the table, sipping coffee and going over bills.

"I'm going to go for a ride," Chloe said, jerking her thumb in the direction of the mini-garage that held almost too much storage crap to fit the car anymore.

"Wear your helmet," her mother said automatically. Then she looked up at her daughter. "Wait? Are you sure you should? What about the police . . . and the Rogue?"

"Screw 'em," Chloe said with a fierce grin. Then she softened at the look on her mom's face. "I doubt the police would even recognize me with a helmet. As for the Rogue—I promise I'll stay in public places. He won't do anything if there are innocent people—humans—around. I really need to clear my head for a while."

"Me too," Anna King said distantly. "This is . . . really . . . unusual stuff for me to deal with, you know?"

"You totally didn't know what you were getting into

when you adopted me, huh?" She said it with a smile, but inside Chloe felt really guilty about it.

"I realized what I was getting into when you were two and you pulled the bookshelf down on top of you. And *then* began chewing on all of my favorite Tony Hillermans," her mom said archly. "I've been reading about other parents with children who want to reconnect with their . . . original *ethnicity*. But none of the case histories in it deal with the supernatural."

That was a strange word. Chloe had never actually thought about it in reference to herself. Well, she tried not to think about the whole dying-and-coming-back-to-life thing in general. It was too weird. Was Sergei in that place of shadows now? Did he exist with the other lion shadows who prowled the darkness in that eternity? Or was there a Mai hell reserved for people like him?

"The good news is, if I get into an accident, I have seven lives left," Chloe said with a grin.

"Don't even joke," her mother growled.

In some ways, Mom's a better embodiment of the Twin Goddesses than Kim, Chloe thought as she pedaled to the park. Like when she made that speech about protecting or avenging her daughter if something happened to her—protective like Bastet, warlike like Sekhmet. Kim was deeply spiritual but didn't really exhibit the qualities of either. If there was something like one of the Muses in the Mai pantheon, that would surely be Kim.

The air was crisp, perfect biking weather, the sun warm on her back. Amy used to make fun of Chloe's helmet when they were growing up—she always ditched hers as soon as they were out of sight of home. But Chloe thought it made her look like a real biker, like a racer or maybe a messenger girl.

People smiled at her as she took a path into Golden Gate Park; other cyclists said "Good morning" or "Great day for a ride." Chloe was both anonymous and recognized, greeted and then forgotten like all of the other people enjoying the nice day outside. A little kid on a pink bike with training wheels tried to race her a few feet and Chloe pretended to pedal furiously until the mom called her daughter back.

It was nice feeling her legs pump, the strange hunch as she leaned over the handlebars. But there was none of the familiar burn in her legs that she normally got, which was kind of ironic, really. The whole reason she'd wanted the Merida was because it had an electric pedal-assist motor and would require little effort on her part to take it up hills. With her Mai strength and endurance it wasn't an issue anymore. *I'll bet I could totally do triathlons now.* Except for maybe the swimming part—she wasn't sure how good cats were at swimming or how much their natural aversion would affect her performance.

She biked past the people who played ultimate early every morning and watched a tall, brown-haired guy leap for a high-thrown Frisbee. Farther on there was some typical San Francisco–style political stuff going on: a shortish blond guy who didn't look much older than she was standing at a table and handing out leaflets on the benefits of libertarianism. Chloe wasn't quite sure what that was, but judging from the jeers of some surrounding grunge types, it probably wasn't leftist.

She swung her bike hard to the north, exiting the park scant minutes later. The destination that had been troubling her in the back of her mind finally surfaced and made itself known: the Golden Gate Bridge.

The place where she had first fought the Rogue and thought he had died. The symbolic gap between her old life and the life of the Mai, holed up in their little mansion across the water in Sausalito. She and Amy and Paul—back when they were just a little younger, back when they were all still "just friends"—used to walk across it and dream of new worlds on the other side. After September 11 legions of National Guard were stationed around it, keeping it safe while making the locals uneasy.

What had once been one of her favorite places in the world had become a source of trepidation for her, of turmoil and serious stomach upset.

It's time to take it back. To reclaim it.

Chloe switched the bike to high gear and pumped as hard as she could, her legs outworking the motor. Trying not to think, she pushed herself forward and closed her eyes.

When she opened them, she was on the bridge.

It was a glorious day: the orange girders shining in defiance against the soft blue sky and cotton candy clouds, a color completely out of place in nature. The bay sparkled blindingly below, a dark blue on which powder white sailboats rode carelessly by. The hills in front of her were different glowing shades of green and dark green, like a watercolor poster in a tourist shop.

Chloe felt like shouting or singing. Since she couldn't really do the latter, she let out a, "WHOOOPPPEEE!" that scared several walkers.

Chloe was filled with a happiness in movement she hadn't felt in a long time. No hunting, no being hunted, no one around she knew to upset this; just the speed, the wind in her ears, her legs moving, the glorious view.

The prayer is the movement.

Chloe remembered something vaguely about Hopi snake dancers who prayed for rain with rattlesnakes in their mouths. The prayer *was* the dance, not a separate recitation or song or spoken verse. That was what she felt like now: all glory and joy in just being alive.

Thank you, Whoever.

The bridge was far too short in retrospect; as she passed over the other limit, Chloe wondered how it had seemed so endless those times she had driven back and forth, once with Brian nearly dying in the backseat.

She had no desire to return home yet, so she crossed over and made her way up the Marin Headlands, waiting to become tired as the hills took their toll on her legs.

It never happened.

As though she were spiraling to the tip of a giant soft-serve ice cream cone, Chloe coasted around the side of the hill and was confronted with another glorious view: the bridge from above, San Francisco in the distance, water and spray in between. There was only a small parking space and a thin coating of grass on the rocky promontory; most people came up, took a picture, and left. Those who stayed were respectful and quiet. Any noise from ecstatic children leaping at the top of the world was whipped away by the ocean wind.

Chloe carefully leaned her bike up against a boulder and climbed on top of it, hugging her knees to her chest and sucking in the view.

I wish I could feel this way forever.

Chloe wished there was some way to store this entire moment, not just the visual image, but smells and feelings and all. Like in a stone or something that she could keep in her jewelry box and take out when she needed to relive the moment.

Chloe leaned back and lay on her back, looking up at the sky. In the sun and the wind and silence the cogs in her mind slowly began to fall back into place; the monkey wrenches and other acts of mental sabotage from the last few months slowly disappeared. The background chatter in her brain quieted. She just *was.*

And there, hidden by the mental graffiti, were the

answers that had always been there. It wasn't a great revelation, a message from the Twin Goddesses or her mom or the beyond; it was just Chloe. Speaking clearly to herself.

She sat up and pulled out her phone, regretful that the moment was over but resolved.

She called information so that her phone number wouldn't show up on caller ID and asked for Whitney Rezza when she was patched through, telling the receptionist that it was Chloe King.

"Why, here's a call I never expected," Whitney said with his usual light sneer, like someone at a yacht club.

"Mr. Rezza, Alexander Smith killed Sergei yesterday."

"Really? Now, *that's* kind of unexpected. Good for him."

Chloe kept her inner calm, refusing to snap or get sarcastic. "Actually, the two were working together. To kill all descendants of the previous *true* Pride Leader. Like my sister. And me."

"I don't believe that for a moment," the older man said promptly.

Chloe wondered briefly if anyone on *either* side had ever seen a spy movie. Of any sort. It was like the idea that two enemies working together for a common goal was preposterous.

"Well, they were. I know: I was there when the Rogue killed him. They both talked about it. But look, that's not really why I called."

"Oh?"

"As the new Pride Leader—the *Chosen One*—I am offering a truce." She took a deep breath. She wasn't overstepping her authority; she *was* the new leader. People like Igor would have to just toe the line.

Right?

"We'll let the death of Sergei be the last violence between us. On my word," Chloe said with resolve.

"Hmmm . . . a fascinating idea . . ."

Chloe held her breath.

". . . but no, sorry, not that interested. This is the first time in years our Order has had a cause worth coming together for; why settle for a truce when we can proceed to wipe out the rest of you? I really should thank you, you know. . . . The little showdown at the Presidio you arranged really did wonders for our morale and purpose."

What did that mean? *There is power in war, that's what that means,* Chloe realized grimly. Their last major strategic maneuver against the Mai was when Whitney lost his wife to a random gang member who was unconnected with anyone. . . . Since then, the Order had been little more than a bunch of violent, slightly overglorified Masons, with secret rules and rituals but not much in the way of actual targeted attacks.

"I mean, good luck as the new leader and all—but really, they're going to be a bit like chickens with their heads cut off for a while, aren't they?"

He sounded so smug. Chloe needed one last thing, one card that would leave him disturbed. Give him something to think about.

"Thank you. By the way, Whitney, how's your son?" And with that, she hung up.

Secrecy. That was the problem on both sides. Secrecy and ritual. If it had been *her,* if *she* had been leader of the Mai years ago when they first came to America, at the first sign of attack from the Order she would have immediately had the top lawyer on racial crimes/crimes of hate on their ass. Blown their cult public. Paul had once shown her the list "Top 10 Things Not to Do as an Evil Overlord" on the Web, and in the top ten was that when the gang of heroes approaches, you do *not* unleash the hounds of hell upon them; you call the local police and have them arrested for trespassing.

I'm telling, Chloe decided, in as whiny and childish a mental voice as she could manage. She called information again and had herself redirected to the tip line that was on the news before.

"Hi? I have some, uh, information on the guy who was murdered in the movie theater yesterday?"

"Can you come down to the station so we can take a full report?" the person at the other end asked in a brusque and businesslike fashion.

"I'd, uh, rather not. I was, uh, buying some . . . *stuff* from a . . . *friend* inside—I saw the whole thing, but I don't want to get involved."

"All right," the woman grumbled, "tell me what you saw."

Chloe told her the entire story, skirting around her own presence as a member of the scene and focusing on the Rogue and Sergei. She described both perfectly—which finally got the other person's attention; it was obvious that Chloe wasn't just repeating what she saw on the news because she described the shuriken that went flying into Sergei's throat. She told them everything she could remember about the Rogue, from his dumb ponytail to the slashes on his arm, and added vague rumors from "on the street" about an insane guy with knives and a penchant for Hong Kong–style fighting. The policewoman thanked her and hung up.

"There," Chloe said, picking up her bike. "I *told.* Deal with *that,* Whitney Rezza."

Abiding by her new policy of no more secrets, Chloe decided to drive to the Firebird mansion that night without bothering to try and hide her tracks. It was ridiculous, anyway; Whitney knew who Sergei was, and *everyone* knew that Sergei ran Firebird. *And for that matter, the same probably holds true for the Tenth Blade.* All of Whitney's friends must have known he belonged to some private club—it wouldn't take a genius to follow him there one day.

Strangely, her mom didn't have a problem with her

borrowing the car. Technically speaking, even though Chloe only had a learner's permit, Anna King decided that her daughter was safer with access to wheels than just showing up in a taxi.

"You call me every half hour," her mother insisted. "If you miss one and I mean *one* phone call, I'm calling the police. You understand?"

"Yes, Mom." She didn't even say it sarcastically. Frankly, Chloe was amazed that her mom was letting her go so easily.

"And let's have a word . . . I know, 'David Bowie.' If you say that, then I'll call the police—okay? Those will be our safe words."

"Okay," Chloe agreed, wondering how she could work the rock star's name into casual conversation while her captors/tormentors were listening. "But I think I might need to stay there overnight. . . ."

"Then call me every three hours after 1 a.m., and I *mean* it, Chloe King. You may be their leader, but you're still my daughter, and you're still under eighteen."

"Yes, Mom," Chloe agreed dutifully. She had already planned on keeping the GPS phone on the whole time. So far, none of the Mai besides Kim and Alyec knew about it.

By the time Chloe arrived at Firebird, the sun had set—and the news on TV had changed.

"I think you'd better look at this, Chloe." Kim had

been waiting for Chloe in the driveway, perched on top of the ornate marble fountain that marked the center of the turnaround in front of the entrance. She looked worried, which panicked Chloe: her friend usually didn't react to *anything*.

No one was in the lobby; no one was in any of the offices. *Many* of the top people were in Sergei's office, their slit eyes wide and dismayed in the half-light, soaking up the rays of the giant TV he had behind a curtain.

There was another reporter outside the theater, talking, but the photos being flashed in the corner when he turned the story back over to the deskman weren't of Sergei—they were of people he had murdered.

Chloe focused on the TV and serious-looking reporter on-screen.

". . . now that the FBI is involved. Investigators report that Sergei Shaddar was a criminal mastermind involved in some Eastern Bloc terrorist organizations. Information from Georgian officials suggest that many of the murders he carried out in his homeland were disguised under the cover of civil violence between the Georgians and the breakaway state Abkhazia."

Chloe looked at Kim. "Keep watching," the other girl whispered. "It gets crazier."

"Shaddar was also involved in a number of other murders in the United States, possibly including the murder of a girl whose wounds and method of murder perfectly match those of Mr. Shaddar."

A photo of the girl who had been Chloe's sister was shown in the corner now.

Believe me yet, jerky? Chloe wanted to mutter to Igor, but that wouldn't have been a very leaderlike thing to do.

Instead she sighed, shook her head, then raised her voice, flipping on the lights.

"Could everyone who isn't Olga, Igor, or Kim please leave the room?"

Everyone turned to face her, blinking against the bright light. A dozen pairs of eyes went back to nearly humanlike round pupils.

"And please ready the, uh, auditorium for the seven o'clock meeting. Could one of you make sure that there's a TV, with access to the news, or a giant projection screen, or something like that?"

Heads nodded: "Yes, Honored One." Chloe tried not to notice how relieved and grateful and hopeful the faces were as they passed and looked at her. Even the receptionist who had sneaked in behind them to watch the news bowed her head.

When they were all gone, Kim closed the door.

"Anyone want to say anything?" Chloe asked, looking back and forth between the three of them.

Olga took the opportunity to start crying. "I never knew!" She coughed. "I can't believe . . ."

Her eyes went slitty again and her claws came out as emotions overcame her; Chloe realized that of all the

Mai she knew even a little, not once had she seen the older woman transform at all.

"I can't believe it either," Igor said softly, but the blank look in his eyes said otherwise. "He was like a father to me. . . ."

"May I suggest a little perspective?" Kim asked in one of the coldest tones Chloe had ever heard her use. "In other orphan cases like Chloe's the human parents have 'randomly' disappeared or turned up dead, like with Chase. . . . You cannot tell me you didn't suspect *something.*"

Neither of the other two said anything. Olga looked vaguely shamefaced, however.

"Don't ask, don't tell, huh? All right, the past is the past," Chloe said. She fought a surge of disgust and anger as she thought of her own mom and the traces of Mai presence that Kim had found around her house. "I am declaring an official moratorium and amnesty right now. In the future, there will be *no more murders.* And if someone suspects something, it gets dealt with *normally* through the police—not covered up, okay? Listen." Chloe looked at her watch. "I have to call my mom in, like, five minutes, but before then I want to reveal some of my secret plans."

Plans that she had worried about and gone over in her head and had found nothing wrong with—but that she still doubted.

"Igor, until—well, until further notice, you're now

acting president of Firebird. Olga, consider yourself CEO." The Mai boy blinked a couple of times at this in a way that wasn't entirely human, shocked out of his snit by the sudden weight of responsibility. Chloe went on. "No matter *what* happens, real estate is not in my future, and human resources is not in my immediate future, as nice as the thought of finding more misplaced Mai may be. I really do plan on going to college. Oh, and let me reiterate one last time—" Chloe fixed her eyes on Igor's. "Sergei. And the Rogue. Were working. *Together.* Which revelation will also no doubt appear in the news sometime in the next few hours after the police release the information."

"How do you know that?" Igor asked, plainly mystified.

"Because *I* told them," Chloe answered smugly. It was true: not in a million years did either side expect the other to go to the police.

The call to her mom was fast, the walk to the auditorium faster. Finally events were catching up with her, the calmness of the afternoon replaced by nerves over what she had to do in the next hour. Public speaking was *not* one of Chloe's finer talents. It didn't help that Kim wore a traditional off-white linen robe and makeup that was sort of Egyptian, kohl black around her eyes and under her chin. She tried to get Chloe to wear a robe, too.

"It's not my thing," Chloe flatly refused. "Our people

should see what kind of a person I really am—not pretending to be."

Kim didn't argue.

The room was smaller than she expected; there really were only a hundred cat people, like a studio audience, ten by ten and packed. While it was a relief, it was also kind of sad: there were only three Prides in America, and this was one of them, and there were so few. . . . Chloe was the leader of a dying people, an endangered race.

Someone had set up the projection TV as she had asked, and all watched, horrified, the news about their old leader flicker across the screen through reporters' mouths and on a colorful banner at the bottom. When she thought they had seen enough, Chloe nodded at the guy in the back—*Mai A/V geek?*—and went out on the little stage, behind Kim.

Her friend, now completely in her role of priestess, held out her hands, closed her eyes, and began to sing. Like the night of the Hunt, when Chloe had first heard a traditional Mai chant, this was just as strange and wailing. It was impossible to predict where the melody would go; Kim changed tone and octave without warning. It sounded as sad and alien as Chloe felt her people looked right then.

Suddenly she *felt* them right then.

As the hymn continued and she looked out at the faces, Chloe could feel the collective emotions of the group. *Fear. Sadness. Expectation. We are so few! We have lost so many! And now this . . .*

Hope, as they looked at her.

Igor was trying to pay attention, but feelings of betrayal and pain were so strong that he wasn't really connected to the others.

She felt strange warmth, like everyone was where they should be: here they were, her Pride, together, waiting for her.

There was one off note, one small thing missing, like someone wasn't there.

After Kim finished, Chloe stepped up, no longer afraid or nervous. Here were her people. She was their leader. She cleared her throat.

"For those of you who haven't met me yet, I am Chloe King, Pride Leader and your Chosen One."

It sounded so stilted and strange, but everyone was listening raptly.

"Sergei Shaddar was *not* your true leader. Though he had good intentions, they were carried out with evil means. The man you thought you were following to some sort of happy-ever-after brought only violence and death. Even those closest to him had no idea of the extent of his activities." *Of course, the kizekh probably had a pretty good idea, since he must have used them to carry out some of his directives. . . .* But she would stick to her line of amnesty and forgiveness.

"When I met with him at the theater where he was

killed, the Rogue was already there, waiting for me."

There was no noise from the reserved Mai, but Chloe felt the collective shock of a hundred people.

"The two had been working together to kill *all* possible Chosen Ones, including my sister. I don't know if Sergei actually killed any himself, but he told the Rogue where she would be and where I would show up, and Alexander did the rest. Once he had me in his sights, Sergei was also no longer any use to him and the Rogue killed him as well."

"I cannot believe a Mai would kill another Mai! There are so few of us," a Mai wailed.

"There are bad people even among us, just as there are good people among the humans, like my mom. And Brian. And Paul and Amy."

Scanning the small crowd, she saw Alyec. Their eyes locked for a moment and he smiled—genuinely, without what had happened between them recently getting in the way. Supporting her. She smiled back without thinking.

"My mother, your previous Chosen One—it was her dream to unite all of the Eastern European Mai, those who had been scattered by war and exile and violence and our curse.

"As your *new* Pride Leader, I believe it is time now that we are all together to embrace our new land fully." There was a little hesitation at this—they were *not* all here yet, and where was she going with this? "Sergei was right about one more thing—you *shouldn't* have to live here like rats holed up. You should be free to pursue your own destinies and come together because you want to, not because you're forced to.

"You're in America now, in some ways no different from any other immigrants. From now on we abide by its laws. That means *no more* revenge and wars with the Tenth Blade. They break the law—they will be punished accordingly. As you might have seen from the news, they are hot in pursuit of the Rogue. And you know why? *Because I told them he was Sergei's murderer.*"

This time there was an audible gasp.

Kim was off to one side, Chloe suddenly noticed, talking with whoever it was running the TV.

"The police will track him down and arrest him. He will be punished for this and his other crimes. . . ."

"Chloe," Kim murmured, coming to her side, "forgive me for interrupting, but Ivan has told me there's something on the news we should see—he TiVo'ed the last few minutes. . . ."

"Put it on." Kim nodded to the back and the projection television came on again.

Somehow Chloe wasn't surprised to see a photo of her biological mother appear next to the CNN guy's face, as one of the dead counted by Sergei's hand.

". . . Anastasia Leon, member and leader of an obscure tribe of Eastern European nomads, originally from Turkey, had returned to her people's homeland.

Investigators are now turning up evidence that she was one of the first of Sergei Shaddar's political murders; the sources are unsure why. . . ."

Anastasia Leon. That was her mother's name. And there she was. A photo similar to the one that Chloe had held in her hand just a couple of weeks ago, of a woman with waist-length black hair and a wide, untamed smile, furrowed brow and determined eyes.

She gestured for the sound to be turned back down.

The Mai looked stunned; some were weeping, some growling. Chloe felt a mix of pity and bewilderment that *none* of them had seen this coming.

"See? This is *exactly* what I'm talking about. Secrecy and survival has forced you to follow a man who *murdered* your Pride Leader. This causeless violence between us and the Tenth Blade ends *now.* All it does is breed more violence and plays for power among ourselves—look what Sergei did to my sister, and look what Brian's people did to *him.*

"I am your new Chosen One, and I will lead you to safety and prosperity—but only through peace."

There was a pause. Were they going to clap? Drum her out? What happened next? Chloe desperately tried to feel the strange empathy she had experienced before, but it had faded to a dull heartbeat.

Suddenly Alyec leapt to his feet and roared. The only time Chloe had ever heard anything like it was when she'd lost her cool with Keira—and scared the bejesus out of the other girl. It was a deep, frightening sound that seemed much too loud and deep for his human frame to produce. His eyes were slit and scary; his claws were out.

Valerie stood up next and joined him.

Soon everyone was standing and howling and roaring, a deafening clamor that should have frightened Chloe but didn't. For just a moment the link was back and she could feel their energy and power and love—the support of the Pride.

Kim didn't roar, choosing to give her a strangely human thumbs-up.

When Chloe retired to give her mom a quick call, letting her know how it went, she was exhausted. *Still not a public speaker,* she realized. Just able to do it when called for. Igor waited patiently close by for her to get off the phone.

"Honored One . . . ?" he asked politely.

"Yes, Igor?" Chloe asked as she set down the phone. Soon she would get back on the bandwagon of making them call her Chloe. It seemed too much to do right now, though.

"I wanted to say . . . I think you are right." It didn't look like he was forcing himself to say this; he seemed full of the stillness and peace that she herself had experienced that afternoon. "Maybe it's because I deal—dealt—with humans more than Sergei, but we should follow their laws. Especially if we stay. And even if we don't stay—nomads can't make asses of themselves everywhere they go. Otherwise we won't be welcomed back." There was the faintest smile on his lips.

"Thanks, Igor. That really means a lot to me." And that was it—it was over. All of the tension between them for the last few days, all of his irritation at her. But the sadness was still there, and Chloe knew that he would be thinking a lot about Sergei in the upcoming weeks, remembering the good things while sifting through them, looking for signs of the ruthless killer beneath. "I never knew my biological father," she added softly. "And my adopted dad skipped out when I was little. Sergei was the third father I lost—and in some ways, the one I was closest to."

Igor nodded, not trusting himself to speak.

"Hey," Chloe said, changing the subject and remembering the absence she had felt at the beginning of the speech. "Where's Dmitry, by the way?"

He was the bodyguard Sergei had assigned to her when she was feeling rebellious living with the Mai, the one who came to protect her when they went out to see *Star Wars.* Along with Ellen, another member of the kizekh—and, she was pretty sure, his lover.

She was expecting a quick answer, like, *Oh, he patrols and guards the upstairs while the Pride meets to keep them safe.*

But Igor's face, blank and confused, told another story.

This is one of those loose ends, Chloe realized tiredly. *One of those unexplained things that's gonna come back and bite me in the ass later.* She was getting so much wiser so quickly . . . and it didn't make her happier.

Sixteen

Eventually Chloe was able to quietly extract herself from the crowd and slip away to the hospital room. Brian was actually reading, beneath a single light floating alone in the darkness.

"Hey," she said, smiling.

"Hey." He put down his book and looked up at her eagerly. There was one thin bandage around his head now, mostly white and unstained. His hair was a little fluffier, like it had been cleaned, and his eyes were brighter, though they were still surrounded by bruises and cuts. But there was definitely something more *alive* about him, pink and healthy, and Chloe felt a little rush of pride that maybe, just maybe, she'd been the one to lift the age-old human-Mai curse.

The book, Chloe noticed as she came closer, was *Blood Meridian*. It looked like a Western.

"Not a lot of reading choices down here," he said, shrugging. "But this is pretty good."

"Are they treating you okay?" she asked, pulling up a metal stool.

"Are you *kidding?*" Brian snorted. "Whatever they think of me, they keep it to themselves. It's all 'Honored One' this and 'Chosen One' that and 'as she desires. . . .' Although the doctor, I think, really *is* good. And kind of funny, for a Mai."

"What's *that* supposed to mean?" Chloe demanded, taking his hand.

"As someone who has been forced to study them most of his life, I gotta tell you: most of your compatriots don't really have much of a sense of humor."

Chloe opened her mouth to disagree, then thought about it. He was right.

She shrugged. "We had a big powwow upstairs."

"I heard. Well, I didn't actually *hear,* but everyone was talking about it. Everything okay?"

Chloe sighed and told him about Sergei and the Rogue and her reporting it to the police and the subsequent follow-up investigations and how he appeared to have killed her entire biological family except for her dad, who no one knew or seemed to really care about. She had to stop once to call her mom, which Brian later teased her about, but he sat quietly, eyes twinkling, while she called.

"Well." She stretched, yawning. "That's about it."

"What now?"

"Now?" She extended her claws without thinking

and scratched at a particularly itchy spot on her head. She hoped it wasn't dandruff. Or whatever cats got. "Now I think I find my old bedroom, crawl into bed, and sleep until hell freezes over—or I have to call my mom again, in about three hours."

"Why don't you stay here?" Brian suggested quietly.

Chloe looked at him. He wasn't kidding. In fact, she had never seen him look at her more seriously. He reached out a hand and touched her lips—a hand that was connected to a really toned arm, peach-colored and muscled. He moved his fingers along her cheek and jaw to run his hand through her hair.

Then she eased off the stool and lowered the metal side of his hospital bed.

"It will be just like a sleepover," he said, grinning.

"No pillow fights for you," she murmured, pulling back the sheet and kissing his neck.

In the morning, Chloe woke up cramped and sleepy.

She had only missed one phone call to her mom—the 4 a.m. one—and Anna King had called her at exactly five minutes past. While it wasn't exactly convenient to answer, the consequences would have been far worse, so Chloe had forced herself to.

Brian made little murmuring noises as she carefully disengaged herself and slid off the side of the bed.

"C'm back soon," he mumbled, trying to open his eyes and failing. "Miss you."

Chloe leaned over and kissed him. Brian smiled but was soon snoring again.

How do I feel? Chloe asked herself, picking her jeans up off the floor and putting them on. They fit softly and nicely, like third-day jeans always did.

Do I feel different?

She made her way through the benches of hospital-y stuff, surprising Dr. Lovsky, who was carrying a breakfast tray for Brian.

"Oh, uh, morning, Honored One," the older woman said, a little shocked when she realized the two of them had been together all night. But whether it was because he was a human or that hanky-panky in general had gone on in her little sterile kingdom, Chloe couldn't tell.

"Morning," she said cheerfully before resuming her thoughts and her progression upstairs. Maybe there was a whole ceremonial day-after-New-Pride-Leader-speech breakfast fete in her honor. That would be terribly embarrassing, but there might be fruit salad.

Sniffing the air and using her Mai hearing, Chloe was sort of disappointed she didn't hear any of the sounds that might be associated with fete preparations, so she went to the kitchenette instead, where at least she smelled coffee.

Kim was in there already, getting her morning green tea.

"Honored One," she said, dipping her tea bag and her head at the same time.

"Chloe," Chloe corrected grumpily, getting a cup.

Since she had been away, they had installed a cool new coffee machine where you could choose a packet of ten different kinds of coffee, or tea, or even hot chocolate—and press some buttons and the machine would make you almost anything. Of course, the packets were made out of nonbiodegradable Mylar, so as soon as things calmed down around here, Chloe would have to start pushing to get rid of it.

Surely a Chosen One could do that.

Her aim was still a little off: as she poured the milk, the coffee overflowed her cup—at least it wasn't plastic foam—and spilled on the counter.

"Damn," Chloe grumbled, carefully lifting the cup to her mouth to sip the excess off. She almost felt hung over.

"Did you sleep well?" Kim asked.

Chloe frowned, looking her friend in the eye, but there were no double entendres. It was an innocent question.

"Not . . . exactly."

Kim nodded wisely. "Did you and Brian have sex together?"

Chloe choked on her coffee and spat it out, spilling some more from the cup as she did. "What the hell?" she demanded.

The cat-earred girl barely hid her smile. "I was just curious."

Chloe had opened her mouth to say something

about the private lives of Chosen Ones when Igor came into the room.

"Honored One." He gave her a quick nod. "You should come quick. Dmitry is back—he's killed someone."

There goes the happy ending that was just beginning. Why wasn't anything easy?

She followed Igor out and into Sergei's office. Kim came padding quietly behind. For some reason, Chloe didn't mind her constant presence, even when it wasn't exactly invited. She was never distracting, opinionated, or full of herself.

Chloe expected to find him standing tall, impassive, scary, threatening—like he normally was. The kizekh were the soldier class, after all—and from what she had seen at the fight on the Presidio, they were quite effective and disciplined in their own scary, catlike way.

Instead he was sitting on a chair, bent over and weeping. Olga was standing next to him, a hand on his shoulder.

"Honored One!" Dmitry whirled around—of *course* he would have heard them talking. His senses were probably almost as sharp as Kim's. The big guard threw himself to his knees at her feet and touched her ankles. "I did not know! That he was a *murderer* of our people—that he—that he—*killed* our Chosen One!" Chloe was confused for a moment before she realized he meant her biological mother. He was old enough to remember her, she realized, and had maybe even met her before he came over.

"What happened?" Chloe asked as gently as she could, considering there was a crazy murdering adult below her wailing and prostrating himself.

"When I learned the news of our Pri—of Sergei's death, I grew incensed and swore vengeance!"

Chloe turned to glare at Igor.

"He wasn't around when I passed along your no-vengeance thing," he protested. "And even if he was, well, tensions were running a little high. . . ."

"I went to a place where I knew there would be one of the filthy human Order patrolling," Dmitry said, a hard glint in his eye as he recalled. "And killed the coward with my bare claws." Then he began to weep again. "I thought I was avenging our leader, our great protector. . . . I knew you were the One, but he was as a father to us in the days between you and the One before. . . ."

"Do you remember which one you mur—uh, killed?" Chloe asked.

Dmitry shook his head. "They are all alike—brown hair, terrible smell—he was one from the skirmish the other night."

He sounds more Klingon than Mai, Chloe noted.

"You've heard my new rule? No more bloodshed, except in self-defense?" Chloe asked.

"Yes, Honored One. Of course. Our duty is to protect the Pride, not declare war." He looked up at her, his crazy face streaked with tears but set with new resolve.

Chloe wasn't sure if he was asking forgiveness; she wasn't sure that she could have given it. There were more important things to deal with immediately. What was it they said on TV? *Damage control?*

She tried to block out the image of the man before her ripping out the throat of some nameless human, tried to forget that there was a murderer at her feet. *Murder.* Someone's life snuffed out because he was in the path of an angry, vengeful cat person. Not that anyone in the Tenth Blade was exactly innocent, but what if it was someone like Brian? Forced to join, not exactly in complete agreement with the tenets . . .

Chloe went around to Sergei's desk and did the only thing that made any sense—she called Whitney. Directly.

"Hello?" From the obnoxious tone in that one word, she could tell he already knew who was calling.

"Whitney, we need to meet *now.* This is the second death in a week from our stupid little war—we need to end it."

"What second death?"

Chloe looked at Igor and Olga and Kim. They all shrugged—whoever Dmitry had killed, apparently his body hadn't been found yet.

"One of my people killed one of your people in revenge for Sergei's death, against my orders. I don't know who it is, but you might want to issue a roll call."

"Son of a—"

"See? I'm *calling* you to *tell* you about it. I'm being open and honest in an attempt to end this . . . *craziness.*" Amy had a much better word, but somehow Chloe suspected Mr. Whitney H. Rezza didn't know Yiddish.

"If you think I'm going to *thank* you for being the first to let me know about the death of one of my Order or break down weeping and beg for a *truce,* Miss King, especially from *you* . . ."

Chloe wondered if it would have been any different if she had been male. Or older. He only called her "Miss" when he was really upset and looking to insult her.

"Listen. Remember how I asked you about your son?"

"What does—?"

"We have him. *Alive*. Barely."

There was finally silence on the other end. This was a gamble; he seemed more than willing to give Brian up to other members of the Order of the Tenth Blade who thought he had betrayed them by helping Chloe. But Brian *was* his son, after all, and she bet that whatever fate he wanted, it probably didn't involve him ending up at the mercy of the Mai.

"If you want to see him again, *alive,* you will come to"—somewhere public, somewhere safe—"Pier 39, at seven o'clock, with all your little cronies or whatever. This whole thing is ending *today,* one way or another, Mr. Rezza."

She hung up on him again.

It was kind of nice.

She looked up—Olga, Kim, Igor, and Dmitry were all staring at her.

"What?" she demanded.

"You don't, uh"—Igor cleared his throat—"sound like the intern we hired a couple of weeks ago, Honored One."

Chloe just smiled, saving her energy for things greater than laughing.

Seventeen

"I have never seen these up close," Kim said, intrigued by the sea lions. She leaned dangerously over the rail, a black baseball cap and her willowy wispiness making her easily mistaken for an overeager young boy.

"You've lived in the Bay Area your *whole life* and you've never seen the sea lions before?" Chloe asked, amazed. Brian tried to stay alert in a wheelchair nearby; Dmitry and Ellen stood guard over him. With his good looks and their weird presence Brian was occasionally mistaken for a celebrity; tourists took candid shots of him, thinking he was *somebody*. Besides this being amusing, Chloe liked having the extra witnesses.

Brian hadn't been completely on board when she told him her plan; he thought it was dangerous for her—and any other Mai involved. But when Chloe asked him what else she could possibly do, he didn't have a better idea.

Amy, Paul, and her mom were with him, too; Chloe

wanted *everyone* who was involved to witness whatever occurred. Alyec pretended to pitch Amy headfirst into the water a couple of times, and Paul even offered to help once. *I'm sure sublimated anger has nothing to do with it,* Chloe thought. Olga was eating a soft-serve ice cream cone, though from her figure it looked like the concept should have been alien. *I wonder if she's also a dairy cat.*

About a half hour after the sun set—it was hard to tell, it being one of those cold gray San Francisco fall days—Whitney strode up with a sleek umbrella he swung like a swagger stick, his expensive raincoat unfurling behind him. There were other people with him, mostly middle-aged, some younger.

"Where is my son?" Whitney demanded immediately.

"I'm right here, Dad." Brian waved weakly.

His father's face went white when he saw the extent of his son's injuries.

"What have you *done* to him . . . ?" Whitney demanded, coming forward, his face now going purple with rage.

Igor stepped easily between him and Brian, arms poised. Ellen and Dmitry loomed forward.

"*We* didn't do anything." Chloe resisted the urge to add, *old man.* "I found him, practically dying, in an alley. *Your* people did this to him."

The old man didn't say anything. He wouldn't deny or confirm it.

"It was Dickless, Dad," Brian said, his thin voice

almost lost in the evening breeze and wails of the sea lions. "He and his little bitches took me by surprise. They left me for dead."

Whitney opened his mouth and closed it again several times. "Richard is dead," he finally said. "The Mai killed him last night."

"Oh," Brian said. "Darn."

"See, this is *exactly* what I mean!" Chloe said, frustrated. "Sergei was killing his own people for power, your people are killing your own people just for—I don't know, old rules. Maybe power as well. And for *what?*" She looked around at everyone gathered there. "What really has been the reason you both have been at each other's throats for so many thousands of years?"

"The Order of the Tenth Blade exists to protect humanity from those stronger who would easily defeat them," Whitney said dramatically.

"Would you take a *look?*" Chloe threw her hand out at her Mai friends. "If your intelligence is *half* as good as ours, you know that there are less than a hundred of us in the West. *A hundred,* Whitney. That's less than the Native Americans, or Tibetans, or Jews, or any *other* dwindling, oppressed minority!"

"Hey," Amy muttered. "I don't think we're dwindling." Paul kicked her to shut up.

"Forget the Tenth Blade: one good earthquake or fire or dirty bomb or terrorist attack and there'd be no more Mai west of the Mississippi. When was the last time, exactly, the Mai actually posed a threat to continued human existence?"

"We have always been there to stop it," Whitney said, drawing himself up. But from the looks on the younger members' faces, he wasn't really convincing anyone.

"And let us not forget the original reason for our existence," a middle-aged woman said, stepping forward. "The villages and cities that were wiped out—"

"Because you raped and murdered one of our sisters!" Igor said, also stepping forward.

"Five. Thousand. Years. Ago. Jesus *Christ,* guys, let it go!" Chloe glared back and forth at both of them. "And may I remind you"—she addressed this to the Order—"the Mai are not *vampires* who prey on the living. You are not vampire slayers who protect the innocent."

"They are fell, foul beasts spawned from the pits," one of the other Tenth Bladers spoke up. "Their existence is anathema to God. Thus they are punished to never have a home and never commingle with true humans."

"You sound like the Rogue," Chloe muttered. "Who, by the way, is an insane psycho killer. And anyway, the whole five-thousand-year-curse thing seems to be over. Brian and I have not only, uh, *kissed* multiple times, but . . ." She didn't want to say it, but if it would further the cause, as it were, well, illusions of her chastity didn't really count much against dead bodies. "Last night, we, uh . . . Look, anyway, the point is, he's *fine.*"

There were shocked looks from everyone, especially Amy. Chloe had *sworn* to her years ago she would be the first to know when It happened. *Technically, it wasn't "It" yet*—she had no desire to get pregnant on top of everything else that was going on in her life right now. But what happened was close enough to It to count.

Brian was blushing furiously, trying to meet his dad's eyes.

"In fact," Chloe said, raising her voice so *everyone* could hear—and hoping she wouldn't be considered a slut, "I made out with *another* human before I ever even met Brian."

"Wait, what?" Brian looked shocked and a little sad.

Chloe ignored him. "And *he's* fine, too. Look, the point is, there is no divine thingy against Mai and humans, uh, loving. We can mix and mingle and mate with no dire consequences."

"The curse seems to have been lifted because we helped save two humans," Kim spoke up, "Chloe's mother and Brian."

Chloe didn't want to meet Alyec's eyes, which were wide with disbelief. No doubt there would be awkwardness and explanations later, even though they were split up.

But her assumption that he was thinking about her was suddenly dashed when Alyec grabbed Amy and kissed her, long and hard. A little too long and hard—Paul and Kim began to look away nervously—but Amy didn't resist. At all.

When they came up for air, Alyec looked her in the face. Amy took a breath, waited a moment, then shrugged. "Nothing. I mean, it was great—but I don't feel weird or anything."

This was not exactly how Chloe had imagined humans and Mai would start to get along better, but hey, it was something. And come to think of it, her usually extroverted friend had been kind of quiet recently. It was only fitting that she steal the spotlight for a moment of silliness during an otherwise deadly encounter.

Edna and Whitney looked appalled, as did other older members of the Order—and Olga and some of the kizekh. Chloe might be mistaken, but some of the other ones looked intrigued. *Not everyone can study sexy cat people without getting a little intrigued.* Opposites attracting and all that.

"The Rogue was just arrested, by the way," Paul interrupted, looking at the news on his phone. "About an hour ago. He's wanted in connection with over a dozen murders. . . . Uh, anywhere else I would say it's the death penalty with the sort of proof they have against him, but I think he's probably going to be committed."

"Welcome to America, lads," Chloe said sweetly to the Tenth Bladers. "And *you* all were born here. This is the way justice happens, not through vigilantes."

"You risk exposing the existence of your own people in doing this," Edna said, but from the baffled look on her face it was obviously a move none of them expected.

"How?" Chloe asked. "You really think that they're going to believe a raving serial murderer when he tells them that all of his victims were actually cats, with claws and slit eyes? Look, I'm still proposing a truce. A *real* truce. You can go on watching to make sure none of the kitties go rabid and start a killing spree, but *no more violence.* If something happens—on either side—it gets dealt with by the police. No more gang wars, no more internecine, uh, necines, and guess what that will mean? *No more innocents gunned down along the way.*" She gave Brian's dad a hard look in the eyes.

"Even if we were to take you up on this 'truce,'" Edna said, covering for Mr. Rezza while he recovered from the remark, "there still remains the little problem of inequity."

"What do you mean? Sergei's dead, Richard's dead, the Rogue will probably go to prison or whatever," Chloe said, thinking furiously. But she came up with nothing. "We're even."

"Not exactly." Brian's dad cleared his throat and spoke up, once again at ease. "There is still the matter of our member who Sergei killed at the Presidio. As far as I can tell, no Mai were even permanently injured in the tussle."

"What do you want *me* to do about it?" Chloe asked

before she could stop herself. As soon as she said it, she knew it was a mistake.

"What Edna said. Equity. The boy Sergei killed and Sergei are dead. But the Mai who killed Richard is still alive. Sacrifice him or her, and we will consider your truce."

Whitney smiled an easy smile of confidence. *I've won,* it said.

"No!" Ellen cried, not with fear, but fierceness. She grabbed Dmitry's arm, her claws extending, her eyes slitting, elongated canines coming out.

As one, the Tenth Bladers stepped back. Chloe could see why just the Mai's existence might terrify some people. Seen this way, they really were kind of like monsters.

"Ellen," Dmitry said calmly, "if this is what the Honored One chooses, this is what must be done."

Chloe panicked. All of her posturing about peace and truce and it had come down to this—a situation she couldn't win. *Leaders sometimes have to make sacrifices they don't like or don't want to, to achieve their goals.* But she couldn't just coldly offer up someone—someone she had watched *Star Wars* with, someone she knew—to die to seal a truce of her making. He even looked willing, as if he was ready to pay for what he had done. Or maybe it was just a look of hopelessness after Sergei's betrayal of the Pride.

With one word, Chloe could send him forward, let the Tenth Bladers kill him, and guarantee a lasting, bloodless future between the Mai and the Order of the Tenth Blade. Wasn't it worth the death of one person?

Yes. But not his.

She *could* offer up someone else, however.

"No, not Dmitry; he was doing what he thought was right at the time." Chloe took a deep breath. "I offer you myself in his place."

Eighteen

A single white gull traced a gentle arc over everyone's heads before heading out over the water. In that one instant, everything was hushed. Then it was over.

"*What?*" Amy, Brian, and her mom all shrieked at once.

"As the Chosen One, I have nine lives to be given in protection of my Pride," Chloe said slowly. "I think this counts as protecting our future. I offer up one of my lives in the name of 'equity' if this will mean a truce."

It was hard to say who was more shocked—the Tenth Bladers or the Mai. The Mai looked more horrified, the Order of the Tenth Blade more confused.

"I hardly think that's fair," someone from the back of the crowd of the Order called. "It's not really like anyone's going to permanently *die* on their side. . . ."

"Oh, shut up, Carlos," Edna snapped. A pair of tourists walked by, well within hearing range, pointing at the sea lions. "Whitney?"

"The choice is yours, Mr. Rezza," Chloe said quietly. "You can let the killing go on or be remembered as the leader who brought peace to both sides."

"And in a group that has a five-thousand-year memory, that's not too bad," Olga added. "For *both* groups."

That was it. That was key. Blood sacrifice, sure, but ego was everything. Whitney was getting old, and it was obvious Brian wasn't going to follow in his footsteps. The line that had ruled as head of the Order ended with his generation. His second choice, Richard, was dead.

The two tourists didn't seem to notice what was going on as they pushed their way through the Mai and the Order to get closer to the sea lions. The kizekh and soldiers of the Tenth Blade shifted uneasily, but after two bright camera flashes the couple waddled off again, happily oblivious.

"Chloe, don't do this," Brian whispered.

It wasn't like she exactly *wanted* to. Dying twice by mistake and coming back was strange—and, if you really put a lot of thought into it, possibly explainable. Her fall from Coit Tower and survival was a miracle. Being shot in the heart and recovering, well, it was really weird, but not completely unheard of. And her little trips to the Mai afterworld? Low-oxygen-to-the-brain hallucinations.

She didn't have the trust in the Twin Goddesses that Kim had. She only had experience.

Chloe hoped her fear didn't show.

There was a long, tense silence as everyone watched Brian's dad, waiting for his response.

"I think it would be . . . amenable to us, this solution you propose," he said slowly. There was something strange in his face as he looked back and forth between Chloe and Brian. Almost like he realized that his son, brutalized by his own people, was in love with a member of the race he hated.

Guess who's coming to dinner, Chloe thought, trying to bolster her courage.

Whitney gestured to a couple of Tenth Bladers. "Make sure no one . . . comes by and interrupts us." Several military-looking men and women slipped quietly into the thinning crowds that strolled by the pier on the boardwalk.

"Do you really want to do this?" Kim asked, approaching her closely. Not saying no, not encouraging; just making sure. A salty breeze whipped around the two of them, muffling their voices.

"I think," Chloe said, trying to control her breathing, which was a little fast and shallow as her heart beat out of control. "I think the Mai's biggest sin is self-centeredness. Being too self-involved. A little too inward looking, don't you think?"

Kim raised an eyebrow, trying to understand Chloe's crazy thoughts.

"What have we ever done for anyone except ourselves?" Chloe added.

Brian wheeled himself over to her.

"Are you *insane?*" Amy shrieked again, also coming closer. "You don't have to do this."

"I really do," Chloe said, taking her friend's hand.

"It will be by ritual dagger," Whitney said, coming forward. He stopped short when he saw Brian holding Chloe's other hand and the terror in her eyes.

"Can—" Chloe tried to steady her voice. "Can it be Brian?"

Both father and son looked equally surprised.

"I don't see why not," Whitney said finally. "It is . . . it *used* to be a high honor, performing this kind of execution." There were hisses and murmured angry noises from the Mai. "It's only fitting for the son of the head of the Order to do it. But the rest of us will be standing around closely to make sure there are *no tricks.*"

"Wow, Dad. *Thanks,*" Brian said sarcastically.

"Brian, I . . ." His father's eyes traced every injury and bruise and scrape and bandage on his son. "I didn't think they would—"

"Try to kill me?" Brian demanded. "What did you *think* Dickless was going to do when you gave him free rein on the 'betrayer'?"

But Chloe was pulled away from the family reunion by Dmitry. "Honored One," he said softly, kneeling on one knee this time, looking her in the eye. "It is my duty—it is my *honor* to die protecting you. Let me do this."

Chloe shook her head, trying to smile but failing. "I'm your leader, and I've chosen. So there it is." *And just one more second of your pleading and I'm gonna wimp out.*

She knelt before Brian in his wheelchair to make it easier for him while pretending to adjust his clothes or something in case the patrolling Tenth Bladers missed some onlookers who might be concerned to see someone's throat being cut. The depths of irony: she was trying to hide her own death.

"I can't do this." Brian shook his head. "You can't ask me to do this."

"It's got to be done," Chloe whispered. "This is the only way to bring peace to the Mai and the Order."

"I can't kill you," he said weakly, a hopeless look in his eyes.

"I can't trust anyone else," Chloe said, kissing his forehead. She tried to ignore the sound of her mother weeping in the background, drowning it out by focusing on the barking sea lions. "I know you'll be careful. Scarring, you know," Chloe added with a smile, although she knew that Brian would understand what she really meant by 'careful'. This was the only way to bring peace, but Chloe couldn't be sure that anyone beside Brian wouldn't slit her throat six more times as soon as she woke back up.

Whitney handed his son the pretty silver dagger. It looked strangely familiar—then Chloe remembered the dream she had where she was her sister and the Rogue cut her down. Same dagger? Or a similar one?

Everyone gathered around them, Whitney the closest, still looking disturbed.

"This is sick," Brian said weakly.

"Hey, I don't trust your old man," Chloe said, her voice shaking. "But I trust you, Brian. I trust you so much."

"I love you, Chloe," Brian said fiercely, a single tear running down his cheek.

"I love you, too," Chloe whispered.

Then he drew the dagger across her throat, and she collapsed to the ground, dead.

Nineteen

When she opened her eyes and saw the strange view of space, the end-of-time galaxies and nebulas spinning above her, Chloe was actually relieved.

It was still a scary place, pitch black with distant echoing roars, on the edge of a cliff with shadows flickering all around, menacing and too close.

But it's better than being dead. Really *dead.*

"Mother?" Chloe asked, getting up and fighting her urge to run. Her voice was lost in the infinitely great space, drowned by the hisses around her like a thousand candles going out. She walked away from the edge of the cliff, toward where the shadows were congregating.

Not that way. Not yet, a voice came to her, growling. A black shadow flame blocked her way. It was both upright and leonine at the same time, majestic and animalistic.

"What do I do now?" Chloe pleaded. "Did I do the right thing?"

You have done the rightest thing our people have witnessed in over five thousand years. Our Pride has never seen a leader like you, not even in me.

"Will we have peace now? Will we be safe?"

For a time—the hearts of both humans and Mai are fickle, Chosen Daughter. You have done the best you can to ensure any peace at all.

"Mother?" Somehow Chloe felt that her time with her mother was coming to a close. "Do you mind me seeing Brian?"

She could have sworn she heard laughter.

Being Mai is a state of mind, a spiritual state as well as that of the body. He loves you, too. What more do you want?

Chloe wasn't sure what kind of answer that was, but her mother didn't seem to be upset by the union.

"Thank you," she said slowly. "I guess I'll be going back now."

Go with my blessings, Chosen Daughter.

There was nothing to embrace, or Chloe would have. The shade of her mother was only fire and air. She turned and faced the edge of the cliff. The winds of a thousand ages blew up it, lifting her hair and stinging her face.

She put her hands out like Superman and jumped.

Twenty

Chloe came to calmly this time, without a jolt or start. *Because I chose to and was ready,* she realized. Her head lay in Brian's lap, sticky with blood. The wound on her neck was already drying up and knitting itself together as she lay there. In a moment, there would only be a faint scar. Like from the bullet. Like from her fall from the tower.

"Chloe!" Brian choked, hugging her as best he could in their two positions.

"That . . . kind of sucked," Chloe said, trying to lighten the mood around them. Then she felt a strange sensation in her stomach. The brave leader and martyr pushed herself off Brian just in time to vomit all over the ground. When her neck pulsed, it *ached* like her worst cramps. One didn't just die and recover immediately; even with Chosen Ones there was suffering in the process. She moaned once, unable to keep it in check.

Dmitry and Amy were at her side, one holding her up, the other holding her hair back.

"Do—do we have a truce now?" Chloe whispered, looking up at Brian's dad. Acid stung her throat.

"We do," the middle-aged man said loudly and authoritatively, but his eyes were suspiciously wet.

Epilogue

This was not exactly how Chloe had imagined attending the fall formal.

For one thing, her dress was kind of last minute—Marisol gave her the choice of one free thing off the racks and Amy had adjusted it for her. Eschewing lace or satin or even cotton, Chloe had opted for a leather bustier and pencil skirt. She felt a little outrageous these days. A red velvet ribbon was tied around her throat as a choker, hiding the scar.

Her date wasn't anyone from her school, and he was in a wheelchair. Brian promised he would try to get up onto crutches for one dance, but Chloe wasn't going to hold him to it. He looked great, actually, very tragic and romantic with his black velvet jacket, pale skin, and luscious dark brown hair. Somehow Amy had managed to scrounge up an antique wheelchair, which helped the image. Brian balked, however, when she suggested a velvet throw over his lap.

Amy was actually dancing with Alyec. They were officially An Item now. And they looked pretty hot together, Chloe had to admit. Her friend was positively gorgeous in the seventeenth-century zombie outfit she had designed.

Paul was sipping spiked punch next to Kim, who didn't bother disguising her ears and eyes; it was a Halloween dance, after all. Everyone complimented her on the "prosthetics." She wore a very prom-y black gown with ruffles and crap, but it actually worked on her, in a sort of otherworldly way.

Paul was still kind of nervous around Kim and Kim was still just drinking in normal human teenage culture; she looked like an orphan suddenly let into a banquet. Somehow Chloe didn't see the two of them hooking up. At least not yet.

"Oh, hey," Brian suddenly said, interrupting her thoughts. "I got you something—I totally forgot."

"*Besides* the corsage?" Chloe teased, fingering the orchids at her wrist. "I'm showered with riches."

As he fumbled in his pockets, she tried to guess what it would be. A little cat figurine? Her name in hieroglyphs, like a cartouche pendant? Catnip?

Instead he pulled out a pin. She squinted at it in the dim light, letting her Mai eyes go slitty for just a moment.

First Woman President, it read, with Wonder Woman standing proudly, hands on her hips.

Chloe laughed. "I think I have all the leadership I can handle right now." She leaned over so he could pin it on. Instead he pulled her forward and kissed her.

"Photo of the charming couple?" Scott Shannon brandished his camera enticingly. There was a portrait area set up in the corner with an actual professional photographer, but he was handling the "action" snapshots.

"That would be wonderful," Kim said excitedly, coming forward and dragging Paul. She beckoned for Amy and Alyec to join them. "Get all of us. I want the tiny ones that fit in a wallet."

"Do you even *have* a wallet?" Paul muttered.

Kim just hissed at him.

Everyone laughed, and the flash went off.

About the Author

Liz Braswell was born in Birmingham, England, and now splits her time between Vermont and New York. Her major at Brown was Egyptology and yes, she can write your name in hieroglyphs. She then produced video games for the next decade, which was the coolest job ever. She likes skiing, sitting third row center at the movies, planting trees, her sister's excellent black boots, and Nutella.